THE FUHRER'S ORPHANS

DAVID LAWS

Print ISBN 978-1-913419-91-2

ALSO BY DAVID LAWS

MUNICH:

The Man Who Said No!

~

EXIT DAY:

Brexit; An Assassin Stalks the Prime Minister

NORTH WEALD AIRFIELD, ENGLAND, 15 OCTOBER 1940

H e could picture the flinty expression, the accusing eyes, could almost feel the hand on his shoulder. It felt as if Father were flying with him. Peter Chesham swallowed hard and strapped himself to the bench seat, but the metallic snap of the belt buckle didn't sound like a signal of safety. More like the clang of a cell door.

He looked at the seat opposite, a slim aluminium ledge that would soon be a vibrating, droning hell. It was empty but in Peter's mind Father was there, sitting as he normally did, watching, judging, disapproving. Father was a constant presence who ruled and charted his life. Peter breathed in deeply. No escape now. No going back from a journey he feared might turn into a fool's fatal errand. His head in a noose? A one-way ticket?

He needed something to do and he stooped once again to check the equipment which lay in the belly of the aircraft. He could hear the crew going about their preliminary checks: ignition master switch on; undercarriage selector lever down; fuel tanks full, flying controls fully operational. Overlaying it all was the hum of the generators.

The only other passenger was Williams, a slim figure in

flying overalls. And Williams was twitching, showing the first signs of fright. Maybe panic wasn't far away, but Peter ignored him, had his own demons to confront. He hadn't relished this flight from day one but he could hardly explain why. They wouldn't have believed him. Surely not! The daredevil Lieutenant Chesham, the parachutist who landed on the upper slopes of a mountain and skied to the bottom, just for fun? How could this man be worried?

What he hadn't told them was the foul-up on his last drop. Just because he was oblivious to heights or the prospect of landing on a remote mountain didn't make him a reckless fool. Moreover, it wasn't just the flight that had him in a state of uncertainty. Images he couldn't suppress kept forcing their way into his mind. The cell, the blinding spotlight, the cruel handcuffs, the screaming voices and the fists of the men in black.

An airman could be seen outside checking the elevators. There was a croak from the bench seat opposite. Williams had found his voice. 'How old is this darned crate?'

Peter shrugged his shoulders as the engines belched into life. One by one they warmed up, revved up and achieved a monotonous and deafening tone. The vibrations matched Peter's nerve-strings.

Williams pointed accusingly at the parachute at his feet. 'What's this? You assured me we're not jumping.'

Peter shouted back: 'It's a promise.'

He knew he should show leadership and cool with Williams. Theirs was an uncomfortable relationship, not the smooth comradeship he had expected and thought necessary. Not the easy-going sociability of his normal friends. Not at ease in this man's company.

The aircraft bumped along the taxiway, then at the end of the strip it roared and vibrated as if every rivet would shoot from its fixing. After several long minutes the brakes were released and speed picked up. The bumping grew rougher until finally the machine grumbled into the air.

Once aloft things did not improve. The din and vibration from the two radial engines did not diminish. Peter, who had once enjoyed cockpit rides, found himself clutching a stanchion like a rookie, muscles tight, arm rigid.

A crew member who'd been hunched over a tiny table with maps and dividers turned around and climbed awkwardly along the gangway. From his stripes Peter could see he was a flight sergeant. His name, Jenkins, announced him on a thin white strip attached to his overalls. 'Must keep low,' he shouted in Peter's ear, as they dipped and wallowed. 'Miss radar and flak. Dog-legs to fool Fritz. Long haul, this one.'

This much Peter knew. He'd pored over the maps.

The exchange helped. Peter made a conscious effort to relax, forcing himself to act as he should if he were to fulfil the role he had taken on. 'Look out of the window,' he shouted at the stiff figure of Williams. 'We should be over the sea by now. Should show up nicely in the dark.'

Williams didn't move. Mumbled something about 'all that water'.

Peter looked away. More uncomfortable images flashed unbidden into his mind: Father's expression of exasperation, the impossible nature of the task ahead and Dansey's sudden and bizarre changes of mood. Did he really trust that strange and intimidating gnomish figure? And what were the odds on success? Given the vagueness of his instructions and paucity of accompanying information, it was difficult to feel confident. Plus the sheer impracticability of the job. Too big, too vague, too elusive. He'd told them that, but they hadn't listened.

Another worry prompted him to change position. He crouched on the step next to the sergeant. 'How d'you know,' he asked, 'that this field is a fit place to land?'

'We don't.' A sardonic grin. 'Relying on the French. Their experts have paced it out. Supposedly.'

Peter rubbed his chin.

'Two nights ago we had to abort at the last minute,' the sergeant shouted. 'Damned great hedge running right across the strip. Useless. A lunatic idea. Moonlight saved us.'

Peter forced himself to concentrate and ask the questions he needed answering. 'How accurate can you be with your navigation?' he said, thinking of the fun drop that had gone bad all those years ago, stranding him on the wrong mountain.

The sergeant pursed his lips. 'Spot on – or abort the mission.'

'How?' Peter asked, pointing at the maps and the pencils and all the criss-crossing lines, remembering the rumours rife in the flight hut about bombers that missed their target by ten miles.

'Visual landmarks, walking the line to the target, plus a bright moon. That's a must.' The sergeant cracked a wan smile. 'And we've one or two other tricks up our sleeve.'

Peter folded his arms and the Hudson bomber continued to judder its way across the Channel and deep over hostile territory. Mountains were his domain, parachuting a familiar routine, even weaponry would not pose a problem – but torture was a different matter. He tried looking through a porthole for distraction but the forbidding image came again of the cell door. Might he break under interrogation? He and Williams had rehearsed it often enough at Fulbrough Manor. Dragged from their beds in the night, tied to a chair and subjected to the blinding light and bullying questions. But that was training. This was reality. Every man fears getting the wind up, they'd said back at camp, and you'll never know how you'll cope until you have to.

The monotonous droning continued. He tried closing his eyes and wished he could be somewhere else – preferably a sun-dappled crisp snowfield – but hell, almost anywhere, digging his father's rock-hard allotment, even shovelling clinker down the engine pits. And if his old girlfriend Gabrielle could see him now in his dowdy suit, he thought, what sharp comment would she offer? Alone with his thoughts across a darkened France, something broke into his half-comatose state. Voices. Anxious voices. The sergeant at the pilot's elbow, all three of the crew staring to starboard. Peter sat up and looked out. Bright flames caught his attention. Orange, evil flames licking from the starboard engine, the prop still turning. More voices, the pilot leaning to one side, pulling open a box and turning a switch, then peering anxiously out at the wing once more.

Peter watched as the flames flickered, stuttered and died. He crabbed forward: 'Okay now?'

Jenkins turned, relieved. 'Fire's out, extinguisher worked, but we're having to feather.'

'Feather?'

'Fly on one engine. That one's dead. We'll have to think about turning back.'

Peter groaned. 'Doing this all over again?' He shook his head. 'How far to the strip?'

'About ten minutes.'

'Can we make it? Let's get it over with. There are people down there waiting.'

A hoarse whisper from behind him. Williams. 'Turn back. For God's sake, this trip is jinxed.'

But Peter knew better, knew his man. Whatever reason they gave Dansey for aborting the mission he would scorn them as failures. As would his father.

The crew in a huddle, the three of them talking in low tones, then Jenkins announcing, 'We'll give it a go.'

Peter back on his bench, shivering, clenching his fists, saying to Williams, 'Nearly there.'

More droning, the plane still flying level, Peter's hopes rising, then another kerfuffle in the cockpit, the co-pilot at the stick, an empty seat beside him.

Peter peered closer. A coughing sound from below, the pilot lying prone on the hard metal of the gangway, retching and shivering. 'He's sick,' Jenkins said, 'the co-pilot's taken over.'

'That's a joke.' A voice from the front, from the man with the stick. 'Flying straight and level under instruction in safe airspace, that's all I've done.'

The pilot's head came up from the gangway. A gasping voice: 'That's it, Larkin, straight and level. Just keep her nose up, okay, I'll be all right in a bit. Something I ate...'

His words tailed off. Jenkins and Larkin were huddled together. Peter could see the sergeant holding the chart. The plane began to circle gently, the novice Larkin easing it around, the port wing dipping for a lazy turn, the two of them staring down, looking for a telltale necklace of light that would confirm the accuracy of their navigation. Jenkins was pointing out landmarks: the river which formed a shining beacon in the gloom, a hilltop church spire, a sharp S-bend on a main road.

'There!'

Six tiny pinpricks of light over to the right. Torches from their reception party.

More murmurings up front. The plane dipped and stomachs lurched as they zoomed over the treetops, scanning the clearing, checking for unseen obstacles.

The co-pilot: 'Give me the checks.'

Jenkins began to read from a manual: 'Reduce to 125 knots, undercarriage down...'

'Right, this is it.' Larkin's decision.

Brave but foolhardy man, Peter thought, listening to the shouted instructions from the manual: 'Mixture rich, flaps down, tailwheel locked, stick right back.'

Jenkins turned to Peter and Williams. 'Ready to brace. Tighten straps. Heads between knees.'

Williams was breathing heavily. 'Told you, didn't I, told you!'

It seemed to Peter unjust that peril should be pressed upon them so soon into the mission. His imagination was running in overdrive, an emotional foretaste of disaster. Instant obliteration, dismemberment, injury; would he be conscious of it? He was too young for this; so much life still to be lived, so much love yet to be discovered.

Another circuit, turning sharply for final approach, the starboard wing seeming to scatter the branches of the trees, then flattening out, air brake extended. Peter got his head down, felt the craft sink rapidly, tensed for touchdown, fearing the worst.

Then contact. Even so he had no conception of the violence of it. A rock-hard fist seemed to punch at the bottom of the aircraft like a giant hand. The noise was shattering and seemed to ring around the fuselage, deafening in its intensity. He was flung heavily against the restraining straps and his body went numb with the shock of it.

Crazily, the aircraft was airborne once again, bounced back into the air by the force of the collision before sinking once more. Another grinding collision and this time the cabin became a blur of flying debris. A cascade of objects, equipment torn from its fastenings, crashed in chaos around him and Peter felt something hard and sharp hit his arm. Through his shock, he was aware of a tearing, ripping sound which seemed certain to smash the flimsy aluminium airframe apart. The Hudson started to slew to one side, as if out of control, then another collision brought it to an abrupt halt. They all jerked forward, straps straining, the breath knocked out of them.

In the silence of the ensuing stillness Peter could hear his own breathing.

'Next time,' Williams said in a higher octave than before, 'I'll damned well jump.'

MUNICH, *Germany, 15 October 1940*

A line of young children bobbed across the schoolyard heading for the gate and the cluster of mothers waiting there. Little ones, bundled up against the cold, sported tiny haversacks and bright woolly bobble hats.

'Goodbye, Fraulein Kellner.'

'Goodbye, Heini.'

'Afternoon, Fraulein Kellner.'

'Good afternoon, Anna.'

Claudia Kellner was on yard duty. She usually was. Most of the staff managed to avoid it but she was happy to be out in the open, nestled in her fur-collared black overcoat, away from the gym hall where Karl Drexler, dressed in habitual storm-trooper brown, was lecturing the other teachers on National Socialist education. He had been the one, everyone knew, who had been the most vociferous in sacking Jewish teachers and expelling Jewish pupils.

Someone was tugging at her coat and she looked down to see Dieter Schmidt staring up at her. His tiny voice piped, 'Mother says, could she speak to you?'

Claudia nodded. They would only have tried it on with her. All the other teachers would have given the stony, formulaic response: *Interviews are for parents' day.* But Claudia stepped around a puddle of slush and approached the school gate with a wide smile.

'I know I should wait,' Frau Schmidt acknowledged, 'but I

just can't. How's he getting on? He's so shy and I'm worried he's being left behind.'

Claudia stooped so she was eye to eye with the boy. 'You're going to try hard for me and Mummy, aren't you, Dieter?'

A tiny nod. Claudia smiled encouragement and stood. She assured the mother. The boy wasn't lagging, and she added a promise to keep a special eye out for retiring Dieter who liked to hide at the back of the class.

Ten minutes more to go. Claudia looked around the playground, touched at the edges by the morning's unmelted frost. Snow was in the air. A cold wind blew off the Alps, not 100 miles distant. Her brow furrowed at another thought and she caught Frau Schmidt's attention once more. She felt a connection with Dieter's mother. 'Erika,' the woman said. 'Call me Erika.'

Claudia pointed across the street. 'Don't let him use that footpath,' she said, looking at the area known as the Maze, a tangle of wild vegetation sprouting from a wasteland of derelict buildings. She would warn the whole class about it in the morning. 'I've been there. On my way back from Brienner Strasse. Something really weird happened.'

'Oh?'

Claudia recounted what she had seen. Movement in the ferns. A child's face. Startled, she'd stopped abruptly. Could there really be little children in the midst of that jungle, exposed to all kinds of hidden perils? An old industrial site full of rusty iron, any number of sharp objects. Then a second face. Claudia had smiled and called 'hello', but the image vanished and did not return.

Erika was reassuring. She knew. 'Don't worry, they're just playing jungle games,' she said. 'Wild ones who've found a hole in the fence. Acting out their wilderness dream.'

Claudia bade farewell to the rest of her class, many well dressed, like Wanda with her blonde plaits and fashionable coat.

It was a mixed catchment area; from the wide avenues with big gates and pompous entrances to the railway cottages and workers' houses down by the big depot. Children were never her problem. She was always bright, cheery, encouraging. It was her colleagues who frustrated her. She glanced back at the school building, a solid and unflinching Wilhelmenian block of stone and glass, trying not to look at the first-floor window, hoping not to see a figure beckoning to her with a crooked finger, drawing her into that dreadful room, the male bastion, the staffroom, the one with overflowing ashtrays, football boots and gym gear. She looked away, licked her lips, her attention momentarily drawn to a horse clip-clopping down the cobbles of the adjacent road, the dray rattling, the wheels grinding. Then relief. The huddle of mothers at the school gate had dwindled to nothing.

With the last child gone, Claudia left for home, slipping away, she hoped, before anyone noticed her absence. She was anxious to get away, yet admitted to herself she had precious reason to rush home, passing a hand over tired eyes. It had been a long day. School started early in the morning and it was a tedious walk along Dresdner Strasse, back towards the railway depot and the room she rented close by. A straight road at least two kilometres long with pools of shadow between large bushes dotted along the roadside.

She shivered, not entirely due to the cold, looked up briefly at the drone of an aircraft passing overhead and decided she didn't like this street. Traffic was sparse. Few people had the necessary petrol. Big villas announced themselves on one side, a curtain of ash, sycamore and sweet chestnut on the other. Munich was not her city. She felt an alien in it. She had few friends, felt cut adrift, left to her own devices, as if her presence were a form of punishment. And she wasn't eating well. Sometimes she was hungry but the desire for food often evaporated as soon as she put it on a plate. Lost in thought, she was surprised when from deep in one of the shadows she heard a quiet voice. Nothing surprising, nothing threatening. Just a polite female voice from the bushes.

'Are you the schoolteacher?'

Claudia moved closer. A slight figure stood motionless and spoke again. 'May I ask for your help?'

A momentary hesitation, a hint of doubt, then, 'Why?'

'My little girl and I...'

Claudia looked again more closely. A tiny figure almost moulded itself into the adult.

'We've had to leave home. We've nowhere to stay.'

At this, Claudia felt a chill of recognition; the feeling that she had been here before.

'Do you know someone?' said the woman pleadingly. 'Somewhere we could stay? With you, perhaps?'

Claudia, stalling, said, 'Why me?'

'You love children. I know. I've seen you with them in the playground. I recognise a truly sympathetic person.'

Claudia took a step closer to examine the woman. She had ratty hair, a shapeless coat and there was something wrong with her mouth. The child too had a sore on her lip. 'What happened?'

'You know what happens to people the state does not like.'

It was a statement concisely summing up the dilemma from which Claudia had been trying to escape. She wrestled with the spot on the nape of her neck, a gesture her mother had warned her about. It was what she did under stress. This was the predicament she hoped never again to have to confront. She had left Prague precisely to get away from the tragedy and dilemma of frightened parents and unwanted children: the Jews, the Socialists, the trade unionists and all the other groups the regime was determined to target and destroy. Even now her unloved colleague Karl Drexler would be preaching this brand of hatred back in the school gym.

Claudia said, 'You know what happens to people who give shelter?'

'We're desperate.'

Claudia, standing in the lee of the bush, sighed deeply and made her decision. A tawdry compromise but the best she could manage on the spot. 'One night only. If we're spotted we're both out. And the rooms are supposed to be for single occupancy only... even if you were a regular person.'

There! Even she was using the dreaded euphemism. *A regular person.* They both knew the situation. This couple were not regular people. They were part of Germany's forbidden society, a legion of lost souls who scrounged and hid and survived below the notice of the authorities in barns and cellars and dusty attics. Submerged, below the official surface.

In the vernacular of the times, Claudia now had two 'U-boats' of her own.

2

SOMEWHERE IN FRANCE

Peter was sitting on an outcrop of rock to await the verdict on the stricken plane. The airmen were on their haunches examining what was left of the undercarriage while the pilot, a man called Mahoney, lay on the ground massaging a twisted leg and clutching a sickly stomach.

The crash landing had been a shocker. Looking at the battered Hudson, Peter could hardly believe they had survived – but survive they had. And he felt foolish in asking the obvious question, but felt impelled to do so.

'Will it fly?'

All he received in response were grunts and shrugs. It didn't look good.

He had already removed his equipment from the fuselage – the radio set, maps, tools, camera, knee pads – it didn't seem much for what they were meant to do. Then he considered his options. Stranded was the first word that came to mind. With some bitterness, he recalled the instructor's dictum at Ringway: 'The best-laid plans do not survive the first shot.'

Peter snorted. Already, things were going awry. Then he began to ask himself once again the even more difficult questions that had plagued him all through the days of training. Questions without convincing answers.

How on earth did I get myself into this?

Just what the hell am I doing here?

He breathed in deeply and recalled that it all began back in Suffolk at his parents' house in Bury St Edmunds, just a few short weeks before. It had been their music night. And he had no idea how it would change his life...

The music had cut off with a sickening brutality. Schumann's piano quartet was in full flood – the soaring strings, the vibrant keyboard, the full glory of the piece given an enthusiastic rendering by Peter, his mother, his aunt and the refugee girl, Helga. Suddenly, as if someone had ripped a string from a bow, it was stilled into a shocked silence.

All four players turned their gaze to the lounge door which had been wrenched open with a rattle of old brass. A tousle-haired figure, of middle years with a thick black moustache and penetrating gaze, stood framed in the doorway.

Charles Chesham said one word: 'Visitor.'

No one argued or protested. There were no pleas for a few more bars or time to finish. Deep sighs marked their disappointment. Eventually, Peter's mother spoke into the sudden stillness to enquire of her husband. 'Who?'

'Andrew.'

'When?'

'Ten minutes. On his way over.'

At this, the players broke up, Mother frowning, glancing in the direction of the kitchen, then giving her sister a wan smile. Klarissa was packing away her cello; Helga was placing her violin in a velvet-lined blue case with inordinate care. Peter too was disappointed. They had begun, sitting in a circle of rosewood chairs, in jocular mood, laughing at their mistakes, especially when Klarissa caught the spike of her cello in the corner of the Persian rug. Peter joined in the laughter but was annoyed that one of the top Gs was dead on the old Broadwood piano. Why were they still using an upright? Father's parsimony? Despite that, they achieved intense, precise, expressive playing. They had plans for Haydn next, then some English folk music, 'The Flowers of Ashgill' and Telemann's 'Surprise Waltz'.

Not anymore. Now they were all out of the drawing room: hugs for his aunt and the girl as they prepared to depart for the house on the other side of town. Klarissa was the jolly one, always fun to be with, quite unlike his serious mother. And Helga, a slim fifteen, was just as dedicated to her music as when Peter had first met her on the day the *Kindertransport* train drew into Liverpool Street station all those months ago.

When the front door closed, Peter's attention turned and he trailed his way to the kitchen, knowing the visitor was someone his mother didn't warm to. She was usually careful to hide her resentment but this had been an intrusion. The music sessions were her delight. Now she was clattering her best Royal Doulton Windsor teacups on the worktop in a mood of irritation. 'What's he want?' she demanded when Peter arrived.

He was Sir Andrew Truscott, Father's high-profile contact at The Works.

'Why call round at this time in the evening?' she said. 'Spoiling our session. Couldn't it have waited?'

Peter put the visitor out of mind, annoyed that his mother's pleasure had been cut short. Music was what lifted her mood, but in recent weeks she had become a worried woman on account of her brother's family in Switzerland. They lived close to the frontier with Nazi Germany.

And then she fretted about Peter.

'I really wish you could have carried on working with Mr Winton. Helping refugees, so much better than this,' she said, running her fingers down the barathea wool of her son's battle-dress uniform. 'You were so good with all those children.'

'Me too,' he said, 'but we've all moved on.' He shrugged. 'No more refugees. The war and all that.'

'Stupid war,' she said, 'what good's it do anyone, just misery and death. I don't want you sent off to some muddy trench to be shot at, blown up, stabbed, or gassed. Just like the last time. When will men ever learn?'

'Not many trenches in the Cairngorms,' he said, giving her one of his crooked smiles.

She stared up at him fondly – her only child, a twenty-three-year-old six-footer with angular good looks.

'I hate it all,' she said. 'Dropping bombs. Senseless, horrible.'

Peter sighed. They were going over old ground. He agreed. Despite the uniform, he was no warrior, but to give voice to such sentiments would bring down on his head a storm of censure. You didn't take a pacifist line in the mess and Peter made sure he didn't say such things around his father. Much to his father's disgust, he had refused to volunteer for the air force, content to be an instructor at the army ski school.

'Still he keeps going on about parachuting,' he said. 'How my experience would be invaluable.'

His mother made a face while setting out the tea tray. 'I don't trust that man,' she said, pointing toward the drawing room where the visitor would be entertained. 'They're too secretive, him and your father. And I'm never told a thing. What's so urgent that he has to come here tonight?'

Peter shrugged. 'Who knows? Talk about my future career after the war perhaps.'

She wagged a finger. 'Don't you agree to anything you don't want to,' she said. A ring at the doorbell put an end to this conversation. Peter knew, of course, that he was fortunate to be on the shortlist for post-war selection to a management trainee course with the London and North Eastern Railway Company, of which Sir Arnold Truscott was the most notable member. Still, it seemed strange that what would probably amount to a job interview should be conducted in his family's drawing room.

Sir Andrew had the appearance of someone always on stage: white hair carefully waved, grey moustache neatly trimmed. He was dressed formally in blue suit, waistcoat and matching tie. A white handkerchief peeked from his top pocket and gold cuff-links and gold rings were on view. He was knighted for services to the nation, designer of iconic locomotives that made the company an emblematic byword for speed and modernity, a leading figure in commerce.

For all this, he had not always been so prominent, knighted or revered. Once, he and Father had been young apprentices in the workshops. Peter grimaced to himself, unsure that his enthusiasm for the company and all its works quite matched theirs.

He was introduced in the drawing room and watched as the two friends – were they actually friends? Or just colleagues? Or conspirators? – talked in low tones by the crewel-embroidered fire screen.

Then came a surprise. Both parents were ushered from the room and Truscott sat in Father's armchair – the one with a moquette-covered golden footstool – and plucked a heavy tome from the alcove bookshelf.

He waved Peter over. 'You're familiar with this?'

Peter looked down at a large line drawing of Isambard Kingdom Brunel's seven-foot broad gauge railway from Paddington to Bristol. 'Known it since childhood,' he said. 'Brought up on it. History all my days.'

Truscott tapped the page. 'That's what I want to talk about,' he said. 'The immense potential of a railway of that size.'

Was this a test? Part of some subtle interview technique? Peter, taking what he thought to be his cue, launched into the subject on which he was fluent. Brunel was a visionary, he said. He built beautiful bridges, fast straight lines and a steamship to America, but the one innovation that didn't last were the hugely wide railway lines. Brunel was forced to abandon these in favour of George Stephenson's horse-cart-sized tracks, the ones everyone is familiar with today. It was the big breakthrough in travel that didn't happen. Peter added a little flourish. What if Brunel had got his way? How might life be different today?

Truscott merely nodded, then lit a cigarillo. There was a smell of musty spiciness about it, tree bark and old paper. Peter felt a stab of resentment at this man's presumption, given free rein to move about the room, the bookshelves and anywhere he wished. Perhaps it was this that lured him into a sudden outburst of dangerous honesty. How could he tell this man he was a non-conformist in an engineering household? That he liked the theatre, ballet, concerts; anything to do with people; people rather than machines. 'The thing is, I've been having second thoughts about a railway career,' he ventured. 'If this is the right path for me?'

The older man's lips pursed, as if Peter had just shouted an obscenity in church. 'Then you'd be a bloody fool,' he said.

'Still, I need to be sure...'

'Not many young men are given this sort of chance,' Truscott said. 'A clear path to senior management of the company. A fool indeed would reject your kind of family tradition, service to the company, service to the country.'

Truscott broke off, anger flushing his features. He turned away, eyes fixed on the bookcase. Perhaps he couldn't bear to look at the ungrateful young man before him. He seemed to be speaking between clenched teeth. 'Despite your last remarks...' He broke off for a deep breath. His next words, it seemed to Peter, were forced by a man who did not normally countenance contradiction. 'Nevertheless, we need to continue this conversation.'

'We do?'

'In the national interest,' Truscott said.

And this left Peter more utterly confused than before. Truscott was making a big issue of secrecy. They had moved to Father's study, checking the windows and blackout curtains and keeping voices low. 'The point is, if Brunel had won the battle of the gauges instead of Stephenson, we'd now be running bigger, heavier and faster services that would have been much more efficient. It's the huge leap forward this country never made.'

Peter was puzzled. Was this it? The reference to the national interest? 'Do I get the sense,' he said, 'that you're proposing to reverse history?' Incredulity overtook caution. 'Surely not? Far too difficult. Ripping the whole country apart to carve out wider tracks? The nation wouldn't stand for it.'

Truscott stiffened, then gave a reluctant nod. 'Not here, not in Britain... but supposing in another country they were planning a vast new network of broad gauge lines to straddle a whole continent? As a student engineer, wouldn't that excite you?'

Peter exhaled quietly. This interview was something else. To play for time, he asked: 'And how broad is broad... in this other country?'

A gleam came to the older man's eye. 'Three metres. Just think of it, nearly ten foot wide. Absolutely colossal. A sea change and a challenge for any engineer.'

'Does this other country have a name?'

Truscott studied Peter for some seconds before saying, 'Hitler's Germany.'

A long pause ensued in which Peter decided this could not

be a test. Just the two of them, Father excluded, talking of Germany, and Truscott discussing a subject with a young man not yet formally indentured to the company? None of it made any sense, so he asked, 'Sir, why are you telling me all this?'

Truscott didn't answer. Instead, he pointed to the large world atlas displayed on the back wall of the study and summoned Peter to watch him make broad, sweeping arm strokes all over the continent of Europe, vast circles reaching into France in the west and deep into Russia in the east, and all of it centred on Berlin. 'Hitler's already begun his new broad gauge network,' he said. 'Calls it the *Breitspurbahn*. Broad gauge. And some lines are up and running.'

'He's done something right then?'

'Amazing, startling even, and fascinating for an engineer,' Truscott said. 'But dangerous, very dangerous for us in Britain.'

'A new railway? How's that dangerous?'

'Don't you see? High speed and massive loads. That means he can take his army anywhere he likes much quicker than we can respond by sea. He could move a whole panzer division on one train straight down to within striking distance of the oil wells in the Middle East before our ships could even leave port.'

Peter's brow puckered. 'Yes, but he doesn't control all that territory... not yet anyway!'

'Soon will! Either by negotiation, threats or military invasion. This is the very latest military intelligence assessment. Officially, I'm not allowed to pass it on.'

'Then,' Peter hesitated, 'why have you?'

'Because certain persons have come to me to ask for my technical advice. And I have to warn you that in the course of our discussions I mentioned your name.'

'Me?' Peter was incredulous.

Truscott nodded. 'I told them about your Swiss ancestry,

your German language skills, your knowledge of railways, parachuting, wing walking, skiing... and they're very interested.'

Peter spread his hands. 'But why?'

'That's for them to tell you. They'll be in touch very soon, so
I've come to tell you before they make their approach, so you'll
be forewarned... and forearmed.'

3

Claudia Kellner's dangerous guests were Lotti Bergstein and six-year-old Anna. She guessed that the woman had been skipping food for the sake of her daughter while hiding out to escape Gestapo round-ups. She had blotchy skin, tugged at a strand of lank hair and her shoulders curved into a permanent gesture of submission.

The girl was equally cowed, refusing to release her mother's hand, burying her head in a buttonless coat. Close up, they stank of their time in the woods.

Claudia ushered them into the bathroom for a clean-up, pointed out her tiny medicine box containing creams and plasters, and then went to hunt down some spare clothing: a jumper, a better coat, some clean underwear. Their past address had been a cardboard box under some trees in a park. Prior to that? She didn't ask.

There was a meal of beans, porridge and bread rolls, the best Claudia could manage from her supplies in the cool cupboard with the porcelain shelf. The flat was one large L-shaped room with a miniscule galley kitchen and bathroom. Resources were scarce but some spare blankets were formed into a temporary bed.

She looked reflectively at mother and child. You didn't seek out too much information, the less you knew the better, yet Claudia could not adopt a distant attitude, her instinct was for sympathy. Lotti's husband, it transpired from gentle probing, had been taken in a night raid but he had been prescient; his wife and child had been prepared, hiding behind the false wall of a large rigid wardrobe. They'd been on the run ever since.

Claudia was upset at the woman's poor condition – spots, sores, hollow eyes, craven posture – and at the child. Despite her best efforts to connect, the girl sank into a fearful, uncommunicative shell. It made Claudia feel guilty. She should stop feeling sorry for herself, she thought, grateful for the relative luxury of her life: she had clean clothes, adequate food, a bath, a toilet, a role. She was above the official surface; she was a 'regular' person. She told herself to put into practice what she preached in the classroom: help and support for those less fortunate than oneself. It wasn't a lesson taught anywhere else in the school.

Her sympathy, however, came at a price. Claudia spent an uncomfortable night twisting and turning with worry. No one was safe from informers. The risk was enormous. Neighbours spied on neighbours, colleagues on colleagues and children denounced parents. The least hint of anything unusual and the block snoop was on it. Frau Netz lived at the end of the row. She was the only one in all the apartments who had a telephone and everyone knew why. Like all the *blockwarts*, she had an official right of entry into every home and the stated reason was to check for inflammables in case of bombing. And the old crone had forced her way in several weeks back, invading Claudia's flat, pretending to go down her list of forbidden items, peering in cupboards and having a brazen nose around.

If she came again it would be fatal.

Sleep would not come. Claudia was sweating, ill at ease, unable to still the knot in her stomach. What if her guests were seen at the window? Heavy, uneven, troublesome breathing from across the room was another indicator of the woman's poor health. She needed a doctor. No chance! She knew U-boats suffered badly from starvation as well as sinking into an animal-like existence forever fearful of discovery. But none were found dead. No householder wanted to explain away a body in the cellar. The implications of all this so appalled Claudia that she couldn't lie still. Unable even to doze, she got up and padded barefoot around the flat: to the loo, the kitchen, the window. Suddenly, it seemed to her, her apartment took on the shape of a prison, a trap, no longer her refuge from troubled days at the school. She thought again about Drexler's ranting in the staffroom. It was bad enough having to preserve her teaching status by subscribing to the party; of having to go to the office in the Brown House in Brienner Strasse to pay her dues. That was when she'd walked down the footpath by the wilderness, spotting children's faces in the ferns. Now she looked for something to calm her nerves but found only milk.

At some moment in the early hours she made a decision. The only thing to do was to act normally and go to classes, cautioning the pair to make no sound and to stay clear of the windows. It was to set a pattern.

Claudia had insisted on a one-night stay but found it extraordinarily difficult to send this pair on their way, even though the risk mounted by the hour. It was an ordeal at school, forcing herself to behave normally, to give away no hint of anxiety, coping with the fractious relationships all around her, knowing that Lotti and her child were hiding out at home. Claudia excused herself from the school dining hall. She couldn't eat lunch. The slightest slip up at home, she knew, would spark

Frau Netz into action. She thought sourly of the *blockwart*. A little person drunk on the power she'd been given over people who would otherwise have passed her by. Was this becoming a sick society controlled by the likes of Drexler, Netz, a weak headmaster and compliant and intolerant colleagues?

Her school agony stretched into a second day. How could she send this desperate pair on their way? Claudia found her concentration in class drifting and at the school gate noticed Frau Schmidt giving her warning looks, but there were no opportunities for explanation or a quiet word. They both knew: you had to be careful what you said in a group.

The anxiety was crippling. She would have to confront Lotti that evening. They must go after dusk – but she had no idea how she would manage such a desperate farewell. Better clothing, food and a little money certainly, but who could she pass them on to? She had no network of friends in this city.

In the evening, however, willpower and words failed her.

It was on the third morning that it happened.

The visitors were still sleeping at five as Claudia dressed and began to brew some of her precious coffee. A knock came at the door and her spoon was stilled in mid-stir. Nobody called at this hour.

She swallowed and went on tiptoe to the window, easing back the curtain just a fraction.

Frau Netz? No, worse.

A cop. A uniformed officer dressed in regulation police green and wearing the Napoleonic-style shako helmet of the regular force.

Claudia let the curtain drop, slid to the floor and shut her eyes. She felt destroyed.

To have been discovered so soon. It was a disaster for all of them.

~

Momentarily frozen into inaction, she lay on the floor, the cop's knock unanswered.

Should she pretend to be out? Hide? Refuse to answer, hoping he would go away? Claudia looked behind her at the petrified expression of Lotti Bergstein and her child peeping out from their blanket beds and decided that running away was not practical. How far would they get? Doubtless, there would be a police squad ready at the back door.

She swallowed, beckoning to Lotti to move out of sight, then put a reluctant hand on the door handle, still hesitating, still trembling. Was this the moment it all ended?

Another knock. Not loud, she noticed. Not raucous. Almost as if this were the postman or the meter man. Not a rap that demanded she open up or face the sledgehammer.

Claudia breathed in. She knew never to show fear to the police. She had coped once before, in Prague, and who could forget those traumatic scenes at the Wilson Station just before the war, sending children out of the country? But dealing with Gestapo officers while on official business was quite a different matter to talking her way out of harbouring a fugitive. Not one but two! A lie began to form in her mind: *she's not Jewish, just a cousin up from the country*. But how far would that wash – with no papers and a woman who looked a mess?

She peeped again. The cop's uniform was immaculate, the creases in his trousers sharp but the expression did not appear aggressive. There was no pout, no overt sign of hostility, no rigid scowl or contemptuous expression. Her hand hovered on the door release. Not to open was merely to postpone the inevitable, or even worse, but to open... that seemed like diving off a cliff. Her mind said she had to open, but her fingers refused to work.

Images of her mother flashed into mind and the promise she had made to her not to put the family in any danger. She longed at that instant for the comforting and safe familiarity of the family home.

But then came a sudden resolve. This she had to do for herself. She breathed in deeply, held her breath and opened the door.

She took in the figure on her step. Her first impression, a surprise, was that he was alone. And nothing in his hand. No stick, handcuffs or piece of paper.

'Fraulein Kellner?' The voice was soft, even polite.

'Yes?'

'Claudia Kellner?'

'Correct.' Would he now produce his piece of paper, the arrest warrant? The instruction to accompany him to...

'I have a message for you,' he said.

'A message?' The incredulity in her voice must have been obvious. And what happened next made her confusion even greater.

The man smiled. 'Yes, a message,' he said. 'Would you be so kind as to call at the depot this morning before going to your place of work?'

'The depot?'

'The railway works, I'm sure you know it, the components department on the north side of the tracks. The far side under the tunnel. Ask for Schmidt. They'd like a word.'

Her surprise must have remained obvious. Perhaps, she thought later, her mouth was agape. In the event, he turned away, the smile still in place and added as he regained the street, 'That is all.'

As she watched him walk away towards the Karlsplatz and the big police station at Ettstrasse – still alone – she had the impression that his eyes had also sent her an unstated message.

Could she be imagining it – or had she read him correctly? *Don't panic, all is well.*

~

The cop in the shako helmet had gone and Claudia slumped onto her sofa, breathing out, trying to calm her heart rate.

That is all, he had said, walking away in the direction of the city centre. But had she read him right? That she shouldn't panic?

Lotti Bergstein looked at her but didn't ask. Her trembling hands said it for her, expecting the worst.

'I don't know,' Claudia said, 'he told me to call somewhere, I really don't know why or what for.'

Was Claudia reading too much into the man's expression? After all, the police didn't act as messengers. You could expect questions, a summons or even an arrest – but not messages. Was this a trick? To lure her out into the open, so they could snatch her from the street? But why should they bother? They weren't normally shy about arrests. 'I really don't know,' she echoed.

Lotti and her daughter rolled into a foetal ball curled up in a corner of the room, two fearful fugitives expecting another knock at the door. And this was the closest Claudia had come to disaster. During all her activities back in Prague, helping to load Jewish children onto the *Kindertransports* for evacuation to England, she had never once feared being picked up by the Gestapo. Her role then had received official, if grudging, approval: to assist with the evacuations. Back then she had regarded the secret police as banal. Secret? That was a laugh, everyone knew who they were. A few obvious thugs, others misfits themselves hiding from authority. None of them outstanding for their intellect. Only the *kriminalrat* had a mind to beware of, but today's brush with the forces of the law seemed quite different. Did this uniformed policeman standing on her doorstep represent peril? Had someone informed on her U-boats?

She considered again what to do. Ignore the message? Run? Disappear like another illegal person? But then the quiet smile of the cop reassured her. She considered herself a good judge of character and thought she had read his unspoken reassurance. After a couple of minutes she decided to trust her judgement.

'You stay here and keep out of sight, I'll find out what this is all about,' she told Lotti, tying on a headscarf. She knew that out on the street she had to be anonymous, inconspicuous. She needed to mask the dark hair that frequently drew admiring glances. In her teens she had been a film fan, an admirer of Lilian Harvey, the Anglo-German star of Hollywood and Germany, whom many said she resembled. She looked anxiously around and her gaze settled on Lotti's brown coat, the one with the missing buttons. She drew in her breath, fighting down her distaste at the odour that clung to the garment.

'Could I borrow that for half an hour?' she asked, pointing.

Then, checking no one was loitering outside in the street, she made her way towards the railway depot. It was a few hundred metres from the apartment and she had to walk close to an immensely high red-brick wall before arriving at the entrance. Hundreds worked at the depot, servicing the locomotives, wagons and rolling stock, and she hoped to pass herself off as just another hurrying worker as she turned through the large black iron gates and across the scuffed and oil-stained cobbled yard littered with a wheelless cart, a stack of broken ties and a truck around which three men were standing in deep conversation.

She almost tripped on an uneven stone and one of the three turned and glanced in her direction. For a moment she feared a wolf whistle, drawing unwanted attention, but the dowdy scarf and brown coat appeared to be a winning combination, marking her out as just another unremarkable item on the human landscape.

The man looked away, resuming his conversation.

She passed under the archway topped by the sculpted lettering DR, the initials of the *Deutsche Reichsbahn*, and stepped into the long tunnel just below the tracks that led to the component store. Ten tracks led out of the *Hauptbahnhof*, the city's main passenger terminus, and it was a mystery to her why the *Reichsbahn* kept all their spares on the other side of the line. She set off down the green-tiled tunnel, feeling vulnerable and wondering what explanation she could offer if challenged. That problem quickly receded. The steel roof beams were just below rail level. The booming thunder of wheels echoed and reverberated up and down the long passage as trains passed overhead. No one could speak or be heard amid such a deafening clatter.

Close to the northern end of the tunnel were several doors but none had any markings. At the end she climbed up the ramp, noticed a general air of dilapidation and recognised the forest of bushes and willow saplings everyone knew as the Maze. Only one building appeared to be in use. She approached, pushed open the door and had the second shock of the day.

'Erika, it's you!'

Behind the counter, dressed in a fading fawn smock, was the mother she had talked to at the school gate.

'Come round the back,' Erika Schmidt said, beckoning her beyond the counter.

Claudia put one hand to her mouth. 'I didn't connect you with this.'

Erika showed her to a corner where there was just room for two stools and a tiny table. 'Comes of having the most common name in the land.'

They perched, eyeing one another. Claudia was recovering from surprise, shock, fear and not a little resentment. 'What's this? That policeman...' She shook her head. 'I thought...'

'I know what you thought. Sorry if it gave you a bad moment, but he's the best messenger I've got.'

Claudia shook her head. 'A policeman as a messenger? From you? How come?'

'He's one of us.'

'Us?'

'Us, as opposed to one of them.'

The two women, once such easy conversationalists at the school gate, now looked at each other searchingly, silently. Warning bells rang in Claudia's head. This sounded like dangerous talk. This looked like a dangerous place to be. Claudia stared back at her friend, seeing her in a different light, trying to read the clues in Erika's expressions to explain this unexpected turn in the relationship. Then she dropped her gaze to the miniscule metal table in the corner of the strange building. What was this place? A component store? It looked like a cross between a warehouse and a workshop. She recalled the conversation with Erika at the school gate – a guarded exploration of each other's concerns: children, school, lessons. Then vague talk about little faces seen lurking in the Maze. Confirmation then, indications of a hidden life somewhere thereabouts. Hints but no explanation. So where was this conversation going?

Erika broke the long silence between them. 'I know what you've been doing,' she said softly.

Claudia was chilled but said nothing.

'It's dangerous. You should be more careful.' Another pause, then, 'They'll send you away, no doubt about it, if they catch you.'

Claudia wore a quizzical expression but wasn't going to admit to anything.

'I know about your U-boat,' Erika said. 'And your little U-boat. A brave but foolish thing to do and one you should stop right now.'

'How? How do you know?'

'Saw you in the street. Saw you two meet, or should I say three? Saw you go off all together, back home. I recognised what was happening. And if I did, maybe others did too.'

Claudia paused. 'So?'

'There's something you should know.' Erika put her head out of the alcove to check that they were not being observed or over-heard. Then she launched into her explanation. The children Claudia glimpsed among the bushes on her way back from the city were not an illusion. They were strays. Lots of them. Little kids, just like the one sharing Claudia's dangerous hospitality. They had lost their parents to the concentration camps, or just became lost with no one to look after them. 'They're a nuisance. They plunder the bins, scrounge food, badger the railway workers and they're dangerous. If certain people find them, they're done for.'

'Why are you telling me this?'

'Nobody wants to risk helping them. We all know the dangers. But the kids are getting more desperate, more daring. Sooner or later, catastrophe!'

Claudia could not help herself: images from her past flooded her consciousness. Pictures of the pre-war days in Prague. Of loading little children onto a train bound for England, of grief-stricken parents parting with their young ones to rescue them from whatever horror awaited them if they didn't go. *Oh no, not again*, she thought. *Not again*! She looked up. 'What makes you think I would want to get involved? Why me?'

Erika checked again for eavesdroppers, then said, 'I've seen you. Clocked you in the playground with the little ones. You're one of the few teachers who really care. Most of them are just parade ground idiots, strutting around in their brownshirts and toy soldier uniforms, yelling "Heil Hitler" and talking nonsense. But you, you care.'

'What are you saying?'

'You know what I'm saying.'

And Claudia did. It was happening all over again. Little children were being made victims by the system. And she was being sucked once more into a mission of care.

'You can't keep your U-boats at home, you know that, don't you?' Erika persisted. 'Send the mother on her way, we can't involve adults, and pass the child into the wilderness, she'll have to survive as best she can.'

'That's horrible, inhuman. I can't just chuck Lotti to the wolves.'

'Listen, Claudia, you have to be tough to survive, your softness will get you killed, we can't start a refugee camp for adults, how long do you think we'd survive?'

'She's had a terrible time. In terrible conditions.'

'It's the best you can do for her child. She'll recognise that. And there's something much more practical you can do.'

'Like?'

'Together, *we* can help,' Erika said. 'Adults we can't support – but we can focus on the children. I've been managing on my own over the past weeks. Put them in the Maze to keep them out of sight, but that isn't enough. They need proper care, before they become a nuisance and a danger to themselves and us. They're starving, not in a good condition.'

Claudia could imagine. She had already seen the state of her own two U-boats.

'I've decided,' Erika said. 'I can't do it all on my own. I need help. Someone to back me up. Caring for them properly.'

She gave Claudia a look that could not be denied. They

knew. They both knew. Claudia acknowledged the moment. Her moment of decision.

She could not refuse. It was her commitment to humanity, to mercy. To be a covert aunt to the strays of the Maze. Hidden, subterranean, beneath the eye of the authorities.

Still she said nothing, took another moment, breathed deeply, felt herself on the brink. The risks were enormous. It was foolish. It was crazy.

Then she looked Erika in the eye. 'Can that cop really be trusted?' she asked.

4

As soon as Truscott had left by the front door and been driven away down Whiting Street in his elegant Jaguar drophead coupe – latest version, wartime headlamp blinds fitted – Peter's mother cornered him in the drawing room.

'Well?' Hands on hips, her stare demanding.

He drew in a long breath. A moment he dreaded. Besides, he had no specific information to give. 'Sorry, Mum, can't say. Sworn to silence. Official secrets and all that.'

She was frustrated, close to tears. 'Just like your father!' she snapped, turning on her heel. He could hear her banging pots around in the kitchen and he felt like a betrayer. They were close, they didn't have secrets. Then he stopped berating himself. Not quite true. What son told his mother *everything*?

During the rest of the day and the next he had an acute sense of foreboding. How were you approached by military intelligence? Another visitor, a phone call, a letter? What could they possibly want? His anxieties grew. He might be a daredevil in the mountains but he knew he was not made for military glory. He didn't want to bomb or shoot people – he wanted to save them. He was a rescuer, not a warrior. He thought nations that went to war were mad. It was as if he inhabited a different planet to his father, who remained gung-ho despite the bitter price the Cheshams paid in the trenches of the Great War. One uncle killed at Gommecourt, the other, Henry, invalided out with a leg blown away. Peter had accompanied the surviving uncle to Thiepval on the anniversary of the Somme: 72,000 men eviscerated in the shelling. Surely, never again! Peter decided there had to be a better way, taking time out after university to play his part in the *Kindertransport* operation.

However, the military had claimed him several months back, as in wartime they were bound to do. His status as a prospective engineer and manager with the LNER cut no ice and he quickly found himself in uniform. He could put all his skills learned in the Swiss mountains to good use at the Cairngorms ski school, the military said. He'd told them about his extended holidays, spent with his uncle, aunt and two nieces, within sight of the German border. What he hadn't mentioned were the fun flights in Stefan's Dragonfly biplane, the wing walking, parachuting onto the upper slopes and skiing back down to the village at Steinach.

'But I'm not a shirker,' he told himself out loud in his bedroom, in a bout of defensive anxiety, conscious of the time he'd spent kicking his heels in Scotland waiting for snow that didn't fall, acutely aware of his privileged status: good food in the mess, better billets than the men, long leaves at home.

Wednesday passed without a word and he awoke on Thursday with a sharp taste in his mouth, like the crab apples he used to scrump as a child. On the following morning there was a letter on the doormat addressed to P. Chesham, Esq. from the Export Trade Department of the Bristol Chamber of Commerce inviting him to a meeting to discuss *a possible change of employment*. When he noticed the venue, he decided someone had definitely got their wires crossed. The Savoy Hotel in London?

His father, when shown the letter, was caustic. 'What were you hoping for? A letter headed MI6?'

'Oh!' Peter slumped, then turned to go.

'And Peter...'

'Yes?' He stopped by the door.

'This is your chance to make a proper contribution to the war effort. To do something worthwhile for a change. To serve your country.'

Peter hesitated, nodded and went to leave.

But his father wasn't finished. 'None of your pacifist nonsense! Leave that behind. And as you're clearly about to meet someone of significance, could you please not turn up in one of those damned white jumpers.'

The Savoy on a wet Friday afternoon at ten to four did not lift Peter's spirits or encourage a sense of eager expectation. When he walked down the steep slope off the Strand, pushed past crowds clustered around a milling taxi rank and stepped onto the black-and-white marble floor of the reception area he wondered just what kind of an interview he could expect.

At the desk he joined a queue. Father had insisted: dark-grey jacket, blue shirt, plain tie. 'You'll be safe enough,' he said. 'The air raids don't start till well into the evening.'

This optimism for wartime travel hadn't survived the journey beyond Ipswich. The train had been crowded with soldiers, kitbags blocking the corridors. At Witham they'd stopped for nearly an hour, the down line blocked by a bomb crater. At Liverpool Street, the site of so many *Kindertransport* arrivals Peter had attended before the war, the terminus was now a shambles, the roof holed, sandbags on the platforms, chaos everywhere.

Out in the street he was struck by an overwhelming sense of greyness and he felt the taste of dust on his tongue. Bombed houses were ripped open to public view and it seemed almost indecent to glance up to see someone's bath, bed and wardrobe teetering on the edge of a second-floor abyss. By contrast the Savoy seemed unaffected. The queue edged forward toward the hotel receptionist and when it was Peter's turn he asked for Mr Rosamond. The receptionist fished around under a ledge on his desk and eventually found a written reminder. 'Ah yes, the colonel.' He looked at his watch. 'He should be there by now. Just go through. By the window on the far side.'

Peter looked in the direction the clerk was pointing. A sea of faces seemed to be staring back at him. Armchairs ringed a room dominated by a huge skylight. The opulence was intimidating. Peter rubbed an ear, stroked his chin. This was not what he expected: white heads, strings of pearls, fur collars, tight waistcoats and parked walking sticks. He passed signs to the Grill and the American Bar, then began to cross an expanse of immaculate parquet, feeling like some strange creature from the other side of the moon come to entertain an audience of the intrigued and the inquisitive. And when he ran out of parquet he stood before a corner table at which a small white-haired man sat alone, arching his fingers into a church steeple and staring back at him with a neutral expression: neither welcoming nor hostile; neither interested nor engaged.

Peter remembered the clerk's form of address. 'Colonel Rosamond?'

'Sit.'

Peter's eyebrows shot up. He wasn't used to this kind of sharp response. Nevertheless, he slid slowly into a seat, supposing he was encountering – if not yet entering – a world where civility counted for little. He dug around his jacket pocket, found the letter and held it out. 'I was intrigued,' he said – but got no further.

'We'll not discuss that here,' the man said, turning and snapping his fingers with practised aplomb. The maître d' hurried to approach, all smarm and anxious to serve.

To Peter, the man said, 'Can I get you anything? Tea, coffee, mineral... or something stronger?'

'Tea would be nice.' Peter remembered his mother's imprecation: *Never drink coffee at an English hotel. Tastes worse than dishwater.*

But then, of course, *she* was Swiss.

'Make it snappy, Emilio, we haven't got all day.'

'Of course, colonel, of course, right away.'

Rosamond – if that was the man's real name, who could be sure of anything about this strange encounter? – addressed Peter with surprising candour at such an early point in the conversation. 'He's Italian. I expect you guessed. Worried about the war, thinks all his relatives will be deported. Thinks I can keep them safe.' A thin smile and a tiny shrug of the left shoulder. 'I don't disabuse him.'

Peter was taken aback by so open an act of manipulation, but then perhaps this was designed to shock. In effect, welcoming him to the secret world.

'So, young man, tell me about yourself. What does the younger generation think of the war so far? Eager to fight? Get stuck in?'

Peter drew in a breath. 'More a case of increasing our defensive capabilities, I would have thought. Aircraft production, supplies, convoys at this particular time.' His voice trailed off, realising this probably wasn't the expected answer. Was he deliberately being put on the spot? An open examination in a public place to test his nerve? Tell all and don't be shy?

The buzz of conversation around them had ceased, Peter noticed. His answers, it seemed to him, had become the focus of attention for those in adjacent armchairs. He glimpsed elegantly-tailored suits, furs, silks, lace, emerald greens, teal blues and magenta pinks. Did these people have nothing better to do? Afternoon tea in the eavesdropper's lounge?

'And what do you think of this place, eh? You approve of us? Our many guests?' Rosamond persisted, sweeping one arm around in a provocative gesture. 'Only last week we had a bunch of East End gentlemen trying to take the place over. Wanting to eat our food, sleep in our beds. What do you make of that?'

Peter worked at an anodyne reply. 'I'm sure we have need of a place for discreet meetings, that kind of thing.'

'Aha! A diplomat!' Rosamond chuckled and bounced out of his seat, beckoning Peter up. 'Come with me.'

Within a few moments they were in a lift travelling to the first floor. For the first time they were alone and the man offered a belated explanation. 'Probably wondering why we met down there. A test. How you'd manage an unfamiliar social situation.'

'Did I pass?'

'I'll let you know.'

They were in a corridor and stopped outside number 21. Rosamond tapped twice, whispered 'Edward' and the door opened. Behind the door was another man, balding, unsmiling and silent. The place appeared to be a standard hotel bedroom. Rosamond perched on the end of the bed and demanded, 'Now that we're out of the limelight, so to speak, tell me everything about yourself. Absolutely everything.'

There followed the rehearsed exposition, the story of his first twenty-three years of life, facts which Peter suspected were not entirely new to this man. Nevertheless, he enumerated all the relevant events: three years and a tripos in mechanical engineering at Cambridge, holidays in the Alps and time out for his role helping Nicholas Winton's *Kindertransport* rescue operation. Then the war: early call-up to the forces, his time in Scotland and the expected career step into railway management put on hold.

Rosamond unravelled a large map of Switzerland and laid it out across the counterpane. Pointing at the mountains, he demanded, 'Which did you climb? And why?'

Peter began to feel more confident. He was on home ground. He reeled off the names – Matterhorn, Monte Rosa, the Jungfrau. Climbing, he said, was fun.

'But why do it?' the man demanded. 'Why take the risk?'

Easy again! Peter guessed this was another test. Simply because he could, he said. Once he'd completed a few ascents it just came naturally. Going up was almost second nature. You saw a good-looking peak or a nice track and you couldn't help yourself. Hadn't done this one before? So let's give it a go. See the sun reflecting from a high ridge and you felt the draw, felt the call. Got to get up there. It was an addiction. Like smoking. Couldn't give it up. Why should he?

The little man kept a poker face but Peter finally sensed approval for his answers. Then Rosamond wanted to know about climbing in bad weather. Peter began to explain about checking forecasts, of gauging risks, but he could tell Rosamond wasn't impressed. Wrong answer?

'What about if you get lost? Ever been lost up on those peaks you've been talking about?'

Peter took a second to reflect. What did the man want to hear? That he had carefully planned each climb, that he made darned sure he wasn't caught out by mist, avalanche or failing light? No, he didn't want to hear that sort of answer, so Peter said, 'Sure, you just need grit and sheer bloody-minded willpower to get you through. That always does it when everything else fails.'

Rosamond nodded approvingly and led him through a second door.

Another surprise. It was the bathroom. The afternoon, Peter decided, was becoming distinctly more weird by the minute. Rosamond perched on the side of the bath and began turning on the taps. Water gushed noisily into the tub but no attempt was made to insert the plug. Instead, the man looked up and said, 'Right, now we can speak with complete freedom.'

Peter, standing, decided to be direct. 'I've answered all your questions, so now perhaps you'll answer some of mine.'

No response.

'First of all, why is it necessary to talk in this bathroom?'

'Bugs.'

'Bugs?'

'You are green, aren't you? Listening devices. If any unfriendly types are trying to listen in to our conversation, the water will drown it all out.'

Peter repressed his surprise and followed up with, 'So why am I talking to the Chamber of Trade from Bristol?'

'You aren't. You're talking to the Z Organisation.'

'The what?' Peter shrugged, then asked, 'And you are?'

'I am Z.'

5

Peter hated being manipulated. He was fast becoming fed up with the truculent little man in the Savoy bathroom who'd suddenly described himself as Z. He was angry at the persistent air of mystery that surrounded this whole interview. Z – what was that about? Such pedantry! Peter glared at the gnomish head, the beaky nose and the huge spectacles that seemed to enlarge the pupils. He drew in a deep breath – then bit back his sceptical impulse, the impulse that would have asked: *why should I take you on trust?* He was remembering his father's plea to commit to some worthwhile act to advance the war effort. With considerable self-restraint, he said, 'I think I'd prefer a more straightforward explanation of your role, Mr Rosamond.'

He added heavy emphasis on the man's name and this seemed to have an effect.

The man stared at him. The magnified gaze was strangely compelling. 'Not Rosamond, that's a cover. I am Dansey, Edward Claude Dansey. And we're an intelligence organisation. We collect military, diplomatic and economic information about countries abroad and pass it on to our government.'

There was something careful and guarded about this statement. Peter wanted to tease it out. Truscott, when he had visited Whiting Street, had mentioned military intelligence, but this Z Organisation did not sound like a properly appointed government body. *Passing it on* suggested a group of outsiders.

Peter said, 'Not official then? Not kosher, is that what you mean?'

'Not completely green, it would seem,' the newly-revealed Dansey conceded. 'No, the diplomats and the regular types are all under surveillance in certain places abroad, therefore of limited use. Comes of operating out of embassies. We, on the other hand, are above suspicion, unseen by the watchers of enemy states.'

Peter waited, let the water gush without comment, drawing out some more.

'Businessmen,' Dansey said. 'People with legitimate reasons for going into factories and key places to pursue their proper trading function... making deals, arranging orders of equipment, tools and so on... but who succeed in the process of picking up all sorts of useful information. That's what we pass on. Or at least, that's what we did – until Germany became closed off to us. But we've still got the neutrals.'

Peter was not impressed. It sounded like the action of a bunch of amateur spies doing a little sleuthing in their spare time, but Dansey must have read him. 'A good deal more successful than the other lot,' he said sharply.

Gradually, Peter came to a realisation of what had bothered him earlier about their conversation: the vagueness, the guarded answers, the hint of mystery. Father had it. Truscott had it. And so did Dansey. 'Like my father then?' he said.

'Like your father.'

'Is he one of your team?'

'We never discuss our team.'

'Not even with sons?'

'Especially not with sons.'

Peter leaned against the bathroom wall. It was hot and steamy and he could feel the sweat running down his back. It was also uncomfortable standing up and talking to the accompaniment of running water. He was damned if he would let this man intimidate him...

'I still don't see how I could possibly fit in here,' he said. 'How could I contribute to the sort of private enterprise spying service you've been describing? Sounds more like a club. A hobby for elderly gentlemen.'

Dansey's stare became glacial. A high voltage charge had entered this tiny room. Perhaps, after all, Peter had gone too far.

'And I had you down as the intelligent sort! Do I have to revise my opinion?'

'You still haven't answered my question.'

Dansey didn't answer. Instead he said, 'What I can't understand is how a young man who is clearly brave, adventurous, a daredevil wing walker and parachutist, a man not averse to risk, is now wasting his time and talents teaching skiing to men who are never going to use it? Such a waste of resources. How can you face yourself in the shaving mirror every morning?'

Peter coloured. 'Adventurous, yes and not afraid. But I have reservations.'

'No one has the luxury of reservations in wartime.'

'Nevertheless, I'm still not keen on hurling bombs down on mothers and children. There are better ways of confronting evil. Surely we're capable of some ingenuity. Specific measures to hobble the German war machine. And the last thing we should do is descend into the kind of barbarity practised by the enemy.'

A period of taut silence greeted this statement. Then Dansey said, 'I'll buy that. Specific ways to hurt the enemy.' He nodded. 'Could be just up your street.' There was another pause, then a visible relaxation, an almost audible release of tension. Clearly, a decision had been made to be reasonable, and Peter deduced that despite all the aggression, this man wanted something. Once again, Dansey reeled out the familiar list of Peter's skills they had already discussed downstairs: skiing, parachuting and trekking. Then came a reference to the family expertise on the subject of railways, which Peter thought overblown but did not contradict. Finally: 'A certain development is taking place on enemy territory which I cannot discuss but which we cannot tolerate. A serious threat to this nation's security.'

Clearly, Dansey was unaware that Truscott had already let slip the basic facts of Hitler's *Breitspurbahn* system.

Dansey said, 'We regard this matter so seriously we've decided to put a man in. A team, in fact.'

Peter was shocked. Were they mad? Entering the Third Reich in time of war? Suicidal! But then his mind clicked back into gear. 'You're an information collection service, not an operational unit, not an active military enterprise, have I got that right?'

Dansey's expression momentarily stiffened, then relaxed. 'You catch on fast. Let's just say, things are changing because of the war. We're getting official recognition and yes we can initiate action.'

Peter winced. Surely, they were not looking at him? No way! He wasn't crazy, even if they seemed on the verge of a precipice. No, his role would have to be advice, information, instruction.

Dansey said, 'We have approval from on high for this operation.'

'To do what?'

'Steal their secrets.'

Peter said nothing.

'And to destroy.'

Peter spluttered. 'Destroy?'

'Why the doubt?'

'Is this thing,' Peter said carefully, unable to spell out his knowledge of the *Breitspurbahn* and the obvious impossibility of destroying a whole railway network, 'is it really capable of being taken out?'

'It is. And we have a carefully worked-out plan. To attack the key component. We have to kill this thing before the Germans can use it. Our plan is for a small team of saboteurs led by a highly qualified man.'

At this point Dansey unfolded himself from the rim of the bath, standing close in the tiny space between bath and wall. Necessarily, close up to Peter. Dansey was staring hard.

Then he pointed. 'Your team. Because you are that man.'

On the train home from the Savoy, Peter wrestled with a clutch of dilemmas: was the scheme feasible? Was it within his grasp? Was he the right man?

The fraught conversation had continued in the dreadful little bathroom, running water gushing freely away, with Dansey giving him the eye, looking for an answer. Was he in – or was he out? It had been on the tip of Peter's tongue to refuse and he was even more shocked when reference was made to an escape plan. 'That's where your Swiss relatives come in,' Dansey said.

Peter balled a fist and jammed an elbow against the train window, furious that Uncle Stefan had been factored in. Could he ever agree to involving the Feissler family? An immediate recall of his many childhood holidays spent at the house on the shores of the big lake, the smiling faces of the little nieces and their two generous parents, only made the point more painful.

'No danger to the family,' Dansey assured him, 'but a certain degree of risk for your uncle. I believe that when you explain the seriousness of the situation he will agree.'

Peter changed trains at Ipswich, his mind awash with images of his mother's furious reaction to such an idea. The risk was too great. Absurd, unfair. This was not their war, the Feisslers were neutrals.

But he could tell her nothing of this. He was under a strict pledge of secrecy. When he arrived at Bury he walked with leaden steps up Station Hill, past the tannery and the maltings and across the big square, past the Boer War memorial with the statue of the sprawling soldier and into Whiting Street. As he stepped into the hallway of number 2 his mother was waiting. She put an arm on his.

'Don't do it, Peter, whatever it is. Say no. I can tell it's something dreadful, or you wouldn't look so torn.'

'So sorry, Mum, can't tell you.' He grimaced. 'Have to give an answer by Monday.'

In the silence that followed Peter realised he was completely on his own. No advice, no soundings, just the big question: could he do this?

Wasn't he an unlikely choice? Surely there were more qualified people, tough guys, people who loved military derring-do? He thought of Gabrielle, whom his mother referred to as 'your latest girlfriend'. Actually, she was out of date, but Gabrielle nevertheless represented the opposite view of life: a taste of the flamboyant, irrelevant fun, a love of theatre. Peter bought into it. Not just the greasepaint and the prompts and the thrill of performing and the enjoyment of being someone he was not, but the whole joyful camaraderie of backstage. He recalled his role as Spettigue, the villain of *Charlie's Aunt*. His mother loved it, Gabrielle thought it quite good, and Father stayed away.

Peter knew he would have to re-establish his standing with his father. The leathery face had been deeply etched in disappointment. Being lukewarm to the LNER was mistaken; passing up the chance of a place at the RAF staff college was crazy; but failing to volunteer for a more active form of service than a home-based ski school was something akin to shameful. Peter knew he could no longer hide behind his past activities with the Winton refugees. He could no longer cite his objections to bombing. An easy billet in the Cairngorms wasn't good enough. And you couldn't stay a pacifist in the face of Hitler's evil.

Father had pointed an accusing finger. 'Now is the moment to redeem yourself. To wipe the slate clean of past shortcomings. Play your part. Serve your country.'

That evening, Peter stayed alone in his room seeking a way through all his uncertainties, his past attitudes cast in doubt. Had he come up short? His core self-belief had taken a hit. Now, staring out of his bedroom window, he made the decision. He would redeem himself. He would pass the test.

However, there were still two barriers he would not cross. He would refuse to imperil his uncle's family in Switzerland.

And there was that other thing... the promise he made to himself at the outbreak of war, even though he had told no one. Yes, he would act to sabotage an enemy capability, but in doing so he would not take a life. Any life.

She was a tall, angular woman with grey hair and a red feather in her hat, and she'd approached him in the queue for the Savoy reception. 'Mr Chesham?' She had a clipped upper crust drawl. 'Sorry, change of plan, new arrangement, would you care to follow me?'

She had accompanied him outside to the taxi rank. As the cab moved into the Strand and navigated the traffic around Trafalgar Square he tried to pump her for information; destination, or the whereabouts of 'Mr Rosamond' but she remained enigmatically silent. Perhaps this was how the mysterious Z Organisation did things. The cab turned a sharp corner into St James's and stopped. He was conducted up a stairway to a blue door boasting a single metallic numeral five. The knock was answered by another woman, at once more elderly and matronly, and Peter was beckoned inside. He was led directly into a large sitting room where he found Dansey sitting alone on a vast chintz-covered settee. Peter was waved to an armchair and a cup of tea was placed almost instantly on a side table.

No running taps this time. The woman was tending the fire. He noted the lush green carpet, deep curtains and ancient, inlaid secretaire. Was this the man's home? The lack of explanation had Peter's mind in a whirl. He was not to know, until much later, that the matronly woman with the coal scuttle was a Mrs Yarwood, housekeeper for Dansey's safe house; that the Z network was being merged into the Secret Intelligence Service; that Dansey's new place of work was just a short walk across the park to 54 Broadway, a building no one outside the service would ever enter.

'Well?' Dansey did not waste words.

Peter couldn't resist. 'Is it safe? Don't walls have ears?'

Dansey waved a dismissive hand. 'Of course they do. Not only the walls. The dinner plates, the tables, the light sockets, the waiters – but have no fear, this is where I conduct my business.'

'Ah!'

'Well?'

Peter drew in a deep breath, made his prepared response. 'I must be slightly mad,' he said, 'but the answer's yes, I'll do it.'

Dansey's smile was a rare thing. 'I knew it,' he said. 'Had complete confidence. Recognise a good 'un. In fact, I've already lined up your assistant.'

'Hang on a minute,' Peter insisted. 'There's one proviso. One condition attached.'

Dansey's expression changed. He didn't look like a man used to negotiating conditions or provisos, other than those he imposed himself.

'My relative,' Peter said. 'If Uncle Stef doesn't agree, I'm not going to twist his arm.'

Dansey's expression was bleak. 'But you don't know yet what we're going to ask him to do.'

'Whatever it is, if there's danger attached, I won't lean on him. Not if he has good reason to say no. He has to decide if he's willing to risk his neck. I might try to persuade him, if I think it's reasonable, but...' Peter shrugged.

After a brief pause, Dansey gave the merest of nods. 'Very well.'

Peter's tension relaxed. His principal objection had been met, but he wanted specifics about what lay ahead.

'Not the way we work,' Dansey said. 'Only when you need to know. Left hand, right hand... only I know how the pieces of the jigsaw fit together. But never fear. At each stage you'll receive your instructions.'

Peter shook his head. Clearly, Dansey and Father were two of a kind. They operated in a world of ethereal vagueness but that wasn't Peter's way. He wanted the facts. In all his dealings with this man he felt something was not quite right, that the man wasn't being totally honest, that vast amounts of vital information were being withheld from him. Peter also suspected his mountaineering skills were more highly valued than his engineering background. Dansey, he decided, was not entirely to be trusted. 'Sorry,' he said, 'I'd still like more concrete details of what's expected.'

Dansey picked up a manila file, weighing it in his hand, then cleared his throat. 'I'll tell you this much. The man behind all this, the mastermind at the centre of this new system, he isn't German at all. An American. An engineer and inventor who's taken his ideas to Hitler because he's been rejected in the US.'

'Charming!' Peter was dismissive.

'Not charming, touchy. A bit paranoid like all these inventor types who've been rejected. Can't handle it – so off he goes to Adolf who thinks like he does, big is beautiful. No, not just beautiful, gigantic. A misguided enthusiasm for all things of monster proportions. A complete pair of loonies. Here!' Dansey passed over the file which was covered in red stamps, all of them including the word *Secret*. 'You'd better read this. What our headbangers have made of him – and it.'

Peter had never seen such a document before but did his best not to be overawed. He carefully trawled through the details and the main point was soon apparent. The broad gauge railway Hitler was building would have been prohibitively expensive but for the engineer Hank Sumner Hoskins. The American was making it possible by doing away with the need for overhead power cables, normally required for electric locomotives.

Because electricity was no longer required to power the trains.

The final paragraph was chilling:

Hoskins' contribution is the key piece of this jigsaw: a new, efficient, self-contained motor of a revolutionary nature, the details of which remain unknown to us. This is the secret we must discover – and destroy.

Peter closed the file and looked up.

'That's your job,' Dansey said.

6

Her day had begun at five o'clock with her usual routine – but not with her normal frame of mind. As she began to percolate the first coffee of the morning, Claudia's head was filled with the problem of Lotti Bergstein and her small child. How could she follow Erika's edict to send them on their way? It was impossible. It was inhuman.

Yet neither mother nor child could stay in the apartment any longer. They'd been inside too long already, yet to eject them like so much human flotsam was appalling. And to separate mother from child was the ultimate cruelty. That situation had played on her mind ever since an earlier episode in her life and now memories of the business at Prague were coming back to haunt her. Every time she formulated the ugly words she would have to use to Lotti, the brutality of the explanation stuck in her throat.

Was she losing her nerve? Had she gone soft? She asked herself again if she could really carry through the task of playing mother to a band of fugitives. Unruly, unkempt, underfed children. In secrecy and in peril. Still in her dressing gown, she began to pour the soothing liquid, her morning cup, a fixture, her unalterable morning routine. We're all hoarders, she told herself – the whole darned nation, everything from secret stashes of coffee to cans of roasted scorpion or tinned potato salad. It was a reflex from the starvation and shortages of the Great War.

Then she turned her mind to the hateful task ahead, beginning falteringly to explain to Lotti the details of the Maze situation. And when Claudia spoke the awful phrase – 'we think this is the only way' – there were no objections, no protests, least of all screams of horror. Lotti was a picture of resignation. She had already glimpsed the sacrifice ahead.

At this, Claudia's fund of sympathy almost overcame her. Images of similar expressions on the faces of mothers and fathers at Prague's Wilson Station came back to mind. She felt Lotti's pain of separation like the sting of a dozen bees, needle sharp, almost impossible to bear and she had to restrain herself from clutching mother and child to her, assuring them she would never let them go. This was the hardest goodbye she would ever know. It was on the tip of her tongue to blurt *I can't do this!*

But then she stopped. Was this act of rejection to be her hardest test, or were there even more difficult challenges ahead?

Claudia left it to Lotti to manage the final heart-rending parting. How to explain to this tiny, clingy person that leaving her mother was her only chance of life?

Claudia departed for her school day, anxious once again about hosting illicit guests in her apartment but hoping for distraction in the classroom. It came – but several times she had to restrain impatience at some of the tantrums of her altogether luckier pupils at the *Landsberger-Schule*.

Anna's departure was timed for the evening, after dark, on the proviso that this would be accomplished with no tears, no sobbing and no sound; that Anna would be taken by the hand by a knowing, streetwise urchin past the school, down a footpath, through a concealed entrance only he knew and into the unwelcoming embrace of the Maze.

When it was done Claudia thrust into the mother's hand a cup of her most precious coffee – not ersatz but the good stuff, the Melitta Gold she'd been hoarding for months. This was a gift she would make to no other, plus a parcel of foodstuffs she could ill-afford and information that there were basements, sheds and long wild gardens to be found close to her doctor friend's place on the other side of the big main road. Crossing this was a peril in itself, but Lotti made no fuss, melting away into the shadows as if she were made for the subterranean life.

Finally, Claudia was alone in the apartment with the incriminating evidence of multiple occupation safely cleared away. She should have felt relief but she didn't. Instead, she decided that the only way she could deal with a sensation of such total wretchedness was henceforth to make the bigger and ongoing commitment to the children of the Maze.

It was part shack, part warehouse. Brick from the foundations to half up the wall, then iron-framed and wood-cladded. Inside, a vast wooden countertop was grooved by the passage of components demanded and delivered over many years. Behind it, mistress of her oily, musty Aladdin's cave of nuts and bolts, Erika Schmidt was in sole charge. She did not sit, constantly on the move, ministering to her lists, charting the ins and outs of rivets, cranks, crank pins, sleeves and rockers. All the artefacts necessary to keep the wheels turning on a dozen elderly steam locomotives stabled across the tracks at the Shed.

Most days Erika, a chisel-faced blonde with a tight bun and dressed in her faded smock, worked alone in her stores. Not today, however. In a small alcove, out of sight of the main counter, she and Claudia were deep in conversation. 'When you get in there,' Erika said, 'you'd better impose yourself right from the very outset.'

'I know how to deal with children,' Claudia said.

'Not this bunch! You won't have come across kids like these before. They're wild. Animals in a jungle. Unruly isn't the word. And you've got to put a stop to those idiotic daredevils in the tower. I can see them swinging around and playing the monkey from right down here. Someone's bound to spot them.'

Claudia nodded. 'I'll manage.' She had risen early that morning to make her preparations before going to school. And now, as dusk fell, she hoisted her burden and made for the Maze. In her big grip was a generous supply of what her mother used to call 'poor people's food': a fried potato dish called *bratkartoffeln*, *frikadellen*, mincemeat dumplings and *bratwurst* sandwiches plus bread and a creamy spread known as quark. The meat, of course, was ersatz and she'd cleaned out her own food shelf knowing full well she'd used up all her ration coupons for the week. Thank goodness she still had some tins! In her haversack: jumpers, cardigans, coats, socks, caps and scarves – a motley collection of cast-offs of various sizes, courtesy of the generosity of the railway wives. And every evening, she knew, Erika put out by the back door a bucket of clean water which would be emptied during the night.

Claudia was cautious, checking she was alone and unobserved. It was crucial no one should see her disappear into the gloom of the wilderness, brush aside a forest of saplings which had sprung up between the long-disused tracks of the old sidings and squeeze around a broken buffer beam. A hundred metres distant, along a meandering path through the myriad of brambles, gorse and broken sleepers, she stepped around the side of a large, weed-encrusted turntable pit and approached the half-moon-shaped roundhouse, shuttered and abandoned these past five years. She avoided a stack of rusty ties, levered ajar one of the tall, grey folding doors and peered into the gloomy interior.

It was ghostly. Irregular patterns of light played out on the swarf-covered floor. On days when the sun shone, little clouds of dust would dance in the dank air. High above, the big old roof was a patchwork of glass skylights, some broken and letting in the light, others intact and blotting out the daylight due to a covering of lichen. The locomotives had long ago been moved to the other side of the tracks in anticipation of building work which, fortunately for the strays, had failed to materialise.

Claudia moved cautiously round the walkway until she came to the engine pits, now boarded over to prevent anyone falling in. Below the boards was a perfect hiding place – perfect, that is, from the point of view of concealment, if not for comfort. She used her foot to tap on the boards and called softly: 'Rudy! I'm Claudia. Come to help.'

Silence. Just the sound of the wind wisping through the gaps in the roof, so she called again. After another long pause she became aware of a small figure standing motionless in the shadows at the back of the roundhouse. The lined face was that of an adult, the skinny body that of a boy. She smiled at him and pointed to her rucksack. 'Got some things.'

He didn't move, didn't reply.

'A nice thick jumper, a hat and some gloves,' she said, opening the rucksack.

'Why should I talk to you?' It was a thin voice, accusative, loaded with suspicion, verging on hostility.

'I'm here to help,' she said.

'You're one of them.'

She shook her head, a little shocked at this response.

'I'm not stupid,' he persisted, 'it's a trick!'

Claudia sighed, realising she was facing the deeply imbued caution of the fugitive, a boy who'd learned to trust no one, who survived on fear of strangers. 'I'm a friend. With Erika. She sent me.'

Another silence and Claudia resisted the temptation to close the gap between them, worried that if she did so he'd scamper away and climb up among the roof beams. 'I wanted to bring a blanket,' she said as brightly as she could, 'but maybe I'll be lucky and find one for you tomorrow.' She knelt to her task of unloading, feeling a fraud. In reality the nice thick jumper was a ragged and threadbare button-up woolly with one arm missing, the best she could offer against the coming frosts of the night. She heard him edging closer, then became aware that he was by her side.

'My back hurts in the mornings,' he said in a matter-of-fact tone.

She nodded, smiled sympathetically and said, 'Shall we look at your bed?'

He leaned down and heaved aside a heavy board to reveal his bed of straw topped by the remains of a tartan blanket. An outbreak of green mould on one concrete wall, a corner wet from a subterranean stream and the usual evidence of multi-occupation, a line of mouse droppings. She pulled out the old blanket, which began to tear as she did so, substituting the jumper, an oddly-shaped piece of rug and a man's raincoat.

'A message from Erika,' she told the boy. 'No more playing up on those roof girders, someone will see you, we don't want that now, do we?'

The risk was high. How long before some small-minded bigot pumped full of the propaganda of hate spotted him and picked up the telephone? How long before the shouts, screams and chaos of a Gestapo raid? How long before all their futures could be measured in a matter of hours?

Perhaps it was her tone. Possibly her concern had convinced him, for little Rudy then consented to be hugged before she stepped outside. Her next call took her behind the roundhouse. She had to be careful. Walking the rails needed precise placement of feet. It was gloomy and there were potholes and abandoned equipment hidden in overgrown places, but she could not risk using a torch, relying instead on Erika's description. Her right foot caught on something metallic. She stumbled, almost fell, wincing, then walking on at an even slower pace. Finally, she identified the remains of a refrigerator car, now grounded in a corner of a once-busy yard. It was minus chassis and wheels, its paint was a lacklustre blue and there was woodsmoke in the air. She went around the side to find the door. 'Why there?' she had asked Erika, before setting out.

'Keeps them safe from intruders. Can only be opened from the inside.'

Claudia tapped out a code of five: three sharp raps, a pause, then two.

For several tense moments nothing happened. Claudia, alone in the fast fading light amid a clutter of moss-covered gravel and clawing brambles, felt vulnerable and foolish standing next to this dismembered hulk encumbered by all her baggage. Then an oil-starved hinge squealed and a face appeared, looking directly at her.

Cuts scarred the cheeks, the hair was in rat's tails and the eyes were wary. Despite that, recognisably a young male.

'Hello,' she said with a smile, 'I'm Claudia.'

There were a group of them – it seemed to her, the wild, the bored and the frightened – seated or sprawled on the floor, dry sticks on the stove crackling and spitting, the remains of a meal in untidy evidence all about them.

It seemed they knew who she was and why she had come, but the welcome was slow in materialising. She looked them over and noted grubby faces covered in sores. Calloused hands and scars. Clothing that was ragged and ripped with missing buttons. One boy had spectacles with a lens gone, yet another a gap-toothed grin. She saw bruised lips, a crude bandage, a chronic limp and evidence of past conflict. She could guess: fights with home-made swords.

All around was the evidence to bear out Erika's word on petty thievery, a boyish Aladdin's cave: a large bell, a station clock, two locomotive nameplates, a silver teapot, three umbrellas and a brass candlestick as well as more prosaic pieces – tarpaulin, sacking, cooking pots, dishes, hammers, wrenches and large tools beyond the ken of normal youngsters. She noticed too the battered toys and a stack of swords next to a bucket collecting drips of rainwater spilling from the roof. She wrinkled her nose: the place stank of unwashed bodies and rotting food.

'Well then,' she said, 'you know who I am, so you'd better introduce yourselves. For a start, who's the daredevil who likes jumping around the tower?'

The ten-year-old with a swagger to go with his rat's tails announced himself: 'Me. They calls me Runner.'

'Oh?'

'I'm the lookout. Anyone comes in the weeds and I'm down here double quick with a warning. Then we all disappear, see?'

A ripple of little grins lit the grimy faces. 'You know when to run, don't you, Runner?' squeaked an admiring voice. 'When to scarper like you was never here?'

'Sure.' A cock of the braggart's shoulder. 'Coppers' sticks, coppers cuffing ears, coppers banging on doors. It's what I know. It's why I'm here.'

Claudia gently delivered her message to cut out the roof antics for fear of discovery. The answer was a sullen glare.

She swallowed. The contrast with her well-dressed day pupils was stark. Her love of children was outraged.

There were other self-styled titles and sometimes these were cruel: Eagle, Cheetah, Mole, Beakie and Wingnut. 'And you?' she asked another.

'Fat Fonzie.'

'But you're looking very lean.'

'How else in here?'

'What have you managed so far?'

'A good day...' Fonzie sighed. 'Fried potatoes, sausage. More often cabbage and treacle, hard bread, soup. Always soup. Very watery soup.'

Another voice: 'I had a dream last night.'

'And you are?'

'Beakie.'

She put an arm around the child, stooping so they were face to face. 'What's your dream, Beakie?'

A lick of the lips. 'Sweet and sour dumplings, beef roulade, *speisequark* for breakfast like my mum did it, loads of blackcurrant and blueberries in a bread roll hot from the oven.'

At this there was a reverential hush, the sort that might have greeted some clerical announcement in church. She looked around the faces. She saw eager eyes focused on her holdall. 'Talking of which,' she said, zipping it open, 'I have something for you all.'

Inertia vanished in a flash. Young figures leapt into a crowding circle.

'One at a time! Don't all rush!' She smacked a hand. 'Don't grab.'

If not yet feral, some of these children were approaching a measure of savagery. Left to their own devices, it wouldn't take much longer. She made them exchange the worst of their ragged clothing for new items, intending to wash or replace as necessary. Cooking was a problem. Scorch marks on the wall described past disasters. Hygiene was almost non-existent, so she promised to be back with a bathtub.

'Are you going to wash us down?' asked Runner.

'I'll scrub you down if I have to,' she said, and her expression killed the smirk. She looked beyond Runner into a corner where two girls lay together, a picture of dejection and lassitude. She asked their names – Elsa and Frieda – and the querulous questions began: What's going to happen to us? When can we go home? Will we have to stay here for ever?

In the ensuing cuddle, she was shocked at how they seemed to be no more than skin and bone. She was frightened to hold them tightly lest they break in two. Such was her emotion she forgot their stink. She wanted to gather them all together and hold them tight, to share their loneliness, fear, hunger and uncertainty. She touched shoulders, arms and fingers. It was a physical welling of compassion, almost maternal, and she prayed that none of hers would ever sink to this condition.

'Is this everyone?' she asked.

'Some others are in the caboose next door,' she was told.

How much worse could this situation get? She was momentarily rendered inactive by a sense of hopelessness and yearning. It was a familiar feeling. Many times in the past she had been overcome by a sense of grief, a hollowed out feeling. On these occasions she felt herself to be the shell of the person she ought to be. Her eyes flickered but when she looked up she saw they were all looking at her, the atmosphere expectant. That was when she knew she had to stay strong. However frightened she might be at her own risk, it was dwarfed by an enormous sense of responsibility. She couldn't run away from this. She and Erika were the only hope these children had.

'Look,' she said, 'I'll visit the ones next door but before I go, listen to this.' Common sense should have stopped her, but she could not hold back from an outlandish promise almost impossible to fulfil. 'I will help you all I possibly can,' she said, 'and somehow I will get you out of here.'

There was a silence as they looked at her. Was it wonder, or disbelief? She knew her statement was foolhardy but her history with the *Kindertransports* was too strong. How many evacuees had she packed off from Prague before the war began and the restrictions were imposed? Did these children deserve any less? Her reaction was purely instinctive. A voice of doubt should have asked if she could pull off such a trick in wartime and alone. Turn a wild bunch such as this into disciplined escapers? She pawed the place at the back of her neck. These children needed more than help. They needed hope. And a future.

'Get us out?' queried Runner.

'Yes, get you out,' she said, adding silently to herself that the *how* of this improbable promise would be dealt with later.

It was a workers' block, tucked away off the main street, washing flapping in tiny backyards, logs stacked ready for the exigencies of winter, a wrecked wash boiler, an outside lavatory. These were mainly depot people, Claudia knew, as she cautiously approached the end door. She could hear a radio playing, someone raking a fire, a mother scolding an unseen miscreant. She moved quietly from the shadows and tapped gently on the door. Through the window she could see a braces-down figure in an upright chair next to a curl of woodsmoke.

The door was opened by Frau Fleischmann. She was

married to an engine cleaner. She was also the collector, the repository of blankets, mostly threadbare, and jumpers with holes, gifts to pass on from her neighbours. Also in the bundle were worn towels, spare spectacles and the odd toy with three wheels and fewer tyres.

'Whatever you can spare.' Claudia smiled her gratitude. 'These are not plentiful times.' She tried a joke. 'Not yet in the land of milk and honey.'

Frau Fleischmann frowned. 'Can't remember the last time I tasted honey.'

She opened a tiny pantry door to add six crumb cakes to Claudia's cache. 'Had to eke out the ingredients,' she said.

Claudia responded with enthusiasm, repressing the memory of a previous offering from the workshop manager's wife. Runner had insisted: 'Tastes like sawdust, nothing like my mum's.'

Frau Fleischmann was one of the more sympathetic house-wives on Claudia's collection round. 'Poor little things, so awful what's happened to them... and you!' She was looking at Claudia directly. 'You don't look well, either. Up half the night scraping the barrel, you must be tired out.'

Claudia assured her she was fine and moved on, but her next call was less productive. 'We're short ourselves, do you expect our own kids to go without?' Frau Demmler had hands on hips. 'And they're not all little angels in that Maze, you know, they've had my bird table away. And a garden spade. Little tearaways!'

Claudia did her best to smooth ruffled feathers. Next would be a cautious return journey. She had to slip out of the depot without anyone being curious enough to ask about her big bundle. These days women carrying bags were common enough. Lean, they were, and always on the lookout. A sudden queue was the signal that something good had arrived in the shops. Empty bags were the norm, bulky ones the exception.

~

First priority on arrival in the Maze was always food. Runner's plaintive appeal – 'I'm always hungry, I can't think of anything but food. Food, food, food... all the time' – had Claudia again raiding her depleted larder and that of Erika and several of the railway wives. Sausage was the staple, plus anything else that could be spared from modest dinner tables. Sometimes little extras appeared, like the large pink cake she suspected came from the works kitchen. And she was sufficiently accepted in the Maze to observe behaviour during this frantic feeding time. There was an overheard snatch of conversation from Runner: 'When the soup comes round I grab my share and pinch a bit of bread off Eagle. He's not as sharp as he thinks.'

Later, she was privy to more of Runner's survival technique. 'Work for each other, share everything?' That had been Claudia's suggestion. Well, up to a point. You had to look after yourself, didn't you? The little ones didn't need all that food. He could acquire a slice or two of theirs when their attention was diverted. He was much bigger and stronger than they, he needed more and they didn't. And when Eagle hid an extra slice of bread under that bit of old carpet he called his pillow, Runner clocked him and later Runner had it. He felt no qualms. He was a survivor, this is what you had to do. To keep going. To stop the hunger.

And hate: Runner loathed all uniforms. They were a menace, they were the enemy. 'The day Horst disappeared I decided: they're not getting me,' Runner said. 'Best lesson I ever learned. Banging on the door in the night, everyone woken up and me, straight into the boiler cupboard behind the big tank. Crouching, listening, shivering. Hearing all the noise, the crashes and shouts and cries. I heard my ma and pa, then all went quiet.'

Runner's eyes were moist. 'The coppers knew about me,' he said, 'and they came looking. But they didn't find me.'

Claudia swallowed hard but decided that talking about their experiences was therapeutic. 'What about you, Eagle, how did you end up here?' she asked, then regretted it when she saw his face.

'I was in the garden,' he said, 'when they took my daddy away and I hid behind the shed. Why did they do that?'

For a moment she was at a loss and the boy added, 'He said some people didn't like him, but why didn't they like him? He was my dad, he was my special dad.'

'It was the Brownshirts, stupid!' Runner was by far the most knowing of the fugitives. 'The Brownshirts, they don't like anybody.'

Claudia looked around, aghast at the state of the children's teeth. Yellowing, jagged, missing, distorted. It was appalling, but there was nothing – no brushes, no toothpaste, no inclination. She thought of the contrast to her own dental regime: at least three sessions a day, once after every meal and sometimes more. Her brother, when they were young, had even accused her of being an obsessive.

The memory was interrupted by a scuffling noise at the end of the wagon, followed by high-pitched yelps and shouts. It was a tussle; kicking legs, flailing arms, swinging fists. The children crowded round. A fight was a spectacle, a distraction, an event. Cooking pots, a cracked chair and several empty buckets scattered as two little furies scrapped.

This was a situation Claudia knew well enough. She'd been there before. She had Cheetah and Wingnut by their collars.

'If you must,' she said, 'do it outside.'

It was a day later and Oskar had an angry boil on the back of his neck. Red at the edges with a hard yellow core. It was the worst she had seen and she'd brought him back from the caboose to deal with him under the electric light of the component store. Claudia was struggling, trying to apply a hot poultice while the boy whined and squirmed.

'Hold still!' she said, trying to pin him to the chair. 'Or it'll all be for nothing. It's taken me ages to get hold of one of these...'

Footsteps made her look up from her work, one hand still on the boy's shoulder.

Karl Drexler was standing just inside the counter flap, staring down at them. There was a shocked silence. Oskar stopped struggling and Claudia ceased her endeavours. She was aghast. Her least favourite person had tracked her down. Her safe haven was exposed.

'So!' he said, one lip curling in mocking triumph, 'this is where you rush off to every afternoon after school. Not very exciting, is it?' He flung a cursory glance around the component shelves. 'What's the big attraction?'

Claudia laid down her poultice, straightened and faced up a challenge. Cold, imperious, hostile. 'Herr Drexler, what are you doing here?'

'Following you, of course. I'm intrigued. You always skip off school at the earliest possible moment, as if you've got some frantic mission to complete. Every day. Ignoring us. Taking no part in school activities. Like you really hate your work. And I want to know why.'

She stepped forward, blocking his view of the child. 'This is private property and I don't see how that's any of your...'

'Oh, but it is. We require more of a teacher than just class-room and yard duty.' He moved, rounding her, staring down at the boy. 'Boils and sores? Very old ones, by the look of them, and he's distinctly unkempt. Who is this child? And why haven't I seen him at school?'

Claudia opened her mouth but no words emerged, fearful that any impromptu lie would incriminate her.

'Well?'

Erika, who had said nothing during this exchange, stepped forward from the shadows. 'He's mine.'

Drexler turned. 'And you are?'

Claudia exploded. 'You've no right! You're not in school now. You have no authority to ask questions here.'

Erika chimed in again. 'He's mine, well not exactly mine, actually he's my nephew, just visiting and he's not normally in this state, it's just that he's been playing, having a good time, rolling around in the bushes and the scrub and playing hide and seek, you know how boys are.'

Drexler's brows knitted. Then he scowled his storm-trooper scowl. 'You should be ashamed. Letting a child get into this state. Look at him! Playing in the bushes? He hasn't had a wash in a week. Probably longer. Why isn't he in school?'

'Just visiting from across the city. Another school.'

'What he needs is a doctor and some good mothering.'

'Enough!' Claudia came up close, her face flushed. 'No more of this! It's none of your business what my friend and her nephew do. You should leave. Now.'

Drexler simply grinned. 'Not before you explain your part in this.' He nodded to the scrub beyond the window. 'And what's out there? What's the attraction?'

Claudia bristled. If Drexler set foot in the wilderness all would be lost. 'Go!' she said. 'Immediately!'

Erika's soft tone interrupted once again: 'Can't friends meet for a coffee and a chat without an inquisition?' She even managed a smile. 'Planning an outing for family and friends.

Nothing more. It's really no great mystery. Nothing to get excited about.'

'But why in here?'

'Why not? As good a place as any.'

Claudia took in a deep breath. Thank God for Erika. Instead of standing on her dignity, as she was entitled to do as the mistress of her tiny domain, she'd drawn some of the sting from Drexler's inquisition. Still, the danger remained. Drexler was peering at the child and then at the wilderness. Oskar was cowering in fright. If he made a dash for the door and vanished into the bushes Drexler would surely guess and their subterfuge would be destroyed. Claudia clutched the boy tightly around his shoulders.

'How did you get those sores, boy? Speak up!'

'Sir,' cut in Erika's gentle voice, 'can't you see? You're frightening the child.'

Drexler glowered, looked from the boy to Erika and then to Claudia and again out of the window at the wavering willows bending in the afternoon breeze. Then, eyeing Claudia, he said, 'I've an instruction from your colleagues. You need to show more commitment to the school. To be involved in our activities.'

Silence.

Finally, he said, 'The teachers' committee instruct that you attend next week's meeting in the staffroom. Wednesday sharp at two. And no excuses for absence will be accepted.'

7

It was Thursday, seventy-two hours after the abrupt meeting with Dansey in the flat in St James's Street, three rushed days of frantic activity. Crammer sessions on morse, suitcase wireless sets, how to place explosives, the power of amatol and, most painful of all for him, the best way to wreck a train.

Dansey, that bullying little caricature of a man, had talked of 'putting in a team'. A team? Peter snorted. The team, it transpired, was a single specialist in electronics, battery technology and electric locomotives. Not an academic, mark you. Not a professor of electronics, nor a wizard from some laboratory or research establishment. Instead, a practical engineer from the Stratford workshops of the London and North Eastern Railway, a man he'd just met that morning on the Ringway parachute tower. Peter had been hooking up his harness, hardly noticing the small man waiting his turn behind him.

'I'm Private Williams,' said a sing-song voice.

Peter turned briefly and nodded.

'I'm with you.'

'Oh, really?'

'I'm LNER.'

Before the conversation could proceed further, the jump sergeant intervened. 'Next!'

Peter gave the required thumbs up and his leap from the tower was as smooth as he always intended, landing perfectly, executing a copybook roll. Easy for someone who'd been jumping out of his uncle's biplane since boyhood.

'You should be doing my job, sir,' said the sergeant with a grin.

'Check out the next one, would you?' was Peter's reply.

Private Williams swung out wide and described a flailing descent, landing in a muddy heap without any of the prescribed rolls.

'Won't get far like that,' the sergeant said.

Later, in a noise-filled Nissen hut, Owen Glendower Williams introduced himself again. 'I recognise you!' he said.

'Peter Chesham,' Peter replied amiably.

'Ah, the boss's blue-eyed boy!' And when Peter did a double take, added, 'We know all about you at Stratford. Word spreads fast. And we'd been warned to be careful, you being under the wing of Sir Andrew and all that.'

In the next few days they came into frequent contact. No mention was made of rank or status as they took to the air for practice jumps from an RAF Anson. Peter's anxiety grew when Williams required the flight sergeant's boot to launch him into space.

Later he asked, 'I take it you can ski a bit, perhaps just a little.'

'Of course.'

Monday found them sitting in a dingy room at North Weald aerodrome, just outside London. A fighter station bristling with Hurricanes. One hangar, however, was devoted to a disparate collection of Hudsons, Lysanders, Whitleys and Martin Marylands, the special ops of Flight 1419.

Peter felt rushed, swamped and uncertain. All along he had nursed doubts about Dansey and his highly personalised espionage set-up. He couldn't rid himself of the suspicion that the little man was a chancer, a flaky personality whose word might be suspect. He even had doubts about his own credentials; how did a degree and a familiarity with railway engineering qualify him for delving into a completely new and unknown technology? There would be no explosives; these were to be sourced on site; his contacts were few; and how would he handle it if the maverick American turned hostile? What's more, he hated involving Uncle Stefan. The operational plan was based on his uncle's ability to use the Dragonfly biplane. Such was his distaste for this idea that Peter even tried persuading the North Weald adjutant to provide a British pilot for the role, and his approach was met, at first, with an amenable nod.

'Sure, we've got all manner of madmen here, just itching to get into the air and try any crazy stunt,' the adjutant said. 'Yanks and Canadians, used to playing dodgems over the Rockies. They'd love to help you out – but it's not part of my job to waste lives on impossible missions.'

Then the adjutant, whose name was Bledloe, took the pipe from his mouth, pointed it at Peter and added, 'And no, we can't let you have one.'

At first, certain aspects of the operation had appealed to Peter's imagination as ingenious, but as they clung to their seats in the fuel-sodden atmosphere of the vibrating Hudson bomber, somewhere over the English Channel reality kicked in and enthusiasm waned into apprehension. He saw jackboots and prisons and all manner of horrors ahead. He'd asked why they couldn't be dropped nearer their target but was told this was completely impractical – 'the fastest suicide note in history'. Peter clutched at a vibrating stanchion and wondered what other problems he would face. That's when the starboard engine caught fire and the pilot was taken sick. Peter couldn't help – he was a jumper, not a pilot. The Hudson wallowed drunkenly and he knew the crew were not in control. When bidden to 'brace, tighten straps, heads between knees', bile rushed into his throat. What a rotten fate, to end up in a crumpled heap in some desolate countryside. Then came the shattering, tearing, ripping collision with the ground. When the din ceased and they were still, he could hardly believe they were down and alive. They stumbled out of the battered fuselage, grateful for their good fortune.

Peter sat on a tree stump, peering at the crumpled wreckage. Two crewmen were crouching to examine what was left of the undercarriage. It didn't look good. Peter rolled out his maps. Despite all the problems they had at least succeeded in skirting around French territory, both the occupied zone and Vichy, and had landed as planned in the Italian zone, a narrow sliver of Alpine terrain close up to the Swiss border.

That they were in the right place was confirmed by the approach of two figures from the shadows. Their reception committee consisted of an elderly miller and his daughter. At last, it seemed, something touched by Dansey had worked.

Peter looked back at the wreckage and asked for the second time in as many minutes, 'Well, will it fly?'

Larkin stood up. 'Sorry, no can do. The thing's a proper mess. This kite has had it, no doubt about it.'

Peter swallowed, knowing it was up to him to demonstrate command. 'Then you know what to do,' he said.

The plane was quickly despatched with a fiery whoosh, courtesy of a Very flare pistol, and Peter, Williams and the three Hudson crewmen, one limping painfully, began to trudge uphill to seek shelter at daybreak at the miller's huge windmill standing high on a knoll. Mahoney, the pilot, was the casualty. 'Still hurting like billy-o,' he said, and Peter confronted his next problem: now there were not two of them, but five. And best the RAF men could expect was to seek sanctuary in the British Embassy or face internment in a Swiss prisoner of war camp.

At the mill, Jules Victor Chappet was reassuring. 'You'll be completely safe here,' he said, 'nobody's been near us in weeks.'

Peter, grateful, nodded, happy to make the man a gift. The miller was a valued Resistance asset, a veteran of Verdun, a man who knew about war and weaponry. Their 'beds' for the day were several floors up a steep ladder to the wooden landing stages of the mill. They might be safe enough for the moment, Peter reflected, but they were still far from their target in the Third Reich, and still stuck in Italian territory.

8

The postcard showed the *Frauenkirche*, the two huge green domes of the cathedral towering over the city which seemed to slumber below, the iconic image of Munich. Claudia was penning an anodyne message to her family, a message of hope and happiness about her new life in Bavaria. It was her regular routine, a different scene each week of the city or the countryside in which she now lived. The bookshop in Neuhausen had a seemingly limitless variety of picture-postcard scenes for the benefit of the tourists of the Reich who came to view their Fuhrer's favourite city.

To her parents it was a carefully constructed message assuring them all was well. It did not reflect reality. Claudia was alone in her small flat with her postcards and her pens and her reassuring fiction, feeling isolated and confined and conscious of the risks she was running. And now, to heighten her sense of peril, Drexler was insisting she face his self-appointed teachers' committee, the party hacks, propagandists and hatemongers she so detested.

One thing was certain. She could not tell her mother any of this. She had promised never to put the family in danger. She remembered the phrases on her departure from Prague: 'Don't be careless with our safety, Claudia.' 'Remember, one unguarded word can bring the house down.' 'Open your mouth too wide and put us all in the KZ.'

The KZ. Typical of Germany. Initials for everything, including the concentration camps. It had started with Dachau and now the KZs spread like locusts across all the occupied lands.

'Even if you don't care about us,' her mother said with her accustomed acidity, 'at least remember your brother!' Robert was in the forces and Claudia knew all about the regime mind-set: the shame of one family member spread to all the others, particularly those in uniform. If she were arrested, he too would be a suspect, perhaps interrogated, perhaps sent to a penal battalion. Mother was frantic to keep Robert out of harm's way at his present obscure air force billet at a North Sea wireless station untouched by war. Mother always favoured Robert.

Claudia's own relationship with her mother had been in the deep freeze since her early teens. She thought again of why she was now in Munich. She had been told to stay out of trouble. It seemed like a form of banishment for that other time of 'getting involved'. There had been rebellion, outspokenness and a defiance of authority. Warning words came back to her: 'These are dangerous times... you've made yourself much too visible to the wrong sort of people.'

Should she now back off to safeguard Robert and the family? Or defy her mother and try to save the children?

She attempted to offset these anxieties by attending to personal appearance. Nails and hair, always neat. Sensible cloth-ing. And no makeup, just as the regime liked it, the one strand of approval they had in common. In the loneliness of her room she sat in front of the mirror and realised the rosy bloom which had once been her trademark had now faded to a washed-out pallor.

She sighed. Never mind, she had plenty to be grateful for. She got up and put a von Weber clarinet concerto on the gramophone. Hers was still a moderately comfortable life. Her voyages into the Maze – scratched by brambles, clothes snagged by thorns – had shown her that. She ran an appreciative finger along the rim of her coffee cup; smooth to the touch, comforting, whole, the blue floral pattern bright and attractive. She possessed fine china. Well, no, it wasn't exactly fine, but compared rather favourably with the unhygienic, broken and split utensils the Maze children used. This, despite denuding most of her cupboard of useful items to pack into a rescue rucksack: cups, pots, pans, cutlery. Added to this had been her school ma'am session with the toothbrushes – all four of them, her very own spares – the toothpaste and the bucket of water. *Do we have to? Yes, you have to.* Their awful teeth were an affront to Claudia.

Her gaze travelled to the other items on her dressing table: the calendar with red rings drawn around two highly-charged emotional anniversaries: a birthday and a departure date. All that, of course, related to that other time before the war when she lived at the family home in Prague, part of the extensive ethnic German community in the Czech capital. She glanced at the painting of Charles Bridge hanging above the fireplace, feeling a little homesick, then at the lapel badge she had worn during her role as helper with the *Kindertransport* departures from the city. Almost involuntarily, she glanced up to the big hat on the top of her wardrobe. She hadn't worn it since ceasing her activities at the station but kept it as a reminder, even pinning on a fresh carnation when an old one faded. The flower was her badge of hope.

She reached for a needle and thread to repair a torn pocket but thoughts of the transports led her instead to open a drawer and to take out the official pass which had given her access to the Prague platforms. The Gestapo ran the operation and back then she hadn't been frightened. She had their grudging permission and felt a personal commitment to the *Kindertransports*, a close emotional link that once prompted an acquaintance to ask, 'Why so dedicated? What's it to you? They're mostly Jewish kids, aren't they?'

To which she had replied, 'They're little children,' with such contemptuous finality that her words silenced any reply.

These memories had her sliding from its hiding place a blank British identity document which she should have destroyed, gazing down at the spaces to be filled in for each child. She studied again the accompanying wording; an approval by the UK government for 'young persons to be admitted for educational purposes under the care of the Inter-Aid Committee', a document requiring no visa and stamped in bold blue ink at the bottom left corner by the 'British Committee for Children in Prague'.

She closed the drawer with a deep sigh and glanced up at the photograph of the Kellner family group: the smiling faces of mother, father and brother Robert. Was the family's good name meant to trump all else? Absent from the picture was the one face missing from Claudia's life: the snub nose and the blue eyes, the same features she had seen a year before with a sense of shock on a sad little boy curled up in a corner seat on the eighth *Kindertransport* departure in Prague. He was on the point of tears. And a dark-haired girl of eight was cradling his shoulders.

Could it be true?

Once again the image swam before her eyes.

They were seated together in a corner, the girl with her arm around the curled-up boy. He was tearful, she was playing little mother. Claudia studied the boy. There was something about him...

For Claudia the day had begun in the waiting room, hot and humid with fear and tears, men and women trying to hide their distress on the day no parent ever wished to see. How do you bring yourself to give your child away? To send them into the arms of strangers?

The talk had been all round the city: of what would happen next to the Jews of Prague. Already deprived of work, schooling and banned from parks and cinemas, worse was feared: round-ups, ghettos, transports to God knew where. No future for a child.

Hence the crowded, sorrowful waiting room at the city's main terminus. With typical cruelty, the German authorities banned parents from the platform, so Claudia was in the middle of this art nouveau masterpiece that was the Wilson Station, named after the American president, dressed for easy recognition in a large straw hat topped off with a pink carnation, ready at the appointed hour to lead a crocodile of 150 children to the waiting carriages. 'All join hands,' she called, clasping tiny fingers, 'and don't forget. Follow the hat!'

It was perhaps twenty minutes later, when she had her charges seated in their allotted places, that she spotted the boy. Blond, blue eyes, a certain set to the mouth, a snub nose. Inseparable from the girl.

Claudia drew in a deep breath and held it. Could this be? Could this be the one?

The girl, who had brown hair tied back in a ponytail, a lacy collar and an earnest expression, produced a sweet from a pocket and the younger child immediately sat up, his face transformed into a smile.

That smile. It was a clincher. It had to be. Now she was sure, there couldn't be another smile quite like it.

Shouts and activity outside on the platform signalled the imminent departure of the train. Now that all the English Kindertransport workers had been sent home, to be replaced by the Prague Institute and the Gestapo, Claudia was the last of the volunteers prepared to be a sympathetic face for the departing children. She looked up. She must get off. She had no business on this train once it left the city.

Then she looked back down at the boy and the girl and read off the names from their ID tags: Luise and Hansi Grunwald. She didn't know the names. She had never known the names. But in that instant, instinct took over.

She smiled at them. She rolled up her sleeve. 'You look so nice together,' she said, pulling her grandmother's eternity ring from her finger, 'and you're taking such good care of your brother. You both should have something extra to remind you of this moment in later years.'

It was a spontaneous gift. She reached for the girl's hand and slipped the ring onto the middle finger. It was loose and didn't fit, so she pressed it into the girl's hand. Then she passed over her wristwatch. 'Look after this for little Hansi,' she told the girl.

More shouts, loud whistles.

Claudia stood, eyes filling, addressing a carriage full of children bound for survival and freedom in England. 'Good luck, everyone, and a safe journey to your new homes.'

9

The first thing they saw, once their eyes became accustomed to the dark, was the sign *Bella Vista* hanging drunkenly from one nail.

Peter frowned. Stefan would surely never have allowed such sloppiness. No sign of the children's swing, either. Then the outline of the chalet came into view, its eaves extending low. Somewhere in the darkness was the gentle lap of water against wood and Peter stood to absorb the familiar smell, a unique mix of lake, mown grass, pigs, cows and lavender. He remained standing, hesitating, relieved to have arrived at the Feissler home on the southern shore of Lake Constance but still concerned. They'd been collected from the windmill the night before, taken across the frontier and driven across Swiss territory in a succession of unmarked cars and vans. It was a slick operation, he had to admit it, and Dansey's Z Organisation had finally proved their worth. They worked, so the contact man Bob Marshall told him, out of a building in Berne quite separate from the British Embassy to avoid surveillance. The airmen had been dropped off at the Z House and now he and Williams had arrived at his uncle's place, but still he remained hesitant. Even in the gloom he could see that the window boxes were empty and the logs uncut. How was he to approach his aunt and uncle, explain his arrival unannounced in the middle of the night and in the middle of a war? Simply walk in through the back door?

He shook his head. The shock effect would be devastating. Instead, he did what he had never done before. He approached the front door and, feeling foolish, gave a gentle knock.

He and Williams waited, eyeing each other, shuffling their boots but saying nothing.

After a long pause Peter rapped again, this time harder. No lights were visible but they could hear a slight movement. Perhaps a wary Stefan was examining them through a blacked-out window.

At last the door opened and Peter peered closely in the poor light until he recognised the slim figure of his Aunt Trudi.

She looked wan. She looked shocked.

'Peter?'

'Hi there!' he said with a huge grin.

'What are you doing here?' An incredulous tone.

Not one Peter was used to. He moved forward. 'This is my friend, Owen.'

There was no response, just an awkward silence.

Then he said: 'Aren't you going to let us in?'

Silently, without a single word, Trudi eased open the door wide enough for them to walk carefully past her and into the darkened hall. She immediately closed the door and arranged a blackout curtain before switching on a dull, flickering electric light.

She didn't invite them further, didn't hug him or give any sign of welcome. Now he could see that she was not the healthy figure of his memory. She had lost her outdoor suntan. Her hair was straggly and her expression gaunt.

'Why?' she demanded, hands on hips, shaking her head. 'What are you doing? How did you get here?'

'I had help.'

That didn't improve the reception. 'Do you know, do you realise, have you even the vaguest of ideas of how dangerous this is?'

At that moment his aunt's exasperated tone was cut off by an inquiring shout from the interior of the house. A door opened and a young female voice demanded, 'Who is it?'

Then they were there, in the hall, two young girls with big smiles, arms outstretched. 'Peter!'

The arrival of his two nieces, Bella and Petra, broke the frigidity of the reception. Peter introduced Owen Glendower Williams using his full title, amid some laughter, and without inhibition they were led into the living room. There was no sign of Uncle Stef, Peter noticed, and there was another worrying sign: nothing bubbling on the big old range.

'Thank God for some new company,' Bella said, 'it's so boring here, so really boring, cooped up in this house.'

'Can't you go out?' Peter asked, before he could bite back the naivety of the question.

Petra made a face. 'It's the war,' she said, clearly imitating a parental instruction, 'and Mummy and Daddy are very worried about it and us.'

Trudi strove to take charge of the conversation once more. 'I'm sorry to sound so short,' she said, 'but you come at a very bad time.'

There were bags under her eyes and Peter noticed straggly ends to a rather dowdy jumper. Where were the exotic colours he had once known? The bright oranges, yellows and reds and the hairdo with the finger waves and rolled curls? 'I know it's difficult,' he said.

'The Swiss neutrality laws are now so strict. So very strict. If we break them we can be arrested, fined, even jailed, and then sacked from our jobs. We might even lose the house. Or the children.'

He grimaced. 'We'll be very discreet.'

Trudi did not look encouraged by his reply. 'We're not allowed to take in strangers, to give aid to any warring country, whichever one it is...' She broke off with a long sigh. 'We're taking enough risks already,' she said.

'Refugees?' Peter guessed.

Her eyes blazed. 'I'm not telling you anything. Anything, d'you hear?'

He tried to make a joke of it, about peas in the family pod, but she cut him off. 'Why are you here? You're family, of course you are, but you represent a belligerent power. So, tell me, what's going on?'

Peter sighed and looked around the room. 'Where's Uncle?'

'Never mind Stefan. Why?'

Peter folded his arms. 'Sorry, all I can say is that I will not put you or the girls in harm's way.'

Trudi studied him for a long minute. 'Why do you exclude Stefan from that promise?'

'Because I have to talk to him.'

'I won't have you involving him.'

When Peter merely raised his eyebrows, she said, 'Whatever it is, I want to hear it.'

'Sorry, Trudi, this is classified. A secret. I'm under orders and I can only talk to him alone.'

'Under orders!' She spat the words. 'So you come here on some devious errand, putting us at peril. I won't be used by anyone. We won't be used. And particularly not by you, you of all people. Is this really you, Peter?'

Her voice had risen to a high pitch. He expected reluctance but hadn't bargained on hostility. The exchange was becoming far too taut for the girls.

'Mummy!' It was Bella, pulling at her mother's blouse. 'Stop going on at Peter, don't be so horrid. Make them some drinks. They'd like tea.'

'I'm glad he's here,' declared Petra, arms folded, a big smile in place. 'And when he gets back, so will Daddy be.'

Trudi's looks were still dark and glowering. She stared at Peter and said, 'You can't stay here.'

'What?'

'You must go.'

'Mummy!' Bella shrieked.

Peter could not mask his surprise but just at that moment he detected a slight noise from downstairs and a tiny vibration. He knew she'd heard it too. More telling squeaks from somewhere below, then the rattle of a door. Her expression was a mix of alarm and relief as she snapped upright and hurried from the room.

And Peter could take a good guess why.

10

As the appointed hour approached – 'Wednesday sharp at two' – Claudia's anxiety peaked. She knew she had to present a strong face to this self-appointed teachers' committee, acting as they were like some star chamber. Claudia felt the weight of an enormous responsibility for her secret charges in the Maze. She had to face these men out. She knew they were planning a grilling, an inquisition. This was more than an ordeal. If she should falter, they represented a threat to herself, her family and her hidden charges. Over the past few days her emotions had roller-coasted between defiance and apprehension. She was feeling the strain of her double life. Once again she heard her mother's voice urging caution and her mind had wandered back over all the events of the past. Two days ago, in the privacy of her apartment, she found herself quietly sobbing, unable to control a sense of uncontainable longing.

Now that the moment was at hand, she refused to play the game by dressing up in something special, instead wearing her usual burgundy jersey dress, as she would on any normal school day.

At two o'clock she entered the staffroom to find them all

there, diehards to a man, lounging in their brown shirts, breeches and jackboots: Hobisch, the PT master now elevated to the status of deputy headmaster, Spindlegger, in charge of training camp and Kuhn, an enthusiast for marching, parades and everything Nazi.

Claudia looked around as she entered the room, feeling isolated and vulnerable. To distract herself, she studied the room and the furniture. Theirs wasn't a modern building, not like the brand-new Bauhaus place for the party elite further into town. Here, heavily-varnished dark-wood panelling contained small decorative squares in which were hung framed photos of parades, notables and memorable occasions, like the annual martyrs march to the field marshal's square. She recalled an old jest from her mother: the army would not be complete until every last schoolmaster has his commission.

That joke, Claudia decided, was wishful thinking. This crew did not aspire to the relative civility of military field grey. Hobisch had his detestable boots on a chair. Once she had liked the smell of leather. Now she hated it, loathed the way these Brownshirt martinets swanked and slapped it with glee and paraded in it, how it appeared to validate their delusions of authority. Their innate absurdity sparked a sudden and bizarre thought which gave her spirits a fillip: how hilarious it would be ·if she could upset their table, see them falling about in chaos, beer and coffee splashing down their shiny leather.

The deputy head spoke first, a voice grating with sarcasm. 'Fraulein Kellner, how nice to see you. We so rarely have the pleasure. Anyone would think you've been avoiding us.'

She smiled, conjuring an unconcerned front. 'Purely coincidental, I assure you.' She glanced around, seeking out her most dangerous adversary, but strangely Karl Drexler wasn't present. Probably, she guessed, drilling 4B on the school square.

Hobisch said, 'Your attachment to your duties in the schoolyard and the children is highly commendable. Such dedication! Would that you'd demonstrate the same commitment to the cause.'

She tried for a puzzled reaction. On no account could she betray nervousness. She had dealt with more brutish types back in Prague but the danger these uniformed posers represented was to be more intelligent. That made their behaviour all the more treacherous, demonstrating the fault lines of their characters; that they had fallen so completely under the spell of a grotesque ideology.

'You are nothing!' Hobisch barked. 'Nothing! The nation is everything. Germany awake!'

'Quite so,' she said.

'But it has been noticed,' Hobisch said, gyrating an accusing finger, 'that there has been a lack of enthusiasm on your part. You shy away from racial science lessons, you don't turn up for party meetings.'

'So busy.' She shrugged.

'You even questioned the story of the brave soldier of Tannenberg. I heard all about your little pacifist postscript,' he said. 'Hospitals, crutches, poverty, hungry heroes without jobs. Hardly what we expect! You're not one of those closet commies, are you?'

Claudia had half expected the war hero story to come back to bite her, wondering which one of her pupils had reported her literature lesson. Required to recite the hero of Tannenberg, she had added a little realistic aftermath to the story of battlefield glory.

Her response was to fix Hobisch with an unblinking stare. 'There's nothing in my closet I'd be ashamed of,' she said, reaping the expected guffaws, hoping to throw them off their track.

But Hobisch was not to be diverted. 'Wild fanaticism,' he

shouted. 'That's what we need. Fanaticism! People ready to demonstrate their commitment to the party, to the cause.' He paused momentarily, as if to regain his breath and remember a prepared script. On another day Claudia would have laughed at the outlandish language – inspired, no doubt, by the high priest of Nazi-speak, Josef Goebbels.

In a slightly more measured tone, Hobisch said, 'It has been decided to give you a test, an opportunity to redeem yourself, to show the necessary commitment. We are fortunate here in Munich. In a month's time there is to be an inspection by the Reichsmarschall. And this school is to be represented in the parade to mark his visit. You, Fraulein Kellner, will carry the school banner and, it is expected, will meet the great leader himself. We, of course, will also be present.'

Claudia struggled to hide her disgust at the prospect of making polite party talk to this obscene voluptuary. She recalled several breakfast-table discussions at her parents' home where the verdict on the leviathan Hermann Goering was unequivocal: a brutal bully masking his murderous intent behind the pose of a good-natured uncle to the nation.

Spindlegger decided it was time to make a contribution. 'This is a great honour we're handing you. Don't let us down. We shall be there. We shall be watching.'

She knew she couldn't refuse, but seethed inside. Talking to Goering? Sitting on a horse-drawn float being paraded through the streets to celebrate some absurd medieval make-believe? The notion of Reichsmarschall Day was beyond laughable. She made a decision. The antics of this trio were hardening her resolve to defiance, to take the big risk and, somehow, to spirit her secret young 'brood' to safety.

'And when is this?'

'End of November. Wednesday the 27th.'

Claudia drew in a deep breath. The best part of a month

hence. Plenty of time, then, to think up her excuses, arrange alternatives, contrive to be absent at the vital moment.

'Of course, you'll have to be appropriately dressed,' Kuhn added, and Claudia knew what this meant: the dreaded Gretchen outfit of peasant dress, lacy top and puffed sleeves. 'Wouldn't be seen dead in it' was a phrase that sprang instantly to mind but had to remain unsaid. Perhaps, she reflected, she should be grateful. The grilling, and their 'punishment' for her lack of patriotic spirit, might have been worse. At least some of the anticipated horrors had been absent.

But her sense of relief was premature. There was a commotion behind her. She turned to see her nemesis, Karl Drexler, legs astride in the doorway, grinning hugely, a tableau of triumph. He was holding something in his paw-like grasp. It was swinging gently to and fro.

Claudia frowned and stared. Then, with a shock, she recognised the object. Her locket. Her mouth dropped open. 'What are you doing with...?'

Her protest was cut short. She gasped. He was opening up the tiny flap and looking inside.

'How interesting!' he boomed. 'A locket with a strand of tiny flaxen hair and the picture of a baby's face. How come, Miss Perfect?'

Claudia rose to take back the locket but he held it in a tight grip, his mouth twisted into a grin.

'My brother,' she said.

Drexler scoffed. 'Brother my foot! At your age? Nobody carries a baby brother's photo around with a lock of hair. Come on! Tell! Who is it?'

'Give it back!'

He was chuckling, a broad smile, the locket held out of reach behind his back. She regretted leaving the locket in her desk drawer. She had stared at it wistfully during a class break.

'A baby brother? Pull the other one! So, what's your shameful little secret? Come along, we'd all like to know. Who's the baby?'

It was too much. This brute grabbing and brandishing her locket, making a mockery of the most vulnerable part of her being. He pushed his big face close up. 'Found you out, Miss Perfect. Is this your guilty secret?'

She blinked rapidly but knew that if she broke this would be tantamount, in the warped judgement of her tormentors, to an admission of guilt. Disaster would surely follow, her reputation and professional standing shot. Claudia clenched a fist until the nails bit into the flesh. She did not do surrender, she told herself. Kellners did not buckle. The women of this family did not slink away in tearful defeat. She adopted her sternest face.

'This is disgraceful behaviour. I have no need to explain anything to you – but...' A sense of the dramatic came to her rescue. She let the silence hang. They were all still, waiting.

'As I said, a family tragedy. Death at nine months from chicken pox.'

Another silence, then Drexler sneered. 'Don't believe you.'

By now she had adopted a fine defiance. Hands on hips, the voice strong, no evidence of inner turmoil. 'A gross calumny. An intrusion. An outrageous invasion of my personal life.' Staring hard and hostile: 'And theft of private property. Is this the proper conduct of a colleague? Appropriate behaviour for a fellow professional?'

'Quite so.'

Another voice. An altogether different tone. Silence struck down Drexler's taunts as Dr Horst Neumann eased through the open door and stood surveying five startled members of his staff. 'Do you not have classrooms to go to?'

She was momentarily grateful for the interruption, but then, did she really want to be rescued by the headmaster? Out of the mould, certainly, a flamboyant dresser, happy to flaunt his blue check shirt and gold cufflinks, but Neumann was a paper rebel. She had not forgiven him for making no protest at the prescribed curriculum of hate and humiliation.

Prompted to end the meeting, Kuhn, Spindlegger and Hobisch leapt from their seats with a chorus of 'heil Hitler'.

Claudia had enough presence of mind to stand stock-still, staring fixedly to the front, extending an imperious hand. She didn't acknowledge Drexler when he dropped the locket into her palm.

Deception had left a sour taste in her mouth and she could hardly escape the protocol insisted upon by the headmaster, so she screwed up her scant reserves of conformity and returned a somewhat dilatory *German greeting*.

But even as she did so she resolved somehow, despite their watchful gaze, to scupper her participation in Goering's absurd party day.

Despite all her difficulties, Claudia knew she had to do more than simply supply her secret fugitives in the Maze with the basics of existence, desperately though food and warm clothing were required. Just keeping them alive was not enough. You only had to watch any group of children in a school playground to witness young emotions at their most raw and unrestrained. Fright, competition, rivalry, contempt, arrogance, aggression.

Then take a group of feral kids left to their own devices with no rules, no discipline and with nothing to occupy their minds and what do you get? Claudia sighed at the thought of it and went to work to collect materials that would engage the imagination. She had been amassing the necessary items for some days: crayons, pencils, paints, brushes, storybooks, picture books, colouring books, nursery rhymes, puzzles. Other items too; a couple of tennis balls, an old racquet and some toys, that would hopefully restore some semblance of normality and civilised behaviour to her fractious brood.

The sack was heavy and full as she made her way once more into the wilderness, but this time there were no cheeses, sausages or bread, no pullovers or blankets. Instead, food for the mind.

As she pushed her way through the saplings and undergrowth she was surprised to be greeted by little voices well before reaching the freezer wagon. Girls' voices. And when they saw her approach, Frieda, Elsa and Wanda crowded around, crying, complaining, pulling at her clothes.

'They burnt my teddy,' Wanda said.

'Played pig in the middle with my Molly,' Frieda said. Molly, Claudia knew, was Frieda's most precious cuddly toy. 'And smashed it all up.'

'Ripped up my picture.' Elsa had a certain grace, even in the face of humiliation. 'My drawing of a tree, I spent a long time on that.'

A noise to one side attracted Claudia's attention and she disentangled herself from the girls' clutches and strode to a cracked and moss-covered concrete platform. Next to it was a deep hole.

'What are you doing down there?' It was her sharpest tone, addressed to a mud-splattered figure beneath the overhanging cliff of a long-ago cargo dock. Eagle looked up at her with an expression of dedicated concentration that would keep him digging for hours. 'It's a tunnel,' he said. 'Going to be my den.'

'If it doesn't collapse on you first,' she said.

Frieda was pointing in another direction. 'Up there,' she called, anxious as any little snitch to point the way.

Up there, Oskar and Beakie were ankle-deep in a tiny brook playing races. Whose oak leaf could race over a tiny dam the fastest. Well, Claudia decided, that was acceptable, almost creative.

Anguished cries led her through more bushes to a scene that shocked her to a moment's immobility. She recognised the back of Runner. His arm was raised. She heard a cry of fear, then the high-pitched threat. 'Will you do it? Say yes or get more of this.'

Drawing rapidly nearer, she saw that Mole was tied firmly to a metal pole that once held a telephone wire.

'Do what?' Claudia demanded, causing Runner to twirl around in anger.

'He wants me to climb to the top of the pole,' supplied the victim. Little lesions and scratches to face and arms marked the progress of this particular torture session.

Claudia's anger erupted, Mole was cut free and everyone directed back to the freezer car. She insisted they sit, no talking, keep still. Her normal demeanour, calm and friendly, was gone, replaced by a stern expression that silenced even the wildest of spirits. She knew she faced a challenge. Unless she could impose order, the anarchy would spin out of control into outright savagery and they would all be lost.

'This behaviour has to stop.'

Silence.

'Any more of this, any more bullying, smashing things up, destruction, being nasty to each other... and it's all over! I'll throw you out of the Maze.'

'I'll tell the Brownshirts,' threatened a still belligerent Runner.

'Then you'll all be in trouble, everyone, including you. You'll be with the police again, back to coppers' sticks, cuffing your ears, dragging you away. Do you want to be taken away? Is that what you want?'

Silence.

'From now on, you will all be partnered with another

person. Someone you must help and treat as a friend, even if you don't want to.'

She was getting out a pen and paper to draw up a list. Penances, partners, tasks and apologies. 'Older ones with a younger one, each boy with a girl, and woe betide anyone who bullies, cheats, hurts or destroys.'

She glared around the crowd, daring a contradiction, challenging defiance. 'This is my condition. If you don't do it, no more food, no more clothes, no more toys.'

Then, in the continuing and conforming silence, she began to unpack her bag.

11

Peter guessed that Aunt Trudi would be scurrying down the ramp to Bella Vista's lakeside moorings. And, as he half expected, the living room door soon opened and a line of cowed and frightened figures were ushered through. Three men, middle-aged, grey-haired and with wet trouser legs; a woman shivering inside a big brown blanket and a teenage girl, the most alert of them all, in an oversized coat.

So, Peter realised, this was behind all the angst. The Feisslers were also running a refugee line.

His uncle's greeting was uninhibited. Arms outstretched, he said, 'Peter! What a wonderful surprise! I'm utterly intrigued. How on earth did you get here?' Bear hugs and fond greetings, then an introduction to Williams. At least Stefan hadn't changed.

The refugees were hustled away – en route to a mountain monastery – and Peter and Williams were given blankets to sleep in a shed. Next day, when there was the chance of a proper conversation, Peter vowed to hold to his promise, not to pressure his uncle. Was it fair to put him on the spot? Was the plan for an illegal flight over the Third Reich the sort of request that should be made? More than that: low flying over the Alps in winter in his tiny aircraft. Peter was torn between loyalty to family and loyalty to country.

Stefan stared out over the lake as he considered the idea. There were the problems: all private flying prohibited because of the war, a lack of fuel and Swiss hostility to refugees in general. Many escapers had been sold back to the Nazis and the Feisslers were scandalised by the behaviour of their countrymen.

The lake was shimmering in shades of silver and grey in a mirror-like calm. Stefan pointed to the far side, the German shore, to which he had sailed his boat on several illicit night rescues. He could cram up to thirty people on board. 'Easier to get you over there,' he said.

Peter shook his head. 'Orders,' he said, knowing his contacts were elsewhere.

But the clincher was Trudi. Stefan said, 'I can tell you, she's all worked up about you being here. It's dangerous for you and dangerous for us.' He shook a reluctant head. 'She just won't countenance anything that puts our family, our house, our lives and our girls at risk. She has our best interests at heart and I can't go against her on this.'

Peter sighed and nodded his acceptance. Later, back in the house after a further conversation, his aunt was no less vociferous: 'You should never have asked,' she told Peter. 'And you can tell whoever it was who sent you, the answer is no. Definitely not. Stefan won't do it. Because I won't let him.'

So that was that. Operation Zilch.

Upstairs, sitting on a straw palliasse and using a book as a desk, Peter compiled a cryptic story in a message to the Z House. A line about a charioteer who had lost his horse. He addressed the note to the Swiss Marine Engineering Supply Company at

24a Knockendorf Strasse, clearly a Dansey letter box, and expected a stand-down order by return.

He was utterly unprepared for what happened next.

It was nearly midnight. A furious knocking at the door. Stefan ignoring. More knocking. Stefan answering. Stefan returning to say, 'Someone asking for you.'

Peter peered at the figure in the porch, then recognised the grinning figure of Skip Mahoney.

'What-ho! How are things?'

Peter did not disguise his surprise. 'You!'

'I'm your replacement pilot.'

'What?'

'I must be slightly barmy, but I'm volunteering.'

'But I thought you were injured.'

'Patched up, old boy. Been under the nurse. Very nice she is too.'

'But you and your crew were going crazy to get home. Your special skills needed back at squadron, you said. Too valuable to waste in a prison camp.'

'Apparently, the home run's a bit tricky just now. We're all stuck. So, here I am, still a bit sore, but all ready to fly.'

Peter drew in a deep breath. This changed everything.

12

She called it Black Wednesday. November 27th, the Reichsmarschall Day parade, was a dark cloud on Claudia's horizon. She determined to duck it. Perhaps she would feign sickness, go on a course, transfer to another school, any kind of a swerve to be absent from the humiliation of parading around before Hermann Goering.

'There's worse,' Erika said on hearing Claudia's angry protests. 'Much worse. You're talking about disgust. I'm talking about danger.'

Claudia stopped and chewed a finger. Something in her friend's expression caught her cold. She'd just had a message, Erika said, from her contact inside the police. Weber, the officer who had given Claudia such a fright the day he knocked on her door, had proved his reliability, warning of round-ups and street sweeps by police and Gestapo looking for U-boats.

'It's all getting much more dangerous.'

'You mean...?'

'I do. How long before they start looking in this direction?'

Claudia had always feared they would not be able to hide and feed their young ones indefinitely.

'We need to do something,' Erika said. 'Before it's too late. Get them away somewhere. To a safer place.'

Claudia scratched the back of her neck. 'Put them all on a train,' she suggested. 'A school party. Some plausible pretext. You can fix it. Send them over the border on a trip.'

Erika snorted. 'You're joking! You couldn't smuggle them over the frontier. You can't hide kids on a train, far too conspicuous. They attract attention. And doing it officially? No way! They'd never allow a school party to cross the frontier for any reason. No reason at all. That's just not possible.'

Another scratch by Claudia. 'Then what about that American you were telling me about? He's powerful, you said. Privileged. Perhaps he could arrange something.'

Erika shook her head. 'Why would he? And what could he do? Besides, he's ring-fenced. Under the wing of the Gestapo.'

'You could tell him about victims of the system. Poor little children. Play on his sympathies. See how he reacts.'

'We'd never get near him.' Then Erika's brow furrowed. 'Although...' She shrugged. 'Not often but sometimes...'

'What?'

'Never comes himself. Sends over a pink slip.'

The pink slip, Claudia knew, was a request for a particular component. When the Engineer required some existing component for his project he sent over the slip containing the serial numbers needed for Erika to locate the item in the stores.

'Trouble is, the escort.' Mostly, Erika said, the slip was brought by the Engineer's morose factotum, escorted by their least favourite secret policeman, Oberscharfuhrer Voss.

'Always?'

Erika thought back. 'No, sometimes in the afternoons when Voss is off shift.'

'Then be ready,' Claudia said.

Claudia was thinking about the sort of man who leaves his country and crosses the Atlantic to work on a secret project for the Third Reich. Its very secrecy and protected status suggested a sinister purpose and foretold an element of danger. What manner of man? Why would he do what the Nazis wanted? More to the point, would he listen to any special pleading from Erika? She wondered what it was that the Third Reich provided that the US did not. Perhaps there was a personal reason. Maybe he was running from something. A weakness? Was that exploitable?

'You could do it,' Erika said.

Claudia blinked. 'Surely not? He knows about you, not me.'

'With these wrinkles? You'd be the better bet.'

It was true. For all her fine attributes, Erika lacked a certain appeal and Claudia began to consider whether to put herself forward. Instinctively, she reacted against the idea of manipulation. Acting the spy, using deceit or behaving dishonestly, these were not her ways. She also disliked the notion of using sexual attraction to entrap a person. Besides, she didn't want to become involved in someone else's politics, she had enough of her own.

She drew in a deep breath and told herself this was different. This was on behalf of her children.

'You can do it,' Erika repeated. 'You've managed your awful colleagues. Survived their inquisition. You've got a hard edge when you need it.'

Claudia bit her lip. That remark made her distinctly uncomfortable. A year or so back she had been a different person: soft, sincere, even shy. Events had changed her. Now she asked herself: how hard an edge will I develop? Shall I abandon all scruples to shield these children?

Erika, meanwhile, had lost her earlier doubts, had now

grasped the idea of approaching the Engineer as the solution to their problem. 'The American, he has to be different to all the others,' she said. 'Up to you, Claudia. Find his weakness, locate his vulnerable spot, pluck his heartstrings.'

Claudia was doubtful. 'It could be fatal. He might be a weasel. He could be a snitch. Saying too much could get us all arrested.'

'Then you'll just have to use that big intelligence of yours to sound him out without revealing anything incriminating,' Erika said.

It happened on the third day. Old Epp came in the afternoon, pink slip in hand and no escort. 'I want you to take this message back to your boss,' Erika told him, and wrote on the back of the pink slip:

The one thing we Germans have in common with Americans is a love of good coffee. My brew is Dallmayr, the very best, taken at 1500 hours in the stores. Consider this an invitation.

It was cheeky, verging on the impertinent to such an eminent man and she, merely a stores clerk. But then he was an American and everyone knew Americans had no side. The casual tone would hook him in, she decided. It would appeal to his curiosity. She had signed the note *Erika*. He wasn't to know she was no Marlene Dietrich.

The following afternoon they were in their private alcove once more. Claudia was wearing her best jacket in a sporty shade of orange with a brown pleated skirt. They were discussing the problems of the Maze. 'Little horrors!' Erika exclaimed. 'Burning things, hurting each other, whatever next!'

'Always going to happen with kids out of control,' Claudia said.

'But have you cured it?'

'Think so. I'll have to keep a firm grip.' She wagged a finger. 'But they were very subdued yesterday.'

Erika made a face, sighed, then looked up abruptly. There was a stagey cough at the inquiry desk. The cough repeated itself. Erika peered under the desk, made a face and whispered, 'It's him!'

'How'd you know?'

'Look at those shoes.'

Brown wingtip brogues. Nobody else in the depot went to work in such expensive footwear.

'Aha!' said Hank Hoskins, grinning, when Erika appeared, 'I smell the coffee. No, no, not just coffee, beautiful coffee. Tell me about this brand.'

This man is probably a connoisseur, Erika decided. 'Dallmayr. Refined here. Ground here. Well, used to be.' Closed for the war – but she didn't say that. 'Kept the beans in huge porcelain jars at their store on Diener Strasse.'

He clapped his hands. 'Fantastic. Far better than the stuff they give me. But then you always get the very best of everything in the stores, eh?'

'The city's very best,' she agreed. 'And my friends think so too.'

'So I see.' Hoskins was leaning over the desk to catch a glimpse of Claudia, still sitting in the alcove.

Erika made her move. This man was in a good humour. 'Perhaps you would care to join us,' she said, 'if you have a few moments?'

'Never too busy to refuse an invitation,' he said as Erika found a third chair. 'Only came to check personally to make sure we've got plenty of these.' He indicated a pink slip. 'But you can see to it later.'

He beamed and introductions were made.

'This is Claudia, my friend from the town,' Erika said and, switching to a station announcer's voice and looking straight at Claudia, she added, 'and this is the star of the show I was telling you about, the big name up in lights who's going to make us all famous at the Depot Landsberger.'

Hoskins laughed, shrugging his shoulders, enthusing over the coffee and exclaiming even more when Erika found three doughnuts in her pantry. 'Tell you what, this is a treat indeed,' he said. 'Decent coffee, cakes and attractive company. Better than old Epp. He's the only one I've got to talk to in that work-shop of mine and, good God, he's a dour old cuss.'

Erika peered around the alcove to check the rest of the department. They were alone. 'I'm surprised you didn't bring your shadows,' she said, 'or are they lurking in the tunnel?'

It was a boldly obvious reference to the Gestapo who normally dogged Hoskins's footsteps wherever he went. It was common knowledge in the depot: the chief engineer was the leader of the Fuhrer's pet project and the men in black were under orders not to let him off the leash.

'Oh, don't worry about them, they're not that close,' Hoskins said. 'Only that young Voss, he's a bit keen on the morning shift. Better in the afternoons when it's Franz's turn. A more relaxed sort of guy.'

Erika raised her eyes and Hoskins added, 'Just now he's probably deep into Schubert. They always have a concert on the Hamburg station about this time.'

'Culture? A musician? Them?' Erika did a double take.

'I know. Doesn't fit the image, does it? Fact is, this isn't Franz's natural territory, more a way of keeping out of trouble. Fortu-nately, he had influential friends.'

'Bully for him.'

'Besides, it's a good posting up here at the depot, they can relax, nothing ever happens, nothing for them to worry about.'

'That's a relief,' she said.

The conversation continued along neutral lines: the pastries, the bread and the specialities of Munich: the famous white sausage that by tradition had to be eaten before noon, the spicy cheese and butter spread *Obatzda*, and then of course, the city and its cathedral. 'Those green domes, they're really something else, aren't they?' he said.

At this point Claudia put down her cup and rose, smiling apologetically. 'Do excuse me, please, wonderful though this is, I must get back, things to do.' She extended her hand. 'Nice to meet you, Mr Hoskins.'

And then she was gone.

Erika kept a straight face. All part of a careful coat-trailing exercise. Don't make the first meeting too easy, they had decided. Give him a glimpse, then see what happens.

Claudia was having second thoughts. 'This really is not me, I don't go putting myself about, engineering dinner dates or appearing eager to socialise. Not me at all. The opposite, in fact. I don't want to be noticed. And the last thing I need is some relationship entanglement.'

'You don't have to act like a nun,' Erika said.

Claudia looked away. She had been careful to avoid male friendships. There was a whole lot more she could say but did not. Instead, she insisted, 'Just part of the furniture, that's me. Much the better for the children. For their sake, I need to appear so ordinary no one notices me. Next to invisible.'

'Claudia,' Erika said with a knowing tone, 'you'll never be

invisible.' Then, 'Just come tomorrow and put on something nice.'

'Definitely not. I won't flaunt myself.'

She had stayed away the next day in protest, then became afflicted by an attack of conscience for letting down her friend. Worse, she had offered no explanation. On the Tuesday Claudia felt impelled to repair her display of bad manners. She painted her nails red – guessing Hoskins wouldn't care about the regime's craze for the 'natural look' – tied up her hair and wore a soft wool jersey dress in forest green. He wasn't to know she'd made it using fabric from two old dresses. Making do didn't mean it had to be plain. She was quite proud of the breast pocket and the roll neck in a darker shade of green. By five o'clock she was sitting behind the counter in the component store feeling nervous but ready.

'He's been asking about you,' Erika said.

'What sort of questions?'

'Who was that nice young woman?'

'What did you tell him?'

'Just that you're from the town.'

'And?'

'Does she have a boyfriend? Married? I said I didn't think so. And hinted you might respond to an offer of a nice meal. Make a change from the rather poor rations we're allowed.'

Claudia made a face. 'Aren't we moving too fast?'

'No, no, this is the chance. He's powerful, lots of status, a cosseted figure. Even the Gestapo have to do what he says. But for all that, this is one very lonely man in need of company. Particularly when it's an attractive young woman.'

Claudia made a face.

'Think of the little ones, Claudia, we – they – need a way out.'

13

I t wasn't so much a roar as an annoying drone. Rather like that of a persistent fly. Peter was used to Stefan's Dragonfly. He had spent several happy daredevil holidays clambering around its fuselage, hanging onto the struts between the two wings and diving off into the snow. It was a modest sea biplane, fitted out by de Havilland with an extra cabin door and wing walkway, and when they crowded in with all their equipment, two of the five seats had already been removed to make room for the cargo: the suitcase radio, two pairs of skis and rations to last two days.

Their departure had been accompanied by subterfuge; fuel bought on the black market, the impounded aircraft freed by bolt cutters, a false trail laid to protect the owner from repercussions. Take-off had been accomplished without incident. Mahoney opened up the throttles of the twin 142 hp Gipsy Majors and the Dragonfly bumped across the ripples of the lake, suction clawing at the aluminium floats until sufficient lift took the aircraft clear. Then it headed like an ungainly insect in the direction of the Austrian Alps. Conditions were rudimentary. No headsets, no wireless, communication reduced to hand signals.

The wind was noisy and biting. Even in his heavy coat Peter shivered. How would this insubstantial, fragile craft cope with perilous air currents above the rocky canyons of the Allgauer and Lechtaler ranges? And how good were Mahoney's skills at crossing mountains?

Moonlight gave the landscape a ghostly appearance. Their route would take them just clear of the tallest peaks but this increased the risk of being spotted by some late-marauding hunter. They were counting on German radar cover being thin. This was the country's back door, after all, bordering occupied Austria, fascist Italy and neutral Switzerland, but thin did not mean non-existent. Then there was the glacier. Locating it called for precision. If something went wrong there was no chance of rescue.

Finally, the jump. The idea of dropping onto a glacier had captured Peter's imagination but extreme conditions made it touch and go. He shrugged off his concerns. Instead, his excitement fed off it. 'Embrace the fear' his instructor had said at Ringway and Peter reflected with a sense of pride that he had been chosen for such a difficult task, even though he knew Dansey had deliberately overlooked a stack of negatives about Second Lieutenant (Temporary) Peter Chesham. Not a natural leader, not a career officer, not a man who said the 'right things'. Never mind, he was doing his bit. He was proving himself worthy. To his father, to the world in general, and to himself. He might be going to war but he wasn't taking to the parachute to kill or maim. It was all about shortening the war. It was all about peace.

～

Mahoney tapped him on the shoulder and pointed downwards. Peter looked out of the side window at the jumble of jagged peaks a thousand feet below, an intimidating vista for all his familiarity with the terrain. Then he spotted the glacier. Hockfelln, right shape, right time.

Peter nodded and gave the thumbs up in gratitude for the pilot's exact navigation. Mahoney had come good. Now it was Peter's turn.

He heaved himself up and out of his straps, checked his parachute pack and pushed open the side door. Immediately, the wind hit him, stopping him for a moment before he eased further out, grasping the struts that kept upper and lower wings together. A fierce thrust from the engine tried to whip his legs away. A loose strap flicked into a frenzied dance. This was no summer picnic, didn't compare with aiming for the gentle snowy slopes around the big lake. Nevertheless, the vista revealed in the moonlight was as impressive and beautiful as it was intimidating in its vastness. White patches contrasted with dark areas of nothingness.

Mahoney was cutting back cruising speed to just above stalling, running in low above the open top of the glacier. Now was the moment. He threw a brief glance back at the white face of Williams, still strapped in his seat, mouthed 'don't fail me!' and thrust himself into space, anxious not to drift over the edge of the glacier and into a chasm. The white silk canopy mushroomed open above him and he floated down, the silence stark, the air so cold he thought he was being sliced open with a knife. Within seconds he had plunged into deep powder snow, cushioning the impact of landing. It was up to his waist. He struggled out of his gear, ripping off a light beacon he had strapped to his belt and switched it on to guide Mahoney round for the second circuit.

Peter held his breath. Could this be the point where it all went wrong? Several large canisters were floating down and Peter was mentally marking the positions where they fell, ready for retrieval, but for the moment stayed with the light. A great sense of relief when, on the third run-in, the aircraft did a sudden bank to starboard and a solitary body came floating down. It landed close by in a straggly heap and bulldozed to a stop in a spray of whiteness.

Williams was in accusative mood when he floundered, grunted and tore at the release straps. 'Never again!' he said. 'Nearly had a heart attack up there. Cold froze me to the spot.'

Peter silently thanked Mahoney. Whether it was a push or the sudden bank that launched Williams into space he didn't know. He contented himself with a nod, switched off the light, and the plane flew away.

Plunging around in the moonlight in waist-deep snow was exhausting. Finding and collecting all the canisters and unloading the gear used up two hours. The snow, once their friend for cushioned landings, now became their foe.

The heavy rucksacks made balance difficult because of the depth of the snow. When they came to move off, Williams over-balanced, not once, but three times and when he did get going it was only to snowplough crazily into another spill. Peter began to worry. Williams, he suspected, had exaggerated his skiing ability so he could join the team. They lay up for a while, awaiting daylight, before crossing a crevasse and spent hours seeming to make little progress. It was desperate stuff. The going was pathetically slow. Williams was floundering so Peter decided on distraction. He didn't want a quitter on his hands and it didn't take much to provoke a response. Recall of a miner's cottage in Wales, highlights of a different life: Friday as payday, Friday nights as pub night, little pots of money on the mantelshelf marked rent, milk, leccy and doctor. Hey! And there's a bath with running water.

Peter trudged on, wondering how two such disparate personalities could have been thrown together, but then that was what happened in this man's army. Suddenly you were up close and personal with people you'd never meet in Civvy Street.

Williams was remarking on Peter's extended family and how 'posh' he was to have relatives in Switzerland. Peter laughed. 'You're just one big bundle of resentments! You're obsessed by this class thing, aren't you?'

'Well, it exists, don't pretend it doesn't.'

'But why all the anger?'

'You want to know? Fine. I'll tell you. I resent your kind. Your class. They know nothing, no practical experience, they don't get their hands dirty, yet they come along, just out of university, and five minutes later they're telling people like me what to do.'

Peter kept his cool. 'All change after the war. Team effort. Just like us now.'

At nightfall they found the wreck of a shepherd's hut and at dawn used an old door as a makeshift toboggan to tackle a steep downslope. Their backs took jarring punishment from hidden rocks and bumps and Peter struggled to keep control as speed built up. It was a beast to steer. Unwieldy, with a mind of its own. A sharp right came up and they just made it round. Williams was shrieking in fright and Peter needed all the strength left in his aching joints to keep them upright. Another sharp turn and this time he knew he'd blown it, Williams disappearing off the rear with skis and rucksacks.

When he struggled back Peter found Williams in poor shape, blood streaming from a cut and a badly bruised leg, two skis and the rucksack containing their food missing.

He strapped the remaining rucksack containing the wireless to the skis, then attached a line to his belt. He'd walk with

Williams and tow their now meagre supplies behind. Progress was painful, limbs leaden, thighs and feet aching, the weakening effect of cold and exhaustion making itself felt. Fingers were numb and his nose felt as if it must belong to someone else. He wiggled fingers, fearful of frostbite, but by nightfall they had reached lush meadows, crossed a bridge over a small river and heard the rumble of a distant train.

'Who'd credit it?' Williams shook his head. 'Trains in this godforsaken place?'

'Exactly why we chose it. The nearest the main line gets to the mountains.'

A tall brick building loomed up and a careful scrutiny revealed it to be their target: the station house at Bergen.

Peter approached the back door. This was a key moment. Was Dansey's information reliable? Did his contacts really work – or was he walking into a trap?

He knocked three times and when the door was answered by a tiny man – bald with glasses, braces over a striped shirt and no collar – Peter stuck to the formula: 'Sorry to call at this time. I'm looking for Maria.'

'What business have you with him?'

Him? Peter's brow wrinkled, but he kept to the script: 'I was hoping to crew the train to the Depot Landsberger.'

The little man emerged onto the doorstep to look Peter up and down.

'You don't look like train crew.'

'I'm a footplateman. Know things only a footplateman would know.'

'Who's the shedmaster at Traunstein?'

'Tannhauser.' Peter felt foolish. Whoever heard of a

shedman with the name of a Wagnerian opera, but he kept an even expression.

'How many wheels on an A-class loco at Rosenheim?'

He was ready again. 'None, because the As have never been shedded there.'

The little man nodded, leaned out further and looked all around the garden, then said, 'You'd better come in. All on your own?'

They were in the stationmaster's parlour, having made short work of fried potatoes and egg with a hunk of black bread. Peter was relieved. Maria, the stationmaster, was their contact at Bergen and hopefully the first in a chain of covert helpers. He chuckled at having to call him Maria but knew it was all part of Dansey's code system based on the forenames of the great composers. The stationmaster was Carl Maria von Weber. Peter, alias Pyotr, was Tchaikovsky.

Then he turned his mind to the problem of Williams. His assistant was now a liability. To do their job they had to be as near as possible to invisible. The requirement was to blend into a crowd, to become just another anonymous face, just another railwayman. A hobbling man with wounds to his cheekbones would soon attract attention. And Williams was at the point of exhaustion. The descent from the mountain had finished him.

Only one option; he had to stay behind, his only utility an ability to operate the radio. He was given an attic room and ordered to 'get yourself healed up – but no doctor'.

Peter, minus radio or any means of destruction save his own ingenuity, would have to go on alone.

By morning Dansey's arrangements proved themselves again. He was issued with an impressive array of new documentation: a yellow *Reichsbahn* staff pass, a green *Reisepass* giving his name as Sepp Bauer, stamped and signed by the town director of Bergen, and to round it off a *Fuhrerschein* (driving licence) on brown felt with a picture of someone looking remarkably similar to himself stapled alongside the endorsement of the *Oberstadtdirektor* who authenticated that the said Sepp Bauer had grey-green eyes.

At six o'clock Peter was putting on the crinkly black hat and blue overall trousers familiar to footplate crews the world over, ready to catch the early train for Munich. On his upper left arm was an insignia patch depicting a steam engine. Which made it official. He was now a driver; a *lokomotivfuhrer*.

Alongside him, to guard against mishap, was another engine man: the stationmaster's son.

'You're expected,' Maria said as he held aloft the white circular staff to give the right of way and Peter, climbing aboard, found this reassuring, giving him a sense of being passed on from one set of secret friends to another.

But then, as the train moved out of the station, a doubt began to form. He had always been acutely conscious of the danger of betrayal. So was this escort really for his benefit? Or to keep track of him, never to let him out of sight?

14

Claudia had expected some discreet backstreet café, or perhaps an out-of-the-way restaurant on the edge of town, but no, Hank Hoskins didn't do small.

They arrived at Brienner Strasse in his Mercedes six-cylinder Super Sport Tourer and made straight for the front entrance of the huge edifice that was the Café Luitpold. The five-storey building with double towers at each corner stretched right across a whole block. Waiters bowed and mumbled greetings as Hoskins walked her through to the most palatial of the twenty inner halls, the royal salon.

While the maître d' scampered off to fetch the dinner menu, Hoskins, dressed in a tuxedo dinner jacket, ran his hand along the back of his seat, under the table and along the rear of their alcove. Then, careful to check that he was unobserved, he unscrewed the light fitting on the table lamp, examined the connections and restored it to its rightful place.

Claudia's quizzical expression forced him to smile. 'I'm an engineer,' he said, 'I like to know how it all works.'

'And the flowers?' she said. 'They're engineering too, are

they?' He was peering into a vase, wearing his still crooked smile, and she knew he wasn't playing straight.

Then the pfennig dropped.

'Surely your friends don't want to eavesdrop on *you*,' she said, stressing the last word.

'You know what they say. Be as watchful of your friends as of your enemies.'

She sighed, acting the sophisticate, and took the gold-embossed menu card. 'What a strange world you inhabit.' She leafed through the list, thinking this exchange demonstrated that Hoskins wasn't an enthusiastic collaborator, nor even a naive one, and that if he was guarded in what he said in the presence of others he might just be open to a different point of view. 'I'm surprised we didn't have an escort,' she said.

'Oh, they're probably waiting at the Torbau Hotel.'

'Won't they be disappointed? A little annoyed? After playing all those tricks with the light bulbs?'

'A lady changes her mind.'

'Please!' she said. 'Don't bring me into this. I don't want to be noticed. Not by them.'

'Fine. Then I'll say I've just changed my mind.'

Claudia did her best to look relaxed. But she wasn't. This was a ploy. This was a game. She had only accepted his invitation after a ritual display of reluctance: the all-consuming workload of a teacher, the marking, the preparations for the following day...

'Oh come on!' he had cajoled. 'A couple of hours won't hurt. Make a change from that dull diet you've been stuck with. Live like a lord for an evening. What do you say to a proper meal with all the trimmings?'

She had him pick her up by the yellow postbox on the Landsberger, not wanting to be seen climbing into a car at the depot or outside her apartment, not wanting to be thought the big man's pick-up. Even so, the flamboyance of the car and their arrival embarrassed her and she hoped no one she knew was watching. And now she was wary, looking for the unseen trap. Had she overplayed her hand? Had he seen through her? Why was he making such a big display of power and position?

They ordered steamed crabs and spinach baked in pastry for him and duck barbecue with mushrooms for her. Claudia had made a special effort with her dress. Her mother had sent her lines of brocade to sew down the seams of old garments, providing a low-cost solution for special occasions. She'd used a two-tone cream and lilac brocade to decorate a deep purple dress fluted at the waist and tied tight with a belt. This emphasised the smallness of the waist. Suitably modest, she decided, but did it pass muster with all those wooden people inhabiting this place?

She looked around her surroundings: all bronze and black marble, fluted pillars and dramatic ceiling art. Musicians played in a neighbouring terrace. 'I can recommend the Luitpold,' Hoskins said. 'As you see, war or no war, they never seem to go short.'

No one seemed to be concerned about food stamps or the ration book in her pocket and she vowed not to be overawed by the occasion or the excessive display of wealth. Remember the Wilson Station, she told herself, remember Prague and the trainloads of little children who made it safely out. And then remember those who didn't.

She still wondered why he was so clearly intent on impressing her. Who was he really? A Judas, a fox, or just a lonely man? She would have to fake enjoyment and delight when the meal arrived, but worried that she might become so nervous she'd throw up.

Then suddenly the bizarre nature of the occasion struck her as funny and her involuntary smile seemed to please him. She had never been to such a place; if her brother could see her now, how they would laugh. Nevertheless, she decided not to over-play her hand. Nothing too obvious, so she asked him about his life: how he liked living in a foreign city, about the difference in the rules of the road, about the challenge of negotiating the Mercedes Tourer past Munich's maze of tram tracks, about his home in America – anything to keep the conversation away from her. But she knew eventually she would have to field some diffi-cult questions. Instinct was to say nothing, to give away no details of her life, but that wasn't realistic if she was to make any kind of human connection, so when he began to ask about her life she gave him as bland a version of school routine as she could manage – delightful children, a rewarding vocation, well-equipped school – and he sensed it.

'Don't worry about being careful,' he said, 'I'm used to it, discretion among my colleagues is a way of life. I understand. It's how it is out here, but you've no worries with me, I'm just a lone-some engineer in need of a change from nuts and bolts. I'm not interested in any of that stuff. Them and their silly games.'

His frankness reassured her and it was understood between them that *they* were the earwiggers, the concealed microphone-listeners and the pathetic army of small-minded informers that any German citizen, or visiting worker, had to watch out for.

'My role here gives me lots of advantages,' he said. 'I know they're under orders not to upset me, because I'm the man who's going to pull the white rabbit out of their hat.'

'And are you?'

'Certainly am.'

At that she waved an apologetic hand. 'Sorry,' she said, 'I shouldn't have asked.'

He dismissed this. 'They're obsessed by secrecy but hell, no harm in giving you the broad outline. Rather nice, actually, to talk to someone who's interested.' He gave a little jerk of the head and a tight smile. 'I have to confess to being really rather proud of it.'

She smiled. 'And why not!'

'And excited by it. Nice to have someone around to share that excitement who isn't bound by some rule or other or who isn't constantly thinking up objections.'

She laughed. 'Pleased and proud?'

'Yes. Buoyed by my achievement, managed against all the odds, despite all the people who refused to believe in my ideas. I know that sounds pretty boastful. Fact is, we're well ahead of the rest of the world. They're just too stupid to take any interest, they're too self-satisfied with what they've already got.'

Claudia risked a personal comment. 'I'm sure your work here is very laudable, but surely, shouldn't you be doing all this in your own country?'

Hoskins paused, tapped his fork on the table and for a moment she thought she'd gone too far. But then he said: 'When your country rejects you, you have to find another way of expressing your talent and ideas, and if you have a big, big idea – as I have – then you need a sponsor, a mentor, an enthusiastic supporter, someone with the will and the money and the machinery to back you. To invest in you.'

'I see.'

Restraint, that's what she had decided. She didn't want to ask direct questions. Stick to generalities that would not arouse suspicion. Besides, she could tell. He was an obsessive. He wanted to talk, wanted to self-justify. So she wondered out loud if his intense dedication to technological progress might have isolated him from the reality of ordinary life in the Third Reich.

'How do you mean?'

'May I be frank?'

'Of course.'

'Very frank?'

'Go ahead. I'm a paragon of discretion.'

'Well...' She sighed and looked at him directly for a long silent moment. 'Many people are worried about what's happening socially. The country may be on the march but there are worries about the increasing numbers of victims of the system. Political as well as racial.'

'You mean, the transports to the labour camps? Can't be that bad, surely, to go and work in the East?' He looked at her carefully, then said, 'But you look as if you don't believe that.'

'I don't believe that,' she said quietly.

The conversation stalled and she felt it unwise to press the point. Too soon, she decided, to risk talking about her secret fugitives. She would try again another time, so she brightened and smiled and returned to his personal life. 'So, how do you find us here? Some nice distractions, I hope! But I can't see the Depot Landsberger as a very fun place.' She laughed at her own joke, smiling. A smile of invitation. She sensed the pent-up personality sitting across the table. Consumed by his work and his ideas, itching to display them to an appreciative audience, to someone he could trust. And she guessed right. Hoskins began to talk. It seemed to her that he was spilling the lot, chapter and verse, and Claudia did her non-technical best to remember the salient points of it. She had the sense that this was valuable information he was imparting and that there might be a moment when the revelation of it would be important. The one fact, however, that registered with her like a clanging fire bell was mention of the Swiss border. She almost jerked out of her seat at this but managed to stay cool, saying only: 'So this all involves lots of travel for you? That far?'

Then he was off on another wide sweep of geography but she was only half listening. The Swiss border! If only she, or he, or they, could find a way to smuggle her stranded children to and across that frontier of safety, what a victory it would be. *But how?*

'You must let me show you,' he was saying. 'Talking about it is all very well. Much better to see the real thing. Would you care to accompany me the next time I visit the workshops?'

15

Peter was acutely aware that he was a man out on his own. Everything rested on his shoulders and he had just one tool: the power of persuasion. He was a soldier without weaponry or the ability to cause destruction. All he could do was talk to the key players of the *Breitspurbahn* – its creator as well as those who sought its downfall.

He swallowed and kept his gaze down. This was the 6.15 workers' train to Munich and the experience grounded him. The excitement of beating the mountain had gone. He was now out of his element and facing a new kind of peril. He knew the smallest mistake could result in arrest and a Gestapo cell. He also recognised that members of the Resistance, like his young escort sitting opposite, were taking an even greater risk. The whole network, including families, stood in danger of being wiped out. He owed it to them to hold his nerve.

Conditions were spartan. The seats were hard wooden slats, the heating non-existent. This was a *Personenzug*, the local stopping train. At first he did not raise his head, his voice barely above a whisper, speaking carefully to disguise his Swiss accent, quizzing young Kurt about life on the footplate. Much the best tactic. Keep the boy talking. After a while he risked a quick glance at the other passengers, curious to know how war was treating Mr and Mrs Average in the Third Reich. Across the aisle were two gaunt-faced women in shapeless smocks and head-scarves. They wore the look of fatigued factory workers about to start another fourteen-hour shift. He'd heard about the armament factories working around the clock.

Body heat gradually misted up the windows and the night frost made it hard to tell the station names, but he clocked Rosenheim and then Grafing.

The power of his new uniform was demonstrated when the conductor merely nodded in his direction. No need for conversation. No need to present his brand-new staff pass – the *dienstausweis* No.44, describing his role, dated and signed by the railway police in Berlin and with three impressive blue stamps showing the German eagle clutching a tiny swastika. His pockets were full of travel paraphernalia. The list was a long one and somebody had been highly efficient. Somebody had been very busy.

His gaze returned again to the others in the carriage; to the one-eyed dog who wanted to get off at every station and to the nun reading the city's *Nachrichten*. Was she studying the sins of society? Peter risked a closer glance. No, she had the paper open at the sports section. Unlike the British, the Germans hadn't cancelled their football league.

Tension rose as they clunked their way through the Munich suburbs. At a sign from Kurt they moved to the veranda end of the coach, closing the gate behind them. Just before reaching the main terminal at Munich, trains from Bergen were required to traverse a sharp right-hand bend to join the main line coming in from the west and north. The wheels squealed, the engine wheezed and speed dropped to dead slow.

The two of them were on the bottom steps, ready to jump. It

was in the closing arrowhead of land between the two converging lines that the Landsberger depot was situated. 'Don't want to risk going all the way to the city terminal,' Kurt said. 'Police in numbers at the ticket barrier.'

They leapt.

Peter stumbled awkwardly when he landed on the trackside ballast but managed to avoid a fall, anxious not to look like a clumsy amateur. Then he did his best to adopt the unhurried gait of the long-serving railwayman as they trudged past a jumble of buildings and tracks. It was a pose of ownership, of kinship, of control, of unhurried competence and he did his best to imitate it.

They entered a control building containing a large crew locker room. Doors were being opened, briefcases stowed, keys turned. It was almost as if the crews were imitating business-men. None had the sidepacks carried by British enginemen, but Peter had no doubt the briefcases contained much the same: lamps, door-openers and flasks of coffee, if not tea. Probably pork, sausage and eggs too, to cook on a shovel held in the loco-motive firebox.

Kurt motioned to approach a slot in the wall. Behind a tiny pane of foggy glass a young woman sat at a desk. She wore a crumpled grey blouse and held a cigarette between two yellowing fingers. A small plaque announced: *Rota clerk*.

She didn't speak, simply jerked her head to indicate she was listening.

Kurt did the talking. 'Replacement crew reporting in for the Stuttgart run tonight,' he said. 'Kurt Fischer and Sepp Bauer.' Then he added with heavy emphasis: 'From Bergen.'

The woman put the cigarette to her lips, drew on it and peered at them through a halo of smoke. Turning slightly, she said from the corner of her mouth, 'Bergen are here.'

Peter then heard another voice. Male, identity concealed by

some kind of screen, the words indistinct. The woman nodded, found two pieces of paper on her desk – journey sheets, Peter later discovered, lined and covered with figures in tiny handwriting – and thrust them through the slot, waving in the direction of the stairs.

'Canteen,' Kurt said. 'Get some food inside us. The Caller can pick you up from there.'

The canteen was a Peter nightmare: cramped, wheezing, smoke-filled. What looked like an ancient samovar grumbled in the corner, several rough wooden benches were scattered with leftovers and a grimy glass case offered doorstep hunks of black bread, the inevitable bubbling sausages and a bin of fried potatoes. The 'menu', however, was not the problem.

Sitting facing them was a man dressed in black, two lightning flashes on his collar insignia, a sharp expression, a tight mouth. An elbow propped one arm on the table, an accusing index finger quickly pointed in their direction.

Peter knew immediately they were in trouble. This man didn't need to announce himself. Peter had mugged up on German ranks, recognising the sig runes of the SS and the two horizontal stripes and a single diagonal bar identifying an *oberscharfuhrer*, a staff sergeant.

'Who are you? Haven't seen you before.'

A rough voice. A man of the street. A man without preamble.

'Kurt Fischer,' Peter's escort piped up. 'And this is...'

'Let him speak.'

'Sepp Bauer,' Peter said.

'From?'

'Stuttgart.'

'Why? Stuttgart crews don't stay over. A straight turnround.'

'Replacements for the late run. Last-minute sickness.'

'You don't sound Stuttgart to me. I know every face in this

place. My business to, and I don't like strangers. Especially Stuttgarters who sound like foreigners. Like a damned Swiss.'

One lesson had been drummed into Peter. A railwayman should always have right of passage on his own turf. Despite a rising sense of uncertainty, fearing that by speaking he would give himself away, he said, 'Local dialect, quiet corner of the country.'

'Papers!'

The two sighed and went through the motions of a slow search of their pockets. This time the staff pass received a thorough examination. 'Fischer and Bauer,' the oberscharfuhrer said to himself, feeling in his pockets and frowning in frustration. Then he snapped his fingers at the canteen woman.

'Pen and paper!'

'Haven't got any,' she said without hesitation, demonstrating a commendable lack of fear.

He turned to Peter. 'Pen and paper!'

Peter shrugged. 'Sorry, engine crew, not writers.'

'Then report to my office in half an hour. Meanwhile, I'll keep these.'

Peter was aghast. He doubted his pass, if checked against central records, would stand up to scrutiny. The numbers were bound to be bogus. 'But we need them,' he said. 'It's the rules. Carry your papers at all times. At all times!'

The oberscharfuhrer glared at him, then threw the passes onto the table. One skidded off the edge. Then: 'Journey sheets!'

'Look,' said young Kurt, 'no need for that. You can check with the rota clerk, she'll tell you. She'll vouch for us.'

'I shall check up on both of you, Fischer and Bauer.' Said with derision as if these names were too absurd to be taken seriously. 'I shall remember you. So make sure you ship out tonight. Off my territory. I don't want to see your faces around here tomorrow.'

As soon as the man in black had stomped down the stairs a diminutive figure with a large head and enormous eyes appeared at the door.

'I see you've already had the pleasure of meeting *Die Pest-beule*,' he said.

Peter, a heart-thumping mixture of fear, excitement and relief, still managed a smile. *Die Pestbeule*, the plague boil.

Claudia was back in Erika's kiosk-like corner of the component stores giving her impression of her evening at the Hotel Luitpold, at the extravagance of the place and the people and all the astonishing detail of the conversation with Hank Hoskins. But it was the contrast between the two venues that struck her forcibly; Claudia, running her fingers over the smooth, gleaming decadence of the hotel dining table as against Claudia running her fingers over the cracked and rough surface of the depot furniture and the plain coffee mug, conscious as not before of the bleak poverty of their working place.

Erika was fiddling with the circular index drum on the big counter but seemed distracted, had no curiosity about Hoskins or any bright conversation about breakfast, *Die Pestbeule* or the oily messengers who called at the counter. Claudia could also sense she wasn't concentrating on the serial numbers of her index.

After a quick glance to check they were alone, Erika broke into the Luitpold story to say quietly, 'Something you have to know.'

Claudia felt a sharp pang of alarm.

'There's things here that you don't know about, things that are going on...'

'Like what exactly?'

'On the other side of the tracks.'

Claudia shrugged. She knew all about the broad gauge system. Everyone with eyes in their head could see the big tracks fanning out of the city. Better than that: she'd just been given a glimpse inside the head of the man developing the system's new motive power. Had, in fact, passed on what she could recall of it to Erika and had been surprised that her friend appeared to know most of the details already. 'Some new secret?' she asked.

'A new secret.' Erika lowered her voice to a whisper. 'Someone arriving shortly who will take all the blame for what is about to happen.'

Claudia spread her arms in puzzlement.

'Wipeout. The new motor is to be destroyed.'

'But why?'

'You don't need to know. In fact, you don't know anything. Remember that. So just don't get in the way, that's all. That's why I'm telling you.'

Claudia was silent for a moment. 'Hank... he's not a bad man.'

Erika shrugged.

'So why? Why destroy something that could benefit everyone? You seem to hate what he's doing but I don't get it. Improving things... surely one of the few actions this regime is taking that you can approve of?'

'You don't understand.'

'Then educate me.'

Erika took in a deep breath. 'You think I'm just nuts and bolts, don't you?'

'No...'

'You think a woman doesn't have an important part to play in major events.'

Claudia stumbled, embarrassed. 'No, of course not, but where's all this leading?'

'Your friend's new motor is a great danger.' Erika waved her hands in the direction of the new tracks. 'You think the Nazis are spending all this money just to make it easier for ordinary people to travel about? Are you that naive?'

Claudia coloured, wondering at this sudden change in tone.

Erika said, 'War, that's what it's for. Not for you and me. To make them great. To give *him* an even bigger war.'

Both their eyes travelled to the obligatory picture on the wall. The Fuhrer, clear-eyed, gazing to some glorious military future.

There was a long silence while Claudia considered this, her brow still puckered in concentration. 'But why do you need someone from outside? Why not someone here?'

'It needs to be a foreign agent to take all the blame. We have to appear innocent and make a pretence of doing our best to save the project. Otherwise, the recriminations will be awful.'

'Sounds hugely high risk to me, treason, if discovered.'

'You know nothing, Claudia, nothing at all. Ask no questions.'

Claudia shook her head. Blew out her cheeks. 'Incredibly dangerous. Haven't we got enough troubles already? I mean, the children! What about them?'

Erika softened her tone. 'You're dedicated to those kids, well, so am I, but you have to realise, there are some things that are bigger even than the children.'

Claudia shook her head. 'You'd be mad to get involved. If I were you, Erika, I'd have absolutely nothing to do with it.'

Another pause. Another stare between them. 'But I am involved, Claudia. I'm part of it. For the duration of this action, I'm to be known as Johannes.'

Claudia stared back at her friend, speechless for many long seconds, amazed and confused at this sudden change in Erika, at the conspiratorial tone. There was a long silence between them and Claudia felt more frightened than when she'd first encountered the U-boats. Eventually, she demanded, 'And who is this agent provocateur? This bringer of trouble to our doorstep?'

'Arriving shortly. To be known as Pyotr.'

'Oh my God!' Claudia had her head in her hands.

'More than that,' Erika said. 'I want you to meet him.'

Peter – or, as he was now known, Pyotr – lay full length on his stomach, strung out across some rafters, trying to keep his body still, not daring to let his legs slip lest they smash through the plasterboard of the ceiling below. All he had for comfort was some sacking, a blanket and a small plank.

His entire focus was on the scene across the tracks, which he could view through a tiny crack in his hide. From his position inside the loft of the two-storey crew bunkhouse, this was his covert introduction to a new world, the world of the *Breitspurbahn*. He had with him a borrowed pair of binoculars and he was watching every movement, trying to put a pattern to the place – timings, frequency, routine. It was good to have something to do. Activity helped steady his nerve. His first few minutes in this place had been a paralysis of fear. After the brush with *Die Pestbeule*, he'd sat in a chair looking at his shaking hands. Stared at them. First the backs, with the smooth skin of the fingers and the lines of the knuckles, then flipped them over, staring at the palms, like some old clairvoyant in a fair, trying to read the map of his future, trying to think his way to control. Duty, the mission, respect, Dansey, his father. When the shaking stopped, he took up his binoculars to make a start and what he saw gave him focus and calm.

Without a doubt his first view of the Fuhrer's new system

was fascinating. Impressive was an understatement. He'd been given the dimensions in London but to see it in action was stunning. These machines were monsters. The locomotives and carriages were as big as houses, dwarfing normal train stock. He knew from his briefing there were gas turbines as well as steam turbines. Some of the steamers had six high pressure and six low pressure cylinders and carried 100 tons of coal and another 100 tons of water. His gaze took him to the new roundhouse, past the water tower, coaling tower and signal gantry, past the lines of futuristic double-decker carriages. The air was full of smoke and coal dust from the steamers and oil and kerosene from the diesels, but then a breeze blew in from the Alps, bringing with it a relieving freshness, before he got another whiff of that peculiar metallic burning smell he knew came from overworked electric motors. He'd first noticed it down the London Tube. More disturbing, however, were the wafts of ash from the wreck of a burnt-out building. He could see the blackened hole in a line of trackside buildings. Obviously, an old disaster.

Through his glasses he identified the chief engineer's workshop, the big loco depot and the carriage construction shed. He had even spotted the Gestapo office, repressing another shiver. On the other side of the bunkhouse, out of his line of sight, were the normal trains – the 'standard gauge' – but he wasn't interested in them. This was what he had come for: the massively-wide trains that ran on rails almost ten feet apart. He could understand now why Dansey had described it, along with all the monolithic new architecture of the Third Reich, as another example of Hitler's mania for all things gigantic. He'd even coined a new word for it: *gigantomania*.

Peter watched the rail movements and he watched the human movements. Men in pairs, men in overalls, men in black uniforms. Then a secretary. Finally, one particular man, surrounded by a team clutching clipboards, wearing a grey suit.

Surely, he reasoned, the Engineer. But at such a distance from across the tracks he could not be certain.

Where, he wanted to know, did they keep the new propulsion unit, the new engine, The Thing – the object of Peter's quest, the device he had come to examine and destroy. It was not out in the open, so clearly they had it locked away.

It was an hour since he had survived his canteen scare with *Die Pestbeule* and been introduced to the little man with the frog eyes. 'I'm the Caller,' he said, 'I run the bunkhouse. Wake the blighters. Make sure they don't oversleep. Don't miss their schedules.'

Despite his easy manner, Peter had gone through the Dansey procedure, inquiring after the health of Sebastian and identifying himself with the same details on the name of the shedman and numbers of wheels he had used at Bergen. 'Sebastian, that's me,' said the Caller, 'but you keep it to yourself.'

It quickly became apparent that Peter's arrival was expected and the Caller had been assigned as his protector. There were a strict set of instructions: keep out of sight at all times and bunk in a spare room. The people 'at the centre', the Caller said, would not speak directly or identify themselves, and information would be funnelled through two conduits – himself and someone called Johannes.

At this Peter protested. 'I haven't come all this way, taken all these risks, to be kept at arm's length,' he said, a little more hotly than intended. 'I'm entitled to meet the top man. Need to.'

The Caller shook his head. 'How long do you think we'd survive if it was as easy as that?'

'You don't understand...'

'Oh yes I do.'

And for the moment there was no way past the outer crust of this cell, but Peter was determined. He would not be cocooned by these placemen. His moment would come.

He spent the first night in his new room to avoid chance encounters with the long-distance enginemen who slept over in the bunkhouse. They weren't a boisterous lot. Faint sounds of radios were the only signs of life. Quiet men. Responsible, middle-aged, family men, anxious to blend in and remain the Great Unnoticed. Peter wondered if any of them had an ear close up to a speaker, sneaking a forbidden session with a foreign radio station for which, if discovered, a jail sentence awaited. Later on, when all was quiet, he crept down to the Caller's tiny office to try again to squeeze from his new mentor as much information as possible: the plant layout, the security, the gossip but most of all, the Engineer's progress on his new project.

But that was a closed secret. 'Tomorrow you may get help with that,' Peter was told.

Next morning, the Caller had ready another set of *Reichsbahn* overalls, dirtier and more frayed than before, plus a pot of grease to smear on his hands, sending him under the tunnel to the stores department with a request for components and the instruction: 'Back off if the contact isn't there.'

Despite his disguise Peter felt vulnerable walking the long tunnel. He hadn't before experienced such a seemingly endless, noisy passage. Fortunately, passers-by were infrequent and incurious and at the counter in the stores building he asked, as instructed, for Johannes. A plain-looking woman in a brown smock was behind the counter. She gave him a long look. It made him nervous.

'And you are?' she said.

Peter scratched his head and turned to go. 'Not at home, no matter, I'll try later.'

'Oh yes, he's at home,' she said. 'Who shall I say called?'

Peter swallowed. Was this going according to plan? How to extricate himself if Johannes wasn't the right contact?

'Pyotr,' he said, almost reluctantly, then looked at the woman closely. The line of her mouth softened a little as she lifted the flap of the counter.

'Come behind,' she said.

Peter walked carefully into a channel between lines of lockers and shelves. She pointed to an alcove by a window. There was no one there. He turned to look at her, puzzled, wondering if he had been tricked. An ambush? Black uniforms hiding behind lockers, ready to pounce? He opened out his hands in a gesture of puzzlement. 'Johannes?'

She grinned. 'Johannes,' she said, 'that's me.'

Ten minutes later, after going through his identity checks, Peter was pumped full of information, principally on the advanced but unready state of the Engineer's new power plant but also on how he should do nothing to compromise the secret of the children hiding in the wilderness outside and the young woman who looked out for them.

'Good grief!' he said. 'Children queuing up to get out? Brings it all back. That last train!'

Erika stared at him. 'What?'

But Peter shook his head and didn't explain. So, he thought, it was happening again. Had it ever really stopped? He thought back to all those children who'd got out. And all those that hadn't.

She said, 'You're worried about the proximity of the children to the depot? Too close?'

'Too close,' he said sadly, staring out of the window at the tangle of grasses, bushes and trees.

'They're on opposite sides of the tracks. Surely no danger from any big bangs?'

'Falling debris. Big lumps of masonry. Plus the *Reichsbahn* may want to reopen the facilities on this side of the tracks if I manage to make a nice old mess of things over there.'

'Oh!'

'Plus drawing the attention of the people we don't like.' Then he softened his tone and gave the woman one of his winning smiles. 'Look,' he said with a confidential whisper, 'my business here is so important I really do need to speak to the leader of the cell. Can you arrange that for me?'

Up to this point she had been co-operative, a willing information conduit, but now she did not reply. Her expression was her answer.

He shrugged, frustrated once again, and pointed to the bushes outside. 'Well then, I may as well go and talk to the kids.'

Johannes snorted in derision. 'You won't find anyone out there. Better than camouflage. They'll see you coming. You're up against masters of concealment.'

Peter grinned. 'I know about these things,' he said. 'I know where to look.'

Children queuing up to get out of the country... harried by a harsh regime... the great rescue and the great tragedy of the pre-war *Kindertransports*. It all came back to him. How the last train, the largest consignment of all with 250 children on board, had been on the point of leaving Prague station when war broke out. Journey immediately cancelled. Children unloaded, never to be heard of again. A bitter pill.

These images returned to haunt Peter as he walked down the path towards a jungle of undergrowth, and now, it seemed, it was happening all over again. But then his mood lightened, anticipating meeting another group of refugee kids, and a happier memory came to mind: one of the successful trainloads which arrived at London's Liverpool Street station and he had been there to meet it.

~

The most striking child in the carriage was a tall girl with auburn hair, bright-eyed and alert and nursing a violin case. Peter gave them all a big smile as his glove puppets went to work: 'Sing a Song of Sixpence', 'Mary, Mary, Quite Contrary' and a brief version of Punch and Judy.

The children followed every movement. He did it first in English, then in German, making a conscious effort to repress his Swiss accent. From the Magic Bag came a funny little shoe followed by the story of the little old woman who lived inside. 'Hey Diddle Diddle' got the biggest laugh when the cow jumped over the moon, then he finished up with 'Ding, Dong, Bell, Pussy's in the Well'.

The girl with the violin case gave him an appreciative smile as, once again from the Magic Bag, out came a series of tiny goodies: a metal Tower Bridge and a miniature horse guard.

A second Winton volunteer extended his arms in a welcoming gesture and repeated the message. It was a three-language welcome. Most children came from Prague but some were from the Sudetenland, their parents having fled the Nazi invasion several months before. Peter filled the time taken by the Czech translation by studying the faces. A tearful little girl in plaits cuddled a doll; a boy in knickerbockers was struggling to put on a tiny rucksack; another lad of ten wore a fashionable jacket with a neat collar and tie.

'Now,' Peter said, resuming his welcome routine, 'you've all had a long journey but it's nearly over. Shortly, I'll take you out of the train to meet your new mothers and fathers. First, we go to the man at the desk and tell him who you are...'

'I know who I am,' insisted a small boy flourishing his name disc.

Peter laughed and the girl with the violin case addressed him in almost flawless English.

'Are you good at music as well as nursery rhymes?'

'I play a little.' He shrugged. 'Mostly the piano.'

'Good, then you can tell me, please, what are the prospects for my musical education?'

Peter chuckled. 'First, we need to fix you up with a home and a school and then...'

'I have a special interest,' she said. 'Elgar.'

'Really?'

'I've read about him. I'm so looking forward to attending a concert at your Royal Albert Hall.'

Peter disguised his surprise. 'Elgar? He's a very English sort of composer, not very fashionable in Europe.'

'When I knew I was going to England I found out all about him. I've been trying out his Variations. They always make me want to cry.'

This conversation stuck in the memory. So many arrivals, so many children – but it was the day Peter met Helga. And Helga was soon to become a familiar part of his life: violinist, Elgar fan, adopted by his aunt Klarissa who lived across town in Bury, a close friend of the family, a frequent visitor to the Chesham household.

Then, another memory, a more recent one: Refugee Helga playing Bach in the drawing room at 2 Whiting Street along with Peter, his mother and aunt, the day Sir Andrew Truscott called to interrupt their jam session and to shatter Peter's calm and uneventful war.

Claudia walked down the path towards the wilderness carrying a faded brown jumper donated by Papa Thorbeck's wife, a hunk of bread from the school kitchens and the last of her own stock of cheeses. As she did so, her jaw took on a determined set.

Relations with Erika had cooled since this new conspiracy was revealed. This morning the stores had been full of people but Erika's swivelled glance had said it all. The agent provocateur had not only arrived. He was in *her* wilderness.

Claudia was in a cold fury. She thought her friend quite mad to be part of it. The adoption of the codename Johannes demonstrated just how deeply she was involved. Claudia was frightened. Talk of sabotage involving the Fuhrer's pet project meant the stakes were huge. Danger had gone sky high. A warning voice in her head, sounding much like her mother's, told her to get out fast before disaster struck.

She swallowed, turning up her collar against the cold, and knew she was in far too deep to run. She couldn't welch on her children and resented her friend's change in priorities. This other purpose? She shook her head. She saw only the desperate and pathetic faces of stranded children. How could Erika fail to put the children first?

She approached a weeping willow whose branches quite effectively disguised what lay beyond. She pushed the foliage aside and found a figure sitting still, partly concealed by moss, grass and leaves.

She recognised him immediately: Kiefer, an eight-year-old redhead from a children's home, rescued just minutes before a round-up. Unusually, he was smiling. And eating. In his hand was an object covered in a bright blue wrapper. As she approached, he clutched the package to his chest and scampered away, as if fearing she might snatch it from him. Little bush rats quickly learned not to risk confiscation.

At the freezer car she went through the entrance ritual and immediately sensed a change in the mood of the occupants. They were attentive, sitting quietly, their usual poses of boredom and hostility gone. Something – or someone – held their gaze. Dry sticks crackled and spat on the stove, the remains of a meal scattered about them.

In the centre of the wagon a male figure sat cross-legged on a piece of matting that served as a makeshift carpet. He looked up at her without surprise. In his early twenties, blond and wearing blue *Reichsbahn* overalls, the eagle at his left breast. His cap was on the floor beside him. For a moment, the children were silent as they looked at Claudia.

Then they turned away and the catcalls began.

'Come on, come on! Finish the story!'

'Who are you?' Claudia's taut tone cut through the clamour. It was meant to, delivered in her most demanding school ma'am manner, despite knowing full well who this must be.

'The story, the story!'

He gave her a big smile and bowed his head.

'What happened to cat?'

'What about the fox? Tell!'

The young voices were insistent.

'Why,' said the man in a rich, intriguing tone, 'the cat made it to the top of the tree when the hounds came rushing up but the fox, oh dear, the fox was not as clever as he thought...'

Claudia, despite her annoyance, found herself lulled into listening. The voice had an inviting, comforting, enfolding quality. Like her father's, a dark-brown, creamy fudge sort of a voice. There was no stopping this storyteller. And at that moment she experienced a sudden stab of resentment, even jealousy. How had this stranger been accepted so completely by *her* children? She was used to being the centre of attention. Perhaps, she realised, somewhat guiltily, she now needed their attention as much as they needed her sustenance.

When the fox, too late, realised his mistake and the tale was finally told, she ignored the storyteller and went straight to little Anna, always the most vulnerable of the children. She knew there would be a wail of discontent. 'I don't like sausage stew.'

'Never mind,' Claudia soothed, 'bread and different kinds of cheeses tomorrow.'

'But they make everything taste funny.'

Claudia nodded sympathetically. She knew why. The cook

was one of the leaders of the gang. Big Jan was an old man of sixteen and showed his seniority by smoking a pipe. His number two did roll-ups. They were both hoping for moustaches. The 'funny taste' was the result of nefariously-acquired foodstuffs – sausage liberated from the canteen, cabbage from gardens, treacle from a broken locker – being consigned to the same big pot and made into a stew. Tomatoes, jam or sugar, anything that could be scrounged or stolen. 'Gives a bit of extra zing,' Jan told her.

'Claudia, isn't it?'

The storyteller was suddenly beside her but she didn't waste words on an introduction. 'You gave little Kiefer, the redhead out there in the reeds, something with a blue wrapper. What was it?'

'Only chocolate.'

Claudia couldn't help it. She might be addressing a stranger but she went straight to the point. 'Not a good idea. He'll get a tummy ache. These children are on a starvation diet, some of the food here is not of the best, and rich things will simply play havoc with their digestions.'

'Just a small bar.'

'Do you intend to play Father Christmas to all these waifs?'

He smiled back at her, not in the least put out by her tone. 'Why, how many waifs do you have?'

'At the last count, approaching thirty, give or take.'

'Thirty?'

'You seem surprised,' she said. 'I was told you knew all about our little kindergarten.'

'No idea it was that many.' He seemed suddenly sad.

'A word please.' She beckoned him outside. When they were on the dirt path and out of the hearing of the children she confronted him, her expression severe, the escalation of danger giving her a sharp edge. 'You,' she said, pointing, 'are my mortal enemy, my worst nightmare, the danger I fear most.'

'Sorry?'

'A peril worse than the Gestapo. You could get me hung and all my little ones discovered. Have you any idea of the disaster you could bring down upon us? Have you any conception? Have you? Worse than a pestilence!'

'Really! No need for that.'

She was still pointing. 'You wouldn't come all this way just to learn how to say a good Bavarian hello. Or rid yourself of that terrible Swiss dialect.'

But the man had regained his composure. 'I know all about you,' he said with a smile, 'I've been told. I understand. You have a very delicate secret to guard. In the circumstances, such anxiety is quite natural. And I've already met some of your young flock.'

'I don't want you talking to my children, filling their heads full of rubbish.'

'Would you consider Grimms' fairy tales rubbish?'

She glared at him for a long moment before demanding, 'Just what are you doing here?'

'You wouldn't really expect me to answer that, would you?'

'I have a pretty good idea. Something dreadful, dangerous and likely to bring the authorities down on our heads. Is that not so?'

'That's a very persuasive manner you have there. I bet you'd get the Devil himself to contribute to the winter relief fund.'

'Don't try getting clever, whatever your name is.'

'Then I should introduce myself. Sepp Bauer at your service.'

She spluttered. 'Yes, and I'm Mary Poppins.'

Coffee was on the table as usual. It was their after-school ritual in the stores but the atmosphere between them was cool.

Claudia did not want to fall out with her friend. She needed someone close, someone sympathetic and with a like mind to offset the fractious atmosphere met daily in the school staffroom. Besides, she could not act alone. She needed help with washing and supplies and for Erika to continue to share the burden of playing mother to the children. But for all that, she was still angry at the intrusion into their lives of this dangerous new conspiracy.

'He wants to talk to you again,' Erika said.

'Really? Why? More nursery rhymes? More fairy stories? Who is this Pied Piper sent to do the dirty deed?'

Erika put down her cup. 'Claudia, you can't keep it up. This hostility, it isn't helping.'

'Children first – in my book.' Claudia knew she sounded petulant but couldn't help it. All the secrecy and use of code-names disconcerted her. She was frightened.

'Mine too, if I had the choice,' Erika said, 'but we're dependent on the goodwill of the depot people for help with the kids. And they want this other thing done. So do I, for that matter. You can't go against it.'

Claudia looked down. 'I don't agree with violence – and Hank, well, whatever he's doing, good or bad, he himself is not a bad man.'

Erika poured another cup and fiddled with the filters. 'I don't know exactly what the plan is. Whether it involves him personally, or not.' She shrugged. 'Talk it through with Pyotr.'

Claudia spluttered. 'Pyotr! All these strange names! Did you know, he calls himself Sepp Bauer?'

Erika's arched eyebrows warned her against such dismissive references. 'They're for his protection. Pyotr for the operation, Sepp for meeting people.' She sighed. 'You know, you're lucky he hasn't reacted against you. You could have come up against someone a lot less friendly.' Another pause then Erika added,

'Actually, I expected someone dour, forbidding, probably a bit scary, at the very least a stuffed shirt. But this man, well, get that smile, a real charmer and so young and good-looking. Don't tell me you haven't noticed.'

Claudia ignored the last. 'The only way to make me happy is to get the kids out first... before he does whatever he has planned.'

Erika shrugged. 'Don't go starting a fight. We need you both. Meet him again. Tell him your concerns. Discuss it with him.'

Peter had done his best but was shocked by Claudia's reaction. Understandable perhaps, but intimidating. However, that wasn't the only cause for concern. The other was the poor condition of the children. It was shocking. Just how long had they been cooped up?

His doubts about his military mission immediately resurfaced. Why had he and Williams made this dangerous trek across mountain and Third Reich territory, defying nature and a torturer's cell, only to confront and now endanger this pathetic collection of walking skeletons? These children needed help: doctors, food, nourishment, care, love. His instincts rebelled at the notion of ignoring their plight, but what could he do?

Back in Britain he would have acted. In the days before the war he had 'done his bit' for the young refugees from Prague and a whole lot more. First, as an entertainer for the young ones at Liverpool Street station when they arrived in England for the first time. Then there were the stranded youths housed in seaside huts, waiting to be placed with foster parents. Who wanted a male teenager when there were girls and babies on offer? However, those boys needed a challenge; sport, conversation and laughter and he had answered the call. He thought too of the refugee girl Helga who had so seamlessly woven herself into the fabric of his family at Bury. He thought of her passion for Elgar – then a kaleidoscope of images flashed before him of the early days of the Blitz: the declaration of war, helping her on with her gas mask, the air raid warden in the street shouting 'take cover', digging a pit in the garden for an Anderson shelter and Helga's astonishment when Father buried family 'treasures' in the foundations of the shelter: his Chablis and Mother's jewels.

What a contrast to the plight of the Maze children. He recoiled at the thought of the indescribable stench of the freezer car. He would suggest it be cleared and scrubbed out. Couldn't they organise a better food supply from the canteen in the works? When Runner had offered him a taste of their homemade 'soup' he almost choked and retched at the foul liquid. What did they put in that pot? Better not to know.

He'd already cleared a patch of scrub for a game of catch, discussed the merits of the latest Focke-Wulf 190 with young Rolf and, stricken by Anna's wails, had delivered an especially soothing rendition of *Jochen and the Beanstalk*, aghast at the fragility of her tiny body.

He was racked by the appalling contrast between the destructive nature of his mission and the vulnerability of the children, separated by just ten railway tracks. A clash of steel and flesh.

Doubt continued to plague him. He knew how to put on a front, how to play a part, how to exude a confidence he didn't feel. A lot of old bull, as Williams would have described it, but Peter thought in theatrical terms. The show must go on – but how would it finish? How would the curtain ring down? He really had no idea. He hadn't learnt his lines because there were no lines to learn, Dansey being a poor stage manager. Peter had acquiesced in all this, taking comfort from his private proviso:

no violence, no rough stuff. He knew it was his patriotic duty to put aside all anxieties and show Claudia a different face. What other course could he take?

~

Cap, overalls, knapsack. He looked like any other worker hurrying about his business in the yard. There were so many of them. Who exactly was who? Few people knew each other. They came from workshops, depots and offices in the standard gauge department, the broad gauge and from across the tracks. The place was a sprawling labyrinth. Apparently, the man known as Pyotr was intent on talking to her again 'as a matter of urgency' so they met in the gloomy porch by the back door of a wheel shed, long since defunct, shielded not only from the attention of passers-by but well out of the sight line of Oberscharfuhrer Voss, alias *Die Pestbeule*.

'Why should I talk to you?' Claudia said as soon as she recognised him. 'You... from an enemy state?' She saw no reason to make it easy. Anxiety gave her hostility a sharp edge.

He smiled broadly. 'Because I'm on a mission of peace.'

She snorted. 'Am I meant to believe that?' She looked away in a demonstration of disgust. 'Your accent and that name, they don't fool me.'

He peered at her, searching for her gaze, forcing her to look at him. He had this disconcerting trait, she remembered from their first meeting, of looking so sincere. 'Today I am not your enemy,' he said. 'Today – and I hope personally for always – I am your friend.'

'And of course I'm silly enough to be taken in by such talk. Like a cheap salesman...'

He cut her off. 'I sincerely hope never to be your enemy,

Claudia, but certainly for now and the next few days and perhaps a week, I am definitely your friend.'

He put his head on one side and smiled at her again, which wasn't the reaction she expected. She didn't seem able to disconcert this man. The school ma'am manner wasn't working.

'Really, Claudia, there's no need to be so hostile,' he said. 'I know our two countries are at war and that's horrible. I hate it. And I know another person standing not a million miles from here who thinks the same.'

Claudia bristled. He knows too much, she thought, and he's far too familiar. It was an unseemly use of her forename. Erika had clearly been talking to him. It must be Erika. Only she knew these things about her. Erika had talked too much.

At that moment their conversation was interrupted by the rattle of couplings from the shunting yard behind them, but as soon as the buffeting died down, he insisted, 'I'm certain of something else too. Most people round here dislike this awful regime as much as I do. The Nazis, I mean. And I think that includes you.'

She stayed silent, measuring him, letting him make the running.

'I want to persuade you,' he said, 'that it would be a good thing for all of us if we were to co-operate.'

She jerked up, as if in surprise, and said, 'Co-operate? How?'

'You could give me your help.'

'Help?' The voice was low, almost a whisper, but Claudia still looked outraged. 'Help an enemy alien? I should report you. Have you arrested.'

'And risk yourself being arrested and your little ones sent to the ghetto – or worse? What would happen to them, do you know?'

She was saved from having to reply by the fireman on one of the huge new locomotives in the nearby *Breitspurbahn* yard. A monstrous geezer of steam screeched high into the sky creating a great cloud of gaseous vapour and deafening all around. The fireman had clearly over-stoked his boiler, raising pressure to dangerous levels and the safety valves had lifted.

When the din subsided she folded her arms and said, 'I hate the military. You say you hate the war, but you're some sort of soldier. Anything you do will draw attention to us. Attention and arrest. I just wish you'd go away and take your ideas somewhere else.'

'What I'm trying to do is to prevent this war from getting any worse.'

'Could it?'

'Oh yes, a lot worse.' He pointed towards the workshops on the other side of the tracks. 'Do you really think they're trying to make people's lives better?'

'I've heard all this before.'

'It's to make war,' he said. 'Bigger and more effective, more bloody than now. It means more countries invaded, more people killed, enslaved, sent to concentration camps. Women and children, just like your little ones. That's what it's for, and we have to stop it before it happens.'

'But...'

'Yes I know, the chief engineer has told you and anyone who'll listen just what a wonderful thing it all is. The man's a fool. He's doing the Fuhrer's dirty work. He has to be checked. And you can help.'

'That's my point,' she said hotly. 'You're here to destroy. Blow things up. And you mean harm to Hank. He's a good man and he's my friend. I don't want anything happening to him.'

Pyotr drew in a long breath. 'That depends on how co-operative he is. How much he can be persuaded.'

'And if he can't?'

'That's where you come in. To help me persuade him. I need

to explain just how mistaken he's been. Get him to see the situation my way.'

She didn't reply, so he said, 'I know you're on good terms with him. Fix me a meeting, but it has to be very discreet, a covert meeting out of sight of the authorities.'

She looked away, then said, 'There's a price.' This followed by a long silence before she spoke again. 'My co-operation comes at a price.'

'Which is?'

'Help *me* get the children away *before* you do anything – then, and only then, will I help you.'

16

It wasn't the sort of invitation she would normally have relished, but given her decision to cultivate the Engineer, Claudia squeezed out a smile when they next met over coffee in the stores and said she'd love to accompany him on his tour of inspection.

'We've really been very futuristic in our designs,' Hoskins said, 'thinking way ahead of our rivals.'

They crossed the tracks before entering the carriage shed and at once she was hit by the pungency of wood, paint and glue. It was a gloomy arena. Strange rectangular patterns of light from roof panels played mystifying tricks with objects at track level: some finished, some skeletal.

Hoskins was running through his list, a non-stop commentary on his repertoire of wagons: gondola cars for steel, wood slat cars for cattle, boxcars for builders and tie-down flatcars for other goods. They went up some steps and inside a VIP restaurant special. It was completely fitted out, all ready to roll. She had also noted the lush green finish on the outside and the flamboyant name in gold lettering on the flanks: The Caribou.

'Isn't that Canadian?' she said. 'Some kind of reindeer?'

'Spot on, teacher,' he said, 'I've had it designed in the style of the Canadian Pacific. North American influence, you see. Reflects my origins.'

Once inside she felt overwhelmed by the enormous space. The wide rails gave it another dimension. There was a sumptuous dining area with a central table covered in red velvet. It was set for a dozen places, had matching chairs and a large sideboard with racks of ivory-handled cutlery and wine glasses. The dinner service was a Nymphenburg porcelain design with the new BB crest: the *Breitspurbahn*, or the big bahn, as Hoskins liked to call it.

She picked up a side plate, circled in yellow with a blue pattern, expressing surprise. 'You've got this far already?'

He gave her a menu card. She looked at the top item: grilled halibut or salmon in lemon butter.

'Wait till you see the next one,' he said.

She stood quite still to take in the details of the second diner: an elaborately-carved ceiling, chandeliers, ornate decor, red patterned rugs, white tablecloths and the most enormous windows she had ever seen. A woman in a smart blue-patterned uniform was kneeling at a cupboard, sorting crockery. 'Sumptuous isn't the word,' Claudia said. 'Like a baronial hall. Like travelling first class on a transatlantic liner.'

He was grinning, enjoying her reaction, proud of his creation. They moved on through the workshop. Someone out of sight was hard at work with a hammer, the noise overlaid by the high-pitched whine of a mechanical saw. In the cinema car a huge screen was being installed and a set of side panels gave the car the appearance of an old opera house.

'Next, the kitchen car,' he said.

Here, Hoskins was particularly expansive. 'The beauty of this system,' he said, 'is that with the increase in size we have such huge capacity for all kinds of refinements and luxuries.

Plenty of space for new equipment to be fitted in the future. Room for everything needed by a top chef on the move,' he said, running his hand over the surfaces. And then, bending, he slid back several panels showing vast storage space.

In the sleeper car progress was not as far advanced. An aproned figure was hard at work with a sandblock but she noticed alcoves behind the bunk beds and cupboards attached to the ceiling.

Hoskins liked to swank. He was proud of his achievements. So she smiled and indulged him.

He touched another panel and said, 'Sealed off for now but it can be opened up later for when the traffic develops and they need even more equipment. Big enough for any piece of equipment we can think of. In fact, big enough for an army!' He laughed, pleased with his joke.

Suddenly the idea came to her. Hit her like a eureka moment.

Big enough for an army?

Big enough for her little band of fugitives!

'Anything the matter?' he asked, seeing her serious face.

'No, not at all,' she said, managing another smile. 'Most impressive, really, a fantastic job you've done here.'

'You can't be serious.' Peter was shaking his head but still good humoured, quietly chuckling. 'An ingenious idea, but no way.'

Until now Claudia had felt hemmed in on all sides, but now a whole new vista opened up to her. The way ahead was suddenly stunningly clear.

'I had you down as a man who loved children,' she said. 'Who told them stories and nursery rhymes. Who could control bullies. Charm them down from the trees. Here's your chance.

Instead of blowing things up, instead of destruction, here's an opportunity to do something worthwhile. To save lives, not destroy.'

He grinned. 'I've said it before, you could persuade Old Nick to give to charity, but not this time.'

'Why not?' Her eyes were big. Appealing. 'Hoskins told me he's taking the train to the border to impress the Swiss, some tactic to persuade them to agree to something, not sure what.'

'Transit, I expect. Either trans-shipment from this system on to theirs or possibly even to build this one through neutral territory, but I doubt that.'

She put her hands on her hips. 'So, you could get my kids across the border. Destroy the train there... but after my little ones have crossed to safety.'

Peter shook his head. 'Even if I said yes, how could you hide nearly thirty young ruffians – scruffy, smelly, unkempt kids who've been living rough for months on scraps – on a long journey on a train full of VIPS? Mostly Nazi VIPs. Kids without tickets or visas. No chance.'

'I told you, in hiding,' she insisted. 'There's dozens of hidey holes in those carriages. Hide them away for the length of the journey, then at the right moment...' She made a springing jack-in-the-box movement with her hands.

He laughed again. 'And what genius is going to create us a secret rabbit warren that can be filled with children in the Fuhrer's most prestigious train? Can you show me the person willing to do that?'

She inclined her head with a slight smile, a gesture that seemed to suggest that anything was possible.

'And how do I get them across the German border? One frontier guard, one train official, almost any German with eyes in his head... if they saw that lot they'd scream *Juden*. And we'd all end up on a train to one of those work camps in the East.'

'You're a clever man. You got yourself into Germany. You have the expertise. You know how to do these things.'

He laughed at her. 'And then there's the Swiss.' He sighed. 'As slippery as the Nazis are brutal. They've got a racket going at the frontier. The border guards sell refugees who cross the frontier back to the German guards for a price. And inside Switzerland there are laws against their own citizens giving refuge. Bribery is the only way. Only you have to know who to bribe.'

She sighed. 'Anyone would think you're a hard-hearted bastard who didn't want to help.'

'Absolutely not, I...' Then he stopped.

'Yes?'

It was on the tip of his tongue to tell her. To explain himself; to justify himself; to reveal his role in the *Kindertransports*. But no. He shook his head and stayed silent. He must play her along while doing his duty. This train would never get to the Swiss border. Hoskins and his new motor were going to be consigned to history, right here in the depot. This train would not leave Munich. He shook his head. 'You're impossible,' he said. 'And it's impossible.'

'Don't fail me, Pyotr. Don't fail my little ones whose lives now depend on you.'

Peter was selecting items of kit, packing them carefully into a fitter's tool bag. The precision of his preparations was vital but his mind was only half on the job. The cruel contrast between mission and children was eating away at him. He shook his head, sighed and picked up a wrench and placed it at the bottom of the bag. He took out a pair of goalkeeper's knee pads and rolled them up his arms until they covered his elbows. Then he checked once again the state of his *Reichsbahn* overalls and rubber shoes.

All was quiet, so he eased out of his hiding place in the bunkhouse and set off at a silent lope for the main office block. It was shortly after eleven and no one was about. He'd already clocked Franz, the railway policeman on late shift, comfortably ensconced in the Gestapo office with his radio set, doubtless tuned to a Hamburg station concert. Haydn tonight, or so he'd been told. He applauded the man's taste if nothing else.

As he crossed the tracks he thought again of Claudia and their conversation about Switzerland and hiding places in the new coachwork. She was trying to pull him into her mad escape scheme and he knew he had to fend her off. He could not allow the mission to be compromised.

He reached a brick wall on the other side of the tracks and located the narrow gap between the document store and the Engineer's office. Both were in darkness. This was his target. During daylight he'd studied the frontage and all that went on there. Large paper plans had been taken from the store and later in the afternoon, returned. He noted the human traffic between the offices and the workshops and paid particular attention to the drawing office staff, the Engineer and his assistants.

Peter squeezed into the gap and looked up to the three windows near the roofline. Hoisting his tool bag onto his chest, he put his back to one wall and his feet on the other and began to wedge-climb using feet and elbows as levers. Just the way Fitzpatrick taught him during his crash course on breaking and entering at Fulbrough Manor. He'd never forget that strangely wizened and evasive figure he suspected of being on day release from Wormwood Scrubs, but Peter had taken to silent entry like the natural climber he was. It had been a case of back to childhood, scaling drainpipes and trees, but best of all was spider-walking up two adjacent walls.

He was panting now with the effort of attaining height and he cursed the serrations of the rough wall, despite the use of elbow pads. Halfway up he stopped to get his breath and he thought again of Claudia. He acknowledged her courage, resourcefulness and imagination but her ideas were utterly impractical. He didn't give them a shred of credibility. A large part of him wanted to help her but he was a soldier now, he had a military task, he had sworn an oath of allegiance and you didn't ditch that at the first hurdle. His overriding aim was to discover the secret of Hoskins's new propulsion unit.

He went back to work, hoisting himself higher, hoping the pain would be worth it. His fear was to be confronted by a safe. There hadn't been time at Fulbrough for safe-cracking.

The windows were old and dirty and one presented an inviting crack. Peter oiled the glass for silent working and went to it with a glass cutter, gently lengthening the crack until it reached the frame. As he worked, he was conscious of the wind and in its mournful moans and sighs he thought he heard the cries of little Anna in her miserable billet. It was, of course, all in his head. The sticky tape and a suction pad produced a neat hand-sized hole. The hook went through next, lifting the latch at the bottom of the frame and giving him an open window large enough to crawl through. The incision was neat. He could glue it back into place on the way out. With luck, no one would notice.

He was in, and by the time his feet touched the floor he had decided he would, after all, try to help Claudia, but in ways more practical than her madcap scheme for stowaways. He began methodically to examine the big stacks of scale drawings, knowing he would have to sift through hundreds. Any big project produced masses of work from the drawing office. He tried to figure their system: carriages, station fittings, mechanicals. He needed time and patience for the trawl but the prize would be worth it. He was ready with the Fulbrough-issue special document camera: a tiny, lightweight Minox Riga using ultra-fine-grain camera film. This would capture the secrets of the new motor. He was concentrating hard, flicking fast through the tops of the drawings, reading off the titles, and almost didn't hear it.

A rattle of keys in the door.

By the time a figure entered the room, closed the door and switched on the lights, Peter was spreadeagled on the open roof beams, feet wedged in a corner, arms supporting his upper body. All in plain sight but working on the precept that office workers, soldiers or even policemen rarely, if ever, look up.

It was Hoskins, the man himself, returning unexpectedly. How long would he stay? How long could Peter remain strung up on the rafters?

Then a new thought came to him. A way of turning the tables. An unexpected opportunity. Wouldn't Dansey, if he were present, urge him to strike while he could? He could drop on Hoskins, using shock tactics and surprise with a leap from the rafters. Then he stopped, the thought rejected before it went further. Such a tactic would not be conducive to the response he wanted. Peter preferred persuasion and an appeal to the man's decency. He had promised himself to forego violence. On the other hand, he acknowledged that an officer should be a man of action, but before he could reconcile this dilemma the door juddered open once more and another figure entered.

Peter held his breath. It would only take one of them to look up. He studied the newcomer and recognised Hoskins's natural antagonist, his rival for technological glory, the deputy engineer of the Landsberger depot, Reinhardt Meyer. Peter relaxed slightly as the danger of discovery faded. This wasn't a watchman's round or a snap inspection. These two were consumed by disagreements. He was aware of the tensions between them and he had Erika to thank for that.

Meyer's voice came up to him, distinct in the silence. 'Glad to have found you,' he told Hoskins, 'I guess we're both working late, struggling with problems. And it's a good moment to talk. Time, I think, for complete frankness.'

'Oh yes?' Hoskins sounded distracted, returned to his search, like Peter before him, and flicked through a stack of drawings.

'I'll be direct. About the 25th.'

'What about it?'

'You'll never make it. Save yourself the humiliation and go for the superheater option.'

Peter knew all about the superheater option. It was a steam locomotive Meyer had developed as an alternative to the new propulsion unit, but what was new to Peter was the deadline – the 25th? Presumably, they were talking about the demonstration run to Switzerland.

'No way!' Hoskins had stopped flicking and was waving his arms. 'No halfway houses, you hear?' Then more moderately: 'I recognise your achievement, Reinhardt. You've pushed steam as far as it will go, a useful refinement of an old technology, but that's not why I'm here. This is a revolution and I am the revolutionary.'

'So you've said.'

'This is the future. It's arrived, here and now. The 25th is the day. The day we're going to prove to the world – not just Germany but to Switzerland and all those others who will be watching – that my system is the future.'

'Too many problems still to resolve. Too little time. You'll never make it.'

'I'm aware you're a sceptic but I'll prove you wrong.'

Meyer became gritty. 'I just hope you appreciate the dangers.

The price you'll pay for failure. The price we'll all pay. This regime does not forgive.'

'Just watch me!'

Meyer exhaled a long, exasperated sigh. 'I want to make sure you realise what's at stake. You're gambling with the future of everyone in this place. Maybe the works. Maybe the whole railway system. Perhaps – very much a perhaps – you'll win the laurels of victory. More likely end up with a striped suit in a camp.'

Peter wondered how Hoskins would respond to this but was not to find out. At that moment the door opened once more and a third figure entered. A man in a grey uniform with eagle runics, plus brown belt, pistol and jackboots. A snapshot of Franz, the railway policeman. Clearly, he hadn't been asleep or distracted by the Haydn concert.

'I thought we had intruders,' he said, 'a break-in of some sort.'

He began to look around.

Would he look up?

'No trouble, Franz,' Hoskins told him, 'we're done here.'

So the regime's babysitter was on first-name terms with his charge. Two men who had history together, Erika had said. Two men who went way back.

Hoskins seemed to make a snap decision, removing a drawing from a pile and walking to the door. 'Reinhardt, we'll speak again in the morning.'

The lights went off, the door closed behind them and the key rattled in the lock. Plunged back into darkness, Peter felt the tension drain, his arms weak with the strain of supporting himself. Nevertheless, he remained in position for several more minutes before descending to resume his search. He stuck at it for the best part of an hour but failed to find the treasure he sought. The drawings for the new motor were nowhere to be found.

Never mind, he told himself, the most important discovery was the day of Hoskins's big demonstration: Monday the 25th and a showy exhibition of the new super-train in Switzerland.

This was now Peter's deadline.

17

It was a struggle to keep disease, sores and depression at bay. Bad food, the cold and exposure were dragging some of the children down. And little Anna was losing the fight. She was bedbound and suffering and her chest sounded awful. Claudia suspected pneumonia and knew she must act, despite the danger of discovery or betrayal.

Then she thought of Peter and decided this was her chance. She needed to hook him in, break down his resistance, make him her ally. She'd work on his empathy with children. She sent a message through Erika and met him in the freezer car where Anna lay hot and distressed.

'I need your help,' she said.

'I'm your worst nightmare, remember?'

'She needs a doctor right away.'

'I can see that, but how can you trust a doctor to keep his mouth shut?'

'There's one. But we'll have to wait until after dark.'

'Now wait a minute...' He came out with the expected objections. Not his job. His need to stay undercover. Why not recruit Erika? Claudia had the answers: she needed a man in railway uniform carrying a suitcase to complete her cover. The perfect family cover. A couple from the depot.

'It's her only chance.'

Peter pursed his lips and hesitated.

No regular doctor would treat a child of the night, Claudia said. An open visit to a surgery would spell arrest and worse. They were reliant on covert medical help as far below the official surface as their own.

Peter repeated his objections, insisting that leaving the depot was an untold risk to his operation, but when the street lamps came on he was there, in DR uniform and cap, and she knew she had scored her first victory.

She passed him a bulging envelope.

'What's this?'

'What do you think? That you can just walk around without papers? Those railway passes of yours won't save you once you leave the depot.'

He withdrew a clutch of new passes, the bureaucratic clutter so beloved of the authorities: employment card, resident registration, food and clothing rations, housing and police registration.

He looked at her, puzzled. 'How?'

'Don't ask.'

Peter drew in a deep breath, guessing at Erika or an insider connection with the police, aware as never before that he was being carried along by the mysterious and unseen hand that stayed frustratingly out of reach while guiding him through the pitfalls of life in wartime Germany. Once again, he had the uncomfortable feeling of being a puppet on a string.

They roused the child, swaddled her in extra jerseys and coats, and walked her out of the depot, across the main road and into the sprawling suburb of Laim, keeping as far as possible to the shadows as they passed tall apartment blocks. Solid middle-class dwellings, a cop might have described the area, no trouble to anyone. Silent supporters of the regime, Claudia would have countered. People content that order had been restored from the chaos of the past but with their gaze firmly averted from the brutality of the regime.

At a corner they passed an ecclesiastical-style building with a vast onion dome. 'Don't they just love their churches,' Peter whispered.

'That's the benefits office.'

At the Friedenheimer Strasse they had no choice but to cross the wide, well-lit dual carriageway. Trams occupied the centre section and it was a legal requirement to wait at traffic lights for permission to cross. Standing on the opposite pavement was a familiar figure, her head cocked to one side.

'Well, hello, Fraulein Kellner! What a surprise! What are you doing out so late? A stranger to these parts, surely?'

Claudia swallowed. Frau Obermeier was all questions and, she knew from experience, not one to hold back. She was one of the older mothers with short greying hair and large earrings. She dressed young with long side slits to a black skirt.

'And who's this?' Obermeier enquired, looking closely at the unprepossessing bundle cowering between Claudia and Peter.

Claudia had her lie ready, unlikely though she knew it to be. 'Just helping out. Her mother's not feeling well, so we're taking the child to an aunt's for a few days, just till her mother gets her strength back.'

'She doesn't look good.' Obermeier was almost poking at Anna's face. 'Definitely a bit peaky. Could do with a good scrub, I'd say. Anyway, what's the matter with the child's aunt? Can't she collect her?'

'You know me,' Claudia said, playing up to her part, 'always anxious for the children.'

'And who's this?' Looking directly at Peter.

He smiled widely and hefted the suitcase, indicating its weight. 'Just a friend.'

Obermeier looked at Claudia, disbelief signposted clearly with a sly grin. 'Been meaning to talk to you, Fraulein, about my Udo. He really needs special help with his reading. Over and above the normal, if you know what I mean. Don't want him falling behind.'

So this was the price: special treatment in exchange for silence. 'We'll talk again,' Claudia said, 'when I have more time. At the school gate.'

'That was a close one,' Peter said when they had vanished back into the shadows of a small avenue of houses.

'She's trouble,' Claudia said.

By now they were into the moneyed quarter. The apartment blocks were smart with bright blues and yellows picked out by the street lights. They had balconies, canopies and sun visors. There were net curtains in the windows and flower pots on the doorsteps. In the next street they passed front gardens, trees and privet hedges and when Claudia heard the swish of a cloak next to a kindergarten she knew they had encountered another problem.

'Good evening, my dear, the school teacher isn't it?'

Father Ostler was a man she did not trust. He had embraced the Nazi church. That was the word in the staffroom. And he preached 'acceptable' sermons.

She gave him her prepared version of events about the aunt, to which he replied, 'What an angel you are.'

She nodded and hurried on, worried that there might have been an edge to his remark. The man was probably an informer. What better source could any state snooper have than an ear in the confessional?

Halfway along the next road they stopped outside an ornate entrance. The oak doors and rounded windows were topped off by a spread of mosaic leaded lights. Before he lost the right to collect state health insurance payments, the doctor lived here. There was a tiny metal box fixed to the wall containing white strips with several indistinct names. Claudia looked behind. No sign of the priest or anyone else who might be observing them, so she checked to make sure all was as before, then pushed the buzzer marked 05, S. Lister.

A speaker crackled and a tired voice said, 'Yes?'

'Hello, Siggie, it's Claudia.'

The door clicked and they climbed a high set of stairs, pushed through another set of doors, and down a passage. The door to number five was already open, a warm fug inviting them in to toast themselves against a coke stove.

Siglinda Lister was a small woman wearing a blue nurse's uniform. 'You're lucky,' she said with a sigh, 'I'm not long back from the hospital. Who's this?'

'Anna. Fever and sickness and I'm worried about pneumonia.'

Lister ushered them through another door. The smells changed: disinfectant and some kind of washing agent. Claudia looked around. This was her second visit, the first had been with another sick child. She remembered the bed, the sink, the chair, and the bucket, but when she looked up at the shelves they were almost bare. Once there had been a plentiful supply of medicines. This, she knew, was the covert consulting room of Nurse Lister, one-time assistant to the district's general practitioner. Such home activities were strictly illegal.

'I'll send my boy to fetch him,' said Lister. 'He shouldn't be long.'

He was Josef Prenzlau. And when he buzzed the front door and was let in by Lister, Claudia was shocked at his appearance. On that other occasion his practice had been amazingly successful, despite his being struck off. He was hugely popular in the district and his patients, mostly the poor on welfare or benefits, paid him in kind: fruit, lettuce, cucumbers, pigeon and turnip preserve. He must have been the most successful U-boat doctor in the city.

Now Claudia saw a different man. In his face she noted the pouchy, bloodshot look of a heavy drinker. There was the smell of cheap cigarettes on his clothes. She doubted he had changed them in the last few days. The toll of the subterranean life, she realised, was leaving its mark.

'Claudia,' he said, 'still walking the tightrope, I see. And looking remarkably good on it. How d'you manage?'

She smiled and shrugged.

'And the little ones?'

'As you see,' she said, pointing at Anna. 'Fever, I'm afraid.'

The child was being examined minutely, Prenzlau on one side of the examination table, his stethoscope at work, Lister on the other. Claudia could hear them talking in low tones. She was surprised when she heard Lister use his forename, something that would never have happened in former times. Then she caught another significant whisper: 'Your hands are shaking, Josef, please, lay off.'

The dynamic between nurse and doctor had taken a new direction.

'She can't go back with you,' Prenzlau said, turning to Claudia.

'She'll have to stay here,' Lister said. 'Until the temperature is brought under control.'

Claudia began to apologise but Lister waved this away.

Prenzlau washed his hands and turned his attention to Claudia. He now lived in the basement of a big house, shrouded by trees in an exclusive avenue. Claudia knew that much. And he only moved at night.

'How are things?' she asked, smiling, opening the suitcase and offering him the ritual bag of potatoes, which he refused.

'Keep them for the kids,' he said. 'I can't grumble. Plenty of people round here are still willing to risk the informers to have me treat them, so I'm lucky. I don't blame anybody.' He shrugged. 'We all have to make our shabby compromises.'

She thought this was going to be a rerun of an earlier conversation, a talk that marked the man's pessimism. 'What would you say are my chances of survival, long term?' he'd asked her then. 'Pretty slim, wouldn't you agree? And you, are you still living in fantasy land? We're doing a grand job, you and I, of keeping your young ones alive, but for what? They'll get us all in the end.'

But tonight there was something different about Prenzlau, more than just the shabbiness and the pouchy face. He'd lost his air of fatalism. He stroked his jaw and his eyes watered. 'To tell the truth, I'm in a bit of a moral dilemma,' he said.

She looked at him directly. Lister was busy tending to Anna, Peter had removed himself to a corner, sensing a private moment. Prenzlau wanted to talk. 'Try me,' she said.

'Quite unbelievably, out of the blue.' He shrugged. 'Fact is, there's a possibility of escape.'

'Congratulations,' she said, 'I'm glad for you. So what's the dilemma?'

'This,' he said, waving an arm around the room. 'This, my patients and you – you and your little ones. I'd be running out on them. Who'd treat them when I'm gone?'

Claudia knew he was right. If he went, there would be just Nurse Lister left, but she still smiled and said, 'Go. Take your chance. You've done your bit for us and the patients. Save yourself.'

'I'm thinking of saying no,' he said. 'Conscience and all that.'

'Don't be a fool!' Claudia was forthright. She thought she could risk speaking frankly. The doctor had selflessly looked after everyone and now someone should be looking out for him. Perhaps that was Siggie Lister, but maybe Prenzlau needed an extra push. 'Don't sacrifice yourself,' she said. 'You've done more than enough. Now it's time for you. So, save yourself.' Then she smiled at him. 'It's great news.'

He nodded but said nothing.

She held her curiosity in check. Like everyone in these troubled times she knew the farewell protocol: you wished an escaper good luck, bon voyage, thanks for times of true friendship and hope they'd make it out.

But what you never asked was when.

And especially not *how*.

18

Peter relinquished his observation post in the loft and moved silently through the bunkhouse, careful not to meet anyone in a corridor. Then he slipped into the cubicle next to the front hall close by the notice to visitors proclaiming in large lettering: 'Silence! Sleeping Crews'.

The Caller, a tiny, wizened figure with a club foot, was seated at a desk covered in printouts and lists. Peter gave him a wide smile and tried again to pump him for information.

'We have to box clever,' the Caller said. 'The cell exists because we're cleverer than they are.' No guesses needed to identify *they*. 'They shut down the union but they didn't destroy it, we just went underground. We're strong, we'll resist them and we have the system. The railway is a complex network, the Nazis think they have it under control. More fool them!'

Peter hoped this monologue was a precursor to identifying the controlling personality and was encouraged when the little man looked up. 'Anyway, there's a message for you,' he said. 'Second caboose on the middle track. The one in yellow. At 10.30.'

'And?'

A shrug of the shoulders. 'That's it.'

'A meeting?'

'Presumably. Good place for it. You can see all around. Who's snooping, who's out there, and you can spot them first.'

'A meeting with who?'

'Didn't say.'

Just before ten Peter set off down the cinder path, keeping between two lines of cars and stopping abruptly every few minutes to check for following footsteps. On the third occasion he ducked under a wagon to change tracks and stayed silent, listening, for three whole minutes. It seemed like an eternity but to test his nerves he timed it on his watch. Then he set off again, crossing over from the wide tracks to the normal ones and a line of nondescript wagons, some gondolas, some coal, some flat cars, which he had noticed earlier in the day. On the far track was an old loco, a shunter quietly simmering away while waiting for work.

Peter crept alongside. He didn't want to be surprised by an alert crew but he need not have worried. Up close to the cab he caught the typical mix of smells – oil, coal and drifting steam – but the footplate was empty. Doubtless the driver and firemen were playing skat in the shunter's shed.

The caboose was a vehicle dating back to the turn of the century, painted in fading yellow, and unlike some in the yard still with its chassis and wheels. The tracks seemed to be full of these old brake vans, obviously long out of use. Its observation tower protruded from the roof like the conning tower of a submarine, except that it was topped by a rather quaint angled roof looking like an old man's hat and two viewing windows. Again, Peter waited on the cinder path listening for telltales. The odd word, perhaps, to betray an ambush? Or the sound of a safety catch being worked? He knew responding to this vague summons was a risk. But life in war is all risk, he told himself, grabbing the handrails and heaving himself up the step onto the gated veranda at the end of the car.

Still no sound, no reaction. He took two paces to the middle of the gateway, past the huge brake winding wheel, and chanced a quick look through the wire mesh window into the interior.

Nothing.

He eased open the door, which squeaked on unoiled hinges, and slid inside. The place looked empty, tidy and unused. There in the corner was the expected pot-bellied stove, once capable of throwing out a comforting heat for brakemen on long journeys. The kitchen table was scrubbed, the bunks empty.

Still no sound.

He moved forward to the centre of the car which housed the stairway to the lookout positions. He approached slowly until he was able to see who might be occupying either of the two seats. He peered upwards.

Left side empty.

Right side occupied.

'Come up,' said a peremptory voice in a Bavarian accent.

Peter wanted to keep one hand on the knife in his overall pocket but found he needed both hands to grasp the handrails. It was a vertical climb. He took four large steps up, his feet slotting into footwells set into the coachwork.

He wasn't sure who he expected to meet: perhaps the chief engineer, perhaps his Resistance contact, perhaps Oberscharfuhrer Voss levelling a Walther PPK.

When he drew level he immediately recognised the man. Last night he had listened to his sharp dialogue in the document store. Close up, he took in the heavy figure with high cheekbones, short hair, brush moustache and bloodhound eyes. Reinhardt Meyer, the deputy head engineer.

'This I didn't expect,' Peter said.

'Don't get the wrong idea,' Meyer said, 'I'm not your contact, I'm nothing to do with the people who are helping you.'

'I see.'

'I have never seen you or talked to you, and you haven't met me either.'

'We're just two invisible men having a chat.'

'I've called you here because I want to make one thing absolutely clear.'

Peter waited, fearing he wasn't going to like what was coming.

'I know your purpose and I do not oppose it.'

Peter's spirits lifted.

'But on no account must it happen here. In this depot.'

'I don't understand. How am I supposed to do the job if not here? This is where the new unit is kept, where it was built, where it was tested, where it's being prepared. Is that not right?'

'Correct. It is under guard in No.1 workshop. Quite impossible to penetrate the security. But that is not my point.'

'Which is?'

'Any act of sabotage in this depot will lead the Gestapo straight to us. Your best chance – and ours – is on the journey to the Swiss border.'

Peter pinched his nose. This wasn't in the plan at all. His brief from Dansey was to sabotage the new engine in the depot, steal the plans and persuade the Engineer to defect. Dansey wouldn't want Hitler's new wonder train showing its paces to the world on the border with neutral Switzerland.

Meyer was speaking again. 'It's all nonsense, of course, the Swiss won't sign up to a deal. Re-bore their tunnels? Of course not.'

'But suppose they do?'

'If they do, they won't be serious. They may sign an agreement just to keep the Fuhrer sweet, then adopt their usual tactics. Endless prevarication.'

'That's no use to me,' Peter said. 'I want to put a stop to it.'

'So do I. And your best hope are the Swiss.'

Peter sighed but Meyer insisted: 'The Swiss are wary of stepping onto Third Reich territory. Can't blame them for that. After all the kidnapping on neutral territory the SS have done. They even crossed the border into Holland to grab two of your people last year, did you know that?'

Peter didn't but he nodded, not wanting to display ignorance.

'Germany's reputation for ruthless tactics proceeds us, so our clever chief engineer Herr Hoskins has solved the problem.' An enigmatic smile. 'He's insisted on building a temporary circuit along the shoreline at Lake Constance purely for demonstration purposes. This is so he can show off his new system to the Swiss who will be able to view it from a boat on the lake without ever having to set foot inside our territory.'

'I don't see...'

'Very light construction,' Meyer said. 'Sufficient only for light loading, sufficient only for the day and the transit of a single vehicle. Hoskins has the Fuhrer's ear so we've had to indulge him, but it's a potential deathtrap. In his manic enthusiasm he hasn't taken account of how fine he's cutting things. And that's your opportunity. We've told him he must uncouple the train and only run the new propulsion unit on the loop, told him he's got to go very slowly, particularly over the bridge because it won't stand speed, but he's headstrong. And it would take only a few loose bolts to fatally weaken the structure... if someone were of a mind to unscrew them. And if he kills himself in the process he'll probably take the whole ill-conceived project down with him.'

Peter looked at Meyer intently. This dour, enigmatic man was smiling. A sudden thought struck Peter. Was he really just the deputy engineer? Despite his protestations, all the ruthless cunning just revealed spoke of something infinitely more devious. Could he be the leader of the Resistance cell?

'Won't worry us if Hoskins suffers a calamity,' Meyer said. 'Foolish man takes all the blame while the rest of us will be in the clear. Nobody will suspect sabotage.' He gave a theatrical shrug. 'It was just a temporary structure and we'll be able to say how we warned him over and over and he took no notice.'

Peter tensed. He knew he was having his plans redesigned for him, but should he go along with it?

'We won't shed a tear,' Meyer added. 'In fact, one great big cheer.'

Peter took a long moment to consider his response. He was reluctant to disobey Dansey's orders, but before he could decide how to react Meyer leaned forward and peered from his window.

'Damn! That looks like Voss creeping up the tracks. Did you have a tail?'

'Definitely not.'

Peter listened intently. He had keen hearing but background noises made it difficult. A rattle of passing trains on the main line, a factory hooter, the clink-clink of buffer stops from a shunting yard. Between these distractions brief spells of quiet confirmed Meyer's warning. A scrape of stones nearby, the sound of light footsteps on ballast.

Then the vehicle swayed as someone grasped the handrails ready to climb aboard.

Peter tensed and put his hand on the hilt of his knife. He

knew the Fulbrough mantra: violence, extreme and lethal, was the right option for dealing with the Gestapo. But could he do this?

Another noise, this time louder, more rhythmic, more constant, someone approaching who was not trying for concealment. Peter held his breath, realising he'd heard this rhythmic sound before. It was the Caller. The little guy was straining his limbs to work a distraction. There was a sharp voice outside – no words – but clearly Voss had issued a challenge.

'Thought I saw someone moving about in the yard.' The Caller's voice was near, loud and clear.

'What's it to you?'

'My yard, my responsibility.'

'Fool!' Voss had given up whispering. 'Get back to your post and stop interfering.'

'So, no cause for alarm then?'

'Go!'

'Good, good, glad to have been of assistance to you, Herr Oberscharfuhrer.'

The rhythmic beat of the Caller's tread gradually died away and the caboose rocked again. The door opened and a loud tapping could be heard on the bare floorboards. Voss was using a stick to poke around the interior, prodding behind the stove and inside the food cupboard.

Peter shrank back, trying to mould himself to his seat, listening to the tap-tap, still clutching the knife. It was his only weapon. He'd dumped the army issue pistol at the windmill in France. Now he recalled Fulbrough's lessons in silent killing; where to stab. He felt the cold steel of the sharp blade. His finger touched the cruel tip. Much like the firearms advice. Shoot your target between the eyes from the closest possible range. It all sickened him and he shook his head. A knife was strictly a weapon of last resort against wild animals or a savaging dog.

He'd promised himself never to use it on a human being. Not even Voss. He slipped the weapon down the side of the seat. If necessary, he'd bluff it out. His German was good enough and he began constructing an elaborate story about a private meeting between old friends.

With one last frustrated whack of his stick Voss retreated to the door. Like so many others, he hadn't looked up, confirming Dansey's maxim that height was always the safest place of concealment.

Peter heard Voss swear and climb down to the track, then footfalls on the ballast.

After a long silence, Meyer whispered, 'That should have taught us both a severe lesson.' And when, after a considerable pause, they clambered gingerly down, both wore distinctly sickly pallors. But there was a big plus for Peter. Meyer handed over the plans for his rival's new propulsion unit and confirmed the date for the VIP train journey: Monday the 25th of November.

He felt boxed in. On the one hand, he had Claudia demanding he place her children first, then the deputy engineer insisting sabotage should take place near Switzerland. Peter was a man alone, he couldn't go against the people on whose help he relied. He didn't know if Meyer actually represented the Resistance but the woman calling herself Johannes, who he now knew to be Erika Schmidt, had made it plain that Meyer's conditions were also her conditions and she was definitely a conduit to the cell. That was another problem: he still hadn't tracked down the leader. It was a continuing frustration. How could he stick to Dansey's plan to destroy the motor at the depot?

There was one obvious avenue still open to him: Hoskins.

But to get his chance with the Engineer he would require Claudia's help in fixing a meeting. He sighed. He was going round in circles.

He went in search of her but found Erika alone in the component store. 'I must see Claudia soon, it's urgent,' he said, but she didn't answer, just smiled.

'I want you to meet someone tonight,' she said.

Peter's spirits lifted. He understood immediately. Another information channel was opening up and he knew better than to ask questions, other than time and place, but it was the latter detail that made him hesitate. Out of the depot again, a long walk in the streets.

The woman was reassuring. 'Don't worry, it's all set up, it will be fine, you'll enjoy it.'

Enjoy? What was there to enjoy?

It was late evening and his sense of unease wasn't helped by exposure to the street. He knew how to operate inside the depot but he was not a professional spy. He didn't have a clue how to throw a tail. That old guy on the other side of the street, was he a planted surveillance operative? A woman standing by her front door was staring straight at him. And those teenagers, giggling and shouting? Did the likes of Voss recruit children?

After the long drag up Landsberger Strasse he approached the beige-fronted apartment block with caution, looking around before getting close to the heavy oak front door. This had a circular window set at eye level and clicked mysteriously ajar as he stepped toward it. He eased the door open and glimpsed a small male figure in the shadows beyond.

'Go on up.' A hoarse whisper he did not recognise. 'Third floor.'

As Peter mounted the top staircase he could hear muted sounds of music. A female singer, he decided. Another door opened and an arm reached out, drawing him inside. He blinked rapidly at the change from corridor gloom to bright interior. It was Erika, dressed not in grease-stained brown overalls smelling of metal filings but a knee-length pink party dress decorated with crimson rose petals. The transformation was complete. She was smiling and he was aware of some kind of scent, possibly jasmine. He looked quickly around: the song playing on the gramophone was 'I Wish I Were a Chicken', from a comedy film that was doing the rounds of the cinemas. People were holding drinks and in a far corner there was a table laden with a ration-busting display of fruit, sausages, things on sticks and quark cakes.

His expression was thunderous. 'What's all this? You didn't tell me it was a party.' He backed towards the door. 'This is crazy. Too many people.' He made a face and whispered, 'Informers.'

She shook her head and placed a hand on his shoulder. 'Ease up! I know everyone here. I can vouch for all of them. Every one of them.'

'Still dangerous!'

'We're fine, this is a completely safe house, this *blockwart*, Irma, she's a friend, one of us.'

He sighed and peered down. 'Look at me, how I'm dressed...'

She took in the *Reichsbahn* overalls and grinned. 'Just perfect! A fancy suit would have looked conspicuous on the Landsberger. Beer, wine or something stronger?'

He looked at the drinks table. A mini-barrel with a tap displayed the sign *Triumphator Doppelbock with* several mugs and litre glasses placed ready. A slop bucket was located below.

'Strong stuff,' she said. 'Try one.'

Reluctantly, and with bad grace, he took a sip of the dark amber beer, noticing a hint of caramel. He picked out several familiar faces from the depot. There were discreet nods from Papa Koller and Hugo Schnee. They had made themselves at home, clutching full glasses in a firm grip. A stranger announced himself as Weber. Some kind of co-operative cop, a man on the inside, he recalled Erika briefing him.

Dominating the room was a huge dark-wood object that reminded him of his grandmother's Welsh dresser. Plates and ornaments were on display, as were rows of cups. 'Family heir-loom,' she said, 'a *Grunderzeit*, a real old Wilhelmenian piece.'

He nodded. It went oddly, he thought, with the Indian carpet, parquet floor and window opening onto a balcony topped by a pink sun umbrella. In the distance he could see a tower crane.

'Always building work somewhere in this town,' she said.

Then, just as he was thinking this had been a wasted jour-ney, he saw her: an elegant figure in purple, clutching a wine glass, standing in a corner next to a spreading pot plant and looking straight at him.

He drew in a long breath and smiled back.

Hank Hoskins downed tools and clutched his forehead. He was working late and a new glitch in the system was wearing him out. He had the beginnings of a headache and he was getting nowhere.

Old Epp, his glum assistant, had already gone for the evening and Hoskins began to regret turning down Erika's party invita-tion. He'd said no because of pressure of work but now, looking up at the big workshop clock registering nearly eight, he decided he had been wrong. What he needed was a change of scene, some congenial company, especially the company of a beautiful young woman. He felt sure Claudia would be at the party. He dearly wanted another dinner date to continue the good time they'd had at the Café Luitpold. He recalled her brightness and engaging conversation and what he now recognised as discreet references to 'victims of the system'. A dangerous subject, but hell, what did he care? He was strongly attracted, she was highly desirable, and that was all that mattered.

He took off his crumpled white coat, straightened his green bow tie, looked in the mirror to check his hair, then put on a rust-brown coat and black homburg hat. Yes, Claudia was just the tonic he needed, he decided, locking up and striding out for the Landsberger Strasse. It might be a surprise to turn up late but he felt sure Erika wouldn't mind.

Peter strolled across the room, pewter pot in hand and offered to refill her glass. The business of ordering drinks, he knew from previous difficult encounters, was a useful ice-breaker. But Claudia was implacable. She refused his offer and launched into one of her inquisitions.

'Most impressed with your ability with nursery rhymes and fairy tales,' she said, a sly grin in place, 'so tell me, how long have you been apprentice to the Pied Piper?'

He tried to match her mood. 'Getting my official badge next week.' He added: 'Anyway, I gather you're in much the same league. An artist in coloured chalks, I hear.'

'An exaggeration, I assure you.'

'One way to make the kiddies laugh. Fat Hermann, a king too big for his helmet, Charlie Chaplin with a brush moustache, Donald Duck in marching boots. Quite the comedian.'

She looked down. 'Someone's been talking out of school.'

'But made the kids laugh, I'll bet. Laugh and you've got them on your side.'

'Your technique too, I've noticed.'

'Weaving a spell to enchant. The way to educate. A shared passion. We're two of a kind, you and I, wouldn't you say?'

If she did, she wasn't saying. A hard one to win over, he decided, so he tried again. 'I'm intrigued to know how you run your double life. What about your kids – the ones at school, I mean, as well as those in the bushes?'

'Children,' she said, her expression serious once more, 'are no problem. It's the adults who are the trouble.' And then she began to open up a little. The official school inquisition after she adapted an heroic soldier story to include a hospital epilogue; mysterious absences when calling the register signifying children who disappeared without explanation; race-hate lessons dressed up as science; drill parades, PT camp... 'I could go on.'

'No wonder you want out.'

'I'm glad we're back to that,' she said.

Peter sighed. Time to try and talk some sense into her. 'Escaping the country,' he said, 'far too difficult. Instead, find a monastery. Or some friendly nuns to take your kids in. Or some other distant, rural sanctuary within the borders of the country.'

She shook her head. 'Full up. Can't take any more, too many children. Do you really think my brood are the only U-boats out there? Of course not, there's hundreds of them. We've simply run out of friendly nuns. Over the frontier, it's the only way.'

Peter looked askance.

'Good people in other countries,' she said, with a knowing expression. 'And across the sea...'

Inwardly, he winced. He had one ace left, just one chance to win her over and engage her sympathy, even if it meant destroying the Pyotr legend and revealing his true identity. A drastic step. Against all the rules of the secret world. But now was the time and the chance. He edged her into a corner, away from the others, and said: 'Pity you couldn't get these children out of the country *before* the war started.'

'Well I didn't, I wasn't here then.'

'A shame. We got a few hundred out, but not enough.'

'We?'

He shrugged. 'Just a bit part in the *Kindertransports*.'

She looked at him. 'A bit part?'

'With the London reception committee, welcoming them, pairing them up with new parents, keeping amused the few strays. Mostly teenage boys, difficult to place. Nobody wants a stroppy teenager. You know of Winton?'

'Of course I know Winton.'

'A great man. I enjoyed working with him. Helping his organisation.'

She looked at him in a strange way. He hoped he was impressing her but she looked as if she didn't quite believe what she was hearing. 'You were one of Winton's men?'

He nodded.

Then the conversation turned. This woman was full of surprises. Instead of sympathy or approval or even just plain old intrigue, he got hostility. 'So how is it then,' she hissed, 'that one of Winton's men is sent over here on a military mission? If you really cared deeply for children like a Winton worker should, you'd know better than to put them in peril. You would be getting them out instead!'

This last sentence was delivered on a higher note and Peter could sense other conversations ceasing. Everyone was waiting for what came next.

'Believe me,' he said, replying with some heat of his own, 'I would if I could. And I'm not endangering them.' He returned to whispers. 'And how is it you know about Winton? Has his fame spread?'

'Everyone in Prague was familiar with Winton.' Her manner was taut, still angry. 'His was a name to conjure with. A man to seek out to get your child on one of his trains.'

'You were in Prague?'

'Yes.'

'But now in Munich?'

'Of course.'

'What were you doing in Prague?'

'Same as now. Teaching.'

'So you heard about Winton's *Kindertransports* when you were a teacher?'

'A little more than that.'

'How little?'

'I helped put them on the trains.'

'What?'

'I played the Good Shepherd. I took the children from the waiting room where the parents were confined and walked them along the platform, put them on the train, made them comfortable and reassured them everything would be fine. Why are you staring?'

Peter was stunned, incredulous. 'You worked the platforms, putting them on the trains?'

'Just told you that.'

He exploded. 'The lady with the pink carnation in her hat!'

'Don't look so gobsmacked. I only wore it so they could find me in a crowd.'

Peter ignored her cool response, seizing her hand and shaking it vigorously. Her reputation in London had been sky high. The large straw hat attained iconic status. The easy recognition device for leading a crocodile of hundreds of children onto the train.

'Stop it!' She pulled away from him. 'You'll put my shoulder out.'

'In London, you were our heroine,' he said. 'Our golden girl. The lady who carried on and did the business when all the Brits got sent home.'

She shrugged away the compliment. 'It was official business.'

'You did it when everyone else had left,' he persisted. 'We knew the situation. You did it in front of the Gestapo. Made yourself visible to them. Might have been official but it was still a big risk. Could have been a change in their policy at any moment...'

Her attitude did not lighten at his recognition. Evidently, she wasn't in the mood for celebration.

He sighed. The ploy hadn't worked. In desperation he tried again: 'Look, things are all mixed up. I'm not certain how it's going to work out. Maybe the Swiss border...' His words trailed off and he shrugged.

For some seconds she said nothing, looking at him through big blue eyes. 'Well?' she said eventually. 'Are you still saying escape is impossible?'

He ignored that. 'And for the new plan to work I need your help.'

'In what way?'

'You know! Fix me a meeting with your friend Hoskins. Alone and in secret. Say we want to discuss...' He looked away momentarily, casting about for a likely subject.

'Refugees?' she suggested.

He nodded.

'Fine. You know my terms,' she said. 'Like I told you before, promise to get my kids away, then I'll help you all I can.'

Erika, pretending not to listen to this conversation, was suddenly distracted by noises from downstairs. A door banging, foot stamping, distant voices. Rising alarm had her peeping from her door and peering over the banisters.

What she saw caused her to shoot back indoors and tug urgently at Peter's sleeve. 'You have to disappear,' she breathed.

'What's up, you've gone quite white.'

'He's here. Downstairs.'

'Who?'

'Him, the Engineer, Hoskins, he's on his way up right now, climbing the stairs.'

'Oh my God!' It was Peter's turn to feel a stab of panic. 'I can't be here, he mustn't see me.'

Claudia protested. 'But you want to talk to him. Now's your chance!'

'Not like this. I need to be in disguise. Not as myself, not as Pyotr.'

Erika was still in a state of panic. 'He'll be here any second.'

'Where's the back way out?' Peter demanded.

'There isn't one.'

'Then I'll have to jump,' he said, heading for the balcony door.

'Don't be daft. This is the third floor. Here!' Erika beckoned frantically. 'Follow me.'

The hammering on the apartment door was persistent.

'Wait!' Erika called, trying to keep the quaver out of her voice, making a great show of opening up. 'Herr Hoskins, what a surprise!' She motioned him in. 'So, you could come after all.'

'Hope it's not inconvenient.'

'Not at all, you're most welcome.'

Claudia stepped forward, as prompted, to join the introductions.

Hoskins held up a hand. 'Do excuse me,' he said, 'very rude, my fault of course, but I must first visit the facilities.'

Erika blocked the way. 'I do believe they're in use at present. Can I offer you a drink in the meantime?'

'Quite urgent! Just show me where and I'll wait outside.'

Erika pointed and, when he was out of sight, hissed at Papa Kuhn: 'Pick an argument! Get him away from that door.'

Kuhn's stentorian tones echoed through the apartment. No one could have missed his words. 'So, Herr Hoskins, is it true? You're in big trouble? Can't get the damned thing to work? Are we all going to be out of a job very soon because of these problems?'

But Hoskins would neither be provoked nor distracted.

Erika had her hands to her head.

Then came the sound of disintegrating crockery. Smashing and shattering noises from the kitchenette were accompanied by several loud female screams.

Hoskins faltered, took a couple of steps toward the kitchenette, saw Claudia picking up the remains of several dinner plates but returned to the lavatory door.

'Ah!' he said gratefully. 'Free at last.'

Erika's gaze followed him. She peered into the corridor. No one was there and the front door was untouched. A frightened expression quickly turned to puzzlement.

Peter reached the bunkhouse out of breath, both fingers bleeding, his back bruised, feeling a complete idiot. Trapped in a flat without an exit? That was a beginner's mistake. Erika had bustled him into the lavatory to avoid meeting Hoskins but waiting like an embarrassed fool for the fleeting chance to creep out unseen was not Peter's way. He'd done the training at

Fulbrough. He had balance and technique so use it, he'd told himself.

The window had been just large enough to squeeze through; the outside sill the narrowest of footholds, his nerve tested to the limit seeking a tenuous grip in the tiniest of mortar cracks. The sill from the next apartment gave him his escape route; a window ajar, a broom cupboard exit, a soundless creep to the front door and a descent of the communal staircase.

His sense of hurt and humiliation at this experience seemed to sum up his progress so far. 'I can't go on like this!' Swilling away the blood, he wagged an angry finger at the tiny washbasin mirror.

It was obvious. He needed a drastic change of fortune – and soon. He wrapped his right hand in the corner of a hand towel, returned to sit on the bed and for the first time was forced to take seriously Claudia's plan to flee the country with nearly thirty children.

Was it quite as crazy as it sounded? He began to put his mind to the problem. Could it be made to work? Sabotage staged during a high-security public demonstration? Surely one would compromise the other. He visualised his reception back at base when he told them of his change of plan. He tried to work out how to word the message to gain official permission to make the children his priority. Then he saw the expressions of his instructors at Ringway and Fulbrough. Heard Dansey's bitter sarcasm. Saw the curl of his father's lip.

They would reject his idea. They'd never wear it. Insist instead he stick to the plan or damn him as an abject failure. His quest to prove himself in the eyes of his compatriots would be utterly doomed. Peter was fighting himself all over again. He sought respect and reputation but not at the expense of a crowd of bedraggled children. If he couldn't persuade Hoskins to co-operate, he would be edged into a corner: follow impossible and destructive orders – or defy them, bringing down on his head the wrath of everyone who mattered back in Britain. It would be an either/or. One or the other. A stark choice.

He was still on a knife-edge next day when he met Claudia. She appeared positively beaming, as if she'd just won a great prize. Perhaps, he reflected, she had.

'There's someone I want you to meet,' she said.

'Who?'

'I've already been introduced. Had a long conversation.'

'What about?'

'And what he told me has me... well!' She rubbed her hands together and gave him a triumphant stare. 'Has me in a state of high excitement.'

'Come on, Claudia, don't be a tease.'

'Demonstrated his amazing ability. Demonstrated amazing devices.'

'Are you going to explain?'

'No. Just be ready to meet at nine tonight.'

19

They met at the back door to the carriage workshop, circumventing security at the front, and once inside Peter was in for a surprise. The man waiting was like no railwayman he'd ever met. There was a shiny bald pate, a red-speckled bow tie and a carpenter's apron with a line of pens and pencils neatly clipped along a wide breast pocket. 'Call me Igor,' he said, introducing himself as the workshop overseer. Peter repressed a smile. He'd never know or ask Igor Stravinsky's real name.

'I gather you need to be convinced,' the man said, 'so let me show you.'

He led the way across a small, neat workshop and into the main hall with its contrasting pools of light and shadow. Peter noticed a pronounced limp.

Igor grinned. 'Not a careless episode in the works, I assure you.'

They turned a corner and Claudia, taking advantage of being out of Igor's earshot for a few seconds, said, 'He got trampled by a mob fleeing the Brownshirts.'

Igor was at a table, unrolling drawing office plans similar to those Peter had already seen and began to point out cavities in the kitchen car, the diner and in the sumptuously-furnished passenger carriages. 'Secret spaces,' he said. 'Enough for your purpose.'

'You know the purpose?'

'I do. I approve. Heartily.'

'He'll do it,' Claudia said.

Peter was still a sceptic. Could the VIP train really conceal Claudia's legion of fleeing children? He said, 'Even so, how do we keep more than twenty kids happy and silent... in these conditions for such a journey?'

'Let me demonstrate.' A prototype hide was already in place: sliding panels, concealed exits, locks and shutters, places to lie, places to sit. A signal system would be installed to reach each space: coloured bulbs would light up to give reassurance; blue for 'all is well' and green for release. Entry and exit could be from both inside and outside of the train. The controlling adults would have special keys.

'They'd never stay quiet for long enough,' Peter said. 'Even if we could induce them to enter in the first place.'

'You could make it possible.'

Peter shrugged and thought aloud about the problems of transporting a large number of children in secret. Of how to provide sufficient comfort and maintain complete silence. First there was air flow but also warmth; bedding, blankets, sacking, pillows and potties. And distractions to keep them quiet: drinks, food, crayons, drawing books, story books, toys, sweets. Plus leadership and control.

'I can build these concealed spaces and the warning system,' Igor said, 'but how you deck them out is up to you.'

Peter nodded, appreciative of the sophistication and willingness on display, at the forethought and easy efficiency. And then the idea came to him: this man had to be more than a compliant overseer turned willing conspirator. The whole idea was masterly. Surely, Igor *was* the leader of the cell? Perhaps, at last, Peter had reached him.

'That's not all, is it, Igor?' Claudia said when they were back in the smaller workshop. 'Not only creating beautiful coachwork but restoration as well.'

Peter pressed and was allowed into an inner room. In the centre stood the most exquisite example of rococo style furniture, a combined writing and dressing table made in France in 1780. Igor knelt to point out restoration work being carried out to the legs and to demonstrate the cog-operated mechanics for opening the desk and a central mirror with side panels. 'Said to be used by Marie Antoinette,' he said with a shrug. 'One of my obsessions. The beauty of the past to offset the brutality of the present.'

Peter smiled and Igor became reflective. He propped an elbow on a ledge and said, 'Let me ask you this. If you succeed in getting them away, what are you going to do with so many children?'

Claudia too, turned to look closely at Peter as he, without any certain knowledge that a *Kindertransport* arrival would still be permitted in wartime Britain, talked about the £50 foster parents who would be ready and waiting at the London terminal.

'So, we're exporting to you the flower of our youth,' Igor said. 'The talented composers, engineers and philosophers of tomorrow. Can't imagine them growing up with fond memories of their former homeland.'

Peter smiled but thought it best to say nothing.

'And I'm grateful to your military,' Igor said. 'That it seems to regard rescue as a valid tactic. Will those children make you a hero? Will you get a medal? At the palace perhaps?'

Peter chuckled. 'Very much doubt it.'

Igor looked at the ceiling and twiddled a pencil between

thumb and forefinger. 'You being here has challenged the comfortable view I have of myself, as a peaceable back-room worker detached from reality. The war? Nothing to do with me!' He stopped. 'True or false? Am I really now a soldier? Is this carpenter's apron a uniform? My pencils and my saws weapons of war?'

How to answer? Peter took a moment over his reply. 'The railway will certainly be a part of Hitler's war machine, but your actions here today will surely compensate for any overt complicity.'

Igor gave several long, sad and silent nods.

On the way out, by the back door to which Claudia had been given a key, Peter took advantage of their close proximity. He spoke low, barely above a whisper. 'I'd like to know,' he said to Igor, 'am I talking to the leader? The brains behind this Resistance group?'

Igor opened the door, looked carefully about and shook his head. 'Absolutely not!' he said.

But Peter thought he detected a mischievous set to the mouth.

His pen jerked into action but the words spilled uncertainly onto the pad: *All action now at Swiss frontier. Only way partners will agree. Necessary pre-condition.* Then he added details of the loop line.

Peter sucked the end of the pen, pensive and aware of the gravity of this message. He could envisage Dansey's reaction. Disapproval turning to choking rage at the next passage, but Peter felt he had no other choice: *Refugees also exiting. Vital arrangements required. Thirty blank neutral nation passports plus Swiss exit visas.*

He added date, time and location, making the bland assumption that Dansey, with his many resources, had the means to obtain such documentation. He intended that the blank passports would be filled in with the relevant details when – and if – the party arrived in the safety of Switzerland. He considered it prudent to omit the word *children*.

He sent off his note to Williams, relying on the Resistance to deliver the message to Bergen. On day one he had been concerned about security but was reassured by the Caller. 'Don't worry, it's absolutely safe. This railway's not just an iron network. It's a human network. Our trusty brotherhood.' Notes came back assuring him Williams had recovered and that the XV suitcase transceiver set was operational.

So it was done. Peter's about-turn. He ran a nervous hand through his hair. He'd once used the word *impossible* to describe the idea of taking a bunch of poorly-clad kids across the border. Now he had committed himself to accomplishing both this and an act of destruction. Igor's active participation was impressive and his plans ingenious, but Peter thought he should be more assertive from this point on. This was to be a military operation. He had plans to make, schedules to draw up and timetables to consult, but when he gave Claudia a long list of items to scrounge and told her they would have to rehearse the children in silent routines she did not react like a subordinate.

She pursed her lips. 'I don't think you needed to tell me all that.'

He had hoped her tone would soften. She was, after all, getting what she longed for. She put a hand on his arm. 'Like Igor, I want to know what happens when they're out. When the children are free.' She looked at him intently. 'Tell me about the *Kindertransports*, what happened to the children at the English end? How were they treated? And organised?'

He was happy enough to talk about Winton. 'We met the

train when it arrived at the station in London,' he said, 'the new parents had already been paired up with the children, they all met up on the platform and off they went.'

'And?'

He shrugged. 'What else?'

'You mean, you didn't look after them. Check on progress? Supervise their upbringing?'

Peter sighed. 'Look, you have to understand. This was a volunteer thing. We all had other jobs. Winton was a stockbroker. He did all this in his afternoons and evenings. A massive organising job to find hundreds of people ready to take children into their homes and stump up fifty pounds. That's quite a sum.'

'But there are no other checks?'

'Don't pick holes, Claudia, we all did our best, gave all the time we could. The paper mountain, the bureaucracy from the government, that all took time. This wasn't an official operation with departments full of children's officers to do the correct thing.'

She was silent for some time and he wondered what was coming next.

'How good is your memory of all those children?'

He shrugged. 'There were hundreds of them.'

'Do you recall the last train? The eighth?'

'Do I?'

'A girl and a much younger little boy travelling together. She about seven or eight. Like glue, this pair.'

'You can't expect me...'

'They were quite special. The girl was dark, the boy flaxen-haired. Blue eyes.'

Peter screwed up his face with the effort of memory. He certainly recalled Helga Lang, the Elgar enthusiast who'd been sponsored by his uncle and was now almost a permanent fixture at home.

Claudia was coaxing him, urging him to remember others: 'These two children, they were inseparable. The girl had her grandmother's eternity ring on her middle finger. And a doll she loved called Gretel.'

Peter gave her a curious look. 'How very specific! Do you have the names as well?'

There was only a momentary hesitation before Claudia replied: 'Luise and Hansi Grunwald.'

He shook his head. 'Sorry. Don't recall. But why d'you want to know? Someone with a personal connection?'

She was silent. She looked down.

This was not like Claudia. 'Someone very special?' he asked quietly.

He saw her swallow, hesitate, open her mouth as if to speak. But no words came out.

'Want to tell me?' he said softly.

But she just shook her head.

Claudia was aware of Peter's eyes following her across the warehouse floor as she left the stores for home, but she had no intention of giving him an explanation. Such a statement would be foolish. It would change their relationship, as it did with everyone.

She hurried on, brushed away a tear and sniffed. Why could he not remember? Was she being unreasonable? But there was still a chance. A fleeting chance. When he returned to England he could enquire about their welfare. She had given him the names. Where were Luise and Hansi now? How were they faring in their new country?

But once inside her flat doubts dogged her. Even if Peter traced the children when he returned home, how would she ever know? Two people separated by a war. 'This vile, filthy war,' she said out loud, then looked quickly around in a reflex of fear before calming down. No witnesses at home. She was as safe in her own kitchen as she could ever expect to be.

She sought solace in activity. She stacked clean linen on the airing shelves, swept the kitchen floor and tidied her table. At least the flat looked clean. Domestic detail helped calm her, but she still worried about the danger of the informer. After the episode with Frau Netz she had been careful to clear away any trace of her work for the Maze – food preparation or a clothing bounty – in case of a surprise visit. She watered her butterfly palm, trying to stay calm, but her heart still felt fluttery. On the sole occasion she had met Siggie Lister socially in town they were careful to talk only in the wide-open spaces of the Hofgarten with lawns flanked by orange marigolds, or the noisy fountains at the Sendlinger Tor or St Jacobs. They would have preferred to chat in the cafés, particularly Rischart's near the cathedral, where you could linger over coffee and *himbeer-schnitte*, tiramisu or fruit tart. However, the pavement cafés in the Rathaus quad, the English Gardens and the Viktualienmarkt were dangerous places. You never knew who might be snooping.

Next day, Claudia needed all her courage to keep her side of a bargain with Peter. Dusk was falling when she arrived at the component stores. Peter was sipping coffee and talking animat-edly to Erika and when he turned she stopped, shocked by the change in him. He was wearing horn-rimmed glasses and had a thick black moustache. And his hair! She did a double take. Brushed forward in a way that changed him. And his face – all puffy and distorted.

'Don't worry!' he said. An awkward grin, twisting his features. 'Still me. Try Hoskins on the phone, would you?'

She frowned and shrugged, then lifted the receiver, the Engi-neer's number scribbled on a slip of paper. She had intended never to use it. Only a fool said anything sensitive on the telephone, but she had an innocuous formula.

'Hello, is that you, Hank?'

'Claudia! What a pleasure!'

'Thought you might fancy some coffee. Brewing now.'

'Oh dear, what a pity. I'm inundated. Got to get finished for the big day. Precious little time left. Sorry. Have to make it another time.'

'But it's so late. Are you there all on your own?'

'They've all left me to it. Even Franz is deep in Schubertland.'

Replacing the receiver, she turned to Peter who was following every word.

'What have you done to yourself?' she demanded.

'He mustn't recognise me – when I see him later,' he said.

She sighed. 'He's there, all on his own and the cop is listening to the radio next door.'

He started to leave, giving her the thumbs up.

'Pyotr?'

He stopped.

'Please, no violence.'

He looked at her. 'Of course, I've already told you.'

'And be careful.'

The depot was almost deserted, and no one appeared to notice Peter crossing the tracks to the Engineer's office. The closed door was chicken feed to an artist in silent entry.

The Engineer had his back to him, working at a draughtsman's easel and it was some time before he looked up and saw Peter standing close by. He was startled, then settled, hands on hips. 'Who the devil are you? State your business. Are you security cleared?'

'I'm your conscience,' Peter announced. 'I represent that part of your brain where your sense of right and wrong should be.'

'What? Who the hell? What right have you...'

'Every right. How is it an American citizen can justify helping an evil regime like this one? A Nazi collaborator? A Hitler clone? Just where is your conscience? Gone to sleep?'

'And you are?'

'An Allied officer come to put a stop to this system.' A dismissive sweep of the hand indicated everything outside.

Hoskins adopted a slouching expression. 'Good God, a damned Limey! You've got a nerve, coming in here, lecturing me, issuing threats. I can call the guard and have you arrested, you must know that.'

'That would be the last thought you ever had. A bullet in the head before you make such a move.'

'So, a common assassin, nothing more. Just forget all that crap about conscience. And you've got it all wrong, buddy, you're the one in danger. Of ending up on a Gestapo slab.'

'I'm glad you know how these people work. Just how brutal is the regime you're so keen to serve.'

Hoskins leaned back. He didn't look scared, more intrigued. 'What exactly is it you're after? Why so bold? Why so foolish?'

'To give you a message. To put a stop to what you're doing here. Helping a homicidal maniac make even more war, kill even more people, enslave the world. To tell you that your card is marked back in London and Washington. Your activities are well known and monitored by the military. And our people can't let you continue here. You have to pack it up and return with me.'

Hoskins laughed. 'Return with you? What the hell for?'

'I'm authorised by the people back home to make you an offer. In exchange for stopping work here.'

'And why the heck should I even consider such an absurd idea? I'm on the brink of a great technical triumph. My life's work vindicated.'

'Serving a monster. Serving a regime that tortures and enslaves and kills on a grand scale.'

Hoskins waved a dismissive hand, almost as if he hadn't time to consider such things.

'You can do your work in London,' Peter said, 'and that is guaranteed.'

The American snorted. 'They blew me out. Your guys and mine.'

Peter didn't falter. 'I didn't come to stroke your ego. This isn't about you. Or your achievements. It's about right and wrong, good and evil, them and us. The pistol in my pocket says refusal will be fatal.'

Suddenly Hoskins became agitated. 'I don't know why I'm still listening to this. Should have you arrested. And if you stand there much longer we'll both be in trouble. They do patrols, you know.'

'Then find a better time and place and listen to what I have to say. You should make no mistake. This is a serious offer. You'll need to give it serious thought. You have a big decision to make.'

A pause, then a grunt. The silence represented a man wrestling with the unexpected, wrestling with loyalty to his new masters, conflicted by doubt, the reference to an immediate pistol shot the decider. 'You'd better come to my villa. No! Too many guards, too many microphones. Anyway, I'm dining out tonight with the Countess of Karlsfeld. If you're clever enough to get here, then you can be clever enough to infiltrate her place and I'll speak to you tonight.'

'And that is where?'

'Her gazebo, well down the back garden.'

'Location?'

'The Stahlmann place, here in Munich.'

'Time?'

'Nine o'clock.'

20

***

Peter took the tram, still wearing his DR fatigues, careful to avoid the central railway station where security was known to be tight. He was nervous. He was not a professional agent and this was his first venture into the city centre alone.

Before leaving the depot, Erika filled him in on the background to the Engineer's friendship with the countess. It was unlikely her villa was being watched, she said, mainly because she had been one of the Fuhrer's original sponsors in his beer hall days.

Peter boarded a tram, avoiding all eye contact but alive to the presence of his fellow passengers. He was aware of the smell of musty clothing, but not everyone was dowdy. Two smart young women in the next row were dressed in the latest Paris styles, one-piece dresses cut just below the knee with wide shoulders.

He stared out of the window. At the *Hauptbahnhof*, teams of brown-clad storm-troopers were aggressively canvassing donations to the winter relief fund. He averted his gaze and spotted a man, hardly more than a youth, hobbling on crutches. At the same stop a girl with long blonde tresses and dressed in the traditional dirndl boarded the tram and drew caustic whispers from the French fashion plates. 'Oh my God, what a Gretchen!'

His journey required a change at the Karlsplatz where he discovered a great commotion. A tram had derailed and crunched into a square of chained-up cycles. A steel mincemeat of smashed wheels and struts was jammed under the front bogie. Several uniformed figures were shaking their heads.

Peter crossed the square, worried he was no longer one of a crowd, and found another stop where services were still running. It was a great relief when a tram arrived but no sooner had he boarded the first car and punched his ticket for seven stops when he had a shock. He could see through the windows to the rear. And there, in the last of the three cars, checking briefcases, parcels and shopping bags were three men. You didn't need to ask. Slouch hats and long raincoats, the sartorial badge for inquisitorial authority.

As the trio moved forward to the middle car Peter made his decision. He couldn't risk an inquisition. Didn't really trust his fake papers. As the vehicle slowed for the next stop he moved to the doors and prepared to step down to the street, risking a quick glance at the middle car. The tall man with a livid scar on one cheek and a contorted expression was staring hard at him. The boss.

The doors swished open and Peter set off at a fast pace down a street running at right angles to the main thoroughfare. If he could make it to the first intersection he reckoned he might lose any tail among the late-night strollers. There were footsteps behind. Obviously, Scarface had despatched one of his men to intercept. He increased pace and crossed the road at an acute angle. Traffic was sparse but there were bins on the pavement, ready for the refuse men. He looked for a parked vehicle behind which he might disappear, but he could see only a black Bugatti coupe with a yellow door and a green Opel Laubfrosch, a sit-up-and-beg cheapie that was far too small to provide any cover. Absurdly, given his situation, he remembered the Caller telling him the tiny car cost only 2,000 Reichsmarks.

His fast walking pace was beginning to tell. His breath came in short bursts and his calves were beginning to ache. An old woman in a floral-patterned apron stared at him from the front door of a big apartment block. Another busybody informer? Several hundred metres still to go to the turning but suddenly there in front of him was a four-wheeled baker's cart, drawn up outside a shop, the deliveryman heaving trays of bread across the pavement while his shaggy pony nibbled at a nosebag. Peter rounded the end of the cart. The door was open. Could he hop in and hide?

At that moment the baker's man in a black striped apron came out of the shop and gave him a quizzical look, so Peter turned and hurried on towards the crowds at the end of the street, almost tripping on some uneven cobbles.

At last, salvation! A straggling cinema queue.

Peter was quickly amongst it. And through it. He glanced behind to see a man in a green felt hat, belted beige overcoat and bell-bottomed black trousers walking up and down the queue resolutely searching the faces.

A short distance beyond was a playhouse with slot machines. Peter vanished into the interior, found some stairs to the first-floor lavatories and disappeared into a cubicle. He climbed on the seat to try the window. It was small and tight but the force of fear and adrenaline had it open and he wriggled through to a fire escape.

Behind him he could hear someone banging doors, searching the line of cubicles.

He took off his boots to mask the sound of his footsteps and padded down the iron staircase to reach the ground floor, finding himself in a tiny walled courtyard.

Doors were still banging upstairs as he tied the laces together and hung the boots around his neck, counted to three, grabbed the top of the wall and heaved himself over.

He landed, surprised, in a bed of hay and found himself looking into the soft brown eyes of a very large horse.

The one heading north towards Milbertshofen where the countess had her villa was an old growler of a tram. It bucked and swayed and jerked along the rails in the main street. This was going to be a long drag. Peter wiped the remnants of some equine dribble off his overalls and wrinkled his nose at something stuck to his boot, but none of his fellow passengers gave any sign of noticing. There were no fashion plates on this journey. Across the gangway was a dumpling of an old woman with receding chin and a tea cosy hat. She must have forgotten to put her teeth in that morning. In the row behind was a wrinkly fellow with a blood-red face, his neck festooned with scarves. He was eating a pork sausage.

Peter was assiduously checking out the names on the tram stops and at Knorr Strasse a large crowd attracted everyone's attention. He could see men in soft caps slouching against walls outside a ring of grey-coated military officers. The passengers stared as the tram drew level and he stood to peer over their heads for a better view.

What he saw were lines of wooden barrack blocks. Several small girls dressed in heavy coats and hoods stared back through the wire. Some sort of building work was going on.

The man with the sausage read Peter's puzzled expression. 'The ghetto,' he said.

Peter did a double take, not wanting to speak.

The old man cackled. 'They call it the Jewish housing estate. Posh name for a transit camp. Waiting for deportation to the East.'

'I heard Theresienstadt,' a low female voice volunteered.

At Neueweg, a shady tree-lined avenue near the end of the line, Peter went down the steps and set off at a medium pace. All was quiet and he began to worry. The countess's immunity from surveillance didn't mean there might not be a carload of watchers parked at a discreet distance.

It was a straight road and he could see far into the distance. Not a car or pedestrian in sight. He checked behind, his senses now heightened to the danger of picking up another tail, but no one had got off the tram with him and he appeared to be alone. Still, a person walking such a street in the evening might be considered suspicious. He doubted any railway worker could afford to live in Milbertshofen. He kept walking, ready to dive into a hedge or garden at the approach of a car. He had been lucky with the weather. It was the *altweibersommer*, the Indian Summer that would any day now descend into the cold fog and rain of a typical Munich November. He had expected to check off house numbers but found only family names. He kept his eyes down, scanning the signs and then the street for lurking dangers. Still alone. Still quiet. He became anxious about his footfall which seemed frighteningly loud. He was wearing the railway-issue boots given to him by the station man at Bergen. There was a smell of woodsmoke from somewhere. Passing a gabled mansion, he picked up the enticing aroma of coffee. A faint drone in the distance could have been a night fighter returning to base. He thought about Hoskins. The man might be a Jekyll and Hyde. Could have a gazebo full of Gestapo waiting for him in a trap. A poor way to end his mission.

Then he spotted it, the seventh property, bearing the legend

Stahlmann. He continued on, doubling back along a parallel avenue to the rear, counting off the houses as he went. When he was sure he had the property parallel to the Stahlmann place, he crept low into the garden, skirted a pond, worked a side gate, trampled a rockery and found a fence. It was wooden and low and he was over in one heave, but he banged his right knee and his boots kicked up a curtain of mud.

On the other side was a pristine lawn. And in one corner a gazebo. Not any old gazebo. This one had a pitched roof, veranda, full-length glazed windows and flowered window boxes. No expense spared for Brigitte Freifrau von Stahlmann, Countess of Karlsfeld.

He stayed absolutely still for what seemed like an hour, waiting for his eyes to adapt, waiting to get in his night vision. Not a sound, not a cough, not a squeak. Peter approached silently from the rear but there was no need. From some distance he could make out the glow of a cigarette and a shadowed figure sitting on a garden chair.

Closer still and he was now quite certain.

'Sorry, chum, no deal.'

The Engineer was vehement, spoke first and wagged a finger as soon as Peter appeared, not waiting for any preliminary. 'And now I'm going to do you a big, big favour, I'm going to give you twelve hours to get clear of this place before I let loose the hounds of hell.'

Peter gave him a long stare, his right hand held tightly against his right pocket. 'Think carefully, this could be a fatal mistake on your part. Have you seriously considered the offer I made?'

Hoskins stubbed out his cigarette and said, 'Look, the people here in Munich, they've given me my big chance of glory... and now you want to spoil it? Forget it.'

Peter kept his hand close to the pocket. 'You're working for the wrong masters. It's us you should be working for. I told you that. A guarantee.'

Hoskins almost spat. 'Don't believe it! Take me for a sucker? Back home they didn't want to know about me or my ideas, nor your people either, now all of a sudden I get the big come-on.'

'War changes things. A change of plan.'

'Yeah, and dump me as soon as I cross the line, just like before? Look, when I'm big with the Swiss as well as the Germans you lot won't dare touch me. And let me tell you something else.' Hoskins was getting into his stride, making his prepared speech. He'd had time to recover from his surprise back at the depot and hone a reaction. 'The world will be grateful to me in the future. For a great future. Faster travel, faster food, a wonderful era beckons. In fact...' Here he ran out of breath, coughed a smoker's cough, gulped for air, then settled for a dismissive finale: 'And you, my friend, have been giving me a load of old Limey horseshit.'

'You're wrong!' Peter found a sudden emphasis. Desperation and an inventive imagination came to the fore. 'I can give you chapter and verse of our preparations. All the figures you're ever likely to need.' An internal voice warned against overreaching himself. How could he hope to provide convincing costings? When he'd tackled Dansey on the point back at St James's he'd received no help at all. 'Promise him anything you like,' the little man had said, 'just so long as you get him out of there!' Now Peter was into his stride, imagination working overtime. He remembered Truscott's broad sweeps across the map. 'Back home,' he said, 'they're thinking big. Forget trying to widen the old tracks. Instead, a completely new set of lines, bypassing all the towns without stopping so as to take full advantage of the tremendous speed. We're talking a definite commitment here. Facilities, workshops, all the rest of it. And if it's money?'

Hoskins waved a dismissive hand. 'Supposing, just for one crazy moment, I were to take you seriously, can you guarantee me I'll be running a broad gauge London to Edinburgh? Eh? New York to Washington?' He snorted in disbelief.

'Look,' Peter insisted, 'I'm as excited about this as you are. The people behind me, them too!' He knew convincing detail was needed, so he began to run through the management structure of the LNER, including Sir Andrew Truscott, who was, he said, leading the campaign for the new project. At least the names were real. Mixing fact with fiction... would that do it?

Hoskins looked at Peter doubtfully. 'Why you? You're a bit young to be their man, aren't you?'

And this was the best part. Embroidering the lie with a veil of truth. 'I've been brought up to it,' Peter said, launching into the map of his family connections to the top tier of management and detailing the role of his father, a man known all around Europe as a dealer in railway stock. 'You doubt my credentials?'

Slowly, anxious not to create alarm, he reached gingerly into an inside pocket and handed over a letter addressed personally to Hoskins.

The Engineer took it doubtfully but seeing Peter's confident pose ripped it open. Peter knew the contents, the key phrases of which included: *the bearer of this letter has my full authority*, and *the project in question has support at the highest possible level*. He knew this because he'd helped write the letter back at Fulbrough Manor and watched a Special Operations Executive draughtsman forge Truscott's signature.

Hoskins shrugged. 'More horseshit,' he said. 'We Americans are not even in your war. It's just you Brits beating about the bush. And forget the threats, man, Hitler's going to win this war.'

'You've been listening to too much Nazi propaganda. Just a

matter of time before the Yanks are in. No way can Hitler win then. And your file back in London – it's growing thicker by the minute. They've had eyes on you for ages. Already has a red tag on it.' Peter was back in the realms of fantasy, but he thought he was making a good fist of it. 'Don't let them put a black marker on it. Because if you turn this offer down that makes you an enemy collaborator. A black marker in the file. A dead man walking.'

'Don't give me all that collaborator stuff. Don't you know, the big corporations, Standard Oil and others, they won't stop trading with Germany.'

'Another fact for you,' Peter countered. 'After the war's over there will be trials of war criminals, and you'll be there, in the dock. And even worse, if you finger me, or if you're responsible for the death or capture of anyone who in any way assists me, the noose beckons, be assured of that.'

The Engineer gave a wave of dismissal, then paused, a sudden puzzlement. 'Tell me, is Claudia in on this? Fraulein Kellner. I'd be really surprised if she's involved.'

Peter bridled. If there had been a Colt 45 in his pocket instead of a box of matches he might just have been tempted, despite his vow of non-violence. Instead, he held a long breath before asking, 'You mean, the teacher?'

'That's her.'

'The teacher knows nothing, absolutely nothing, except for the long line of victims your friends the Nazis have created. Like most sensible people, she's scared you're going to create even more victims if you continue. Women and little children.'

There was a pause, a long silence between them, and Peter thought he had scored a telling point. Claudia's good or bad opinion seemed to matter. The Engineer stroked his chin and looked at the floor. Then he said, 'All right, I'll give it some thought.' He looked up and about him. 'In the meantime you'd best be going. You're in great danger and we've been here long enough. I told the countess this was just a fleeting assignation. No doubt she'll want a full description of my lady friend, but you don't look a bit like a voluptuous beauty.'

'Then use your imagination,' Peter said, turning to go. 'Start with Marlene Dietrich.'

Owen Glendower Williams was becoming agitated at being stuck in Bergen, bemoaning his fate at being far removed from the action. He sent Peter a series of notes that arrived in the Caller's office, saying he had recovered from his injuries, that his leg was now fine and that he would like permission to travel to Munich.

I feel completely isolated and out of it, he wrote. *Pretty bloody useless too, sitting all day in this man's spare room, poor sod.*

But Peter was adamant. He required Williams to be his 'pianist' to work the radio back to London well away from any interceptor vans that might be working the city. He waited with considerable trepidation for Dansey's reaction to his message announcing the proposed change of plan, shifting destruction of Hoskins's motor from Munich to the Swiss border.

A reply was not long in coming. And it was terse: Keep to plan. Destroy on site. Get drawings out, man out, forget rest. Williams on way.

Peter entertained a momentary wobble. This rejection and its peremptory tone were to be expected when a junior officer disobeyed orders, but his fear lasted only a few seconds before he became annoyed at the terseness of it, seeming to override both himself and his co-conspirators. As if Peter could demand the Resistance do his bidding! Dansey was being ridiculous. So he composed a reply and sent it off to Bergen: Complete co-operation of partners required for success. Pre-condition destruction at border, plus exit route ready on same day with thirty blank passports and visas. Have been warned: all off without agreement.

There was a certain satisfaction in being in control, the bullying Dansey helpless to dictate terms from London. Peter wondered if he would ever be exposed in his big lie – the one about the passports and the escape being an obligatory part of the deal – but he didn't care. He was going to do his bit for Claudia and the kids. She was right, they deserved to get out. He, after all, was still Winton's man.

Shortly, a further note arrived from Bergen saying Williams would be arriving with his wireless on the morning train.

The wireless message that Peter didn't read was the one sent from London marked *Strictly Williams' Eyes Only*.

It was from Dansey: Imperative you arrive operational area soonest. Exercise surveillance. Ready any eventuality.

Williams knew what that meant. Quite appropriately, he had been cleaning and oiling his Welrod silenced pistol as he read the message. Typical, he thought, they always give the dirty jobs to the plebs. Just like down the valleys and in the mines it was, just so the bosses could keep their hands clean.

He had seen Peter at the French windmill, thinking himself unobserved, leaving his weapon in the hands of the miller, knowing they would not be returning. Peter was crazy to go on this kind of operation unarmed, but that's how he was. Thought he could achieve everything by the gift of the gab. So what were his chances? Would the 'charm school' technique work on the Yank? It was obvious; at least a fifty per cent chance Hoskins was a traitor. Could such a person be persuaded to change sides? Whichever way events turned out, Williams didn't intend to be a lamb to the slaughter. He wouldn't allow himself to be an easy victim. His upper crust colleague was putting his head in a noose and his public-school education was leaving him well short on street sense. He wrapped the Welrod carefully in a cloth and inserted it at the bottom of a railwayman's briefcase. Then he packed up his other things and the priceless radio and prepared to move out according to instructions. Even if Lieutenant Chesham didn't, Williams knew what might need to be done.

He arrived off the morning train. Peter met him on the triangle track and bundled him straight into the bunkhouse. Crewmen normally logged into the control centre and left their bags in the locker room, but Peter wanted the radio set where he had immediate access.

'Smaller than a henhouse,' Williams said, when he saw the tiny room they were to share.

'You get a blanket in the corner,' Peter said. 'What did you expect, en suite?'

Williams refused to be put down. He was trying to be optimistic, happy to have made it to Munich without mishap, but when the subject of Peter's contacts with Hoskins came up he was blunt. 'Sounds like a complete fruitcake to me. A glory-seeker with a big chip on his shoulder. Under pressure from the nasties to succeed. You do realise, don't you, he could be conning you, stringing you along, just to inform on you later and we'll all be in the can?'

Peter was dismissive. 'I'm the one doing the stringing along,' he said.

Williams was even less enthused when he heard about the children, the escape plan and his role in looking after them. 'Not sure I signed up in this army to end up playing scout leader to a bunch of scruffy kids.'

21

Sweat ran into her eyes, her chest heaved, her thighs ached and her feet throbbed. There seemed to be a hundred different ways to make the life of a teacher in the Third Reich more difficult: parades, camp, an appalling syllabus, lessons in hate. And now this.

Claudia was in a forest somewhere south of Munich on a cross-country run as part of the school's month-long compulsory physical training camp. Every teacher had to take their turn, the headmaster insisted.

She had objected because of the staffing crisis in the elementary department. There were so few staff left, she told him. Many had quit, others excluded because of race, still more gone to the forces. Her classes were already up to sixty and it was absurd to absent herself at this time.

But rules were rules, the head insisted. At least for the day.

She hated PT camp. She wasn't especially sporty. She liked tennis but found the physical demands of running a burden. Besides, she was convinced the camp had no educational value. Its army-style discipline did little for learning and the officially approved familiarity of the pupils bordered on the impertinent.

She thought the 'mucking in' ethos simply an excuse for party propaganda and warrior training. It was typical of the new regime, conditioning the children for a future marked out as cannon-fodder.

Claudia stopped running, gasping for breath and came to rest on a fallen tree that made a convenient seat. She had inevitably dropped behind the main body of runners while negotiating dales, forests and fields. She remembered passing a fallen signpost, a tethered wooden hawk on a long wire dancing in the wind and a scarecrow with birds sitting on its outstretched arms. Soon she was running alone. Drexler, her detested colleague, was well out in front. The idea of trekking through a forest alone was a little scary but the path and foot-prints were plain to see. A distant hum of traffic reassured her that civilisation still existed over to her right.

A crashing of twigs behind caused momentary alarm. She turned to see a skinny kid with spindly legs and a runny nose loping into the clearing. When he spotted Claudia, he hesitated, stopped, then joined her on the log.

'Beni, isn't it? Beni Hofer?'

The boy nodded, for several moments incapable of speech.

'Finding it hard going?'

A gasping nod.

'Never mind. We'll run together when you've got your breath back.'

Beni wasn't in her class but she'd seen him in the play-ground. Small for his age, she suspected he'd been bullied. He wore a threadbare shirt and his shorts were ripped.

He saw her looking at his thick mop of black hair. 'I'm not Jewish,' he said.

'But you're having a tough time?'

Falteringly, Beni's story emerged. His parents had disap-peared and he was living with his uncle.

'Just as well your uncle lives close by,' she said.

'Well, not really an uncle. I call him that. He was my dad's best friend and told me to go to him if anything happened.'

'So what did happen?' she asked, fearing she knew already.

Beni hung his head, silent.

She put an arm round his shoulder. 'Taken in the night?'

He nodded, but that wasn't the end of it. 'My friend, Erich, he's been taken. Mum and Dad have been gone for ages but Erich just the other day. Police got him. He was sheltering. In that old house by the bridge at the Donnersberger. I saw it. He was screaming and shouting. Didn't want to go. And do you know where they took him?'

'How do you know?'

'Everybody knows. Where they always take them. The ghetto on Troppauer Strasse.' Beni looked up at Claudia. 'He shouted to me to save him but I couldn't. I'm just a kid, but you...'

Beni looked at her imploringly. 'You're a teacher. They have to take notice of you.' The long stare was unrelenting. 'Please, Fraulein, can *you* get him out?'

Claudia bristled at Beni Hofer's story. It appeared that several other orphans had been sheltering in the disused house by the bridge and had got away, but Beni's friend Erich had not been quick enough to evade the net.

She had heard such tales before but somehow this one seemed more personal, more unjust. It was as if the police had just stamped their jackboots all over her doorstep. Little Beni and his friend were close to home. It felt like an affront, but could she really consider rescuing a child from a ghetto?

'Please, Fraulein,' Beni had pleaded. His desperate faith in her abilities tore at her. She couldn't rid herself of his image or his entreaties. He kept repeating, 'I know you can do it.'

When Claudia floated the idea to Erika, her friend listed all the obstacles. 'First, you've got to get in, find him, then smuggle him through the wire. You'd only get away with it at night, far too visible in the day. And then there's the business of travelling with a scruffy, smelly child through the streets and on the trams late at night. Asking for a police check. Or interference from some busybody.'

'Then what about a car?'

'And where do you suppose that's coming from?'

Claudia had no idea. But two days later word arrived that a certain Herr Weber would be available in a black Opel round the corner from the depot at 11 o'clock on Wednesday.

She decided that first she would carry out a daylight reconnaissance, so after school on the Tuesday she took the tram north to Milbertshofen. Peter had passed that way several days before and gave her the location. She approached on foot along the main road, the Knorr Strasse, passing the Café Waldeck at which several hardy customers taking coffee at pavement tables gave her lingering looks. Next time, she vowed, she would dress in a headscarf and dowdy coat.

At the corner she hung back briefly before turning into Troppauer Strasse, taking in every detail. A line of peak-capped figures in long, grey, belted greatcoats stood to one side like a screen, staring through a wire fence at ten large wooden huts. Behind the wire, at the end of the line, a new hut was being constructed. An elderly man in white shirt, tie, waistcoat and black gloves was pushing a wheelbarrow. Another white-haired jacketed figure was holding a spade. Others stood uncertainly about. It was immediately plain that these were men unused to manual labour and she recalled Erika's parting remark: 'They even make them build their own huts.'

Claudia risked approaching the wire where two young girls stood staring out at the world they had so recently vacated. They wore fur hats, thick coats and gloves. Both had puzzled, pathetic expressions.

'You there!'

A peremptory voice hailed Claudia from behind.

She turned. The tallest of the grey figures advanced toward her. She half expected a sword-slashed scowl to go with the skull cap badge and the double runic collar tabs of the SS.

'Get away from the wire. No talking to those people.'

Claudia bit back her instinct to challenge.

'What business have you here?'

She noticed the smooth, almost feminine features, a child-like pout and the aroma of lavender water.

She shrugged and turned, waving at the wire. 'I've never seen anything like this before.'

'Damned gawper!'

It was then she spotted a black clipboard under one arm and the top of a gold fountain pen clipped to his greatcoat lapel. She faked a beguiling smile. There were times to be cautious, she knew, but there were other moments when meekness merely encouraged aggression. She stepped forward and in one swooping motion reached up and whipped the fountain pen free.

'A Montblanc Meisterstuck! Fantastic! I've always wanted one of these,' she said, sighing and turning it over appreciatively in her hand.

'Hey!' The SS man did a double take, looking down at his now empty coat lapel.

'Can I try it out on your clipboard?' she said, fingering the black resin barrel and stroking the three gold rings like a new pet kitten.

'No you may not!' He took a deep breath – but whatever

outraged reaction was to have followed was cut off by a guffaw from one of his colleagues.

'Getting cosy with the girls again, Wolfgang? Another admirer?'

There were chuckles from further down the line of officers which effectively deflated the pomposity of the man. Claudia thought she picked up an undercurrent of mockery, perhaps teasing out an uncertainty about this man's sexuality.

She turned her attention to the others, flipped a shoulder like the impulsive flirt she was not and held up a hand in a gesture of fake surrender.

More laughter. Deflated, the baby-faced officer contented himself with snatching the pen back.

'Be on your way!'

Next evening, she made sure she was ready and waiting in a street adjoining the Landsberger. The Opel, when it arrived, looked every bit a cop car, all black with four doors, the sort she normally shrank from. With some trepidation, she opened the passenger door.

At first she didn't recognise the driver, dressed as he was in a grey trilby and a civilian suit. Then she saw the trademark wan smile. This was the officer who'd given her such a fright the morning after she had picked up her two strays.

Claudia breathed in doubtfully. Wary of a trap but remembering Erika's assurances that Weber was "one of us", she climbed in beside him.

He handed her a stamped and signed pass. 'Permission for you to be in the area to visit a relative,' he said, then produced a pair of wire cutters from under his seat. 'Officially, this place is not a ghetto,' he said as they pulled away from the kerb. 'Munich is much too proud and embarrassed to have such a thing on its doorstep. So, no ghettos here. It's just a transit camp for deportations to the East.'

'Same difference,' Claudia said tartly. 'Barbed wire is barbed wire. You can't argue with that.'

Along the way she wondered about this man, an off-duty police officer driving her on a covert mission. Perhaps she should be reticent but eventually asked, 'Why are you helping?'

'I have my reasons.'

Claudia gave him a quizzical look and after a short silence he opened up: his wife had been dismissed from the civil service because of the ban on married women and his daughter refused entry to university because of quotas. 'And some of my old colleagues disgust me,' he said. 'Clever men who've moved into the security sections.' Claudia recognised cop-speak for the Gestapo. 'Who not only should know better but *do* know better. They have degrees in jurisprudence but choose to ignore all the correct procedures they practised under Weimar. Now they lower themselves to the level of untutored thugs.'

Weber parked the car one block away in Bischoff Strasse and stayed at the wheel while Claudia approached on foot. The temperature had dropped appreciably and she was acutely aware of her own footfall in the silence of the late evening. She walked along Knorr Strasse, lit by just a few desultory lamp standards, vanishing into vast, enveloping pools of darkness. The daytime buzz of background noise had gone and she could make out the distant rumble of a train and an occasional metallic boom echoing from a factory. Weber's wire cutters felt clumsy, weighing down her coat pocket and banging against her thigh but she dare not hide them in her wicker basket. This was filled with flowers and fruit, a deliberate focus for attention to distract any stop-and-search squad. The darkness matched her mood; a momentary doubt about the wisdom of what she was about to do. What right had she to take this child? What could she offer him beyond uncertainty and discomfort? The wind plucked at the scruffy coat she wore as a large DKW passed her in a dazzle of headlights. She listened to its echoing drone, thankful it had continued on its way. She ploughed on, wishing she had better shoes to cope with the uneven cobbles, spurred by the urgent beseeching of Beni on behalf of his friend Erich. In case of interception she had several excuses ready: delivering gifts to her aunt and calling at a nearby kiosk for Greek cigarettes.

When she reached Troppauer she was relieved to find there were no guard posts and all was silent. No lights showed at any of the huts and Claudia wondered about the condition of the occupants. She knew about the eight o'clock curfew. She also knew about the restrictions they had suffered before being ordered from their homes: banned from their businesses, parks, restaurants and stations and forbidden to buy newspapers, flowers, coffee and fruit. But did this insistence on lights out require the inmates to lie in the dark? Such was the pettiness of this regime.

She stopped by the wire. Nothing stirred. Rattling the metal strands might attract unwanted attention, so she found a fallen tree branch and poked it through the wire, gently tapping on the nearest window.

Then again, a little louder, fearful she might wake some slumbering sentry. It seemed impenetrably dark. Her eyes were not yet fully accustomed to the night.

'What do you want?' a low voice issued from a few feet away.

'I've come to collect a young boy, name of Erich.'

'Wait.'

Some minutes later a portion of wire was prized open from the inside. She ducked through into the compound, entered a darkened hut and found herself surrounded by a group of people she could barely see. Those close by still wore their street clothes. The place was cold. She could glimpse no furniture.

'Why take this boy?' a woman asked.

'He's an orphan, he has no one of his own, and he doesn't want to go.'

As if to prove her point a little bundle of squealing energy rushed to her side, clutching her round the middle as if to save itself from drowning.

'Please, Fraulein!' whispered the boy, Erich. 'Take me out of here.'

A small man came close enough for her to see and she tried not to wince. He had bad breath, a crumpled jacket, wavy hair and an authoritative manner. Was this the wheelbarrow man she'd seen the day before? She put out a sympathetic hand but he brushed it away.

'Erich will be better off with us,' he said. 'Better than the life of a U-boat! We're being taken to a labour camp. He can muck in. We'll look out for him.'

Erich protested once more. 'Please, Fraulein, please get me out of here.'

'Can I speak to you privately?' Claudia looked at the door. 'Outside?'

She didn't believe in Nazi fables about labour camps. It didn't add up. Why would anyone send children, ageing grannies and the lame to such a place? Logically, they would only take the able-bodied. Forced labourers were already appearing in the Reich from the occupied territories and they didn't bring their families. She swallowed. How brutal should she be with this man? Was it better to allow him to go on believing?

He was reluctant at first to leave the hut and she had to insist they talk well beyond the hearing of the others. She said, 'You really shouldn't get your hopes up. Can you expect acceptable conditions for your wives, old people and children in a labour camp? Fair treatment for those who cannot work?'

The small man's tone grew coarser. 'You've no right to come

in here scaremongering, trying to frighten us. If we co-operate with the authorities I'm sure everything will turn out well. Don't cause them any trouble, I say, don't antagonise them, that's the best policy.'

'Think about it,' she said. 'Given their cruelty and their utter ruthlessness.'

'You're just saying that. You don't know. You can't know.'

'I've seen them up close. How they think. How they work.'

'Go,' he said, pointing. 'Before you start frightening the others.'

She put up a hand of resignation and took a step back, hugging Erich, ready to return together through the gap in the wire. 'Sorry,' she said, 'I fear for you all but I can't help. You are too many. The most I can do is to take this boy.'

The man hitched up his oversized jacket and snorted.

She insisted. 'Can't guarantee it, of course, but I think he's got a better chance with me.'

There was a long pause, then a shrug, before he led them to the wire.

22

A towered masonry heater made up of two dozen oval brown tiles spewed out a glow of hot air from the corner of the component stores. Peter, who was keying in fast to the black humour of the Third Reich, courtesy of the Caller, was propping up Erika's counter, enjoying her fund of stories about the oversized Hermann Goering, his boasts, his medals and his uniforms.

'A Goer is the maximum amount of tin a man can carry on his chest without falling flat on his face.'

Peter chuckled and brought out his cigarette packet. There was a warm fug in the room, enhanced further by the Junos he'd taken to smoking as a conversation enhancer. He lit another, managed not to cough, and offered his host one, which she refused.

'A water main bursts in the cellar of the air ministry,' she said. 'Told of the mishap, Goering demands: "Fetch me my admiral's uniform."'

Then there was the Goering promise to change his name to Meyer if Germany was bombed. Air raid sirens were now known as Meyer's bugle-horn.

Peter grinned. He wanted more. Humour, he'd decided, was his best way in. He was still frustrated at being kept on the outside in his quest for inside information.

He said, 'Heard a story of my own last week, what one of the wives found in her husband's pockets.'

'Husbands' pockets,' Erika said, 'like panning for gold.'

Peter grinned but still felt under pressure. Williams had arrived from Bergen, feeding him Dansey's blunt imperatives toward a single-minded act of destruction. He needed more information. Surely, Erika knew the secret of the directing mind of the Resistance? Would humour unlock it?

'Of course,' Erika said. 'Going through his pockets, that's completely normal. Just the usual thing. Don't want to wash his money or his diary or anything he's left in there, do you?'

'Naturally.' Peter grinned. 'But this time amongst all the usual stuff she finds a piece of paper with a telephone number scribbled on it.'

'His fancy woman?'

'That's what she thought when she gave it a ring.'

'And?'

The spell of the story was broken when the door opened and Epp, Hoskins's assistant, entered the stores bearing a pink slip. He ambled to the counter and Erika took the slip, looking down the list, preparatory to flicking through her rotary index for the requested part numbers.

'And,' Peter said, appearing to take no notice of the interruption, 'guess who answered the wife's telephone call?'

Erika, one hand poised over her machine, looked up. 'Surprise me!'

'Not the fancy woman at all.'

'Who then?'

'The dog's home.' Peter cackled at his own joke. 'It's true. He was going to buy her a puppy for her birthday.'

Erika kept a straight face. 'Pull the other one. The mistress probably worked there.'

Peter turned to Epp and spread his hands. 'What do you say? To all these suspicious, doubting wives?'

But Epp was saying nothing and looked away.

'Cigarette?' Peter still had out his packet of Junos. A man proffering free smokes was not to be ignored, so Epp gave Peter a quizzical stare before taking one.

This, Peter knew, was his other big chance. He'd been hoping for this moment – meeting Epp unescorted in the stores – even though Erika had cast doubt on the likelihood of opening him up. Silent Hans they called him. Peter's match flared and they both lit their cigarettes.

'How's it going over there?' Peter wheezed through a halo of smoke.

Epp said nothing.

'Can't keep it a secret for ever, you know. Got to come out some time... Like when you show the train to the wide world – and soon.'

Epp wet his lips and leaned forward.

Erika looked up, as if intrigued by a rare moment.

Epp said, 'Wait and see.'

'So when is it then? The big day. Monday next week, so I hear. Going to be all ready for it then?'

Epp seemed to be chewing his gums. His tongue was doing a route march. But no sound emerged.

'Thing is,' Peter said, 'I heard there's a problem. Might not be ready in time.' A quizzical expression.

But Epp looked down, then up, then sideways.

Erika was pushing bulky items across the counter. There was the sharp tang of freshly-oiled metal. She said, 'All done! Mind you don't drop.'

'Here!' Peter said. 'Let me help. That's a heavy box. I'll walk back depot side with you.' And so saying, he grabbed the bulkiest box, weighed it rather dramatically, tucked it under his arm and moved to the door. Out in the tunnel the two of them set out for the far side, Peter trying again: 'What do you need all this stuff for?'

But no answer was forthcoming and soon the thunder of wheels passing overhead ruled out any further conversation. It was a long walk. Water seeped and dripped down damp tiled walls, forming little puddles on the cobbles which Peter was careful to skirt, but then he stumbled on a loose stone. 'Damn!' he said, looking down and behind. 'Somebody should do something about this old tunnel.'

'Don't know why the stores are still over here anyway.'

Peter was pleased. At last he'd managed to provoke the taciturn Epp into speech. 'Ah, that's because it's always been over here,' he said with a chuckle. 'Don't change a thing, isn't that the usual way? A reflex, wouldn't you say?'

But it didn't work. Epp resumed his habitual silence, trudging wordlessly onward toward the little portal of daylight in the distance. Peter's feet began to feel sore from wearing the big boots he had been given at Bergen. He was also conscious of the roughness of his issue overalls. Nothing like the smooth feel of an officer's barathea tunic.

He tried again. Could Epp be the man, the silent mastermind? Peter just wanted a sign, a clue, some gesture of recognition. 'I admire your silence,' he shouted, 'but I can guess what it means. You're the one with his finger on the pulse.'

He waited for a reaction, hoping for some physical, if not vocal acknowledgement that he was on the right track. About halfway, Peter stopped. 'Another smoke?'

They lit up in silence, then trudged on. At the far side a familiar figure seemed to block the exit. Closer to, Peter recognised the military policeman on afternoon shift. Franz was the name. Said to be a music buff. Once again, Peter clocked the grey uniform, eagle runics, pistol and jackboots. Greetings were exchanged. Peter knew he was courting danger but decided his only tactic was to continue to play the depot gossip. 'Just saying to Epp here, heard there's a problem over in his department. Could be a delay.'

Franz was impassive. Not hostile like his morning colleague, more an enigmatic, almost an avuncular figure. He too was smoking and Peter was conscious of another tobacco smell mingling with the usual Juno haze, but couldn't place it.

'You can't ask him that,' Franz said without apparent rancour. 'Herr Hoskins would be most displeased if he were to answer. Besides, you must understand, all new things are beset by difficulties. In fact, they're performing absolute marvels over in that workshop. Amazing achievement. Naturally, there are a few little problems. A case of try this, then try that.'

Peter was relieved at this mini-eulogy but mystified why Franz didn't react like other cops. He turned his attention back to Epp, hoping all this comment would provoke some useful response, but found himself looking at a retreating figure.

Clearly not the mastermind then.

With a shrug Peter turned to retrace his steps through the tunnel, noticing that Franz too had walked away.

Erika was in a strange mood: reflective, talkative but sad. She looked as if she'd been consumed by some dreadful problem, but then problems were a daily occurrence for all of them.

'I've been watching you,' she told Claudia. 'You're bringing those kids along brilliantly. Less feral, more obedient. You're a natural. They're going to be one lucky bunch if you get them away.'

Claudia smiled, but she didn't like that little word, "if".

'I've also been thinking,' Erika said. 'Thinking hard about the future of my Dieter.' Dieter was still in Claudia's class at the school. 'He's really taken to you. Ever since you've been keeping an eye on him. You're good for him.' Then she swallowed before adding, 'But his long-term prospects around here are pretty poor, wouldn't you say?'

Before Claudia could answer, she added in a small voice: 'No one likes to let go of their child...'

Her voice trailed away and Claudia began to frown.

'Like all those other mothers you told me about at the Prague station,' Erika said.

'Where's this all leading?' Claudia asked.

'Maybe you ought to add my Dieter to the list. Get him out of this place with the others. Free of this poison. He'll be better off with you.'

Claudia moved closer to her friend, put an arm on her shoulder. 'Are you sure about this?'

Erika's eyes were clouded with tears. 'You've got to think of what's best for him, haven't you?'

Once again Claudia marvelled at the selflessness of motherhood; the willingness to surrender a child into the hands of strangers for the greater good. She sighed and shook her head. 'We'll see,' she said, deliberately tentative, knowing she was reaching the limit of the numbers they could deal with. Peter had definite ideas on the count.

But she also knew she couldn't refuse her friend. How could she? The two of them sat together, arms linked, saying nothing. There were few words for what they were thinking.

Later, when Claudia told Peter about this conversation, he reacted as expected. 'We're up to our limit,' he said. 'If he comes aboard, Dieter will have to be the last one. Makes it twenty-seven, plus three adults, absolutely no more.'

She gave him a look that said he could squeeze a few more, that he could be more flexible for the sake of young lives.

'There's a very good reason for being precise about the numbers,' he said. 'Best you don't know. So I'm afraid it means you'll have to turn away the next child who wants to join.'

She made a face. 'And how do I do that?' she said.

23

Hoskins glided into the component stores. It was nearly three and Erika was making coffee, as she always did at this time. He leaned over the counter, accepted a cup, and said, 'I had a visit last night from a young gentleman proposing a very interesting idea.'

'Oh?' Erika stopped her filtering and looked up. 'And what was that?'

'Something about moving my work to somewhere else.'

Erika put the sugar bowl in front of him and said, 'Moving? Oh dear. No more coffee and doughnuts then?'

But Hoskins didn't join in the jovial banter. 'You haven't noticed a stranger around the place? Full head of hair, black moustache, glasses?'

Erika tucked into one half of a cold Nurnberger, dabbing it with French mustard and munching a pretzel. 'Doesn't sound like anyone I know,' she said, keeping her eyes averted from the Fuhrer's picture on the wall and shrugging her shoulders, mouth still full. 'But I'll keep an eye out.'

'Thanks.' Hoskins sipped his coffee. 'Trouble is, I need another meeting. Need more detail.'

Erika's voice was muffled by the big sausage. 'Detail?'

'Of course I know this won't mean anything to you, but there was an intriguing moment when the subject of guarantees was mentioned.'

She shrugged. 'You could leave a note on my wall,' she said, pointing to a clutter of staff messages on a corkboard.

He shook his head. 'I'll wait.' Then he changed the subject. 'Where's your young friend? Haven't seen Claudia for days. You and she, the only sensible people I get to talk to around here. Plenty of common sense and not too scared to say what you think.'

'Straight out with it, that's us!' Erika chuckled through a mouthful. 'All sorts of people drop in here for a chat. I'll ask around about your stranger.' She took another large bite. 'Perhaps a little later on?'

At five Hoskins appeared once more and she handed him a small folded note with a pin still attached. 'Found this stuck to my board,' she said.

'How would anyone know I'd be here today?' he said sharply.

'Must have seen you.'

He gave her a long look, took the note and unfolded it. She knew full well what it said.

Direct and to the point. *Shedmaster's office, 1830 hours.*

At exactly half past the hour Hoskins approached the office. He'd been there once before and was surprised the shedmaster might be involved, but after knocking at the door and getting no answer, he entered to find the place deserted.

He grunted, annoyed.

He looked at his watch. Dead on time.

He looked around. Clear desk, office chair, just a telephone perched on an old directory. Then he looked out of the window, wondering how they had managed to get rid of the shedmaster. Slowly, the realisation came to him: there must be more than one person involved in this intrigue. Could he be up against some well-organised cabal?

Another grunt, another look out of the window. He considered storming out in disgust. He was a busy man. He didn't like people who were late and he didn't like being stood up. But a sense of anticipation kept him there another few minutes. 'I'll give you exactly three minutes to show yourself,' he said under his breath, wondering if someone could hear him. Was his mysterious late-night visitor hiding nearby, listening to a hidden microphone, observing, checking that he had no tail? These people were security obsessed, he thought. Perhaps, in his case, with just cause.

On the dot of three minutes Hoskins turned angrily to the door. He'd already clasped the handle when the phone on the desk began to ring.

He stopped, wondering. It could just be a call for the absent shedmaster. He wasn't going to play at factotums, passing on messages. Then another thought occurred to him. He turned and walked back to the desk.

It was still ringing.

Slowly, with some deliberation, he lifted the receiver, said nothing but put it to his ear.

'Hoskins?' said a voice, and he recognised it immediately.

'What's all this secrecy thing?' Hoskins said sharply. 'Can't you meet me face to face?'

'Not in this place.'

'What is it you want?'

'The other way round, my friend, you wanted to ask me some questions, I understand. Something about guarantees?'

Hoskins ducked around the desk and sat on the chair. 'Are we really going to conduct business in here over this phone?'

'Yes.'

Hoskins hesitated, then said, 'What sort of guarantees are you offering? That's a mighty big leap you proposed last night. I'll need something pretty solid in place to entertain it seriously. It's too easy to issue a bland verbal assurance. Anyone could do that.'

In an office just out of earshot down the corridor, Peter was speaking into the phone. 'Okay,' he said in a tone of complete reasonableness, 'but you surely weren't expecting anything in writing on this side of the border. You'll have to trust me on that, but as soon as we cross the frontier you will get your guarantees the moment you arrive.'

'How can I possibly trust that sort of promise?'

'Because I've already sent the necessary message to start the process rolling. They're expecting you. They'll meet you on the other side and discuss what arrangements and facilities you require. But before then, there will be an upfront payment of 50,000 dollars before you even start work, as an article of our good faith.'

Peter's imagination was roaring into top gear. He was enjoying himself. It amused him to wonder what Dansey would say if he could hear what his agent was pledging on his behalf. Would the Treasury, or whatever funding source MI6 used, ever agree to such an amount? He had no idea. 'I'm sure you appreciate,' he said, 'that it would be very dangerous for both of us to put anything in writing now, but I can assure you I have the authority to make this upfront payment. It's all ready and set to go, that much detail I do have.'

'What currency? What bank?'

'Dollars and Switzerland obviously.' A pause, then he said, 'Do you have pen and paper handy?'

'Thought you were against anything written.'

'I'm sure you can bury this particular piece of paperwork.'

'I'm listening.'

Peter began reading out a series of letters and numbers. The first were the opening set of the international banking code identifying Switzerland – CH followed by two numerals. He followed with five more numbers that referred to an individual bank, in this instance, the depot's branch office in central Munich, which he had copied from a supplies receipt discovered in the shedmaster's desk. There followed three more numbers that he could remember from his uncle's bank account in Bern and the rest were pure invention. Having counted the digits in a genuine number, he made the total up to twenty-one.

'What's all this?'

'Your new Swiss bank account number. Just been set up for you. Check it as soon as you can.'

A pause while the man considered this. Peter hoped he was as mercenary as Dansey had suggested.

'I still need something concrete, some firm reassurance,' said the voice.

'Can you phone abroad?'

'Possibly.'

Peter paused. His powers of invention were in full flow. 'Then call the British consulate in Bern at nine tonight and ask for Charles Wightman, the trade delegate. He'll fill you in on what they have planned for you.'

Was there such a man? Probably not. He would have to get Williams busy on the radio, instructing Dansey to set up this elaborate subterfuge.

'Still not enough.'

'Perhaps the initial payment could be raised to meet your requirements. I'll see what can be done. But these are already generous terms. And remember what I said last night, the alternative for you is dire indeed. You'd be a fool to refuse.'

Hoskins said, 'I want guarantees. Copper-bottomed assurances that I'd be working on a broad gauge, not the old one, I need to know how serious you really are.'

'Look,' Peter said, 'first we have to focus on your new propulsion methods, that's your unique gift.'

'Not enough. I want the whole package.'

Peter sighed. This was getting out of hand. He couldn't, while retaining credibility, promise the moon. 'Okay, I'll see what can be arranged. First, we need to talk to the chairman of the company, Lord Chelmer.'

That brought an immediate response. 'Not him! I won't talk to him!'

Peter was momentarily nonplussed. 'Why?'

'Chelmer? He's the guy who blew me out! A dinosaur. Committed only to steam.'

Peter winced. In for a penny, he thought, and galloped on: 'Well, I can tell you now, I know for a fact, he's changed his tune – on government orders.' He repressed a chuckle. The lies tripped effortlessly off his tongue. It was as if he were in a play, speaking someone else's lines, talking in another voice. 'I'm in touch with the people at the very top,' he said. 'Influential people, like Sir Andrew Truscott. You must know him, a household name, the most renowned locomotive designer acknowledged the world over for his streamlined expresses...'

Hoskins hit back again. 'He hates me. And he stole all his ideas from the States.'

Peter didn't baulk, carried along on his tide of fantasy. 'I can tell you now with utter certainty that if there was once scepticism it has now been reversed. You know as well as I do, war changes everything.' He subsided, pleased with his punchline.

'How is it then, they've sent a boy to do a man's job?'

Peter waved a fist at the receiver while keeping his voice even. 'I'm part of the team. A big set-up. All ready to go as soon as we get the green light.' He swallowed, breathed in and decided he needed to sound tough. 'Look, you've seen my letter, you must know by now this is a major policy decision by the British Cabinet. I can assure you I do not approach this matter lightly. Wheels are turning. I can disclose that over the water an experimental test bed is being set up at a special location, even as we speak.'

Hoskins exploded. 'I don't need a test bed, I've proved my system works.' He was shouting, cursing. 'You can see that for yourself, for Christ's sake! Lines starting to spread all over the Reich.'

'Hang on! We'll still need test facilities to check each new vehicle as it rolls off the construction line, then we'll proceed from there. However, if this should prove insufficient, Sir Andrew assures me he is prepared to put extra facilities at your disposal.'

There was a silence and Peter decided he had to bring this thing to a close. 'Now, have I not been reasonable? I've tried to meet all your legitimate concerns on a practical level, there's a great future to be had here but we need to take one step at a time. So, Mr Hoskins, are you now ready to come on board?'

'I'll think about it.'

'I need a decision. Ring Bern tonight, then come back to me tomorrow. Same telephone, same time, for our final terms and your reply.' Peter tried to inject menace into his sign-off. 'Think carefully now about your personal position.'

'Tomorrow's too late,' Hoskins said. 'The party big shots and their hangers-on, they'll be all over me by then. Too many people. I'll have no opportunity to speak without eyes and ears all around me. Make it at ten tonight. And you'll have to have something better than this.'

With that the phone went dead.

~

Peter returned to the bunkhouse to find Williams. 'Send this message,' he said, handing him a scribbled note.

Williams looked askance. They had a rule: no WT usage from the depot because of the danger of wireless interception. They didn't want to spark a search and focus unwelcome attention on the Landsberger district.

'Have to take the risk,' Peter said, 'otherwise the whole con job may fall through the floor.'

Then he spent the next few hours worrying whether Hoskins would check on Peter's fictitious trade delegate – and whether there would be anyone primed and ready in Bern with the right script.

Had he gone too far? Maybe Hoskins already had a Swiss bank account and would know from the configuration of his own number that Peter's was a fake. Had he gone over the top and endangered everyone? What did disaster look like?

He suffered a quick stab of panic. The image was paralysing: wholesale arrests, screaming children and the image of Claudia at the mercy of a team of sadists in some Gestapo basement. He swallowed, sick with apprehension.

24

Two men reclined in deep armchairs, silent and watchful as a third, dressed in well-pressed black trousers, jacket and gloves, banked up the fire, leaving the scuttle in the grate half-full of coal. The man in black stood to inspect his work. The flames were coming through nicely, he thought, the room warming in response. Satisfied, he turned to go, glancing as he did so through the high window which gave a brief view of the ducks swimming on the pond in the middle of St James's Park. There was a certain subtle beauty about London in the autumn, he decided.

Then, with a bow to the two silent figures, he withdrew, closing the door noiselessly behind him. The silence continued for several more minutes until a stage cough presaged the start of a conversation. Sir Stewart Menzies, pronounced *Mingis* by those in the know, and who also knew him as C, sat up, swirling around in his glass a favourite malt, savouring pleasures to come. This was his favourite drink; this was his favourite room. But first there was a distasteful task to perform.

He turned his attention to the other man. 'I thought it best to get away from the clamour of events. Away from the hustle and bustle. Now to dispense with the diplomatic language.'

A chuckle from the other chair. 'Dispense away, old friend.'

This last description was an overstatement. Dansey ran his own closed ship within Menzies' organisation. The two rarely spoke.

'Edward, it has come to my notice that you're running an operation which, until now, has been quite unknown to the rest of us. And it transpires that the arrangements for this activity leave much to be desired. You could have saved everyone a lot of trouble if you'd used normal channels.'

'You know me.' The grating voice from the other chair was like the rattle of rusty nails. 'I don't like channels.'

Menzies, looking like a country squire in tweeds, grimaced. 'Fortunately, I do know you, and I have to say this operation has all the hallmarks of your string and sticking tape approach. No proper preparation, no backup.'

'How d'you make that out?'

'I'm only now hearing some of the details. Two operatives sent into enemy territory, both inadequately prepared, with only one succeeding in getting to his operational area. Unarmed and without equipment. And the other – well, he's been left miles behind with his wireless. Both are now out of touch with each other except by handwritten notes carried between them by enemy nationals.'

'Someone's been shooting their mouth off.'

Another cough from Menzies. 'Never heard the like of it. Not at all sure what the PM is going to say.'

'Does he have to say anything? Does he have to hear?'

'What do you think?' Menzies looked down at his glass and added, 'While the objective of this operation seems admirable, the means much less so. What arrangements have been made for our American engineer friend to come across?'

Dansey roused himself. 'Unlikely, to be frank, and my second man has the necessary orders in the matter of disposal.'

Menzies was quick to reply. 'His Majesty's government does not conduct its foreign policy by means of... disposal, as you put it.'

'That's what you said back in '38 when you had the chance to knock off a certain Adolf Hitler. A sitting duck, as I recall, while leaning over the Reich Chancellery balcony. And now look where that's got you!'

'Recriminations, hardly helpful.' Menzies took a sip from his glass. 'As it happens, I've had several representations about this operation of yours. The boy's father and an important figure in the transport industry.'

A groan from the other chair. 'I don't want your people inter-fering! I have every confidence in the abilities of my man on the spot.'

'That's not what I hear. No stomach for the fight, refuses to handle his weapon, even left it in the custody of a French Resis-tant. Haven't done very well so far, have you?'

'I run a lean outfit,' Dansey insisted. 'Always found the fewer people involved the better.'

Menzies spread his hands. 'What can I say?' After a moment he asked, 'So, once again, this American, can he be bought?'

'Doubtful.'

'Then I think he may need a little more encouragement. We need to raise the sum involved.' C sat erect in his chair, his earlier languor gone, and pointed an accusing finger. 'Come to that, I think your men in the field need an extra helping hand. And then again, I think you too may need some assistance in this matter.'

≈

Peter had spent the intervening hours wondering if his Hoskins subterfuge would work and at ten o'clock precisely he upped the stakes. He knew the man was sitting by the phone because hidden watchers close to the shedmaster's office had given him the signal.

'Are you alone?'

'Of course.'

'Good. Spoken to Charles?'

'Yes – and he was a damned sight more to the point than you. Did you really think I'd fall for that bogus bank account dodge? No, sir, we've sorted it. They have MY account details and they've made the sum seventy-five.'

Peter swallowed. Good God! So the fictional British trade delegate Charles Wightman now appeared to be flesh and blood and possessed of the authority to stump up 75,000 dollars. Peter drew in a long breath. Don't sound gobsmacked, he told himself. Maybe Hoskins was lying too. So, two can play! Keep the fantasy on the road!

'Fine, I've got an update on some of the details.' Peter had been working on this new story for hours. 'Charles is planning a separate set of workshop facilities at the Stratford locomotive works in London, one of the most modern we have, and you'll have available a small workforce, we thought initially, ten fitters, plus two assistant engineers. This can be expanded as necessary as the work proceeds, plus a fully-equipped drawing office, and the necessary steel can be obtained once you've drawn up a list of your precise requirements.' Nothing could stop the unfolding of Peter's fantasy. 'You'll be heading up a new group called the Broad Gauge Planning Group, there will be a house with a manservant, your own car with chauffeur and if it all works out, probably a knighthood. So far we have a test bed, a fleet of road vehicles ready for supply and they're already manufacturing broad gauge axles and wheel sets for you.'

'Size?'

'Three metres, of course.'

'Hold on, how d'you know I won't want to change my mind?'

'Why would you? After your present success?'

Peter heard Hoskins mumbling to himself. Had he guessed? Or was he taken in? A pause, then Hoskins said, 'I still want assurances I'm going to be working on a broad gauge, not the old one, I need to know how serious you really are. I want the whole package.'

'Sure.' No pulling out now. This was the moment for Peter to play his last card – the big secret of the new motor, as told to him by Meyer in the caboose.

'We'll have two tankers on standby, one hydrogen, the other oxygen, and a dozen gas cylinders available for immediate use,' he said, anxious to impress with the insider view of Hoskins's new technology. 'Plus the usual ancillary electrical gear.'

'Tankers? I'll need a whole gas production plant to make this thing work.'

Even Peter's fertile imagination was beginning to run dry but Hoskins saved the moment by switching subject. 'And how am I expected to proceed with this frontier crossing?'

Now he was on firm ground. Peter said, 'Everything will remain the same. Start the inaugural journey on the 25th and carry out your schedule as planned. Don't change anything. Then, at the right moment, you will be contacted with precise instructions.'

'Will your people be on the train? How will I recognise your people? Wearing what, for instance? Some clue as to identity.'

'We'll be on the train. We'll be watching. Eyes on you throughout the journey. And at the right time you will get a message. That's all you need to know.'

A long pause.

'Are you with us, Mr Hoskins? The preparations are under

way in London. We're all ready for you, so are you now ready to come on board?'

Another pause.

'Very well, young man. I can see you've been working hard on this and I shall look forward to discussing the fine detail when we next meet.'

'Then, can I take that as a yes?'

'Sure. Sure thing, it's a yes. I agree.'

Peter cut the line, rubbing his chin. Fake or sincere? That was the question. On balance, he thought Hoskins was probably genuine. The man's fear of discovery from the shortly-to-arrive party of VIPs was genuine enough and that seemed like a good sign. It was natural for him to be on edge.

Williams' opinion on the matter, however, also flashed into mind: 'Watch him! He'll sell you out. I wouldn't trust him further than I could chuck a stoker's shovel.'

One thing was reassuring. The first part of Dansey's mission looked set for success. He'd have no trouble smuggling out the secrets of the new propulsion unit. He had already used his tiny document camera to snap a series of shots of the outline drawings that Meyer had given him, the plans themselves being far too big and clumsy to smuggle out.

However, there was a worrying caveat, issued by Meyer when he and Peter had first talked about Hoskins in the caboose: 'He's very secretive, they're only outline plans, make of them what you will. But I can tell you, there's a lot of hydrogen involved.'

'Hydrogen?' At that time Peter had been completely adrift.

'Highly inflammable. Dangerous stuff. He's already burnt out one workshop. And you do know, don't you, it was hydrogen that put paid to Zeppelins and the airships? Remember the Hindenburg fireball in '37?'

The biggest hurdle of all, it had to be said, was Hoskins himself. What if the man resisted or betrayed? Kidnap was out of the question. That would have required resources Peter did not possess. An ambulance or hearse, Dansey had suggested when broached on the subject back in London. But he'd been no help at all. 'Afraid we can't provide either, facilities short on the ground, you understand, leave it to your own resources, a bit of vehicle theft called for.'

'What, from a hospital?' Peter had exclaimed.

'Try an undertaker. Pretend it's contagious. The Germans are frightened silly by diseases.'

Then, as now, Peter had dismissed this. Dansey was by far the biggest fantasist in this operation. As for the man's other option, a resort to firearms, absolutely not. Peter would stick to his promise. He would not waver. Not for nothing had he left the pistol in the custody of the French Resistant at the windmill. Violence, for him, was still out of the question.

25

They should have been relieved and pleased. Anna was back. It was the little girl's good fortune that the suspected pneumonia was not as bad as first thought and Nurse Lister had restored her to health. The child had been returned to the Maze.

Claudia, twisting a strand of hair round and round in her fingers, knew what was coming when Peter received the news.

'That makes twenty-eight, one over the top. You know I can't take any extras. There's a very solid reason for the limit, twenty-seven kids and three adults, absolute maximum.'

They both knew: one child would have to drop out, a stay-behind, a sacrifice to whatever peril the wilderness would present once Peter's plan had wrought powerful destruction to the Nazis' favoured project.

'How do you do that?' she asked. 'How do you explain to a child they're to be abandoned, their protection withdrawn, while all the others are free to go? How do you send a kid back to the horror of the cellars?'

Peter was shrugging, blinking away his lack of an answer. 'It's what we both feared. Sooner or later we'd face this dilemma.'

But Erika was different. She had the answer. 'You don't send them to the cellars,' she said. 'Anna goes with you – and my Dieter stays with me.'

Claudia swallowed, embarrassed, bowled over. 'Erika, are you sure?'

'And if there's another stray on the last day, they come with me, we're making plans,' Erika said.

'We?'

'Dieter and me, I've been thinking about this for a while, we can't leave anyone out there in the wilderness. There's going to be a frenzied backlash once Pyotr gets to work. Far too dangerous to stick around.'

Claudia's brow furrowed. 'But it was you who told me Pyotr was the one who'd take all the blame.'

'Too serious for that now. It'll be poisonous around here. We need to be gone. I'll get them to a safer place.'

Claudia glanced in the direction of the railway cottages. 'You know the wives can't take them,' she said. 'They can't suddenly acquire a fully-grown child, especially one of ours.'

'All things are possible,' Erika insisted. 'Lots of movement in and out of the depot. Work people transferring to different jobs, different locations. Paperwork gets lost. The railway is a vast and complex network.'

Claudia looked at her friend, usually so talkative but now clearly intent on saying no more. She had turned away to attend to her dockets and you didn't ask questions in this kind of conversation. Everyone knew that. But still Claudia could not contain herself.

'Mystery upon mystery,' she echoed, 'just one little boy and you. Or maybe two little children and you...'

Erika said nothing.

～

The demonstration train, now in finished condition with its paint gleaming, luxurious fittings in place and embossed badges proudly resplendent, had been coupled together for the first time. Hoskins, Epp, Franz and their team of engineers were inside, checking all was ready for the test run. Departure from the Landsberger was scheduled for 19.36.

The journey included a rehearsal for the celebration meal. The chefs and their kitchen assistants were also on board, making preparations, and had no idea that a few feet away behind wooden panelling Claudia lay prone on a bed of rough blankets and sacking collected over the past week from all corners of the depot.

She was alone. Peter had wanted to do the test run but she refused. 'I'll do it,' she insisted. 'I want to know just what I'm going to be putting my little ones through.'

She shifted position, lying first one way, then another. The carpentry was unforgiving. The smell of new timber might have been tolerable had it not been for the pungent combination of many new paints and a shimmer of dust to plague her confined air space. She had masked her entry using a crafty rearrangement of obstructions. The workshop was a constant muddle of machinery and equipment. Time dragged, waiting for departure. Voices became more strident on the other side of the panelling. Her position close up to the kitchen provided one of the bigger hides Igor and his carpenters had constructed. She looked at her watch, expecting the usual timetable precision, when suddenly there was a massive jerk. This threw her head-long from her blanketed alcove right across the rough floorboards.

She lay still, fearful the noise had alerted someone on the other side of the woodwork. She waited. Would they begin investigating?

Departure time had obviously been brought forward. The

train began to move. It was 18.44. She was conscious of the whining of motors, of mysterious grating sounds, accompanied by a gentle swaying motion. Plenty to cause distraction to the people in the kitchen. Speed increased and the wheel noise grew from a hum to a howl.

Claudia breathed out. Overlaying the din was the occasional metallic clash of pots and pans. The kitchen staff were clearly focused on the business of the day. A full menu was to be worked, only tonight there would be no VIP guests, merely a grateful train crew. Fine for them.

She thought again of Peter. He had wanted to accompany her but she insisted the risk of discovery was ever present and that it would be foolish to risk them both.

Her mind went back over the past couple of days to their hurried preparations: the scrounging of supplies for the journey, the washing and smartening up of the children; new clothes, new bandages, extra coats and scarves, cushioning material and the assembly of snack meals for the hours of confinement.

The train was picking up speed. Despite the wheel racket the chefs were becoming noisier. Kitchen utensils were being clanged about and someone was attempting to sing snatches of 'Ave Maria'. A high-pitched voice seemed to be exhorting the crew to greater effort. She had anticipated confinement and discomfort but not the high volume of noise. Being so low seemed to magnify the racket from the wheels, plus the rush, whistles and hoots of passing trains. Strangely quaint was the intrusion of distant church bells into this world of bedlam. Pace increased again, evident from a more pronounced swaying. She was also hit by a pungent odour that could only be a lineside cheese factory and alarm at the acrid smell of burning, the ignition somewhere of some quite unpleasant material.

The cold would be a problem for her young ones. Draughts kept her shivering. The children would need extra layers and some greater form of insulation. She couldn't expect more from the wives; they were already giving what they could. It was obvious they would need to widen the search, scour every workshop and outhouse, trawl other depots. This was the message she would take back to Peter and Erika.

She began to long for the end of this ordeal so she could crawl out when all was clear and slip away unnoticed into the outbuildings of the Landsberger. She dreamed of a soothing bath; of the simple pleasure of sitting upright in a chair.

But she had to wait for her opportunity and that wasn't to be for several more hours.

26

They had arranged to meet in the wheel drop foreman's hut, a tacked-on brick and corrugated iron addition to the old roundhouse. Erika's component store was now considered too risky a place for a rendezvous. Claudia was fingering her locket, twisting the chain, caressing the smooth surface of the tiny gold heart. Her release from the test train had been an agonisingly long and tedious affair. She was still bruised, aching and tetchy but she now had much more to think about than the requirement for extra blankets and insulation material.

Hoskins had been in touch.

The door of the hut swung open and she looked up to see Peter enter. This was the moment, she decided, when she would be tougher and more resilient. 'I've made a decision,' she said, before he had time to sit. She ignored his surprise. 'Hoskins wants to see me again. Keeps inviting me places. Restaurants, his villa.' She made a face. 'And now he wants me to join his VIP party on the train to Switzerland.'

A sharp intake of breath, then Peter asked, 'As a VIP guest?'

'His personal guest, yes.'

'Problem!'

She nodded. 'If I say yes, how can I be with the children, down inside the carriages and hidden away with them?'

He considered. 'You can't say no.'

'I know. Refusal would put his back up. And we need to keep him sympathetic.'

'Absolutely. You being with him – actually, it could swing it for us if there's a problem on the journey.'

'Much against my instincts,' she said, 'I've told him yes. So that puts extra pressure on you to care for the kids during the journey.'

Peter was silent for a while, no doubt thinking through the consequences while she thought through her role as a Hank Hoskins guest. Dressy and in the public view. She sighed. She didn't want to socialise. She wanted to be with her children.

'Next problem!' Peter said. 'If I also go into the hides with the kids it'll restrict my activities. I won't be able to control events.'

'No alternative.'

'But I can hardly pop out all of a sudden when needed. I should really have a public presence as part of the train crew, to be there when I'm needed.'

Claudia shrugged. 'Well then, you'll just have to dip in and out as and when you can.'

He went silent and she began thinking about the man sitting on the hard plastic chair next to her. Was she right to trust everything to him? She'd met his partner, Williams, and the conversation had been forthright. 'My boss is riding for a fall!' In Williams' view, Hoskins was a viper, a Nazi fellow traveller who was stringing Peter along.

The man himself, sitting beside her, said, 'Maybe Williams could be roped in to look after the kids.'

'I thought he was going to be the cinema operative, marked out to keep the VIPs off our backs.'

Peter sighed. He was twisting his fingers. So, she thought,

was this man too trusting? Out of his depth? That thought was one that had lain dormant at the back of her mind for some time, but with Williams' uncomfortable perspective ringing in her ears, she began to think that Peter did, indeed, appear to be a most unlikely person for the job. She read in him a taste for adventure without the necessary ruthlessness. There was a boyish naivety about him, she thought, much like her own brother. Mothers' boys the pair of them.

'I suppose,' Peter said, 'we could have a rota. Check out each hide, say every half hour.'

'Possible,' she said, and looked about her in disgust at this junk-filled hut with its strange and unfathomable metal shapes clamped to the wall. Rust, dust, clinker and dirt. It permeated everywhere around the depot and contrasted with the spartan cleanliness of her own apartment. And since she couldn't stand any more of the sooty squalor Peter had imposed on her in this abhorrent place she did what she never did – what she told herself was absolutely out of the question.

She invited him home.

Williams reluctantly acquiesced in his unexpected role as Pied Piper. He took the kids food, blankets, coats and sacking, but he lacked Peter's linguistic connection as well as his repertoire of nursery stories. However, he was pleased to discover during his stay at the depot that the VIP train was a lettuce leaf full of holes. There were places on that train you could hide a body. A body that might be Hoskins.

Better still, the new arrangements included a nursing station with a fully-equipped set of cubicles for passenger emergencies. White coats for the operatives, basic first-aid equipment, blankets, a stretcher and more.

Williams' pack contained two special items. One was the Welrod, the other a canister containing a large hypodermic needle and a phial of liquid, the exact nature of which he didn't know or enquire.

'Enough to make him very sick for twenty-four hours,' Dansey had said back in London. 'Should be more than enough for your purposes.' And he talked about a fever case needing to be moved to the local hospital. 'A treble dose, mind, now that could be terminal.' The conversation concluded with a stage wink and a reference to secrecy and the need to know.

Such as it was, this was the fall back.

He looked at his watch and thought about the departure date: Monday the 25th. Two days to go.

'So Pyotr, or is it Sepp... how do you come to be here?' she said with a grin. Claudia's mood had changed. She seemed less remote, more assured amid the familiarity of her home.

'Peter, please,' he said. 'You know those others are just my code names.'

She smiled. 'Peter.'

She'd turned on her radio. The Berlin Philharmonic was playing a Beethoven symphony. 'I'd really like to know,' she said. 'Here you are in Germany, in Munich, mixed up in all this. How does a Winton man get involved in military sabotage?'

He grinned. 'Do you have anything to drink?'

'Sorry,' she said, 'I'm a miser when it comes to coffee. Hogging it all to myself. Gold dust to everyone in this country, you understand.'

'Fine, I won't ask for tea then.'

She was looking in a cupboard. 'Jagermeister, apple schnapps or apple juice?'

'What's that first one?'

'Herbal liqueur.'

'I'll take the schnapps.'

While she organised the glasses, he glanced at her wind-up gramophone and the record labels. Top orchestras and opera singers like Christel Goltz and Heinrich Schlusnus. 'Very highbrow!'

'Not entirely. I'm big on Zarah Leander and 'The Merry Widow', even 'Falling in Love Again'.'

'Ah, the ubiquitous Dietrich.'

Then he examined her 'people's receiver', one of the Goebbels radio sets that were turned out in their thousands and made of Bakelite and cardboard with little swastikas on the tuner knobs.

'Can't you cover them up?'

She shook her head. 'Too risky!' And pointing downstairs, added, 'Snoops.'

Despite her outward familiarity, there was still a distance between them. Peter felt himself to be under another kind of interrogation while sitting on her kitchen chair. He knew his first visit to her flat was something special. She'd guarded her privacy fiercely, and a stealthy entrance had been necessary to ensure his presence went unnoticed. He gulped back the schnapps, saw her quizzical expression and said, 'Why me? That's what you're saying, isn't it? A Winton worker but I'm not exactly what you expected.'

'True,' she said, 'I sense something different about you. In fact, you don't add up.'

He was taken aback. 'Meaning?'

'Meaning you don't seem the ruthless do-or-die soldier type.'

'Maybe,' he said. 'Not my natural forte, but I'm here partly because of my background in civil engineering. I'm familiar with railway technology, you see, been around it all my life, at least the conventional sort.'

She looked at him closely. 'Somehow, you don't strike me as an engineer, either.'

He laughed. 'So what does an engineer look like? I assure you, it's true. My family has been in it for years, it's the natural outlet, I'm all but signed up as an apprentice at the big works when this war is over. Been brought up with it, the railway is all around us in our little town.'

She nodded and said, 'Then tell me about your family. It's a different world. I'm intrigued.'

'And yours? Fair exchange?' he said.

She shrugged. Less than an agreement, but probably all he was going to get. He wasn't sure how to read her and wondered if his presence in her flat represented an improvement in their relationship. Ever since he'd discovered she was the Prague heroine with the pink carnation he'd been in awe of her. And he soon found himself abandoning all caution and talking about the Chesham family household in Bury – about father, connections with the company and his pre-planned career path; about his mother, the *Kindertransports*, the refugees, about the many friends in amateur dramatics, about the joyful experiences that seemed to irritate his father. 'He has no time for the stage, for theatrical costume and fancy dress.' Peter stopped suddenly on mentioning his father once again. He hadn't meant to be so open.

'Sounds to me,' she said, 'that you're compensating for a harsh childhood. Trying to please a dominant father but craving approval from your mother for the things that really matter to you. Look, I've seen you with the kids. My crazy ones. You're a natural. Nursery rhymes, stories. Maybe you should be an actor. But better still, a teacher, not an engineer.'

He laughed. 'A teacher! That would please the old man!'

'All this fatalism, resignation about your future,' she said, almost crossly. 'You seem to be drifting helplessly into a career you don't want, just to please him.'

'That's what someone else said. Going into the workshops would be like disappearing into a black hole.'

'And she was right!' She pointed a knowing finger. 'It was a she who said that, wasn't it?'

Peter's rueful grin confirmed it, acknowledging her perceptiveness. Gabrielle it was who said it. He remembered the words. The black hole, the dark dungeons she had called the long line of ill-lit wooden sheds down by the station. 'You don't want that,' Gabrielle had told him one afternoon when they were examining his colourful jackets. 'Never again cut a dash in a smart suit! Forget the blazers and the waistcoats! Work in that gloomy place? With all those boring men in greasy overalls, baggy slacks, dirty hands, filthy fingernails? Grubby faces and sweaty armpits.'

He laughed ruefully at the memory of that conversation and then noticed Claudia's intense expression.

'You're an only child,' she said. It was more a statement of fact than a question.

'But not anymore,' Peter replied brightly, downing his glass, 'now that young Hannah has arrived from Prague I have a sister!'

Mention of Prague seemed to stop Claudia in her tracks.

'And what about you?' he said, 'why teaching?'

There was a silence before she said, 'I suppose it's also a form of compensation.'

He shrugged, bewildered, but she looked away and rose to clear away the glasses and he guessed that was all he was going to get. There was still a distance between them. She was keeping herself contained. She was erecting a wall. However close he wanted to get to her, however powerful her draw, she was running and hiding and holding him at bay.

Should he persist?

The dilemma of what to do next was solved in a way neither expected.

~

'Bad news,' Erika announced when she had been ushered in. Her knock at Claudia's door had caused consternation until a twitch of the curtains had revealed her identity. 'I've come to warn you,' she told Claudia, 'to stay away from the stores.'

Voss, it seemed, had already acted, sending a snoop to 'assist' Erika in her duties.

'Soon sussed him,' Erika said, 'asks too many questions. Trying to be casual but I got out of him that you'd been seen out in the streets late at night. They've noticed you, Claudia, time to be invisible. Don't be seen again at the depot.'

Claudia clenched a fist. 'Father Ostler, I knew he was a danger. Just a common informer! You can't trust anyone, not even a priest.'

'What have you done about your stool pigeon,' Peter asked Erika.

'Spun him a nice story. He wants to know what's going on, so I've hinted at the black market. A drip, drip of little morsels. Tomorrow I'll say it's coffee then, Dallmayr, then there's a big consignment of the stuff coming in on the day after you're due away.'

No one spoke. Each considered the consequences and dangers of increased suspicion and heightened security and how they might cope. Claudia would have to use the hole in the Maze wire. The silence was broken by another knock at the door.

This time it was their cop in civilian clothes. Officer Weber, the man who had given Claudia such a scare on that first day.

'More trouble?' Erika demanded.

'Just got word.' The cop drew in a deep breath. He'd been hurrying. 'They've changed the day for the Reichsmarschall's parade. Advanced it forty-eight hours because of some problem with Goering's diary.'

Claudia looked stricken, clutching a hand to her forehead. 'Oh no!'

Weber nodded. ''Fraid so. It's a clash. Both events on Monday.'

She said, 'Our departure day! I'll never be able to get away.'

'Go sick,' Peter said immediately.

She shook her head. 'They're watching me at school. Like tigers waiting for a kill. It's so important to them, they're manic, they'll check up on me. I'll never get away with such an obvious excuse.'

Peter was reassuring. 'Don't worry, our departure time is early in the morning, we'll be away before they miss you.'

She shook her head. 'You don't understand,' she said, 'they have early callers too, we're not the only early starters. They'll be around my door before five in the morning, knocking me up to make sure I'm ready. Probably escort me. I won't be able to escape them. They're onto me, they know I hate it, they're persecuting me over this damned parade.'

'Then stay in the Maze overnight,' Peter suggested.

But she would not be mollified. 'If I try a dodge like that they'll suspect it's got something to do with our train and come looking. Maybe force a cancellation or delay. Search the train.' She shook her head. 'This gets worse!'

Heads dropped.

Then Erika spoke. 'Never fear!' The confidence of a woman who dealt in solutions. 'We'll think of something.'

One day to go.

~

They were clustered around the warm stove in the fridge car. Runner's sores had been soothed, Eagle's cuts bandaged and supper had been dispensed: thicker-than-usual potato soup with hunks of bread. Claudia and Peter were both present and the children were quiet, expectant. They'd picked up on an unspoken sense of purpose between the adults. It was understood among them all that there was to be a talk.

As bowls were grounded and the meal finished all eyes turned to Peter but it was Claudia who spoke.

'I've got something to tell you,' she said. This was a statement of ownership. These were her children, this was her moment, she was in charge. 'I wanted us all to be here so you could share this together.' She took a deep breath, almost a sigh. 'We're going on a journey. A long one, and we're not coming back.'

Complete silence. No one asked why or where. The atmosphere was charged. Only the little ones did not realise this statement would define their lives and futures – if they had a chance of either. All their besieged existence in the Maze these past few weeks had led to this moment.

She said, 'We're going to leave this place – not because you've done anything wrong. No, no, far from it.' She opened her palms in a gesture of conciliation. 'You've been wonderful, so good at keeping hidden and staying quiet.' She took another deep breath. 'But you can't go on living here like this for ever. We have to try to get away to a better place.'

Runner was the first one to find his voice. 'Is this why we've had these lessons? To speak English?'

Claudia nodded. 'We have to get you out of this country because you're not really safe here. You know that, don't you? You've all got reasons to know that.'

A tiny voice, almost a wail. Little Ingrid. 'I don't want to go, I'm frightened.'

'Can't we stay?' Anna, a pleading expression.

Claudia adopted her most reassuring manner. The teacher who comforted, who would keep everyone safe. A difficult task when explaining peril without causing an outbreak of fright. 'I'm afraid it's not really as safe here as it's been in the past,' she said. 'So far, we've done well, really well, but as time goes on it becomes less so. It means we can't stay. We must move as soon as we're ready.'

'This other place?' Runner again. 'An enemy country?'

'Not to those who seek shelter, as you are doing.'

Another voice, Blondie: 'Who'll look after us in this new place?'

'A new set of mummies and daddies who are waiting for you to arrive.'

Ingrid: 'I want my old mummy. Why did she leave me?'

Before Claudia could respond Frieda asked, 'Will I get to have nice things? Do they eat *bratwurst* there? And *bratkartoffeln*?'

'Kind of.'

Eagle had a deep frown. 'How will we go? I mean, without them spotting us and taking us away.'

Claudia smiled and pointed. 'Pyotr here will explain all that in a moment.'

'What games will we play?' Blondie wanted to know about her new life. 'Can we go to the park again?'

And the others followed. 'Can we go to the pictures again?' asked Leo.

Beakie: 'And a new school?'

Claudia spread her arms and smiled. 'Yes, yes, yes... and now I'm going to take you all outside and teach you a new game for a new park.'

Peter, who had remained silent all this time, murmured, 'Intriguing. And what game might that be?'

She shot him a quick mischievous grin. 'Jealous? One you couldn't possibly have heard of or know anything about.'

'Like?'

'Cricket.'

~

Drexler thought he had scored a great hit. Claudia not merely acknowledged him, she approached him in the drill room where he was helping to organise drum kits and banners, ready for the great day.

'Karl, I wonder if you'd be interested. Friends of mine are having a party.'

He grinned. So, his expression said, our session with the locket in the staffroom and the mystery of the baby's face have not only melted the ice maiden, they've also got me an invitation. 'What sort of party?'

'An eve-of-parade celebration. To mark the big day. A beer party. My friends brew their own and they're very keen to try out a new recipe.'

'A welcome change of attitude.'

She smiled and gave him the sparkling eyes. 'It'll be quite different from what you're used to. They asked me for some volunteer tasters who'd be willing to give their opinion and I immediately thought of you.'

'If you're going...' he said.

'Of course.'

~

Erika's courtyard was decked out with three strands of red, black and yellow bunting, a couple of picnic tables and a mini-barrel with tap and slop bucket located at a small trestle. Several mugs and litre glasses were placed ready. Papa Koller and Hugo Schnee from the depot had not taken much persuading; they already had full glasses. Claudia herself was at an upstairs window, watching out for the approach along the Landsberger of her new-found friend. She had already made her other move, persuading the one teacher colleague she trusted to take her place in the parade next morning. Hubert Techtow, an historian who could talk fascinatingly about the life of Napoleon, was as dismissive as she of the myths of an ancient Aryan civilisation and other National Socialist fantasies. Claudia had once stifled a giggle on learning that the boys of Techtow's class spent their entire drill lessons playing football. The most important thing, however, was that the teacher committee should not know he had taken her place in the parade until it was too late for them to react. It was necessary that their entire attention be directed elsewhere.

Her thoughts were interrupted by a shout.

'He's coming!'

Claudia moved to the door.

'Karl, how lovely of you to come.'

The smile was wide, the arms welcoming. 'Come in and meet everyone.' She guided him through the house into the courtyard, steering him to a table sizzling with frying bratwursts, pans of pommes frites and pots of mayonnaise. 'Just the thing to start the evening off.'

'I know why you're doing this,' he said through large mouthfuls, 'why so friendly all of a sudden, why you've changed your tune. You don't want me to tell.'

She stood in front of him, hands on hips. 'We've got off on

the wrong foot, Karl, that's awful. Time to make a new start. Colleagues should be on good terms.'

A sly smile, then he looked around. 'Not many people, not many girls.'

'This is something special,' she said. 'We invite only three tasters at a time. Would you like to start? The brew's a dark hop and the strength eight per cent. Can you cope with that?'

'Of course I can cope with that. No problem!'

She already knew from her police contact, Officer Weber, that Drexler and his Brownshirts habitually boasted of their drinking prowess, of their bottomless capacity for the dark-brown stuff, the double *dunkel* of the city's speciality brewers. Claudia worked the tap, filling a grey porcelain stein with the new brew, handing him his drink with a wide smile.

Drexler drank, nodded guardedly, gulped some more, nodded again. 'Not bad, not bad at all.'

'Let me top you up,' she said.

'You still haven't said. Who's the child in the locket?'

But she didn't answer, running a finger along the Sam Browne belt strap across his chest, as if she now approved of the uniform she once found so distasteful. Then she gave him the sparkling smile once more.

He gulped, a picture of anticipation.

You're playing a risky game, Erika had warned her before the party, but Claudia was determined. She needed Drexler to be the focus of attention at tomorrow's parade.

'I still might tell,' he said slyly, enjoying the moment.

Claudia nodded as if in agreement, turning to refill his drink. Her body obscured his view of the tap as she said, 'But we can be friends, Karl, can't we?'

'Oh yes,' he said with relish, 'we can be friends,' and that was when she slipped the contents of a little sachet of white powder into his stein.

27

They stole aboard like little warriors, hand in hand, silent, stealthy, not a whisper, not a hesitation. Peter led the way, his pairings deliberate: Runner holding onto little Anna, Eagle with Frieda, Cheetah with Walter, and Beakie with Leo; each hide leader in charge of a younger child.

This was Monday, November the 25th, the big day of Hoskins's demonstration, and it began in the dark before dawn, long before anyone at the depot had stirred. Peter and Claudia led the children Indian file out of the Maze, not daring to use torchlight, guiding their way by feel and familiarity with the landscape. Down the long tunnel they went, under the railway tracks and through a rear door into the overseer's empty office.

Peter glanced briefly through a window at the shape of the resplendent new train, locked and immobile in the immensely tall shed. It was ghostly and, quite unlike every other occasion on which he had seen it, chillingly silent.

Igor, their collaborator from the carriage works, was already in the overseer's room, the wide floor space clear of its usual detritus. As the children entered, there were chalk lines marked out in rows headed by cardboard signs, each bearing a number, one to five.

Dressed in top coats and hats and clutching sandwich bags, they sat cross-legged on the floor below window level. The order was complete silence. No chattering, no footsteps. Claudia had drummed it into them. All fully prepared and knowing what to expect, with animal names for hides, leaders assigned to teams and the ultimate prize kept keenly in mind.

At a signal from Peter, Runner and his team rose and crept silently through the door, along a gangway, past a set of wheels and under an open hatch. This was the baggage car. This was Dog, Hide No.1.

Runner scrambled in first, looking around, deciding his position. There were slabs of the bright blue *Breitspurbahn* moquette cushioning and strips of carpet laid on a wooden floor with enough head room for Runner to crawl in and find a back rest against a beam. He beckoned to Anna to follow, apportioning her a place, followed by Ingrid carrying a faded brown satchel containing crayons, picture puzzle books, games and soft toys, nothing metallic or wooden allowed. Fat Fonzie came next with a bag of cakes and Blondie with the sandwich bags.

'All set?' Peter whispered, peering in from the outside, studying the irregular shapes before him: alcoves, nooks and recesses filled with pipes and cables. He kept a cheery face and a reassuring manner but doubts began to form over their stamina for the ordeal to come. The children had one sleeping bag between them and would take turns, the little girls two at a time, with hours to snooze before the train moved. The journey would be short but the wait would be long. Could they make it? Anna managed a wan little smile and a wave and Peter whispered, 'Remember, no noise, complete silence all the way until you're called, just like we told you, okay?'

It was a reminder he would repeat at all five hides. He had

worried about a timid child creating a scene, of refusing to enter, backing up to a catastrophic traffic jam, but clearly Claudia had instilled sufficient discipline to avoid this kind of chaos.

Runner gave him a double thumbs up. Frightened faces, little people trying to be brave. Reluctant nods.

These kids were tough, he assured himself again. These kids would make it.

He closed the hatch door, clicking it into place with a key turner, supplied by Igor. This gadget would gain him entry to all the hides.

The same silent routine was followed with Eagle and his team scrambling into Giraffe at the side of the restaurant car, Cheetah into Cat in the cinema car, Beakie into Horse in the lounge car and Mole into Lion under the kitchens.

With all the children settled Peter was pensive. Claudia had done a thorough job on discipline: instant obedience throughout the journey. She had also done her best for the time beyond this day, teaching first aid, cooking, mending and English. 'They have to speak the language of their future,' she said. 'This country, sadly, is now their past.'

The operation had been a rush – the scrounging, the collection of supplies, the scrubbing, washing and smartening up of the children – conducted below the scrutiny of preparations for Reichsmarschall Goering's parade. She'd been losing sleep, leading a double life, spending night hours in the Maze while school days were occupied in acting out the part of an Aryan princess she would never play, dressing her class in fake outfits and decorating the float in the absurd trappings of a bogus history. She felt sad she couldn't risk warning her day children she would be absent from the parade. Now, in the silence of the pre-dawn, Claudia came close and frowned at Peter. 'I'm worried about Drexler,' she said.

'Don't be.'

'There'll be a great frenzy when they find I'm gone. And when Drexler wakes up he's going to be a very angry bear with a very sore head.'

Peter shook his head. They'd laid out Claudia's unconscious antagonist the night before amid the drum kits and flags in the school stores, delivered late in the evening using a closed railway parcel van. 'He won't be coming after you and he won't be going on any parade,' Peter said. 'All the angst will be directed at him for messing up their big day. Erika assures me, he'll be out of action for hours. A clever woman, your Erika.'

She felt empty. Hollowed out and consumed by fears. Powerless now to help her children. Claudia had always expected she would join them in the hides to share their ordeal, allay their fears and comfort them during their long incarceration. But now another role had been forced on her as Hoskins's guest.

She left the shed, knowing that soon Hoskins, Franz, Voss and their team of engineers would be arriving to check all was ready. Shortly after, the train staff would move to their positions: conductors, waiters, hairdressers, cocktail bar attendants, nurses and a host of ancillary staff. Departure from Landsberger was due at seven. And all through these preparations the children would have to remain completely silent. Could they do it? Was she expecting too much?

She thought too about the tearful farewell with Erika the night before. They had clung together for several minutes, each about to embark on fateful and uncertain journeys. When she thought of all they had shared – the risks, the endeavour, the intense commitment – it seemed a cruel twist that they would never meet again. But given the toxic atmosphere that would envelop the depot the next day, this was accepted and they did not speak of it. Still, Claudia was intrigued by her friend's involvement with events 'on the other side of the tracks' and the mystery of her means of exit. And the departure wasn't confined to Erika and Dieter. There were two more ragged and starving strays – teenage Rosa, who'd been living under the staircase of a water tower, and nine-year-old Alfred, inside the arches of a railway tunnel. Erika's parting comment: 'I live for the day when this nightmare is over.'

By now Claudia was due at the city's main station to join the select band of high-profile guests. She had never before mixed in such company. What did you talk about to the functionaries of a regime you detested? She still feared repercussions from her absence from the Goering parade – and then there was Hoskins, the sympathetic man she had dined with at the Café Luitpold expressing concern for 'victims of the system' but who still insisted on devoting all his considerable powers to promoting the *Breitspurbahn* project. She wondered if he still trusted her or if he had guessed her connection with Peter.

She breathed in deeply, trying to calm her nerves. She still wore her locket, twisting it continuously between her fingers.

A special VIP lounge had been installed at the *Hauptbahnhof* so the main party could join the train at the city terminus when it had been shunted in from the depot. Claudia eased past all the private function notices and pushed open the door, wearing her hat with a fresh carnation and her one and only party piece, the purple dress with the cream and lilac brocade, the one she'd worn to dine with Hoskins at the Café Luitpold. Inside the lounge it was all gilt and dark-wood panelling. At first, she recognised no one. Drinks were being served by uniformed waiters and she took one, if only to look the part. Then she spotted Hoskins at the centre of a large crowd. They were listening intently as he spoke.

She moved forward to the fringe of the group and Hoskins recognised her, quick to react, breaking off immediately. Faces turned, eyes focused on her as he came to her. She had a fleeting glimpse of cold stares, appraising looks, hints of jealousy at one so young and slim.

'Wonderful,' he said, grinning broadly, a hand on her arm. 'So glad you could come.'

She ignored the others and gave him one of her sad smiles.

He said, 'The dress is lovely. And the hat.'

In a low voice she said, 'You've seen it before. The best a poor teacher can manage.'

'You'd look good in anything, but you look especially good in that.'

Someone asked Hoskins a question and he looked away to answer.

'And who are you?' An imperious demand, flung at Claudia from a large woman clinking with rows of beads, bangles and necklaces. If not an interloper, the tone implied, then someone who did not quite fit.

Hoskins broke off his conversation and slid an arm around Claudia's waist. 'She's my special friend and guest for the day,' he said.

A knowing look passed across the woman's face and Claudia gritted her teeth. She did not enjoy the role in which they had cast her.

But then, did these people matter if she had his protection? She was relieved that his welcome appeared enthusiastic but her doubts persisted. Had he seen the light? Did he suspect her? Would he defect – or would he betray?

∼

Peter kept well back in the shadows for the ceremonial departure from the city's main station. The train, Hoskins's new hydrogen locomotive was festooned in black, red and white bunting topped off with a giant swastika flag. Bands played as Schumann, the city's gauleiter, cut a tape. Bombastic notices around the station proclaimed the inaugural international journey of the great new *Breitspurbahn*.

Most of the crew were happy to join the welcome party to show off their smart new uniforms – a bright red jacket worn over a dark blue waistcoat – but Peter, conscious of the heavy police presence, kept his back turned, checking dials and equipment. The security detail manifested all its attention on the station concourse and the throng of onlookers. Clearly the train itself, with its closely controlled guest list, was regarded as secure, but Peter still had to beware of Voss and Franz who were expected to be on board. He was relieved when the whistles blew and the train moved off. Having taken on board its party of Nazi notables, it left amid much pomp. He became aware of a slight rocking motion as it picked up speed and left the city through the western outskirts. He began to patrol the corridors, anxious that his hidden human cargo should not have been frightened by all the noise and commotion at the station. So far, however, Claudia's regime of discipline appeared to be holding.

He looked out of the window, aware that what might appear to be a modest speed of perhaps forty miles an hour would probably turn out to be twice or three times that much. He looked at his watch and calculated. He had been in the Caller's office to consult the maps and knew the route: at full speed, if they managed it – 350 kilometres an hour, it was claimed – it would take less than an hour to reach the Swiss frontier. Please! He issued a silent plea to the hidden children: just hang on!

Claudia passed Hoskins in the corridor, this time a smile their only contact, and again the agony of not knowing if he would defect.

She stalked the corridors, listening, fearing, hoping. How long could the children last? Few adults would cope with such a cramped and uncomfortable journey and some of her brood were as young as six. Almost babies! What a torment she was putting them through. She shook her head, stricken by guilt, but knew her job was to mix with the other guests, playing the Engineer's favourite.

She forced herself to make an appearance in the VIP lounge. They were all there, drinking in the luxury, the privilege and the alcohol. Wall-to-wall waiters revolved around the room like a human conveyor belt dispensing cocktails – 'have the latest from America, a champagne punch' – dark chocolate and pistachio truffle cakes and peach melba tartlets. A pianist tinkled gently under the glass roof which flooded the place with natural light, the sky seeming to skim past at an astonishing rate, but few appeared to notice amid the clink of glasses and bright chatter. Scented candles and silver teapots were trinket gifts on a side table. The transport minister's wife was next door having her hair done, the assistant's wife a new set of nails and the minister himself was one car away in a deep steam tub.

Claudia found an empty armchair – the moquette had changed, she noticed, from standard blue to a deep red. The big woman with the beads was holding centre stage. Blonde tresses were piled high and a display of lipstick and thick rouge were a clear defiance of the regime's fashion rules. But then most of the wives of the top Nazis defied them. It was common knowledge, a joke that did the rounds. Propaganda minister Josef Goebbels had been forced to sack his own wife from her editorial position at the Nazi fashion magazine for ignoring party dictates. She preferred Paris fashions.

Claudia looked closer. The blonde, whispered to be the wife of works minister Fritz Todt, wore an expensive blue afternoon dress with batwing arms and a large bow tied at the waist. Flaunting her wealth – and so in love with herself she kept on her high-brimmed hat and red silk gloves even in the heated carriage.

Todt himself was the real star. His were the work gangs that laid the track. At the far end of the bar, looking hunted and hawk-like from beneath beetle brows, was the Fuhrer's personal representative, Reich minister Rudolf Hess. A social misfit if ever she saw one.

She frowned then. With Hess present, Claudia wondered, why wasn't her grotesque hate figure, the ghastly Reichsmarschall Goering, also on the train? Then, of course, she realised. He, as the gilded representative of German aviation, would never have lowered himself to glorify a mere railway train, however feted.

Claudia gave little away in conversation beyond generating the necessary enthusiasm for the big occasion. Finally, she could bear the contrast no longer: the luxury versus the sawdust and unforgiving boxlike carpentry of the children's hides. When heads were turned she rose and slipped away.

Peter couldn't stay in the shadows for ever. He had to act normally as part of the train crew, moving along the corridor, nerves sharp and raw. He kept his expression blank, masking an accelerating heartbeat. Out from the safety of the depot bunkhouse and into the open under the gaze of party officials, guests and railway personnel, he had only the uniform and his change of appearance to protect him. He was counting heavily on the invisibility of the new outfit and its flamboyant sash, expecting outsiders to pick up on the bright colours and overlook the man. 'Flunkeys are dehumanised, become part of the furniture,' his instructor at Fulbrough had said when lauding the role of waiter as a suitable disguise. 'No one ever sees the face, only the fancy dress.' Could the *Breitspurbahn* uniform, created to promote the new train, do the trick? Peter looked down at the waistcoat, embossed on the left breast with the initials B-B in gold, and at the gaudy pink sash. At the bright yellow lettering announcing '*B-B*, the world's first super-train' in French as well as German.

He'd persuaded Williams to borrow scissors to give him a Prussian-short haircut but couldn't do more. Voss knew what he looked like.

He walked purposefully into the restaurant car, stopping at each end to record on his clipboard the readings on the vacuum brake dials, testing the interior panels on his vibration meter and averting his gaze from the danger zones. Don't meet the eyes! Don't look into the faces. Don't engage the interest of the inquisitive or the suspicious.

Instead, he nodded to one of his new colleagues, young Otto from Leipzig, a man too lame for the forces, and another anonymous member of staff, and was rewarded with a grin and a nod from both. With the train crew, Peter was everyone's friend. He'd worked on this the evening before, insinuating himself into a discreet eve-of-departure staff party as Sepp Bauer, the new man from Stuttgart.

In the lounge car he held his breath, hearing the voices of Franz, Hoskins and Voss but without seeing them, proceeding with his pantomime inspection, checking for faults in the new system and monitoring progress. What he was really looking for were signs of distress from below. How were the children faring in their cramped and uncomfortable hides? Most probably bored, hungry, tired and frightened. Had he and Claudia overestimated their endurance?

'You there!'

Peter swallowed, dropped his eyes from the panelling and focused reluctantly on a finger-pointing VIP. The clipboard felt sweaty in his grasp, the restaurant car hot and clammy.

'How can I help, sir?'

'Another glass of champagne.'

Peter nodded, backed away and directed the nearest waiter. He passed through another passenger car, picking up snatches of conversation about coffee, the price of sugar and the soaring divorce rate. Later, back in the restaurant car, all was quiet, dining complete, and Peter decided to risk breaking cover, knocking three times on a panel to check on progress in the hide called Giraffe.

Mistake! Almost immediately it slid back, a loud childish wail made him jump and he hurriedly shushed the tearful complainer. When he looked closely, he wasn't surprised. Little Frieda. She was constantly close to tears. 'My back hurts and I want to come out.'

'Think of your new mummy and daddy,' Peter whispered. 'They're waiting for you at the end of the journey... they'd want you to be a good girl, to stay quiet and safe.'

More tears.

'Sweets,' he said to Eagle, who was nominally in charge but looked more like a parent fed up with trying to mollify the most obstinate of offspring.

'Why did I get stuck with her?' the boy complained. 'She just won't listen, keeps going on and on.'

'It's your job,' Peter retorted, more urgently than he intended. 'Do you want us all to be caught? Sent away like your parents?'

Eagle shook his head and Peter reproached himself for the

harsh tone. These were young fugitives who had lost their parents in the most traumatic of circumstances. He forced a smile.

Then came the dare. 'You should try it!'

Eagle, fed up with being in charge of Giraffe, was provoked into the challenge.

How to respond? A dictum leapt into Peter's mind – what the instructor told officer trainees at Fulbrough: 'Never ask anyone to do anything you can't do yourself... at least as well, and preferably better.'

Peter looked behind, then lowered himself into the hide. He knew it wouldn't be pleasant but the reality was an ordeal. Shoved up tight in the only vacant space, he found his head jammed against a beam.

He closed his eyes to blot out a moment of panic. The roaring and vibration were insistent. The whirr of the wheels sounded just inches away; screeching and howling, reducing his hearing to a great mush. He couldn't rid himself of the image of wheels as shears or guillotines. Might they not come crashing through the woodwork? This cave was a thunderbox with a battering effect on the brain. How could he have put the young ones through this?

He managed to turn to view the rest of it. A bigger space for them, thankfully, but Frieda was still crying, her clothing awry, one finger bloody where she'd scraped it on a rough edge, crayons and books scattered about. Peter edged away, achieving an upright posture. He felt in his pockets, found a bar of chocolate and some biscuits acquired from the riches on offer in the VIP lounge. 'Here,' he said to Eagle, 'work some magic with these. And tell her a story.'

Eagle didn't look like a storyteller.

'I'll be back to see you later,' Peter said, 'with more.' Every nursery rhyme he'd ever known had fled from his head.

He sighed and raised himself from the hide to climb back into the corridor.

Then froze.

Otto was in the corridor, staring at him like a scared rabbit.

Peter slid the panel shut, cutting off the childish cries, shutting down Giraffe once more, then rose and smiled.

'Don't worry,' he said, 'just some little kids who stowed away. No bother, I'll deal with them at the other end.'

Otto began to stutter. 'But we should report this...'

'Leave it to me, no need to create a fuss.'

'But we can't just ignore them and walk away.'

Peter shook his head. 'We don't want to cause a commotion, not with all our guests on board, now do we? No harm done and don't worry, you haven't seen anything.'

Otto still looked dubious. 'Don't involve me in any of this.'

'Don't worry,' Peter insisted. 'Everything's fine. You didn't see anything,' he repeated, patting Otto on the back reassuringly, turning the young man around. 'Nothing happened here. Just carry on as usual.'

Claudia's frustration increased. Peter was nowhere to be seen. Perhaps he had gone into one of the hides. Perhaps there was trouble.

She retraced her steps towards the VIP lounge, anxiously scanning the faces of the crew, nodding and smiling at those she did not know. She was startled by the drumming of forceful footsteps behind her and quickly found herself overtaken by Hoskins, bustling past with a large folder under his arm.

'Come and listen to this,' he called, giving her a quick smile and holding up his folder. She could see maps and papers as he passed. 'Something of interest.'

Inside the VIP lounge he was a bubble of energy and excitement, captivating his guests. Here was the master of ceremonies on the brink of his greatest triumph. Claudia joined the crowd, doubts building. Could this really be a man about to defect?

He ordered champagne glasses to be refilled, then set up an easel, as if in school, on which he placed a large map of continental Europe. It showed those parts controlled by Germany and her neighbours. His arm swept dramatically along great red slashes over the map. These, he said, represented the new *Breitspurbahn* network, a few short pieces of route already built and operational but dwarfed by the sheer length of the extensions he had planned. These reached out from Berlin through France to Spain, eastwards to Moscow and Asia, south through Yugoslavia and Greece, following the old Berlin-to-Baghdad line to the Middle East. Claudia recalled her staffroom conversations with Techtow, the history buff: the Middle East, the region that had caused so much disturbance in recent times. Revolts, revolution, war.

'Negotiations,' he said, 'are proceeding with our neighbours for these extensions and when completed we will be able to deliver vast numbers of people, freight or armies anywhere we like in a matter of hours.'

A polite round of applause greeted this statement. Hoskins looked up at the faces around him. He was beaming but, Claudia thought, he was also searching. He needed the approval of his audience. His eyes found hers. 'Is that not exciting?' he asked, appearing to put his question directly to her.

She drew in a breath and told herself to play the part. 'Those vast distances!' she said. 'I can't believe the scale of it. Truly fantastic.'

Several faces turned to stare. She had expected adulation for his demonstration, or at least enthusiasm from the party faithful but she saw only a muted response.

This is why he wants me here, she told herself, *he expects this of me, I'm to be his public supporter*. 'A brilliant plan,' she said with as much enthusiasm as she could manage, staring back at the blank faces around her.

Hoskins bustled out of the room, all smiles, with a parting declaration: 'Today will be the decisive day in which we persuade the world to see the future our way.'

In his absence there were a few sober murmurs. She looked at the presentation map. The line to Spain had stalled close to Switzerland and diverted to a transhipment depot at the border. This, she knew, was their destination. She also knew Peter's doubts about Hoskins's scheme: was it credible the Swiss would co-operate? That Josef Stalin would also agree? And then the technical doubts: the sheer scaling up of size presented all kinds of engineering problems. The steam locomotives, he'd told her, were not performing well and used inordinate amounts of precious fuel.

Claudia picked up a quiet but significant murmur of scepticism from Todt and the minister. They had turned away from her. She heard Todt say in a low voice, 'We can't afford electrification, too expensive and uses up too much steel needed for the arms factories.' He patted the polished mahogany of his seat. 'The key to making this thing a practical proposition is his new propulsion unit. So does it perform as well as he claims?'

A shrug of the shoulders, a grunt. Or it could have been a snort.

'And today, we shall see.'

No one paid her any heed. They turned their backs. Claudia's enthusiastic endorsement clearly counted for little among the official party, so she walked quietly from the room, trailing

Hoskins, sensing that he too was on a hair trigger of excitement. His mood was clear. He was ready for action. Clearly, he had made up his mind about what to do and she had to know.

She found him in the compartment he called his control centre. He was alone at a desk, arranging papers, folding maps. Looking up, he said, 'Not far now. Just getting ready for the next announcement. My Swiss audience.' He grinned at her and stood. 'Thanks for what you said in there.'

This was her chance. She had him to herself. The time for subtlety was gone. Time was running out. Time to be direct, to stop the dance and risk him guessing she was part of Peter's scheme.

'Have you thought about what I said?'

His puzzled frown prompted more.

'About victims. About collaboration?'

He grinned. 'Constantly.'

'Made any decisions?'

'Like?'

'Not for me to say.'

'What kind of a decision were you hoping for?'

She allowed a slight smile. Mocking now. 'It can't be for a mere teacher to suggest to so eminent an engineer how to proceed.'

'So coy.' Hoskins smiled back. 'But I think you have a very clear idea.'

A pert expression that could be a question or confirmation or whatever he made of it.

'You wouldn't by any chance,' he asked, 'be in league with someone who wants me to jump ship?'

Now they had reached it. The key moment that meant success or failure. 'Jump ship? What ship? I'm not familiar with this expression.'

'Some friend of yours from another country, perhaps?'

'Now that would be a strange thing to suggest.'

His playful expression was gone. 'Claudia,' he said, looking at her hard, an expression that said he was both serious and concerned, 'it would be a very dangerous thing indeed to become involved in anything like that.'

A sharp pain in her side. How to stay cool? Not to react. Silence her only response.

'Stay with me,' he said gently, 'and you'll be all right.'

'All right?'

'Safe from the ill winds that sometimes blow around these parts.'

Peter, fearful of what was happening in the hides, looked urgently for Claudia, hoping she could share the task of checking on the condition of the children. He found the Lion hide adjoining the kitchens and was relieved when Mole assured him all was well. He blew out his cheeks and looked at a tiny pocket map. At 350 kilometres an hour, it was impossible to read the station names on the adjoining standard gauge track or pick out any significant landmark, but he thought he knew roughly where the train had reached in the race across the territory of the *Oberschwaben*. They'd begun at modest speeds to clear the Munich suburbs but had picked up since then. Just ten or fifteen minutes to go, he thought.

Just hang on in there, kids!

His cover story was to keep the corridors clear, check the vacuum brake dials on the ends of each coach and to make sure the cooks in the kitchen car delivered on time.

His other big problem was Oberscharfuhrer Voss.

Disguise was a trap. A complete disguise, if detected, would earn instant arrest. The highly suspicious Voss had already clocked Peter as the Stuttgart crewman, so cheek pads or moustaches were too obvious and too dangerous. Instead, he relied on the smart *B-B* uniform and gaudy sash, and for the rest, his close-cropped haircut.

But it didn't work.

In the corridor between the kitchens and the restaurant car Peter saw Voss approaching and contrived to adopt a pleasant, innocent expression.

'You!' Voss came to a sudden halt, face flushed, pointing an accusing finger. 'Who let you on board?'

'They chose me.' Peter tweaked his sash, putting on the act of the proud crewman. 'And very privileged I am.'

Voss stood close, glaring into Peter's face. 'That haircut doesn't fool me. I'd know you anywhere. And that phoney accent! You were supposed to return to Stuttgart. I never liked you.'

'I did return, but the rota people thought I'd be good for this job too, so they sent me along and here I am.' At this he tapped the blunt end of a long pencil against his clipboard, angling it so that Voss could see a forest of diagrams and grids.

Voss ignored him. 'There's something wrong about you and I'm going to find out what it is.'

'Please,' Peter said, 'just doing my job. They wanted someone to fill in. A last-minute sickness.'

Voss was grabbing him by the sleeve. 'Never mind that! You're not on my list. Nobody gets to ride this train who's not known on the list. Who's not security cleared.'

Peter twisted away, tapping his clipboard again, looking urgently about. Just in time he spotted a dial. 'You see, it's essential to monitor the brake pressure in each of the coaches. That's my job. Vital to check the safe passage of the train.' He was reaching up, tapping the glass, scribbling down the numbers on his pad. Meaningless numbers to him, but vital numbers all the same. 'Everything's so new, you see.'

Voss stood close. He seemed to be examining every inch of Peter's face. 'I have a feeling about you in my gut. I can feel it. Smell it! I warned you to stay away but you couldn't manage it, could you? But this is too sensitive a place for the likes of you. You're coming with me.'

'I'm part of the team,' Peter insisted. 'Absolutely necessary to do these checks. Everything must work properly. Essential to the safe passage of the train... and you wouldn't want anything to fail now, would you, Oberscharfuhrer? Not on this of all days! Wouldn't look good. Could wreck the whole operation if some fault were to develop.'

Voss was hissing. 'I want you off this train!'

Peter turned away and did a dramatic double take. 'Ah! Just spotted it. The next pressure gauge. Must check.' Pointing toward the end of the coach, he marched off in the direction of his supposed task, leaving Voss behind, open-mouthed and uncertain how to react.

28

The fate of his operation hung on a knife-edge. Peter had seconds, minutes at most, to act. Should he run before Voss reappeared with handcuffs? Disappear into a hide or brazen it out?

He looked at his watch. Perhaps five minutes to go until arrival, at most ten. Play for time, he decided, they'll be distracted when the train stops and has to uncouple. He went for the hare tactic. Race away in a straight line, then double back and hide close, where your pursuer least expects.

Peter was a small-town country boy. He knew about chases, and in this case there was a bonus. Snuggled into a tiny gap behind the parcel office, he was close enough to hear Voss ranting. It was a raucous no-holds blast in full volume. So how would Hoskins react if he was on the point of defection?

'This Bauer!' A pause. 'I want him off the team! He's not to be trusted.'

A softer reply. Hoskins's tone. 'What's the problem?'

'He's trouble. I can smell it. He should be put off at the next stop.'

'Your evidence?'

'Instinct. I just know it. And how did he get on the list? Who chose this man and why?'

'Late replacement.'

'There's something not right about him. That accent. It's not Stuttgart. Like a foreigner. He's not to be trusted.'

A louder reply now, shorter, offhand, dismissive. 'Speak to Franz about it, he's your man.'

Peter let out a deep breath, puzzling over Hoskins's attitude. If he was so dismissive as to shuffle off responsibility for Peter's fate to another functionary, what did that say? He didn't care, a defection not his intention? Or simply a way of avoiding a confrontation with Voss, playing pass the bureaucratic parcel?

Peter had an uncomfortable image of Hoskins's sly looks during his own presence in the VIP lounge. Had the man guessed? Had he seen through Peter's moustache-and-glasses disguise at the villa? Then he thought about the American's outfit: a houndstooth check jacket, patterned red tie and what Peter considered to be absurdly flamboyant Oxford co-respondent shoes in white with tan caps. Was this the dress of a defector? Or that of a showman?

The shouting had ceased and clearly the next hurdle was the reaction of Franz. Peter began to trawl back through all the information he had gleaned about this man, clearly no ordinary official. Franz was said to have special status. He spoke with the authority of the mentor, guide and recruiter of the American engineer. It had even been hinted he had the Fuhrer's favour. If true this would be the ultimate power, enough to block even the Gestapo.

Speed was slackening, their destination close, and there had been no stamping of angry footsteps in any direction. Just when he thought it might be safe to come out of hiding he heard a light tread outside.

He held his breath, peering through a crack.

Claudia.

He made a light shushing noise and leaned out to catch her arm. He saw her startled expression, then they were squeezing together in his tiny hiding space.

'You're lucky,' she whispered, 'Franz has just vouched for you. Told Voss he has complete confidence in the loyalty of every member of his team. Personally checked every one.'

Peter blew out his cheeks. 'And Voss?'

'Still angry but thwarted.'

Peter made a quick assessment. 'So Voss doesn't have unlimited powers. Maybe even the junior partner in terms of policing.'

'He could still make trouble,' Claudia said, 'force Franz's hand.'

He gave Claudia a hard stare. 'If anything happens to me, go to Williams for help. He's been told to do whatever you ask.'

'Is he still in the cinema car?'

'Yes.'

'There's something else,' she said. 'I think Hoskins knows about us.'

'How?'

'I tried to pump him about what he's going to do. Told me I mustn't get involved, that he'd protect me.'

'Protect you?' A short pause, then Peter said, 'That means he IS a Judas. Protecting you means he'll betray me.'

At that moment Peter was aware of a change in the background noise. They stopped talking to listen. The drumming of the wheels continued but some other element was missing. For a moment he was puzzled, then he had it. The clatter from the cinema car was absent. The film must have ended. No more music, no more Wild West shooting, no more dialogue. The sheriff finally triumphant, the bad guys in the chokey.

'Williams will be changing the reels,' he said. 'Let's hope

what comes next engages their attention at least for the next few minutes.'

His elder brother Emlyn had been the projectionist, the two of them had spent many hours together high up in that little room at the Rex watching the flickering images on the big screen down below. Mickey Mouse, Donald Duck, Roy Rogers, the Lone Ranger and hard-boiled sheriffs of the Wild West. This was the stuff of happy memories for Williams from a childhood spent in Aberdare. He almost laughed. Here he was again, regurgitating much the same sort of material for the select audience in the cinema car.

He peered through his spyhole. All was well. Sitting quietly, no chatter, no fidgeting, entranced by the screen and no bother to anyone. Just how the boss wanted it.

'Keep them occupied, Williams,' he'd been told. 'Keep them quiet, I don't want them wandering about in the corridors.'

Williams had volunteered his skills with the projector. Although never his job, he was familiar with the techniques. A back-room boy was how Chesham described it. Much the best place for a man who didn't speak the language. They'd managed to persuade the official projectionist to become a member of the audience. He peered again into the auditorium with its huge carriage-wide screen. Hitler, the briefing went, was a once-a-night film obsessive who loved Mickey Mouse, *King Kong* and *Mutiny on the Bounty*. And now his minions were similarly captivated, insulated from the outside world, unheeding of the train's progress, unheeding of what was happening in the corridors and interior of the other carriages.

Williams roused himself. The film had wound to an end and he needed to stop dreaming and get to work to change the reels.

Carefully, not hurrying so as to make no mistakes, he went about his business.

~

From their hiding place, Peter and Claudia were aware of a new set of sounds. Footsteps, slow and light, and then high-pitched female voices.

'Good God,' Claudia hissed, 'sounds like that dreadful old trout.'

'Who?'

'Frau Todt. Demanding, inquisitive, complaining.'

Peter was cursing under his breath. The voices grew louder, shrill and insistent. Clearly, Williams hadn't been quick enough switching films to quell the impatience of the Todts and assembled company, who could now be heard quite clearly. They were close by and out in the corridors where Peter did not want them to be.

A woman's querulous voice: 'What is it? What's that tapping sound?' A higher pitch. 'I can hear funny noises behind here. Things moving. Behind here... somewhere.'

'It's her,' Claudia whispered.

Then a man's voice. 'Sounds like a legion of rats.'

Todt's voice: 'Surely not on this new train! Not already, with the paint still hardly dry?'

'Certainly it's not mechanical.' Another male tone.

The kerfuffle increased with the sound of running footsteps. Through his spyhole Peter could see Voss, pounding down the corridor, shouting, 'I can hear them. Someone moving about. Crying. Complaining. First the lounge, now here!'

This was the moment to act. Peter arrived on the scene, intent on creating a diversion, saving the operation from disaster, but Voss was kicking like a man possessed at a panel which was bending and warping under his blows. Wood splinters cascaded, fabric cover ripped, a hole appeared... then a tear-stained tiny face.

'Raus, raus, you little rats!'

Time to intervene. Peter moved close to the splintered panel. 'Allow me to deal with this, Oberscharfuhrer.'

'You, Bauer! Appearing again like some ghost. I should have known you'd have something to do with this. Are these your little vermin?'

Peter was at the panel, stooping. 'Leave this to me,' he said. 'Just some stowaways. I'll deal with it. No need to panic.'

But Voss could not be placated. 'Get them out! Out! Get these vermin away from our special guests. We'll all catch something. It's an outrage. Sabotage! Wrecking the big occasion.'

Peter crouched down and beckoned to the gaunt face of Runner, his team leader at Dog, the first hide.

Voss was swinging his boot, ready to hit out. 'I'll have the train stopped and you'll all be put off together.'

Slowly, with reluctance, Runner emerged, blinking in the light, the sores on his face a contrast to the elegance of the guests. Behind was the frightened face of Ingrid, who began to sniff.

'Stop that bawling, child. Get them all out of here.'

Peter smiled at the third child, Blondie, and he realised how she must look to the bystanders: a coat far too large, a piece of string making up for missing buttons. Three young ones dressed in a collection of dowdy greys, blacks and assorted browns.

'Disgusting little wretch,' said Frau Todt. 'How can you bear to touch it?'

'Good God! We'll all catch something,' echoed her husband.

Peter was reassuring. 'Never fear. I'll remove them to a spare compartment at the other end of the train.'

Another child emerged into the subdued light of the

baggage carriage. This was Fat Fonzie, looking a shade less ragged in a big fluffy multicoloured jumper that some good-hearted wife had spent hours knitting.

'They should be in prison,' Voss said.

'Sorry,' Runner whispered, 'the lights went out,' but Peter ignored him, beckoning out another, a tiny girl with tears on her cheeks and looking on the point of more sobs. It was Anna Bergstein, Claudia's first U-boat. She was always going to be difficult.

'I want my mummy.' She'd been saying that ever since Claudia had sent the mother away. Even though scrubbed up, Anna looked waxen and tarnished by her long history in haystacks and barns. 'Horrid in there.' She sniffed. 'Cold and dark and dusty and the sandwiches didn't taste nice.'

Claudia eased her way gently to the front of the crowd and knelt to help the children. Anna clung to her.

'Oh dear, they seem to know you,' said Frau Todt. 'How on earth is that, I wonder?'

Claudia looked up. 'Just a sympathetic face,' she said, 'I'm a teacher, I'm used to this, a natural response.'

'But you'll catch something. Spoil your dress.'

Another stir caused heads to turn. Hoskins had arrived, demanding, 'What's all this?'

'Stowaways,' Voss spat, 'disgusting, dirty children, ill-dressed, ill-kempt, probably Jews from the look of them, hiding behind this panel.'

'I'll deal with it,' Peter said.

Hoskins looked askance at the ruined panel, then at Peter, a knowing smile creeping across his face. He pointed an accusing finger. 'Oh, never fear, I can read this situation. I know what's happening here.' He chuckled, pointing again. 'Hard luck, chum! Nice try but your pretence ends here. Your disguise didn't fool me for a moment. You forgot one very important fact, you can't change a voice. I recognised you as soon as you opened your mouth.'

Voss looked puzzled, then angry. 'What is the meaning of this?' He hated being out of his depth.

Peter spluttered, shrugging his shoulders. 'No idea what you mean.'

Hoskins focused on Peter. 'You took me for a fool, didn't you? No written guarantees, you didn't want any plans, didn't want any information, just me out of the way so you could play your little escape game.'

Peter shook his head in a gesture of puzzlement. It was all he could do. 'You've made a mistake, I've really no idea what you mean.'

'And I'll tell you something else!' Hoskins was enjoying the moment, baiting Peter, ignoring his guests, ignoring Voss. 'This brilliant railway scheme would certainly never have happened back in London, even if your promise had been genuine.'

Peter spread his arms. 'You must have mistaken me for someone else.'

'The English and the Americans,' Hoskins insisted, 'they're all lagging so far behind it's not true. You will soon see how right I am when I demonstrate my system to a major international audience.'

Voss forced himself into this exchange. 'I must insist, Herr Hoskins. What should be done with this man?'

'Arrest him immediately, that's what should be done. He's a British agent pretending to tempt me into defecting to the West.'

'My God!' Voss shouted, unclipping his holster.

'But never fear. It's all a pretence,' Hoskins said. 'All is now revealed. The defection was a trick. This is his real purpose. The escape of these scruffy children. The illegal flight from the Reich of these ragamuffins. How romantic! How pathetic!'

~

He'd already taken a swipe to the side of the head and several kicks to the back of his legs. Now he felt the blunt, unforgiving steel of a pistol barrel pressed to his ear.

'Move!' Voss was at the edge of hysterical, and Peter stood motionless, paralysed in dread. This paranoid man could pull the trigger at any moment.

'Move!' Another kick to the back of his legs.

Peter flinched, went down in pain, felt himself half pushed, half kicked into motion. He staggered to his feet and stumbled forward.

The ultimate humiliation, the ultimate defeat.

Plus the man's constant neurotic shrieking. 'An enemy agent! We know how to deal with them! We have special ways with people like you.'

More kicks behind the knees, which made him stumble again, more shoving, then shuffling slowly, a reluctant voyage along the corridor, still with that sharp metal barrel banging painfully against his head. Had the man released the safety catch on the weapon? He shuddered. Another jolt could prove fatal. Would he know anything about it?

'Okay, okay!' Peter mumbled, anxious to dampen the frenzy.

'Move!'

The absurd procession stumbled towards the front end of the train and another thought entered Peter's head. An absurd thought, given the circumstances. His father's ridiculous talk about 'the enemy' and how they didn't like cold steel.

Did anyone?

By now they'd stopped and Voss was kicking open a door. Peter's collar was grasped, he was spun around and pushed roughly through the gap. Another kick sent him sprawling.

The door crashed shut. A key rattled and Voss shouted through the woodwork, 'I shall return!'

'Don't hurry yourself,' Peter shot back, looking around a vacant compartment without windows. He felt battered and bloody, his uniform ripped, the sash long gone. This was his lowest point. The mission, the children – all defeated. Like a punch to the solar plexus. He closed his eyes and had an uncomfortable preview of Dansey's scowl when he learned of his failure. Then, an even darker image: a close-up of his father's expression.

Peter opened his eyes and scanned his surroundings. A bare space, a store of some sort, devoid of paintwork but with the door firmly locked. This was his recurring nightmare: sitting in a cell awaiting the attention of the Gestapo. He swallowed. His only chance was to break out before Voss returned. The here and now, he told himself, don't wait to be enclosed by bricks and mortar, attack Igor's carpentry.

He went looking for the weakest point. He knew the carpenters had been under immense pressure to complete their work on time. Had they skimped on fixings? It was obvious from the lack of finish that Igor's men hadn't wasted too much energy on this compartment. Maybe, he hoped, they'd skimped on battens or cross members.

He sought out the largest panel, feeling with his fingers until he located a tiny crack, but the timber was more resistant than he expected.

Time? How much of it did he have? How soon before Voss returned? The energy and force of panic coursed through him. He tried shoulder-charging the panel but it felt like hitting a brick wall. He tried kicking it without result. He looked around, spotted a metal shelving unit weighed down with all manner of heavy objects and decided to use it as a battering ram. He had an image in mind of a cop using a sledgehammer to smash his way through a front door. His legs felt weak as he unloaded boxes, containers and pots of paint onto the floor. It still needed a supreme effort to drag the unit to the panel. He loaded up again, lay on the floor with his back against the far wall and the bench against the other and used every ounce of energy he could muster to kick hard against the bench, smashing it against the wooden panelling. Pain shot up his legs where he'd taken a beating but the wall appeared undamaged.

Try again! More pain, no result.

He drew in a deep breath. Another kick, a yell of pain.

He crawled to get a closer look at the panel. Just a dent. He swallowed, took up his position again, closed his eyes, then delivered a third kick with all the vigour of a desperate man.

That's when it gave.

As tears cleared from his eyes, he peered into the space beyond. A collection of unused nails and several large pieces of timber lay scattered in the next cubicle. The carpenters had indeed left in a hurry.

Peter considered. Voss was a paranoid freak, capable of any excess but incapable of being duped by soft words or persuasion. You couldn't con this man with sweet reason or a good story. When Voss returned there was no choice. Physical resistance was the only recourse.

Claudia was doing her best to ignore Peter's ignominious departure and concentrated everything on the children.

'Claudia,' Hoskins asked, 'you know these little wretches?'

She looked up. 'I'll look after them,' she said, 'there's a spare compartment in the last wagon, well out of everyone's way. You won't have any trouble.'

'How very clever of you. To be so naturally in control of the situation, a fine quality, don't you think?'

Just then the train gave a jerk and Hoskins's attention was instantly diverted. Brakes were being applied. Hoskins looked at his watch. 'Almost there!' he announced, and Claudia glanced through a window to see dozens of tracks and spare coaches. Clearly they were about to enter the *Reichsbahn*'s specially constructed transhipment depot next to the Swiss border. High fences topped with razor wire were now visible as the train eased into a dock and glided to a stop. The VIP guests were putting on their coats, eager to disembark to join the special party allowed to watch the international demonstration. They had no fears about crossing the frontier. No one would question the presence of officials from the Third Reich. The discovery of a group of scruffy children was a minor matter soon forgotten in the anticipation of the big occasion. This was to be the highlight of the day, to be seen from a unique viewing platform, a luxurious steamer on the Swiss lake. More champagne would be flowing, perhaps lavish Swiss treats, perhaps caviar too.

Voss was back, returning fast from the control coach where he'd found a stores compartment in which to lock his prisoner. Now he was all questions, vying for Hoskins's attention.

'That man, Herr Hoskins? He threatened you? Is there still a danger?'

'Not at all. I played along. He wanted to prise this new technology away from the Reich – so he said.' Hoskins shrugged. 'But he's no engineer. That was all hokum. I never once fell for the blandishments. I knew it was a trick. Would you believe? Who in their right mind would offer 75,000 dollars without a shred of proof?'

'Bribery!' Voss shouted.

'A pretence. He doesn't have the money. Instead, it seems he's really some kind of latter-day Pimpernel.'

'We must protect you and the system,' Voss insisted. 'I'll arrange for the prisoner to be collected and subjected to proper interrogation. Seal off the train. Conduct a proper search.'

'No! No time.' Hoskins waved a dismissive hand. 'I will not tolerate delays or any loss of focus. I'm due on the Swiss viewing boat in twenty minutes. Nothing must cause the slightest problem. No snags, nothing! Everything must go exactly according to schedule, is that understood? There I shall demonstrate the superiority of my system for all the world to see. Nothing must stand in my way. Nothing!'

'I still think...'

'Deal with it later. In the meantime, Franz will be in charge here in my absence. Take your orders from him.'

29

Williams knew it. This was the moment he had to stop thinking of himself as number two. With the boss under arrest, it was time to step up. Time for the Dansey solution, the Welrod option. Time to redeem his pledge to the little spymaster back in London. He recalled Dansey's uncompromising expression in the flat at St James's: he was not to let Hoskins slip away. A defection or shoot.

Knowing this moment might arise was one thing. Actually confronting it was another. The pistol was a single-shot, close-range weapon issued to the Special Operations Executive specifically for assassinations, but he couldn't use it in a crowd. Not in front of the Gestapo officer and assembled VIPs. He'd need to get the man on his own and with a decent chance of escape.

When Hoskins announced he was about to depart the depot for Swiss territory, Williams realised this was his chance, trailing his quarry out of the carriage and walking fast towards the front of the train. Once free of bystanders Williams intended calling the man back, but Hoskins was too far ahead. Before he could get within effective range the Engineer had climbed into a car and was gone.

Dispirited, he began to walk back, thinking his next best option was to shoot Peter free.

But how to do that and survive long enough to lead the children to safety?

'Stand to attention in front of me!'

Voss was a bundle of conflicting emotions. Triumph, outrage, hatred, excitement. He wasn't sure how he was going to cope. Sure, he'd taken part in round-ups and arrests before, but they were mainly soft targets, frightened old men, crying women, whimpering kids. Never before had he such a prize in his hands: a real-life active enemy of the state. How best, he wondered, to maximise his role and prestige?

He was taken by surprise by the enemy's attitude. Not at all deflated. And moving forward.

'Stand still!' he ordered.

But the enemy agent didn't look cowed or compliant. Voss expected shouted commands to achieve instant obedience, but this was strange. He was used to craven, frightened prisoners. People under arrest by the Gestapo did not act like this. Defiance was a foreign country.

Suddenly the agent darted forward. How could this be?

'Stop!'

Voss unbuckled his holster. But not quick enough.

Voss's right hand was on the holster. Peter was quick on his feet, using the jagged end of a length of timber he'd been hiding behind his back. He lunged at the area of the man's right arm, desperate to prevent the weapon being drawn.

Voss staggered back. Peter had missed the arm but connected with the man's face. With a shock he saw blood on the cheek, the man clutching a wound just below the eye.

'Resisting arrest, striking an officer!' Voss swayed a little, then tried again for his pistol. 'You're a dead man!'

For an instant Peter was shocked by what he had done. He'd never before caused bloodshed. Voss was unsteady and slow but managed to get a grip on the Walther.

Peter reacted, striking fast before the pistol could be brought up to fire.

Another quick jab to the arm knocked the gun clean out of Voss's grasp. It clattered to the floor and skittered across the bare floorboards. The safety catch must have been off – either that, or the force of the fall had done it. As soon as the weapon hit the doorway there was a loud concussion and a bullet whizzed somewhere into woodwork.

'You'll die for this!' Voss was staggering but still voluble.

Against all instinct, Peter knew he had to incapacitate his foe and drew back the makeshift cudgel for another blow – then froze, staring into the space beyond.

The look on Peter's face must have done it, because Voss also stopped and turned.

That's when they both saw the frightened face of the woman.

Voss recognised her. She was the person who'd been with all those scruffy kids. It was that Claudia woman, framed in a pose of alarm, staring back at them from the open doorway.

Her children. That was all that mattered. She would not let them down, so near to the Swiss border and yet so far. She wouldn't let the escape plan end in miserable failure.

Claudia had been shocked by Peter's arrest. It was a shame.

She was sorry for him but he was a soldier. He knew the risks. She understood Williams was also on the team but didn't think he could rescue the situation so now, she decided, she was the only one who could stave off disaster.

But how? She considered. Acting alone, simply taking the children off the train would achieve nothing. They would never get out of a freight depot ringed by high fences. Peter would know how to do it. She needed him free. But what could she hope to achieve against a Gestapo officer like Voss?

She drew in a deep breath. Force of personality, match aggression with aggression, find the weak link. There had to be a way to dent his confidence. She knew from her time in Prague, every bully is a coward waiting to be unmasked. She'd confronted Gestapo men before. So what was this man's secret fear?

The answer came quite easily. Shame. That would be his weakness: why wasn't he serving in a fighting unit? Was he scared? Was he a weak man hiding from the war?

She stepped into the corridor and made for the coach where Voss had his office. She had her speech ready. She would question his courage; suggest to anyone around that Voss be transferred to a front-line unit. 'Why is an able-bodied young man doing a nothing job like this?' she would accuse. 'Surely a job for a wounded veteran. My granny could do what you're doing.'

But then she stopped, shocked by a loud report. It sounded like a gunshot.

Frightened by what this might mean for Peter, she ran forward to the open door.

Framed, there were two figures, static as if in tableau: Peter holding a large lump of wood; Voss, face bloodied and wild-eyed, looking at her.

Then she looked down and saw it. The gun on the floor. At her feet.

Voss turned and stepped towards his fallen weapon.

Peter yelled at Claudia, 'Pick it up! Don't let him get it.'

Voss came on, reaching for the gun.

All her prepared speechifying flew out of her head. This was elemental. This was personal survival. Instinctively, she knew that Voss, if he gained control of the weapon, would kill them both.

Claudia stooped, picked up the gun and held it high, pointing at Voss. He stopped his lunge, a shocked expression replacing earlier determination.

'I'll shoot,' she said.

Voss ignored her, reached for her, and once more instinct took over.

Claudia snatched at the trigger.

She was stunned by what she had done, the body of Voss slumped face down at her feet. She could hardly believe her own actions. It was as shocking to her as if one of her tiny charges had been eviscerated. She shivered. She looked into the distance, held her breath, then breathed deeply, rhythmically. Her hand shook but she kept hold of the gun.

Then she looked up at Peter. He was standing immobile, rigid with shock. He too, she realised, had crossed a line, breaking his taboo, forced by circumstance into taking violent action.

They stared at one another for several long seconds, then back down again at the body sprawled before them.

Finally, Peter breathed out and swallowed. 'You didn't have any choice,' he said, placatingly. 'Don't feel sorry for him.'

'I don't.'

He shook his head. 'I know you'll feel bad about it, but we just need to be practical.'

'Have you shot anyone before?'

Peter was crestfallen. 'Actually, no.'

'Well then, you don't know how it feels.'

He bent down and began to lift the body. 'We have to get him out of sight as quickly as possible.'

Claudia nodded.

Then, while grasping Voss's arms, he looked at her and said, 'You know, you did the only thing possible, you saved my life. And probably the children's too! So, for their sake, you have to stay strong. Don't get the shakes.'

'Have you ever seen me go to pieces?'

'Well... no.'

He let go of the body and reached for the gun. 'Best,' he said, 'in case of accidental discharge.'

She avoided his arm and brought the gun up, levelling the barrel at him.

A shocked expression clouded Peter's features. 'What are you doing?'

'Are you another Judas?' she demanded. 'We've just had Hoskins, now this customer. And are you another one? Using my children as a cover for your wrecking operation? Another dirty trick to leave the kids stranded?'

Peter sighed. 'How could you think that of me? Of course, I'm going to get the kids out, just as soon as...'

'No!' she said. 'Starting now, we'll do it my way. The kids go first. First, you hear? Before anything else at all.'

Peter sighed, hesitating, then nodded. 'Okay, the kids go first.

But now, will you just help? We've got to move Voss out of sight before someone comes and finds him here.'

But someone had found them.

Williams was at the door. 'Jeepers, Peter, what's happened here? I heard a shot.'

'Never mind!' Peter was feeling around the bottom of the timbers, searching for another loose panel. 'Just help me move him under one of these...'

There was another movement in the doorway.

All three looked up. Standing there, studying the scene, was the railway policeman they both knew as Franz. Impassive in his uniform, the embodiment of authority.

30

Franz was immaculate in his uniform, the sort of man who remained unperturbed by any turn of events.

Peter started to jabber. 'Look,' he said, 'this is not what you think. It was just an accident. His gun just went off...'

'And that's why she's still holding it, is it?'

Peter closed his eyes. He was more than an enemy agent now. He was implicated in the killing of a Gestapo officer. He could already hear the swish of the noose on some KZ parade ground. Perhaps, just a matter of a few days. And in one sense, Franz was more threatening than Voss. Clearly intelligent. No possibility of bluff.

'It's no good putting him under there,' Franz said. 'He'll stink and soon be found.'

Peter gaped. He was expecting arrest. Had he heard correctly?

'Move him to the propulsion unit,' Franz said. 'He can go down the ravine with the rest of the wreckage.'

Peter's frown increased. He stared at the cop, puzzled, disbelieving. 'You?' he said.

Franz nodded. 'Yes, me,' he said.

But before the conversation could continue, two other figures appeared behind Franz. Frightened faces drawn by the noise of gunshots. Peter recognised Otto and another member of the train crew he'd met but whose name he'd forgotten.

Franz reacted first. 'Stand back, will you? Return to your duties. There's been an accident and we're dealing with it.'

Otto's was a frozen stare. A man rooted to the spot, gawping at Voss's body.

'The *Ober* isn't feeling well.' Franz turned on Otto. 'Give him some space, some dignity, will you?' Then to Peter: 'Is the sickbay ready?'

It took a second, then Peter reacted. 'Ah, yes, they're standing by. Sending a stretcher.'

'See that bloodstain?' Otto's whisper could be heard in the silence.

'Fool!' Franz was emphatic. 'It's a paint stain. Just had the painters in, or hadn't you noticed?'

A doubtful silence. Then orders from Franz. A crisp issuing of instructions; for closing of all doors and windows and readying the train for its return journey; for assembling in five minutes' time in the cinema car for fresh orders. The bystanders shrank back before the authority of the military police.

Peter was crouching over the body, not wanting to reveal its limpness before witnesses. Once they were on their own Franz had Voss by the feet. 'Right, let's drag him through to the front.'

Without further word, Franz, Williams and Peter half dragged, half carried Voss through a now empty train to the leading car. Peter's wrists were bloody, his hands weak. The other two had taken most of the burden by the time the body was dumped on the floor of a compartment.

Franz stood back, sighed, reached into his uniform pocket and produced a cigarette case. He lit up.

Cool, Peter decided, very cool, and the resulting aroma

reminded him of something, some previous memory he couldn't quite grasp. A familiarity he couldn't specify. Then he had it. The crisp issue of orders.

'That voice,' Peter said. 'I recognise it. I've heard it before, behind a screen in the control centre. And when I met with old Epp at the end of the tunnel...'

'Slow, aren't you?' Franz said. 'Not figured it before? I've been looking after you since the day you arrived – arrived, that is, empty-handed, no weapons, no explosives, no plan, no clue. Not very impressive. Not clever. How do you think you've got this far? All your own work?'

Peter was nonplussed. Staggered by the calm way this turn-about had been delivered. Even tones, as if betraying his masters was a matter of complete routine. Franz was deadpan, ice cubes in his veins.

'But aren't you going to be for it?' Peter asked. 'When this little lot hits the bottom of the ravine?'

'Of course, anyone in any way connected will be executed. A KZ at the very least. The Fuhrer's vengeance will know no bounds. Hoskins knows this, I've warned him often enough, and if he doesn't take my advice... well, that's down to him. He's big enough and ugly enough to look after himself.'

'But you?'

'I have my exit route firmly in place, thank you. All my family are in America, so the nasties will have no one on whom to take their revenge.'

At that moment attention switched away from Franz. Both he and Peter turned to look at Claudia. She was present but was silent. She looked frozen. She looked ill.

She knew she had to be strong. She must get her children away. But the nightmare of what had just happened in that dreadful cubicle caused Claudia to seize up inside. Never in her life had she thought herself capable of such a deed; of even touching a weapon of war, let alone using one; of taking a life.

It had all happened so quickly without time for a second's reflection. Hers had been an instinctive reaction. She'd understood the necessity of it and had stayed calm at the critical moment, but now a sense of shock set in.

Had she really done it? She blinked, felt unsteady. She put out a hand to grasp the wall.

Franz said sternly, 'This is no time for nerves. You have a job to do.'

So he knew. All the time he had known what she – and Peter – were about. All along he had been the one pulling the strings. The realisation was shocking, belittling even, but then, strangely, also reassuring. His role made her feel better, less alone, more of a team. She swallowed and stood straight, making a supreme effort to restore self-control. This was no time to lose it. She hadn't let herself be intimidated by the likes of the terrible triumvirate of Hobisch, Spindlegger and Kuhn back at the school. She had said it then and she meant it now: no *Kindertransport* worker would cave in and run at a vital moment. Her little ones were depending on her.

Franz spoke again. 'Fraulein Kellner, I suggest that right now you prepare your children for the next stage of their journey.' He drew in a deep breath. 'And you might also want to know that all my friends back at the Landsberger, those with key roles and in danger of recrimination, are at this very moment making themselves scarce. Off to the remotest corners of the country. So, Fraulein, whatever else you do, do not go back to the depot. Tomorrow it will be a nest of vipers.'

Claudia looked at him, puzzled. 'Your friends?'

'People known to you,' he said.

'Ah! Thought so! Erika!'

'Frau Schmidt and Dieter will be among those evacuated.'

'I get it!' Claudia said. 'It's you and she, isn't it? All along, you two have been in this together, running the show.'

His very inscrutability was a form of answer.

For a moment Claudia felt choked and bit her lip. She had already said her goodbyes to Erika and this moment signalled the final point of departure on their intensely emotional journey. They had achieved so much together, defeating the forces of darkness, saving young lives. 'Wish her the very best from me,' she said, 'safe journey to wherever.'

Then she turned to go, heading back along the corridor, back in control, her mind focused once more on what she had to do.

31

He had the face of a ferret. A little man who kept cocking his right shoulder, as if he were just about to launch a boxer's jab. Someone clearly not agile with words but confident about what he did. No, more than confident, Peter decided, proud almost to the point of a simmering arrogance.

'Definitely not!'

The man looked at Franz and Peter as if they had just issued the insult of a lifetime. 'I am the driver of this train,' he said. 'It's always been understood, the job is mine. As lead driver.'

Franz issued his soothing smile. 'Bauer here has been specially trained. For this one demonstration drive. Just for today.'

'No. The job is mine.' Then, the little man pointing at Peter, demanded, 'What's this training you've had?'

'Classified,' Peter said. 'Can't tell you that. A secret, understand?'

'No!' Another shake of the head. 'Only Herr Hoskins has control of the drivers. And you're not one of them.'

Peter put a placating hand on the man's arm. 'This is far too risky for you. This particular part of the journey around the loop, that's what I'm here to do. To relieve you of any danger. To keep you safe.'

The propulsion unit was being uncoupled from the rest of the train as they spoke. It was understood by all: the bridge on the temporary exhibition loop was not up to carrying the weight of a full load. Especially not the giant coachwork Hoskins had assembled, so the propulsion unit would be the only vehicle allowed across and then at a severely restricted speed.

None of Peter's words cut any ice. The driver shook his head. 'I've always been number one. This is my job. My duty. My special day. And I'm quite sure there is no danger... if the job is done properly at the correct speed.'

Franz turned his attention from the cab window and stepped away.

Peter, desperate to save the man's life, looked at the driver imploringly. He tried charm, smiling at the man, asking him about his service. Mathias Adler flicked a shoulder once more, pleased that at last his sense of self-importance was being recognised. It was a privilege to be chosen for this special job, he said, recounting his years working on experimental projects. The man was puffed up, proud but fidgety, anxious to be on his way. He stared resolutely ahead in the direction of the lakeside loop, hands firmly on the controls. 'I'm waiting,' he said in a hard voice. 'Ready and waiting for the right of way.'

Peter moved out of earshot and confronted Franz. 'Well? We can't let him go. It's a suicide run.'

Franz shrugged. 'He's obdurate. He'll only make trouble if we shift him.' Another shrug. 'A necessary sacrifice. Surely, as a soldier, you must recognise the necessity?'

'No, I don't.' Peter was stricken by the negation of the promise he had made to himself. There was already one casualty down to this operation. 'Not what I wanted at all.'

But the signal was given. Hoskins had demanded it, timing

was all, and there could be no further delays. The propulsion unit received the green light.

Peter reluctantly stepped away as the locomotive moved off and continued to watch in horror as the rear of the vehicle disappeared round a bend, distraught at the scene shortly to follow: the machine derailing, the bridge toppling, the locomotive falling, the driver screaming and Voss's lifeless body locked in the rear cab tumbling with the rest of the wreckage, smashing itself to pieces on the rocks at the bottom of the ravine.

Yes, the machine would be wrecked – his job done – but the thought of the driver's needless death paralysed him. He was still in a state of glazed shock when he heard Franz give a startled cry.

'Good God, it's back!'

Peter could not believe it. The propulsion unit had negotiated the dangerous loop, completed the circuit and returned to the depot in triumph. The bridge had survived.

'But how?'

'I thought you'd warned your people!' Franz snapped. 'Can't they even manage that? Just knocking out a few bolts?'

Peter swallowed. Yes, he'd sent a WT message to Dansey giving date, time, location and details of the loop. There had been ample time for the spymaster to organise a wrecking mission. It should not have been difficult – a temporary wooden trestle bridge, surely short work for someone who knew their business? Another Dansey shortcoming!

Peter's head was in his hands. This was a disaster – because there wasn't a disaster. Failure because of Hoskins's success. The nadir of all his hopes. Hitler triumphant, the rest of Europe eating out of his hand and Britain's worst fears confirmed. All the efforts of the Resistance were now at nought.

It seemed to him that however hard he tried failure dogged

his every footstep. He sank into a posture of gloom, total and abject.

32

Through his misery, he was aware of voices. Peter, looking up, saw Adler, the driver, the little man now a lot less confident than before. In fact, he was almost gibbering. 'You were right, Herr Bauer, that loop is a deathtrap, I nearly had it over there.'

'But you made it.'

'Only just, it was wobbling, vibrating under me, I could feel it, it's just a whisker away from disintegrating. You were right. I should never...'

Peter put out a consoling arm. 'Am I glad you're back!'

The driver stared at him, puzzled.

'You need to calm down,' Peter said. 'Take a rest. Go to the crew room and I'll bring you something to make you feel better.'

Franz was answering the telephone. When he put it down, he gave Peter a long look. 'Just got word from the boat.'

'The boat? How? Have they got ship to shore radio?'

'No, a breathless messenger in a rowboat.'

Peter shook his head, still relieved for the driver but anxious for everyone else.

'Our luck is in,' Franz said. 'We've got a second chance!'

Peter gaped.

Franz snorted in derision. 'Hoskins thinks it's been a great success. A wonderful demonstration, the fool! He wants the loco round again to impress his audience, only this time faster.'

'Mad idiot!' Peter was both shocked and elated. Then worried. Would the bridge hold up long enough to stage another demonstration run?

Franz cut him off. 'I'll give Adler a sedative, put him to sleep. We should be grateful. He's done us a huge favour. So!' There was a rare smile. 'Speed is what Hoskins wants. Speed is what he's going to get.'

33

––––––––––

Claudia still felt shaky, but who wouldn't? There was an inexorable logic to events and once started there was no going back. Forward was the only way. She and Williams scurried through the deserted corridors. They had four other hides to release. The children would be worried now that the train had stopped. They would be afraid and clamouring for reassurance.

As they passed the cinema car loud guffaws could be heard from inside. The staff leisure period was already in session. It was an irresistible lure; something saucy, something forbidden, something from under the counter. Hurrying on, the train fell into silence. All the attention of the VIPs had been switched to the lake. The train was slumbering and the depot asleep. Even as she prepared for the final hurdle of the escape and perhaps her greatest test, Claudia's mind locked onto Franz's revelation, astounded at the part played by Erika, at a single stroke transformed from best friend status to a figure of mystery and intrigue. She had always been mystified by the apparent absence of a partner from Erika's life. Gentle probing on the subject led nowhere. In her flat there were no photos, mementos, nothing that indicated a male presence. Not even a razor in the bathroom cabinet! Erika was a woman completely self-contained.

And now Claudia knew why. Her past had been deliberately expunged, washed clean to prevent any link being detected in the event of a search. There would be no evidence to find.

Clever! Claudia recognised just how silently effective the Resistance movement had been. Erika and Franz! What a surprise.

Struggling, jostling, kicking, chattering, laughing, crying. The corridors were a chaos as Claudia and Williams ran the length of the train, opening hatches and freeing Eagle from the restaurant car, Cheetah from the cinema, Beakie from the lounge and Mole from the kitchens.

'Stay together!' It was Claudia's cry as the children clambered from their hides but some serious swaps were taking place. 'I can't stand her anymore!' Runner was adamant, even though older children were meant to stay paired with their younger partners. Very quickly Eagle acquired Anna and Runner had Frieda. Younger ones suffered most from their prolonged incarceration. Arms and legs were stiff, shoulders hurt and stomachs grumbled.

'You'll all feel better in the fresh air.' Claudia was at her most reassuring. 'As soon as we begin our walk, arms and legs will feel better, you've just got cramp from being cooped up for so long. It'll be lovely, a delight to be outside and away from this train.'

Williams was on a pillage mission, acquiring all manner of treats and delicacies from the kitchens and capturing a postman's trolley from the mailroom. Claudia worried that the younger ones might not be able to complete the long walk ahead, little Frieda in particular being her biggest concern, and

Williams indicated the trolley as a possible solution for later. He'd also equipped himself with a makeshift rope sling and a large empty rucksack. Claudia also worried about footwear and whether the children would cope. She'd done her scrounging best back at the depot but she had no idea of the conditions they would face, only that they were embarking on a trek 'cross country'. Her own court shoes were hardly suitable and she feared her dress would look out of place in the countryside.

An impromptu reward system was rapidly worked out: chocolate eggs would be handed out in the afternoon and even more wonderful treats were for supper.

It didn't seem to matter that the children were creating an uninhibited din. The cinema audience were enraptured by their illicit fare. The only staffer encountered outside, Otto, worried about 'trouble ahead' when the bosses returned but was quietly placated. There would be no children on the return trip, Claudia promised him; he should deny all knowledge of their presence and, if necessary, plead 'obeying orders'.

After a frantic counting of heads, laces were tied, coats buttoned up, hats pulled tight, and the crocodile restored to order. Claudia went to the rack in the ladies' cloakroom and emerged in her big hat, placing herself at the head of the line. In the brim: the fresh carnation.

Echoes of all those other days and the earlier departures.

Finally, they were ready. And once again the instruction was passed down the line: *All join hands and follow the hat.*

Williams wasn't sure Dansey would approve. He'd have a hard job persuading the spymaster that playing nursemaid to twenty-seven scruffy kids constituted an operational necessity befitting of a British military mission... if, on top of all the other disasters, he ever reached home soil to give such an explanation.

He shrugged his shoulders and brought up the tail of the long crocodile crossing the tracks, stumbling over dumped ballast and catching the trolley wheels on crumbling sleepers. They continued down a line of wagons, alongside a parallel track, past huge metal dump containers and straight to the big wire fence and an unmarked exit gate. He stole a quick look back but there were no signs of alarm. Progress had been masked by lines of rolling stock. The key Franz had issued fitted perfectly and turned a well-oiled lock. You could always bank on German efficiency, he told himself. Just as well, the close-mesh fence was ten feet high. As the last one through, he buried the key by the second stanchion, according to instructions, then followed the crocodile down a slope and out of view to some trees.

They were walking Indian file again and once within the treeline he caught Claudia up. She was as focused as he on maintaining progress and he had to admire her composure, given everything that she had been through. He held the map, a German walkers' guide to local footpaths called a *wanderkarte*, and he knew their destination, a planned rendezvous point well ahead. Peter had released this much of the secret; it had been set by the Z-men for their escape.

Shortly, they crossed a stream and started up a rise towards another line of trees. Some of the children carried small parcels, remnants of the sandwiches and treats they had set out with. The rule of the march was the same as on the train: complete silence. If they passed walkers on the path they were to smile and wave as a way of disarming curiosity. And say absolutely nothing.

Williams kept the pace steady. There were views from the path through the trees. He could see fields leading down to the big lake. They passed a remote cottage with a notice about dogs but heard nothing, then a field occupied by several horses, some sheep pens and a concrete dip in a farmyard.

At a stile he had to hand the small children over the top along with his trolley and he cursed the loss of time. He knew they must allow no straggling, so when one of the youngest began to lag and cry he placed her in the trolley, pushing hard to keep pace. However, they were slowed by mud and pools of rainwater from the night before. In the distance he heard a tractor and the drone of a plane. By a grassy slope the girls wanted to stop to pick buttercups but he shooed them on.

The smallest began to lag and Williams was forced to hoist a complaining Frieda into his makeshift papoose. After another mile he peered back, wondering what was happening at the depot. There had been no clues, no signs of alarm, no explosions, so had Peter succeeded in getting away? Two low-flying aircraft were the only sign of unusual activity.

He urged on the line once again, considering the likely prospect that his boss might not make it out. He grimaced to himself; that too could be the fate of them all. He tried not to think of having to play hide and seek in the woods with a Gestapo search party. Not a thought on which he wished to dwell.

34

This was his first time. Climbing into the cab of the new propulsion unit was something Peter hadn't been able to accomplish in all his days at the depot. On the outside, dazzling speed stripes made it look glamorous, but inside the equipment was spartan.

He took his place in the second driver's swivel seat and tried to adopt the calm approach of a career railwayman. Despite that he felt a fluttering in his chest. He was so wound up he found it difficult to concentrate. He was also conscious of a smell resembling burnt cables, in some ways similar to that he'd noticed at the depot.

No expense had been spared on passenger comfort but the exuberant designer style ceased at the front end. They had hard seats before an all-metal, unpainted control panel, cold and unforgiving to the touch. Peter kept his coat on. The only dashes of colour were two large red buttons on a side panel.

Franz was in the driver's seat, checking over the controls. The tension never seemed to get to this man. Not so Peter. Here he was, at last at the beating heart of this futuristic machine. Strange to think it was doomed, even though it represented the future. In one sense, he would have preferred to save the machine for posterity, but that was impossible. Would the sabotage work? Would the train destruct? He could see his future – success or failure – being decided in the next few minutes.

Franz had taken off his watch and placed it between two dials so he didn't need to take his eyes from the controls. Timing was everything. Hoskins had issued a new timetable and expected strict adherence. The loco unit was to appear on the lakeside viewing loop at a precise moment in the Hoskins programme. The VIPs standing on the deck of the boat on the lake would be expecting a grandstand view. And Franz was going to ensure they had an event to remember. The disaster had to be witnessed by all.

Not too soon and certainly not late. This was the German way. Exact timing not just to the minute but to the second.

'Ten minutes to go,' Franz said.

Peter, full of doubts as well as nerves, at last found his voice. 'There's something I don't understand,' he said. 'I have to ask.' An inner voice demanded it. 'How is it that the person who recruited Hank Hoskins and the promoter of this new broad gauge system should turn out to be the ultimate means of its destruction?'

The answer, when it came, was in the same matter-of-fact tone.

Franz arrived from the US as part of the Hoskins project, welcomed to the Third Reich with accolades, status, uniforms and unlimited funds. 'I was never a real enthusiast,' he said, 'just the appointed agent in America ordered to recruit him. And as time has passed it's become brutally obvious just how noxious this regime has become. Hank Hoskins is a romantic given to ignoring everything outside his own closed view of the world. He knows but doesn't want to know. The new motor is a case in point. The reality is, it isn't ready. Needs years more development to make it work properly but you should know by now how this regime operates. Five years? Three? Two? They haven't got ten minutes. Once that was obvious, my course was set and the means of resistance were at hand.'

'And the children?'

Franz shrugged. 'Felt sorry for them. Didn't have the time or means to deal with them... until Claudia came along. Until you came along.'

Peter was silent, shocked and a little angry at how both he and Claudia had been manipulated.

'Now!'

Franz had not taken his eye from the watch. He yanked the horn, released the brake and pushed open the throttle. The big machine inched forward towards the exit gate that led out of the enclosed compound of the rail depot and down towards the lake.

The gateman too had the new times. The big wire door drew slowly back on its runners, powered by an electric motor, rather like the sliding doors of an aircraft hangar, and the signal turned to green.

Franz gave the gateman a wave as they slid smoothly out of the compound and down the meandering slope. Onwards towards the moment of doom.

Up here, sitting high and viewing the passing countryside, there was a strange mix of emotions: the almost reassuring sense of being in control against the excitement of what they were about to do. The eerie quiet was broken only by a faint hum of the motors slung beneath the bogies and the kiss of the wheels far below. They moved smoothly round several bends and began to slow towards an unscheduled stop two kilometres from the ravine bridge. The unit was coasting gently to a stop well out of sight and sound of the gateman.

Peter found his voice. 'I hear there was a problem on the journey here. The driver mentioned it.'

Franz said, 'Overheating. This thing is not a done deal. Actually, it's pretty much played out. Bottom of the ravine is the best place for it. You can see...'

He pointed to a dial directly below one of the red buttons. 'Almost at danger point. Oh, don't look surprised. This kind of loco will work eventually. Hoskins is well ahead of his time, he just needs a lot longer.'

'And those red knobs?'

'To shut everything down before she wrecks herself.'

'So even this tiny shunt is dangerous?'

'Only if we push it.'

'But we're about to do just that, aren't we?'

'Yes.' A thin-lipped smile. 'We just have to hope it will last a few more minutes.'

The uncertainty had Peter's heart racing. Might it burn out before they could jump?

And then there was that underlying but persistent sense of mistrust. The fear of trickery and betrayal. Was Franz really what he said he was? The suspicion of some kind of a double-cross never left him. Peter looked over at the man, still calmly studying his watch and the controls, but it was hard to harbour doubts about someone so obsessed with the precise timing of the task.

'Right,' Franz said, 'this is where you get off.' The machine had stopped rolling. 'No point in both of us having to jump. Wish me luck!'

It was this last remark, tying Franz into some kind of a conspiratorial union, that convinced him. Without knowing it, Peter and Claudia had been in the hands of this man right from day one. It was time to trust.

He pulled open the door, climbed down the ladder and

landed on the track. The big machine moved off and Peter stood immobile, looking at the disappearing rear of the loco as it picked up speed and began the descent to the bridge – the bridge over a deep ravine with a sharp bend at each end.

Suddenly he went rigid. A panic attack at the prospect of being duped. Speed had built up and still no one had jumped from the cab. Was Franz still at the controls, planning a slow demo run to show off the train – a Judas despite everything?

Then Peter saw something fall from the driver's side.

Surely he would be injured by such a fall.

Peter started to run towards the spot but he hadn't gone more than ten paces when the figure unfurled itself from the trackside, stood and waved.

Relieved, Peter waved back.

The train had gone and Franz was now out of view.

That was the last he saw of either.

Peter turned and began to jog back the way he had come, looking for the path that would take him out of sight of the depot and on to the footpath that Claudia, Williams and the children should at this moment be using.

35

The pace was slackening and daylight was fading, so Claudia decided to take charge. She sent Williams back to the rear to make sure there were no stragglers and to be ready to issue a warning signal – a double owl hoot – if they were approached by strangers. At least they had travelled far enough to be out of sight and sound of the depot and the boat.

But little voices were complaining: 'My feet hurt...' 'I'm not used to walking...' 'I want my mummy...' 'I'm hungry... can't we stop?'

There were other requests: for a story, for a nursery rhyme, for a bed. 'We're on the last part of our journey,' she said, 'out of that horrid train, but we must keep on, a man is waiting up ahead, ready to help us.' The crocodile was becoming painfully slow but it was necessary to keep moving, not only to get to the rendezvous but also to get as far away as possible from the depot. When the alarm was raised – and at some point that was inevitable – would they come looking for the children? Would they care? And if so, in what direction would they search? The most obvious places to check were the road crossings on the border and the ferry terminals, all, thankfully, in the opposite direction. Claudia fervently hoped there were no border patrols up here on the hills beside the lake. Surely, the frontier police would consider this 'safe' territory.

Her thoughts were cut short by a double owl hoot and she immediately stopped the trek and moved the crocodile into deep shadow. Then she hid herself, alarmed by a heavy foot-pounding and laboured breathing.

The noise stopped almost by the tree she was using as cover.

'It's okay, you can come out now,' said a familiar voice.

Peter was still panting. He'd been jogging most of the way from the depot to catch them up.

'Well?' Her tone was a shade caustic. 'Are you a hero?'

'No,' he said between deep breaths, 'so far, just a saboteur and a thief. I'll only be a hero when I have you and the kids across the lake.'

'We didn't hear much,' she said, 'only some planes flying really low.'

'A lot more than that. I could hear hooting and sirens from the boats but of course I didn't stick around for the finale.'

'Why a thief?' she queried.

He grinned. 'We may have lost Hoskins but I still have his plans somewhere safe.'

She gave him a quizzical look.

'Under my socks.'

She did a double take. 'But those drawing office plans... they're huge...'

'On film. A tiny camera, slotted in a tight recess in my shoe.'

'Well, make sure you don't get it wet.'

They were on the move again and eventually cleared the trees. Over to their left the lake was an inky blackness stretching into a misty horizon. They didn't talk much. Claudia was putting all her strength into the long walk. This might be his thing, but it wasn't hers. She checked behind, cajoled the stragglers, played march marshal, but part of her mind was on other things. On whether they would be caught by pursuers. Or whether they would succeed in escaping her native land. This last began to colour her thoughts. The glimpse of another life; a different life with different prospects. She was sure the children would adapt to new surroundings. The young usually did, but would she? Did she even seek it? Instinctively, she fingered the locket, recalling the brutal occasion when Drexler had made fun of her. So what about Hansi and Luise? For the first time, she realised, she had reversed the order of their names, reflecting the way in which she thought of them.

She looked ahead to Peter, striding out, peering at the horizon, checking his map, acting the scout leader he undoubtedly had been in boyhood. She recalled their revealing talk forty-eight hours earlier in her flat; of his privileged life, his circumscribed ambition and the domination of his father. This would be the last lap for him. Perhaps he was thinking about home at this very moment while she was contemplating a final leave-taking of hers. Was he the man to whom she should attach herself? She sighed, maintaining her reserve, then looked again to see him stopped, scanning the darkening skyline.

'Got it!' he said, pointing. 'See up there, far up on that hill.'

'What am I looking at?' she said, stopping to study the line of hills stretching away inland.

'There, on that little rise. A brick tower. A folly. Some nineteenth century clergyman's dream lookout.'

He handed her a tiny black pair of binoculars and she made the spot, murmuring noises of recognition. Then she shrugged. She wasn't in the mood for spotting items of interest.

'A landmark,' he said, 'what I've been waiting for. Keep close behind me from now on.'

Claudia was reluctant to cede control but only he and Williams knew the location of the rendezvous. However, when he took a sharp left from the main path she objected. She pointed to the walkers' map and the land around the foreshore. 'Look,' she said, 'we should keep going straight on, past this headland and down to the shoreline. Surely, the pick-up point is down there.'

'Trust me!' he said. 'We've reached the turn point. I know what I'm doing.' He tapped the map. 'We'd never fix a pick-up from such an obvious place. That's a public landing stage you've got there. Think about it! This is a covert operation.'

She shrugged and got the children moving again, following him over a broken fence and squeezing between two concrete posts, then descending steeply down a stony, rock-strewn gulley between two hills. It was rough going and some of the little ones slithered and fell. She too felt herself sliding in her uncomfortable shoes.

'Are you sure about this?' she asked, setting them upright.

'Can't you hear it?' He pointed.

Yes, she could hear it. Water slapping vigorously against rocks.

'Not far now.'

At the foot there was a double S-bend around a cove-like gap in the cliffs and then they were there, staring at a levelled space next to a concrete ramp leading to a dock carved out of rock. Fifty yards inland a high cliff fissured with layers of granite-looking stone and gaping holes showed where tunnellers had once worked.

'Spooky!' Claudia said. 'Scary, no wonder there was a fence

higher up, I don't think we're meant to be here. What is this place?'

'It's a bit stark, I'll give you that,' he said, 'but that's because the light's fading fast. This is an abandoned quarry, the workers long since gone but leaving us lots of hiding places, should we need them. And an ideal pick-up point for our boatman.'

'When?' she asked.

'Two deadlines,' he said. 'Both after dark. First at 1830, second at midnight.'

'Midnight? That's an awfully long way off.'

'Fallback, in case of problems.'

'Two hours to go to the first,' she said, peering at her watch.

Williams arrived, looking shot. He'd been pushing and carrying children for much of the way. Claudia glanced at Anna, one of the more timid of her charges, and her spirits lifted at the welcome absence of tears. Finally, this small person stood on the threshold of freedom and safety. Claudia's sorrow was that she had not been able to avoid abandoning the child's mother to the perilous uncertainties of Munich's subterranean life.

Peter said, 'This is what we'll do. Get the kids settled, share out what we've got left...'

'Precious little.'

'Keep them quiet and comfortable, post a guard...'

She looked at him, waiting for the end of the sentence.

'And then you can tell me all about your little secret. The one you've been hiding from me since way back.'

Claudia took one look inside the tunnels where quarrymen once mined granite for porticoes, fireplaces and town hall facias and refused to put the children inside. The ceiling was low and propped up by four metal pillars. The ground was rocky and smelled of pigeons. The place was miles from the nearest habitation.

'I wouldn't put Hank Hoskins to sleep in there,' she said. 'The whole lot looks like a catastrophe waiting to happen. The roof could come down at any minute.'

'Lasted the past twenty years,' he said.

'No way!' Instead, they turned their attention to part of the yard that contained the ruins of a quarry office. Huge stone blocks remained at doorways, there was a rusty glassless window, broken jibs of an old crane, a smashed staircase, fallen masonry and exposed steel girders. One corner, however, remained standing. A canteen, by the look of it, or perhaps the boss's office, it was hard to tell.

'We'll move them in here,' she said, asserting her authority even though she knew she was nearing the point at which she could no longer exercise control. Once over the water, she knew, she would be totally reliant on others. At least these bare walls would shield the children from a chill wind blowing off the lake. 'No more walking!' she announced. 'We've arrived, a man is coming with a boat. Won't that be exciting?'

'I'm scared of water,' said Blondie.

'Not long now,' Claudia said. 'Soon you'll be warm and safe with nice people to look after you.'

'We want you to look after us.'

She smiled.

'I don't like the dark,' said another voice. 'This is a horrid place!'

Claudia spent some time talking about the wild flowers growing in the many crevices. That diverted attention for a while. She could identify the blue cornflower and a wild rose and thought she'd found a willow herb. 'Pick just one each and take it with you,' she said, 'and when it's light again we'll see if we can say what they are. In the daylight. Tomorrow...'

Tomorrow?

Tomorrow was another day; tomorrow was another land. But for the moment she was happy to ignore the prohibition on interfering with wild flowers. You had to keep a sense of proportion when your future was in the balance.

36

Everyone who was anyone was right there. The top deck of the steamer Bodensee was the place to be if you wanted to be noticed. She was a gleaming three-decker with stainless-steel interiors and picture windows, a sleek, white mini-liner of the lake.

All eyes were supposed to be focused on the shoreline where a spindly wooden bridge spanned a deep ravine, officially declared as the prime viewing point for the big event of the day.

In reality, the focus was on each other. There had been plenty of time. The VIP guests had been waiting patiently for the arrival of the train.

To the left was the German ambassador and his wife, flanked by his minister plenipotentiary and the chargé d'affaires, all hemmed in by an anonymous security detail.

Centre stage, with the best view of the bridge, was the President of the Swiss Confederation, Marcel Pilet-Golaz, and three of his Cabinet – one for posts, one for railways, one for home affairs, and sundry government officials.

To the right, just off the train, were Hank Hoskins, deputy engineer Reinhardt Meyer and Siegfried Uffelmann, the deputy architect. No one asked about the chief architect. They were too polite.

At the rear of the crowd, mingling with the nameless also-rans, were two observers barely welcomed, merely tolerated: a plaid-shirted figure who, had he spoken, would have revealed the cadences of the East Coast of America, and an even more anonymously-suited figure who had begun his day with an acerbic briefing from Dansey, speaking down a secure telephone line from London.

Set out on a large table in front of the VIPs was a diagrammatic map of Hoskins's *Breitspurbahn* network, as envisaged for a Europe-wide, then worldwide future, plus a large cut-out of a three-metre carriage and another of the hydrogen motor unit.

Hoskins was in full flood. 'Now, Mr President, Mr Ambassador, ladies and gentlemen, we still have ten minutes before the main event, so let me explain the new system.' He was throwing out facts and figures faster than a BMW salesman. 'To appreciate the staggering increase in size of this system, you need to know that one train will pull as much freight as an average-sized cargo ship – but at a much greater speed. So, to pull this train, we have various forms of motive power. First, the traditional steamer.'

He looked around, hoping for attentive faces. The ambassador's wife, dressed in a large blue floral frock, was fidgeting. When he'd pumped her pudgy hand a few minutes earlier, Hoskins already knew she wouldn't be marvelling at the six high pressure and six low pressure cylinders he was going to talk about. She had her eyes on the refreshment deck and had set her heart on apple strudels and cherry cheesecakes.

'Impressive, truly impressive, a wonderful advertisement for our country.' Her husband, Ludwig Freiherr von Marquardt, a small man with a receding hairline offset by elaborately coiffured waves around the ears, was loudly doing his best to proclaim the reputation of cutting-edge German engineering before the assembled company.

Certainly the Swiss president looked impressed, but then Pilet-Golaz was almost a Hitler puppet. He looked the part: short black hair and a brush moustache. Eager to please, he'd allowed sealed German military trains to transit Swiss Alpine tunnels, banned criticism of the Fuhrer and blocked all attempts to accept anti-Nazi refugees. Under him, Switzerland was less of a neutral, more a client state.

'Shortly,' Hoskins was saying, checking his watch, 'the new hydrogen motor unit will travel down our special loop line and cross the bridge you see before you, to give a grandstand view of this futuristic technology. You've seen it once, just a slow initial demonstration, and shortly it will repeat this performance at normal speed.'

Grandstand was the key word. For all their enthusiasm for the 'New Order', the Swiss were wary of stepping onto Third Reich territory. They'd seen how the SS invaded a Dutch border post the year before to kidnap two British agents and put them on trial in Germany. They'd seen how Hitler intimidated and threatened the Austrian Chancellor before invading his country. Hence the Swiss viewing boat positioned on the neutral waters of the lake.

'Standby, your attention, please.' Hoskins again. This was his crowning moment.

All eyes turned to the line by the bridge.

Hoskins held his breath. Everything would go exactly according to plan, wouldn't it? Of course it would.

Then he saw it. An instant stab of alarm – even before he heard the intake of breath from those around him.

Why wasn't it whistling, sounding the siren as planned, to draw attention, to add that little touch of grandstanding? Worse still was the alarming speed with which it approached the bridge. They'd settled on fifty as the optimum, but this looked like half as much again. He cursed Herr Adler, the driver. Clearly, showing off. He'd have to brake very sharply at the last moment before rounding the bend.

But the loco didn't.

There were more gasps from the crowd as it swerved around the sharp curve on the approach, rocking and swaying, and continued at an outrageously excessive speed across the bridge.

For heaven's sake! Hoskins could hardly repress his reaction. Hadn't the stupid man listened to his briefing? He'd been didactic to the point of boredom. The bridge was just a temporary structure erected for the day. It wouldn't take this sort of pounding.

'My God!' said the president. 'The whole structure is wavering. Can't you stop it, Herr Hoskins?'

But Herr Hoskins was frozen in a trance of horror. The bridge was swaying, first one way, then the other. He knew instinctively that disaster was upon them. The loco was, for some unfathomable reason, out of control. At the sharp turn at the end of the bridge it simply disappeared. He knew it would happen before it did, even as he hoped against hope for some miraculous deliverance, but the engineer in him was logical and knew that certain things were beyond the limits of possibility. The loco had jumped the track and disappeared into the ravine.

Hoskins gripped the table, helpless and stricken, and then came the boom and crash of the machine hitting the rocks on the valley floor.

That wasn't the end of it. The bridge, fatally damaged by the rampaging monster that had assaulted it, sighed and splintered, collapsing like some giant, incompetent Meccano set into the ravine, burying the wreckage of the locomotive.

Hoskins looked down and closed his eyes.

He let out a sob.

Why? Why hadn't Adler slowed up? It was inexplicable. He began to contemplate the size and scale of the disaster and the wreckage of all his work, ambitions, dreams and hopes.

He was hardly aware of those around him, immune to the atmosphere of shock and embarrassment. No one said hard luck. All the Germans felt the shame of failure put on public display and shrank into a corner. Only the Swiss were sympathetic, issuing condolences for the loss of the driver.

Hoskins had never felt so alone.

He found himself guided to a side room by diplomatic Swiss officials, then once more facing the president and having a conversation he never imagined possible.

'Herr Hoskins, my sincere commiserations. I think you should take a moment's reflection before you decide on your next step.'

'I must get back,' Hoskins mumbled, 'to find out what went wrong. To put things right. I can make it right. Really. It's not the end.'

But even as he said this, Hoskins knew that it was.

'Please, pause for one moment,' the president said. Pilet-Golaz would have described himself as a pragmatist. Certainly, he was a realist and whatever his political leanings, he knew about life on the other side of the frontier. 'I think you should consider your position. I have a very definite feeling that a certain leader will *not* be inclined to forgive what has happened here today. I think severe recriminations are likely. You should expect to be in great personal danger.'

Hoskins looked doubly shattered. Something Franz had said to him several days before echoed this thought. He slumped, uncertain how to respond.

'You wouldn't be the first victim of this new railway,' said the president. 'We had to help your architect.'

So that was it. Solved: the mystery of the missing chief architect. All Hoskins knew was that the man had been on the point of nervous exhaustion because of the Fuhrer's constant changes of mind.

So, another victim. The man had simply fled through neutral Switzerland.

The president put an arm around Hoskins's shoulders. 'If it should cross your mind to seek asylum in another country, or perhaps a return to your own,' he said, 'there is a gentleman wearing a plaid shirt in the next room with whom you should discuss such a possibility.'

37

Claudia fussed among the children, getting them to sleep, making sure they were warm and reassured, telling a couple of her own impromptu stories. They were tired. It had been a long traumatic day. Perhaps she was being a little too conscientious. She knew Peter wanted to talk and she wasn't sure she wanted to answer his questions.

Because she hadn't yet made up her mind.

Instead, she thought about risk. Would the boatman show up? Would they cross without being intercepted? Her recurring nightmare was for the children to be discovered and arrested, either in the wilderness, on the train or the lake, all her good work in keeping them safe undone, the little ones sent to ghettos or deportation trains to the East.

She was also in danger. If caught, she would stand condemned, not only for an illegal escape attempt, but also for consorting with an enemy national.

Not that she considered herself anything other than a patriot. It wasn't that she wanted to co-operate with an enemy; she simply wanted to get her children away. She had no intention of acting against the true interests of her country, but humanity and decency were being traduced every day in a comprehensive betrayal of the true nature of the nation. She could only hope for a change in the regime.

She entertained the vague hope that when that happened the children might return to their original homeland. At that point she stopped herself and reality kicked in. This sort of fairy tale didn't happen, she told herself.

But what was staring her in the face was her own chance to escape. She was sure the children would be better off in England, but that created a dilemma for her. It was a choice that had played on her mind from the moment she'd met Peter. She asked herself again and again: should she go?

She found him at the edge of the dock, staring out into the inky waters of the lake. 'Forty minutes,' he said, 'an hour tops.'

'I've a question,' she said.

He turned to face her, all attention.

'How would Mr Winton cope if relatives of the *Kindertransport* children turned up in England unexpectedly? Turning up, I mean, to reclaim their children?'

Peter frowned. 'Difficult,' he said eventually, 'a situation still to be resolved. I guess, in truth, we don't expect any relatives to survive the war. Sorry to be frank.'

'But what if one did? You must have a policy?'

A long pause for thought, then he said, 'How would you feel, if you were a child and some strange person turned up claiming to be your mother or father, a person you couldn't remember and didn't know existed?' He looked at her quizzically, then added, 'Depends on the age of the child. In the case of the very young, bad idea! If the child has no recollection of its biological parent, no. But for a teenager, especially one who might not have settled so well and who *did* remember...' He shrugged. 'Maybe. Why do you ask?'

Claudia ignored the question. 'Yes, I can see that. In the case of young ones, it could be unsettling. Cruel even. Better not to disturb a loving home relationship.'

Peter said, 'A decision would have to be made in each case according to the circumstances.' He looked at her closely. 'Now, are you going to tell me? Explain all these questions? This is more than just an academic interest. It's personal, isn't it?'

Her instinct was to parry. To avoid his enquiries. Every day she thought about the child whose picture she carried in her locket. The snub nose, the delicate mouth. To fill the void in her life, that would be a wonderful thing. To deal with that missing part of her that was akin to a lost limb. She felt it nearly every day.

'Well?' he said, still probing.

She got up suddenly. A crying child needed her attention and saved her from having to answer.

She had been sitting propped in a corner, eyes closed, awash with anxiety, when suddenly she was aware of him next to her. She opened her eyes and he gave her the look that said he was going to keep right on asking his questions.

She sighed. She wasn't ready for the inquisition and her deflection technique was second nature. 'What about this boatman?' she asked quickly. 'Another British spy? How good is he? And are the children still in danger?'

He shook his head. 'Not really.'

'They could be intercepted,' she persisted. 'Turned back by some Customs or police boat.' She looked anxious, stricken. 'It would be awful to lose them now, so near to Switzerland.'

'I trust everything to my Uncle Stef,' he said. 'If anyone can do it, he can.'

'And tell me now. Why only twenty-seven?'

'Simple. The boat isn't big. Only takes thirty, that's three adults and the kids.'

She nodded. 'I see. And your uncle... he's done it before?'

'Many times.' Peter began to speak of the incident, just weeks before, when he saw his uncle ushering four bedraggled refugees from his boat.

'What happens on the other side?' she asked. 'Are they friendly?'

Peter sighed and began to explain the complexities of the Swiss situation: that unsponsored refugees were officially outlawed; that getting out of Switzerland was almost as difficult as getting in. 'That's why I've asked for twenty-seven neutral passports,' he said.

She frowned. 'Why neutral?'

The authorities would not allow British passport holders to travel, he said, because of the country's belligerent status, but neutrals, as one to another, were free to go. Nicaragua or some-where in South America would be fine. The children, given neutral passports, would be driven south to Spain or Portugal and put on a ship, or perhaps a plane at Gibraltar, and sent to Britain.

'It's all arranged over there,' he said, pointing across the water. 'My aunt will be waiting. Hot soup, sandwiches, warm beds... she loves kids.' He scratched an ear reflectively. 'Trudi can be fierce at times but underneath, she's a big softie.'

'So!' Claudia said, 'good old Uncle Stef and Aunt Trudi. Now I know the real reason you were chosen for this job. Relatives close at hand!'

He looked deflated. 'There were other reasons.'

'Tell me,' she said, 'about when *you* get back home. What are *you* going to do about *your* life? Stumble on in the same old way, doing what you're always told, or are you ready to change? To assert yourself?'

Peter looked at Claudia, then up at the looming cliff towering above them, sighed, drew in his breath and looked back at her. 'It's you, you've done this to me,' he said. 'You're so damned confident, so certain of yourself, so damned decisive.'

'Meaning?'

'I've made a decision.'

'That must have been hard.'

He gave her a warning look. 'When – and if – I get back and meet my father again...'

'This I want to hear,' she said. 'Yes, so what are you going to tell him?'

Peter swallowed, breathed hard, gritted his teeth and rehearsed for the hardest speech of his life. 'That I'm not joining the company. That I don't want to be an engineer. That I'm out of the company training scheme.'

She managed to look shocked. 'Wow! Some resolution. But what then?'

'Well, I might not be the next greatest acting talent in the country, I know that, but I love the excitement of the theatre. I want to be backstage, involved! The bright lights, everything about it. London was a vibrant theatre land. All stopped now, of course, because of the air raids, only the Windmill Theatre is still going...'

She interrupted. 'A theatre still plays during the bombing?'

'Yes, but they're not my cup of tea.'

'Why not?'

'Just high-kicking dancing girls.'

She laughed.

Peter said, 'I want to be there when this is all over and the West End theatres open up again. In front of the lights or behind them, I don't care, just so long as I'm involved – and not covered in soot or oil or stuck in a railway drawing office.'

'Peter, it's no good telling me this if you're going to duck it when the time comes. You must not be browbeaten. Don't go back on your word.'

'I won't.'

'Remember, this will be the most important conversation of your life. Assert yourself. Don't be in your father's shadow. And I shall be a fly on the wall, I shall be there, listening, checking you keep your promise. Remember that.'

Just what was she doing, toying with this great temptation? Claudia was back with her insoluble problem. Had she forgotten her solemn promise to her mother, made all those years ago, never to interfere in the adoption process? A promise was a promise. A tenet of her upbringing was never to break her word. And it had been easy to give such promise when there wasn't a realistic prospect of making contact, but Peter had provided an unexpected opportunity by opening up the route to England. This was her great temptation, the great danger, the great foolishness.

She allowed herself to think about him, to dream of another future. At heart, a good man and an attractive one. She loved the dimple in his chin. Well-intentioned, brilliant with children. Perceptive too, on familiar subjects, such as Winton, railways and the stage. She was grateful for his clarity on the *Kindertransports*. Amused too at his romantic engagement with the theatre. She hoped he wouldn't be disappointed if he got the chance to pursue it. Despite all this, however, she could read in him immaturity and naivety. Just a boy, really, despite his years. Easily manipulated, she suspected, by the military, his father and other authoritarian figures.

And what would he think of her, if he knew? It was the question she asked herself every time she met an attractive male.

They would all run, she was sure, as soon as they discovered her shameful secret. She wondered if she would ever meet a person with whom she could start afresh; if ever she had the realistic prospect of a conventional family life.

She made herself sit quite still. This was the moment of decision. She thought of all she had done for her twenty-seven young strays – and then made up her mind. She sighed. Now it didn't matter if Peter knew. This time she willingly opened herself up to his unending curiosity.

'Tell me,' he said, when she'd made herself visible in the old ruin, 'the ponytail girl called Luise and the little boy called Hansi. Luise, the one with the eternity ring and the doll called Gretel.'

She shrugged apologetically. 'I know, there were lots of them...'

'Hundreds.'

'They were such a distinct pair. Little mummy, tiny boy,' she said.

'Two very special children. Now, we've got ten minutes before Uncle Stef makes landfall and we're nearly through this nightmare. So, fair's fair, you've put me under the microscope and now it's your turn. Time to explain.'

Should she? Even now, after all this time? She sighed, stayed silent for some seconds, then she said in a low voice: 'My son. My baby.'

He looked at her for a while before saying, 'Just the boy was yours, not the girl?'

She nodded.

'Want to explain that?'

'No.'

'Oh, come on!'

She looked at him again. Shame or not, perhaps it *was* time.

'My baby was given away at birth,' she said. 'Part of the arrangement with the other family.'

'Why?'

'Wouldn't do for a teacher to have an illegitimate child. Would have been the end of my career.'

'Would you have minded?'

Claudia shrugged. 'Wasn't given a choice. I had brought shame on my family. Had to go away to have the baby, then a Jewish family, the Grunwalds, fostered him. The arrangement was: the girl and my boy would both get out together. On the *Kindertransports* as a pair. Luckily, they just made it on the eighth. That's why I asked you.'

'Shame on the family? That's a bit harsh.'

'Isn't it the same in England?'

Peter thought for a while. 'I guess so, but I've no direct experience. Anyway, who decided all this? Why didn't you have a say on the matter? Your life, your child!'

'My father was okay but mother was very firm.'

'Super strict, is she?'

'On this.'

'But you regret? Resent it? A lingering anger?'

Claudia hesitated. 'Regret but acceptance – until now.'

'Harsh words between mother and daughter?'

'No, she acted for the best. I have to believe that. Actually, I don't – but I have to believe it.'

'Is that why you were in Munich? Banished from the home?'

'In a way, I suppose, yes. But mainly it was to get out from under the noses of the Gestapo. I'd made myself too visible with the *Kindertransports* in Prague. This was my new start.'

'Still close to your family then?'

'Postcard or letter every week.'

'Will you go back when you can?'

'Hope so. I hope we can get back to being close once again, like we were before.'

'Your mother, she should have forgiven you by now. How old is the child?'

'Just over six.'

'And what about him – the father of your child?'

She shrugged. 'Faded from the picture. Probably never knew about the baby. Shrouded in secrecy. My very foolish youthful mistake.'

Peter stroked his chin. 'Redemption, forgiveness, peace in the family. I wish you well with that.' But he wasn't finished. He looked at her quizzically. 'So, we have sitting here two very anxious people with two highly proscriptive parents – my father and your mother. I seek assertion, you seek redemption. Two problems so close to home.' He chuckled. 'So, fly on the wall, I think your redemption might take a little longer than my one volcanic meeting.'

She heard him murmuring into the radio, indistinct at first, then louder and more urgent: 'Stonemason to Fairweather, come in.'

Could things go wrong at the final moment? She took several steps to the edge of a protruding rock and looked out at the water. There were lights twinkling on the far shore and she knew there were villas and houses and churches and little towns over there that represented normality and safety; behind them a screen of trees and beyond the screen, mountains with touches of snow. More lights away to her left, the direction from which they had walked, random and without discernible pattern.

'Stonemason to Fairweather, I repeat.'

She turned up her collar, then saw something moving in the distance, fast and purposeful. Other lights moved more slowly. After some minutes she became aware of a drone, getting louder, a plane. Something was happening back where they had come from, activity that told her Peter wasn't exaggerating when he said the train had duly played its part in the disaster plan. She looked down. The lake didn't seem like a millpond to her. Little waves slapped at the stones and the rocks. Did all this activity represent a threat? She still worried about the crossing.

Peter said, 'Stef has the quietest boat on the lake. No lights, grey paint, very hard to spot in the night and practically noiseless.'

'What about the motor?'

'It runs off a battery. An electric passenger launch.'

'Didn't know such things existed.'

'A leftover from the twenties. Originally intended for a Bavarian lake where motor boats are banned, but it got left behind here. It's the ace smugglers' boat.'

Another voice crackled on the radio. She didn't catch the words but Williams was quick to whisper in her ear: 'Five minutes to landfall. Better get the kids ready.'

She went into the ruin. Thank goodness they hadn't needed to go into those fearful caves. 'Get up, children, the boat is coming. Let's be ready to move.'

'I'm so cold,' said a small voice.

'And hungry,' said another.

'I don't like the dark.' That was Mole, even though she couldn't see him in the gloom.

'I don't like boats.'

'Come on, Eagle, you have to be a big boy for me now,' she said. 'Remember how brave you were in the wilderness.'

There were male voices, low and urgent, outside and she was surprised to see, when she arrived at the dock, that a long low launch had glided noiselessly into their little hideaway and a man with a sailor's cap was tying ropes around stone bollards on the rocks.

She went closer. Peter was talking to the sailor, a much older man with a leathery face. He was introduced as 'Stef'.

'How was the crossing?' Peter's voice betrayed his anxiety.

'So many sightseers the patrols have lost it. Everybody who's got a boat is out on the water getting an eyeful. Not every day you can watch the Nazis making idiots of themselves.'

'Is the crossing going to be difficult?' Claudia asked.

Stef looked at her and grinned. 'The German police boats are buzzing round the crash site trying to keep photographers at bay and the Swiss are busily gawping at them, just like everyone else. Everybody wants to get a good look.'

'Yes, but?'

Stef put a reassuring hand on her shoulder. 'Ideal confusion for us,' he said.

Williams was already hoisting the children over the gunnels. The wood creaked, the straining and stretching of the retaining ropes sang a song in tune with Claudia's fractured nerves as she checked all twenty-seven of her charges into the boat. The children, she noticed, were sent immediately below deck. Runner was the last of the children to climb into the launch. 'Now you,' Peter said.

She sighed.

Now for the moment.

'Sorry, Peter,' she said, 'I won't be coming.'

He jerked upright, looked as if he'd taken a punch. His mouth opened and closed and he took a pace closer. 'Why?'

'It wouldn't work,' she said. 'You were right. The children, Hansi and Luise, they've never known me as a mother. I'd be just another stranger to them. Better with their new parents. I'll keep the promise I made to my family. I won't interfere. I'll let them go.'

Peter shook his head. 'Come with us anyway! At the very least, save yourself!'

'No.' She was adamant. She was being her resolute best. 'There's work to be done back in Munich. Do you think these twenty-seven children are the only U-boats in the city? Of course not. Loads more! Hidden all over the place.'

'Claudia, think!' he said. 'You won't survive the Gestapo sweep. Someone there will snitch on you, the police will be all over it, Franz has already warned you, have you forgotten that?'

She put a hand on his arm. For a second, she thought to hug him, then stepped back. 'Don't worry, I'll steer clear of the depot. Maybe the school, like nothing happened. Acting the innocent.'

'School will still be a danger zone.'

'Peter, this was meant to be.'

Stef had stood close, not saying a word, but now he broke his silence. 'Sorry, but we can't stand here debating. Too dangerous to hang around.'

Peter was insistent: 'For God's sake, Claudia, don't risk it, come with us, you'll never be able to pull off the escape trick twice.'

She shook her head.

'We must go,' Stef said.

'Please, Claudia.' Peter was begging, almost in tears. She desperately wanted to hug him. He said, 'I can't leave you here, this is madness.'

She stepped away from the boat to signal the finality of her decision. She had no formed idea of how she would return to the city, still less how to achieve another rescue. 'It's what I'm meant to do,' she said. 'Just promise me, you'll never abandon our little ones... you're their future now.'

Stef was casting off his lines and she called out, 'I pass to you the mantle of care. As a Winton man, I couldn't have wished for anyone better. Peter, I'm relying on you.'

He was on the prow as the launch reversed out of the tiny dock, its motor just a hushed purr barely audible above the ripple and slap of the water.

'Time for an English nursery rhyme,' she called, 'what about 'Little Jack Horner'?'

Then she heard a broken, fractured voice she hardly recognised as his. 'Children, say goodbye to Fraulein Kellner, loud enough for her to hear.'

'Goodbye, Fraulein Kellner,' came several young voices.

'More!'

Then a desultory, 'Auf Wiedersehen.'

A slight mist hung low over the lake giving it an ethereal quality. Finally, a chorus of tiny voices floated out across the water and echoed faintly around the man-made cove carved out by long-gone quarrymen. The launch was still reversing, then changing course before setting a zigzag pattern towards open water and the other side of the lake. Switzerland and safety.

Most of the twenty-seven managed to make their voices count.

'Farewell, Fraulein Kellner, farewell.'

THE END

AUTHOR'S NOTE

Inspiration for this story sprang from the Kindertransports, the thousands of children saved from Hitler's evil regime *before* the Second World War began.

The statues of refugee children at Liverpool Street station in London attest to one such operation, by Sir Nicholas Winton, which ended on the day the Nazis invaded Poland. Getting children out after that was strictly forbidden.

Another fact used in this story is the Fuhrer's plan for a system of monster trains to straddle the continent and elsewhere. The Breitspurbahn was an engineering absurdity but planned and modelled down to the finest detail.

And if anyone thinks it impossible to parachute onto an Alpine glacier and ski down it in the midst of a winter night – well, several crazy men did it and succeeded in assisting in gaining peaceful surrenders at the end of the war.

Finally, a word about geography. My characters live in the town of Bury St Edmunds and I've sometimes been taken to task for bending a few streets here and there. As the author Jack Higgins said in a preface to one of his novels, fifty per cent of the facts in this story are true. It's up to the Reader to decide which is which.

Printed in Great Britain
by Amazon

54384895R00203